A Maid for All Seasons IV

T0382428

A MAID FOR ALL SEASONS IV

A MAID FOR ALL SEASONS IV

GREEN EYES, SCARLET CHEEKS

DEVLIN O'NEILL

BLUE MOON BOOKS
NEW YORK

A Maid for All Seasons IV
© 2005 by Devlin O'Neill

Published by
Blue Moon Books
An Imprint of Avalon Publishing Group Incorporated
245 West 17th Street, 11th floor
New York, NY 10011-5300

First Blue Moon Books edition 2005

ISBN 978-1-56201-463-6

9 8 7 6 5 4 3 2 1

Printed in Canada
Distributed by Publishers Group West

A MAID FOR ALL SEASONS IV

Chapter One
After the Storm

Leaves, boughs and twigs strewed the back yard as if a giant hand had shaken them from the trees. Three men piled storm wrack onto tarps while an ax clunked *moderato* beneath a strident chainsaw melody. Dylan Travis, founder, headmaster and entire faculty of Red Blossom College at Red Blossom Cottage, stood by and frowned at the battered oaks.

"Not much left of them, Frank."

"They'll be OK." The man took a paper box from the pocket in his bib overalls and shook out a Marlboro. "They're pretty scraggly now, but the boles are sound. I lopped off all the cracked branches and tarred over the wounds . . . couple three years they'll fill out and you won't be able to tell they was ever messed up so bad." He flicked a wooden match with his thumbnail and lit the cigarette. The professor nodded.

Dylan stood five-eleven in his black wingtips, and his dark brown hair had flecks of gray at the temples. He wore a white cotton shirt, the top button undone, and the trousers of a blue Pierre Cardin suit. A gray silk Abboud tie hung loose at his neck.

"I hope you're right. They were here before the cottage was built."

"Yeah, I figured." Frank blew smoke and glanced over his shoulder. "You know the Martins, there on Bush? Lost three maples . . . wind yanked 'em right up and tossed 'em in the street."

"I saw that . . . so it could have been worse."

"Any storm that could pull these oaks out of the ground would of took the house too."

"Somehow that doesn't make me feel better. I had six young women huddled in the bathroom with me until four in the morning."

"Yeah? I was in the basement with my wife and her mother." He winked. "So I guess you got the better end of the deal."

"Perhaps . . . but I don't look forward to another blow like that one."

"I've seen worse around here . . . but not many." He pointed the cigarette at the wall along the rear of the lot. "You want me to cut back them weigela bushes while I've got the crew here?"

"If you have time."

"Sure . . . I'm about caught up from the storm mess. How come you waited so long to call me about the trees?"

"I wanted the ground to dry out. There was a pond back here for almost a week."

"You need more drainage . . . I could put in some pipe out to the street gutter if you want."

"Good idea. Send me an estimate, would you?"

"I'll do that. Anything else?"

Dylan smiled. "I'm sure I'll think of something. Thanks, Frank."

"Any time." He stubbed out the Marlboro on his heel and tossed the butt into a leaf pile, then reached down to pick up a short, thick log. "Hey, Professor . . . you wanna keep this?"

"Why? What is it?"

Frank pointed. "There was a rope swing on this bough. See the marks?"

"I don't remember . . . oh, wait." He took it and examined the indentations in the bark. "My great-uncle put that up for his son. There were only a couple of strands of frayed hemp left by the time I saw it. Yes, I'll hang onto it."

"Thought you might. I'll give you a holler when we leave."

"Thanks again. I'll be in the study around front."

Dylan carried the log through the kitchen door, set it on the table and stared at it. He sighed as he pulled a cell phone from his belt and thumbed a speed-dial key. The phone at the other end rang twice.

"Hi, Dylan! Can you hang on? I just walked in the door."

"Sure, Gwen. Take your time." He smiled as he listened to rustles and clunks.

"Hey! What's up? You OK?"

"Of course . . . I just wanted to hear your voice."

"Mmm . . . that's sweet. You're not calling to tell me you got blown to Phoenix by another tornado?"

"We would most likely be blown *east*, not west, and don't be a smart aleck. What's in the packages?"

"Um . . . what packages?"

He grinned. "The ones you're backing away from even as I speak."

"I wish you wouldn't *do* that."

"Do what, Princess?"

"*That* . . . that eyes in the back of your head thing . . . it's really annoying."

"Oh, *is* it? No eyes involved . . . merely superior detective work."

"Nuh *uh* . . . I think you hid cameras in my house 'cause you always . . . ." She stopped and bit her lip.

"I always *what*? Know when you've been naughty?"

"But I *haven't* been naughty."

"Then why won't you tell me what's in the packages?"

"'cause it's none of your *business*."

"Gwendolyn! You know better than to talk to me that way."

"Not *Gwendolyn*, OK? Did you call just to yell at me?"

"No." He puffed his cheeks and blew a breath. "I was feeling a bit sentimental, that's all."

"How come?"

"I found a relic of times past in the storm debris and started thinking about Jake."

"Who?"

"My cousin . . . *second* cousin . . . the one who died in Viet Nam."

"Oh . . . yeah, you told me about him. So what did you find of his?"

"An old rope-swing . . . well, evidence of it . . . when they were cutting out some broken branches."

"So, um . . . you got all the storm damage taken care of? The roof and the windows and everything?"

"Yes . . . all done. Sorry I've been so busy lately."

"That's OK . . . I understand. So do you have time to tell me what happened? All I got was bits and pieces."

Dylan settled into a kitchen chair and leaned back. "Sure . . . if you do."

"Uh huh. Don't mind me . . . I can listen while I change clothes."

"OK." Hangers scraped a closet rod and he smiled. "I told you we were stuck in the bathroom for twelve hours, didn't I?"

"Yeah . . . you and the *girls* . . . so what did you do all that time, or do I even want to know?"

"Gwen."

He drew out the syllable and she bit her lip.

"Um . . . it's kinda chilly for this early in October . . . maybe I'll put sweats on, what do you think?"

"I think you'd better behave, young lady."

"But I *always* behave . . . so, um . . . what were you saying?"

"Not the yellow sweats. You look like a banana and if I'm not there to peel you. . . ."

She giggled. "OK, I'll save them for later. How about the peach?"

"Much better. We talked."

"Huh?"

"You asked what we did for twelve hours . . . we talked. Well . . . I did most of the talking, to calm the girls . . . um, young women."

"Oh, yeah? What about? You didn't just keep going with the lesson, did you?"

"No . . . I talked about you."

"Say *what?* Ow!"

"What's the matter?"

"Nothing! And it's *your* fault!"

"What did you *do*, Princess?"

She grumbled and shifted the phone to her other ear. "Well . . . I was pulling down my pantyhose when you said that and I lost my grip and snapped sort of a tender place, OK?"

"I'm sorry. Should I kiss it and make it better?"

"Yes you *should*, and right now. So why were you talking about *me?*"

"I *try* to keep my social life separate from business, but it seems the more discreet I am, the more certain parties want to know what I *do* when I leave town."

"You mean Teresa?"

"Among others."

"Yeah, well, you should have known . . . they're barely out of high school and there's nothing high school girls like better than gossip about a teacher."

"I know . . . but I hadn't counted on being that close to them for so long."

"So what did you *say* about me?"

A glass clinked and the refrigerator door opened when Gwen went to the kitchen. Dylan got up and walked to the study.

"That you're a bigger brat than they are and I spank you even harder than I do them."

"You did *not!* Why are *you* being such a brat?"

He chuckled. "Don't put so much ice in the glass or you won't have room for the cranberry juice in your Cape Codder."

"You are just *horrible,* and I'll have as much ice as I want. Anyway, what *did* you tell them?"

"Only the basics . . . you studied financial forensics with Dad after you got your MBA, and then fell hopelessly in love with me the minute we met."

"Dylan Travis, you just back the truck *up!*"

"What?" He grinned as he poured single-malt into a crystal low-ball and sat in the desk chair. "Wasn't that the way it happened?"

"You didn't really say that, did you?"

"No . . . I embellished the story of our first date, though . . . but only in a travelogue sort of way."

"Yeah? So you told them about all the *nice* restaurants you drove past on Wilshire Boulevard when you took me to lunch . . . at a *taco* place by Santa Monica pier?"

"You didn't even think you'd *like* fish tacos, but you said you did."

"They were *OK* . . . but I only went out with you 'cause you were my mentor's son and I wanted to impress Will with my open-mindedness."

"Right . . . and *not* because you wanted to cruise LA in a drop-top Firebird?"

"Oh sure . . . and breathe that *wonderful* LA smog, driving around with a forty-year-old juvenile delinquent? I was only thinking of my career."

"I was thirty-eight, if you don't mind."

"OK, a thirty-eight-year old juvenile delinquent!"

He laughed and sipped whisky while Gwen guzzled vodka and cranberry juice. "So . . . while we were eating fish tacos under the umbrella, it didn't occur to you to *lie* when I wanted to talk about your overextended credit cards?"

Gwen pouted hard to suppress a giggle. "That was your *dad's* fault. He already spilled the beans about it at dinner, and um . . . not to speak ill of the dead . . . but geeze! The man had *no* discretion in social situations."

"A fact of which I've been painfully aware all my life . . . but you looked so *cute* that night . . . the way you wiggled and blushed when he asked you about it. I just *had* to follow up."

"You did *not.* You made me feel so *guilty* . . . looking at me with those big blue professor eyes . . . I wanted to jump in the *ocean.* That was worse than when Sister Ignacious *glared* a confession out of me in fourth grade for spilling Coke on my arithmetic book."

"But didn't you feel better after you invited me to your hotel room so I could spank away all the nasty guilt?"

"I did no such *thing!* God, what a selective memory! I invited you up for coffee, *not* to spank my bare fanny."

"Oh, that's right . . . the spanking was merely a bonus."

"Dylan! I *hated* that." She giggled and slurped her drink. "And I just *bet* you told those girls how you spanked an innocent young woman you hardly knew."

"Uh . . . we're still talking about *you,* aren't we?"

"I was *so* innocent . . . and my credit cards weren't any of your business!"

A truck horn sounded. Dylan turned to the window and waved at Frank. A diesel engine roared and the stake truck, its bed piled high with leaves and twigs, rolled away.

"I believe you said as much at the time . . . repeatedly."

"Yeah . . . while you *repeatedly* smacked my sore bottom. So is *that* what you told them?"

He finished the whisky and poured another. "No . . . they had their own sore bottoms to gossip about."

"You spanked them during a *tornado?*"

"Of course not . . . it was before the tornado alarm."

"How come you spanked them?"

"Because . . . let's see . . . four of the girls blew off their assignments entirely, Teresa sent me half a page of drivel, and Ashley stole her essay off the web."

Gwen blinked as she counted. "That's the whole *class*. God, you're a mean teacher. I suppose you paddled them *bare*, too, huh?"

"No, I let them keep most of their clothes on . . . except Ashley."

"I *meant* on their bare . . . what *about* Ashley?"

He shrugged and sipped. "I had her disrobe completely before I spanked her . . . to increase her embarrassment."

"*Geeze!* That's not just mean, that's . . . *disgraceful!*"

"I believe she felt that as well . . . but plagiarism isn't something I take lightly."

"No, but . . . how *awful* for her. Did you make her get n-naked in front of the other girls?"

"Yes . . . why?"

"And . . . and you *watched* her take off her clothes?"

"Of course." He grinned. "Why do you ask?"

"Well . . . I mean . . . *God,* Dylan! I just want to fall through the *floor* when you take off all my clothes to spank me, and I can't *imagine* how horrible it would be if . . . if . . ."

He licked his lips. "I think you *are* imagining it . . . how you would feel if I undressed you in public . . . and then paddled your little round bottom in front of other people."

"I'm not *either.*" She drained her glass and slammed it onto the counter. "You . . . you're being n-nasty, so *stop* it."

"All right. I won't tell you anymore about how humiliating it would be if I had to scold you in class and then bend you over the desk, lift your skirt and pull down your panties to . . ."

"*Please,* Dylan . . . don't *tease* me! You *know* how much I miss you already and I'm just so . . ."

"Shh . . . I miss you, too . . . and I'd be on the next plane to Logan if I could."

Gwen sniffled and cupped a hand between her thighs. "Really? What . . . what would you do when you got here?"

"Well . . . after I kissed you for a long time, we'd have to discuss those packages you brought home."

— 7 —

"I don't *wanna* discuss that." The whine tickled her throat, and she reached inside her pants to caress plump, moist lower lips.

Dylan smiled. "But you know we *have* to, Kitty Eyes. You stopped at Macy's on the way home from work, didn't you?"

She stared at the bags on the kitchen table and gasped as she looked around. "I . . . I had to take some things *back,* and how the hell . . . heck . . . did you *know?"*

He chuckled. "Because I know my little princess . . . and if you *returned* things, why do you have packages, young lady?"

His voice hardened as he spoke, and the scolding tone tingled her ear. Cool, crisp fire glimmered in her vagina and she gasped as she stroked the hard, quivery bud.

"What was that, Princess?"

"But I . . . I *needed* new shoes, honest!"

"What you *need* is a long, ouchy reminder, with my hard hand on your soft, bare bottom, *not* to spend money on nonessentials."

"No I *don't.* You . . *?*you already reminded me *lots* of times and I remember 'cause I'm a *good* girl."

"You're a *naughty* girl, Gwendolyn . . . and your naughty little fanny is going to pay for all those things you bought today."

"Nuh *uh* . . . you . . . you *can't* be mean to me!"

"When am I ever mean to you?"

"Ah . . . all the time, 'cause you just . . . like to see me squirm!"

"That's true . . . you're so *cute* when you squirm . . . like you're doing now. Where are your fingers?"

"Huh?" She yanked the hand out of her pants and coughed to clear the huskiness from the throat.

"You heard me . . . were you toying with that special little button, by any chance?"

"No! And anyway I don't know what you're *talking* about!"

"Don't fib to me . . . you *know* what happens when you fib."

"Dylan! It . . . it's your own *fault* for . . . for . . . well you know how I get when you scold me . . . so just knock it off!"

He chuckled and sipped whisky. "You're giving me *orders* now?"

"No . . . sir." She wished he could see how hard she was pouting. "Um . . . so when *are* you gonna come see me?"

"We're still on for New Years, aren't we?"

"Yeah, but that's so *long.*"

"You can't come for Thanksgiving?"

She sighed. "I already signed up to work in the church kitchen. Why don't you come *here?*"

"I fed chestnut-and-oyster dressing to every homeless person in the diocese last year so . . ."

"It was *two* years ago."

"What? Are you sure?"

"Uh huh . . . *last* year you were a grump and spent the holidays working out your dad's estate."

"Oh . . . right . . . that *did* take some doing . . . and I was kind of a grump, wasn't I?"

"Yeah . . . but you're over it, aren't you? So why can't you come *this* year?"

"I have Fel and Teresa to take care of now . . . and Lisa is planning dinner at Swayne's house, for us and her family . . . and any of the girls who don't go home. So it seems I have a prior commitment. You're still invited, though."

"Humph! It seems I have a prior commitment."

He grinned. "It's just one day. *The poor will be with you always.*"

Gwen's jaw dropped. "That's not fair . . . atheists aren't *allowed* to quote Jesus."

"Really? *The devil may quote scripture.* I thought that gave me permission."

She giggled. "Like you *need* permission to be annoying. Why don't you go do something constructive and let me decide what I want for dinner? I'm *starving.*"

"OK . . . I'll call you Sunday."

"Why don't you call me Gwen?"

"Gwendolyn!"

"No . . . *Gwen* . . . my good-girl name. Sure . . . but don't call too early 'cause I'm going out with Deb Saturday night."

"Do I need to remind you to take a cab?"

"Oh, geeze . . . no, sir, Professor Dylan, sir. I'm a *big* girl now and I know all that stuff, so you don't need to . . ."

"All right, all right. 'Bye, Princess. I love you."

"Love you too . . . and thanks for the scolding!"

The phone beeped when he thumbed it off. He stared into space and smiled while he finished the whisky.

CHAPTER 2
A GATHERING TEMPEST

COLD NOVEMBER DRIZZLE smudged windshield grime on Dylan's new Blazer. He thumbed a wand and fluid squirted the glass. Wipers slicked it away as he pulled to a stop behind a baby-blue Datsun hatchback at the curb in front of Michael Swayne's house just as darkness fell. A black Pontiac coupe and a red Toyota pickup were parked in the driveway, and he glanced across the street at Jill Scott's BMW.

"Looks like quite a crowd." He switched off the engine and slipped out of his harness belt.

His half-sister Felicia sat with him in the front seat. She was twenty years younger than Dylan, a late-life surprise from their father's second wife. Her bright blue eyes looked like his, and she stood nearly as tall, but her complexion was fairer and her hair a shade lighter brown. Felicia's stepdaughter Teresa sat in the back seat with two other college students, Delia and Christa. All three young women were born and raised in Germany, and became friends after they moved to the small Midwest town to attend university and Red Blossom College.

Teresa stood five feet four in her low-heeled shoes, weighed a bit under one-twenty, and had green eyes that glowed with curiosity and mischief. Her father Gerhard was a widower and a close friend of Dylan's. He married Felicia, with Dylan's hearty

approval, even though she was only twelve years older than Teresa, but then he died in a small-plane crash when Teresa was fifteen. Even before Gerhard and Felicia were wed, Teresa called him Uncle Dylan and relished his frequent visits to their home in Hamburg, where he pampered and spoiled her as only a non-parent can. Now almost twenty, Teresa still loved her uncle but it galled her when she had to call him Professor at school.

Delia and Christa were cousins from Frankfurt whom Dylan had agreed, with some trepidation, to accept at his college. Both were just over twenty-one, grew up together, and had a long history of misadventures that culminated in problems with drugs and alcohol. Less than two months after they arrived in the States, Dylan punished them severely when they got drunk and took Ecstasy at a party. Teresa was appalled when he bared the girls' bottoms to take their temperatures, and most empathetic when she visited them the next day and discovered he also gave them enemas and then spanked them with a belt, because she had often incurred his keen displeasure and felt its effect on her bare behind.

Dylan turned to Felicia. "I didn't think there were any Datsuns *left* in this part of the world."

"It belongs to Mandy . . . Lisa's sister," Teresa said. "Her dad bought it for her."

"Really? That car's older than you, sweetie . . . but it's in great shape."

"Yes, but Mandy hates it . . . she says it is a beater."

Felicia laughed. "That figures. I've *heard* about Mandy."

Teresa shook her head. "She is not so bad . . . only a little spoiled."

"Not like anyone we know." He winked and Teresa stuck out her tongue. "I see Greg's new pickup has a fresh coat of wax."

"He is very proud of his truck, Uncle Dylan, so do not make fun."

"I wasn't, sweetie . . . but I was thinking that *this* truck could use a good wax job. Shall we go in?"

The group shivered and chattered to the front door and Felicia rang the bell. Lisa Carlson grinned and waved them inside. Warm odors of sage and roast turkey filled their nostrils as she took their coats. Lisa stood almost five-one in her sensible shoes, and her blonde hair hung down her neck in a short ponytail. She had light

blue eyes set wide apart above a short, turned-up nose, so she always appeared to be looking for something.

"Hi, guys . . . happy Thanksgiving . . . *Michael!*"

"Yes, yes . . . I heard the bell, for heaven's sake!"

Michael Swayne smiled as he hurried across the living room to shake Dylan's hand. The transplanted Englishman owned a real estate brokerage firm that he ran from his home office, and also acted as co-trustee of Lisa's trust, which included a chain of boutiques called Lola's. He had a full head of gray hair, stood two inches taller than Dylan, and had eyes the same color blue. The men grinned at each other like fraternity brothers about to embark on a road trip.

"Thanks for inviting us, Mike."

"Not at all . . . I'm relieved you're here. The other men are engrossed in American football and I'm afraid that at any moment one of the women will enlist me to help in the kitchen."

Dylan laughed and turned to his entourage. "You remember Felicia, don't you?"

The man bowed. "I recall the name . . . but it was attached to a skinny twelve-year-old the last time we met."

Felicia grinned and shook his hand. "I was *sixteen*, Mr. Swayne . . . and I've *never* been skinny."

"Ah! Then it must be Dylan's *other* little sister I was remembering."

"I don't *think* so." She held up her arms and they hugged. "Because you were a terrible tease *then* . . . and you haven't changed a bit."

He smiled and squeezed her. "Then you *do* remember me. How very sweet."

She giggled and backed away but held onto his arm. "You know Teresa. . . ."

"Hello, Teresa."

"How do you do, sir?"

"Quite well, thank you. Have you and Lisa finished your homework for next week?"

"Suh—*sir?*"

"Michael!"

Dylan laughed. "Hush, Lisa . . . Teresa, you just heard what a terrible tease he is." He took the quivery cousins by the hand and

– 13 –

pushed them toward Michael. "Delia . . . Christa . . . this is Mr. Swayne, your host. He's a nice old guy, way down deep . . . and you have my permission to ignore anything he says that annoys you . . . at least for today."

The girls bit their lips as they nodded. Michael made a grand bow and then winked at them.

"And you have my permission to enjoy the hospitality of this house whilst ignoring your pedantic and overeducated tutor without fear of reprisal . . . at least for today."

"Oh, *really?* I wouldn't be nearly as *pedantic* if someone offered me a drink."

"It's *my* experience that liquor merely exacerbates the problem . . . but we'll sample what's in that decanter nonetheless."

"Well all *right,* then."

The two men marched across the living room.

Lisa chuckled. "They are so *weird* when they get together. Come upstairs, guys. That's where the real party is."

The petite blonde, nominally Michael's maid but in fact his ward and protégé, led them to the study and ushered them in. She introduced Jack Carlson, her father, and Mandy, her younger sister; then Beth Trelawny, Michael's executive assistant; and finally Greg Bentley, Lisa's boyfriend. Jill Scott, Dylan's friend, advisor and part-time housemother to students at Red Blossom College, sat in an armchair and nodded. The woman was in her late fifties, medium height, slender, and had brownish gray hair that framed a pleasant face.

A forty-inch TV, set into a bookshelf, mumbled a college football game. Lisa went to the credenza and poured wine for the newcomers, and then perched on the arm of Greg's recliner.

"Who's winning?"

Greg stamped his foot and grunted. "Iowa State *was* . . . until you guys came in." He was slender, six feet tall, and in his early twenties. Blonde hair swept back from a high forehead and green eyes glimmered above a nose that was a bit too long for his lean face.

Lisa grinned and kissed his cheek. "So it's *our* fault, huh? You take these games way too seriously, you know?"

"Yeah whatever."

"And did you know that if you stew prunes like applesauce they taste more like tomatoes than rhubarb does?"

"Uh huh sure."

Teresa laughed and sipped merlot while she sat on the end of a brocaded chaise next to Mandy. Delia and Christa drank their wine by the credenza. Beth sat in a wingback chair next to Jill's. She got up and told Felicia to sit, then ambled to the door.

"I'll go check on dinner." She shook her head when Lisa looked at her. "I've got it . . . you take care of the *boys*."

Lisa giggled and slid off Greg's chair. "Dad?"

"What, honey?"

"Do you want another beer?"

"Uh huh."

"OK . . . you want it in a coffee cup with ice?"

Jack blinked at her. "*What?*"

"Just wanted to see if you were paying attention."

"I'll pay attention to your smart-alecky butt in a minute." He grinned and yanked her onto his lap. "Now what's so important you gotta interrupt the men's football game?"

"We're gonna eat in half an hour or so . . . are the *men* gonna join us?"

He laughed and kissed her cheek. "I expect we will . . . long as you weren't kidding about that beer . . . and get Greg another one while you're at it."

"Certainly, Father . . . and be sure to yell real loud if you want anything else."

"I'll do that, Daughter . . . now move it. I just missed a fumble."

Lisa dodged a swat he aimed at her bottom as she jerked to her feet and went behind the desk to open a Coleman cooler full of iced bottles.

Teresa turned to Mandy. "Do you enjoy football as well?"

The girl shrugged. "It's OK . . . as long as Iowa State wins."

"You wish to attend this school?"

"I guess . . . but I'd go to college in Podunk, Alabama if it got me out of *this* dump."

Greg and Jack yelled and shook their fists at the TV. Lisa grinned and knelt beside Jill's chair.

"Hi . . . can I get you anything?"

The woman shook her head and smiled. "I'm fine." She glanced at the German cousins and sighed. Lisa followed her gaze and bit her lip.

"They're um . . . still mad at you?"

"'Fraid so. They just *glare* at me every time I stop by to do curfew check."

Lisa pouted. "Well that's not right . . . you didn't *do* anything to them, and anyway it happened over two months ago."

Jill sipped Diet Coke and nodded. "But I was *there* when Dylan . . . did what he did . . . and they can't seem to forgive me for that."

"How much does he pay you for putting up with them, anyway?"

"Lisa!" Jill chuckled and patted the girl's arm. "You know better than to ask that . . . and it doesn't matter because I'd do anything he wanted for nothing."

"Yeah, I kinda figured." Lisa grinned and winked. "Maybe you should have some wine and get to *know* the girls, huh?"

"I'd just pass out . . . but it's sweet of you to offer."

"Uh huh . . . I better go see about them. Maybe they could use some more wine."

"I don't think Dylan would appreciate you pushing. . . ."

"Shh! I won't tell him if you won't."

Mandy's scowl caught Lisa's eye and she squatted beside the chaise.

"Hey! Why so glum?"

"None of your business."

Lisa looked at Teresa and she raised her wine glass.

Mandy leaned toward Lisa's ear. "How come *she* gets to drink and I don't?"

"'cause Dad's right *there*, you moron," Lisa whispered. She squeezed Mandy's hand and winked. "Let's go see if we can help in the kitchen, OK?"

"Why would I want to . . .?"

"Where the wine cabinet is?"

Teresa giggled and stood as Lisa yanked Mandy to her feet. Lisa pushed them to the door and then turned toward the credenza. She emptied the merlot bottle into Delia and Christa's glasses.

"Thank you, Lisa. This is very excellent," Delia said.

"Thanks . . . so you guys feel better now?"

Christa turned to her cousin and frowned, then looked at Lisa. "Better about what?"

"About how awful it was the last time you drank too much wine and got in trouble with Uncle Professor."

"But we . . . he was so . . .." Delia followed Lisa's eyes, then nodded and looked at Christa. "Perhaps we are unfair to Ms. Scott . . . to make her feel bad for what *he* did."

"Yes . . . perhaps." Christa turned to Lisa. "But if she tells Professor Uncle we are drinking too much now . . ."

"She won't . . . I promise." Lisa smiled. "Go talk to her . . . and call her Jill, OK? *Ms. Scott* is what Dylan calls her to make her sound official, so she *feels* official when you call her that." She picked up a plate. "Here . . . take her these sugar cookies . . . and you guys eat some too, all right?"

"Yes, this is a good idea. Where are you going?"

"To get my sister some wine."

"But there is wine right. . . ."

"Shh . . . I kinda have to sneak it 'cause she's underage."

"And Teresa is also."

"I know . . . but Dylan lets her drink when they're together and that's sort of got Mandy's panties in a knot."

Delia spat cookie crumbs when she laughed. "Pardon me, but that is *such* a strange saying!"

Lisa grinned. "Go talk to Jill . . . I'll come get you when dinner's ready."

The girls dragged the chaise closer to Jill and offered the plate. The woman smiled and took a cookie. Felicia waved them off, but then leaned over to take one.

"Thanks. I was just thinking it would spoil my appetite, but maybe I *should* spoil it . . . so I don't pig out on turkey and dressing."

Christa shrugged. "But it seems like this is the *point* of the holiday . . . to overeat."

Jill nodded. "That's what they *want* you to believe . . . so you'll buy lots of food."

Felicia chuckled. "Thanksgiving is a conspiracy by the grocery store owners?"

"Well, sure." Jill winked at Delia. "And the weight-loss clinic owners . . . and the diet food makers . . . and the fitness clubs . . ."

Delia laughed. "It is a good thing there is the exercise room at our apartment . . . so I can work off this overeating."

"Yes, if you only will *do* so." Christa wrinkled her nose when Delia stuck out her tongue, then she looked at Jill. "Did Britney and Ashley go to their home?"

"Yeah . . . Dylan called me last night and said they made it OK, but I guess it was kind of a rough flight to California."

"From the bad weather?"

"Uh huh . . . and the plane was completely full. I'm glad I don't have to travel on the holidays."

"The professor has made our reservations to fly to Frankfurt for Christmas."

"Are you anxious to see your folks?"

Christa sighed. "Yes . . . we have missed them."

"I'll bet they miss you, too."

Jill patted the girl's knee and Christa smiled.

* * *

Michael and Dylan sat in armchairs next to the fireplace, a crystal decanter on the lamp table between them. Oak slabs flamed and popped between the firedogs. Beth lounged, wine glass in hand, on the sofa. She was the high end of thirty-something, had long legs and a full bosom, and auburn hair that spilled down her back in a loose ponytail. Teresa, Mandy and Lisa clambered down the stairs and stopped in the middle of the living room. Dylan smiled at them.

"How goes the game?"

"Pretty close," Lisa said. "But I think it'll be over in time."

Beth chuckled. "If it's not we'll eat without them."

"*Sure* we will." Lisa led her sister to the kitchen door. "Can I get anybody anything?"

Michael shook his head. "We're all right, thank you."

Teresa went to sit on Dylan's chair arm. "This is a wonderful fireplace, Mr. Swayne."

"Thank you. We were just talking about the ones in Los Angeles."

Her nose wrinkled. "I do not remember seeing any . . . but I only went there once."

Dylan patted her leg. "The ones in my dad's house all had potted plants in them. . . ."

"And the ones in our apartments had ceramic logs and a gas-jet flame." Michael sighed and poured whisky into his and Dylan's glasses. "Most unsatisfactory."

Teresa nodded. "This was where you lived when you were at school with Uncle Dylan?"

"Yes . . . in fact he and I were neighbors. Did he tell you that?"

"Your apartment was near to Grandfather Will's house?"

"No, sweetie . . . I rented a place by campus so I didn't have to drive across town every day . . . and Mr. Swayne's apartment was right next to it."

"So . . . this is how you met?" Dylan nodded and Teresa frowned. "But I thought no one in Los Angeles *knew* his neighbors."

Michael laughed. "You're thinking of New York. It's almost the same in LA, but when we discovered that we left home at the same time every day . . ."

"Headed in the same direction . . . ."

"And had lunch in the same café at the student union . . . ."

"Even a stodgy Brit and a self-absorbed Angelino cast caution to the wind and we introduced ourselves."

Teresa giggled and sipped wine. "You had no classes together?"

Dylan shook his head. "We had very few formal classes, except the ones we taught, since we were both graduate students."

"Oh . . . um. . . ." She licked her lips. "I do not mean to be impolite, but . . . you are not the same age, are you?"

"No, sweetie . . . I'm *much* older."

"That will *do*, Travis." Michael winked at Teresa. "Your uncle was a callow youth, barely in his twenties, whilst I was a mature man of the world with degrees from Oxford and real work experience."

"Oh, *that's* right . . . I must have forgotten. But I had to teach him how to drive."

"He *means* he taught me how to drive on the wrong side of the road . . . and I taught *him* to appreciate beer made to be served at the proper temperature."

Teresa nodded. "Like Guinness and champagne?"

The men looked at each other, then glared at Beth.

She puffed her cheeks and stood up. "I'll see what's happening in the kitchen."

"Sit *down*, Ms. Trelawny." Beth sat and Michael leaned forward. "What *have* you been telling these girls?"

"Nothing! I . . ."

"It was not *she*, Mr. Swayne, I only. . . ." Teresa bit her lip.

"Only *what*, sweetie?" Dylan smiled.

"Someone told me there was such a story . . . about you and . . .

and Guinness and champagne, but she would not tell me more because she said it probably was not true."

The men laughed while Beth sighed. She stood again and shook her head.

"If you'll *excuse* me . . . I hear a wine bottle calling."

"So . . . what *is* the story, Uncle Dylan?"

"There isn't much to it . . . but it got blown out of proportion."

Michael nodded. "The tale grew in the telling, as it were."

"But what *did* happen?"

Dylan looked at his friend and they shrugged. "OK, sweetie . . . what *really* happened was that we went to a party and had a bit more to drink than was good for us."

"You drank Guinness and champagne?"

He nodded. "A delightful but dangerous combination."

"Indeed . . . and thought to be hallucinogenic." Michael smirked.

Teresa gasped and Dylan chuckled.

"Not really . . . although it's certainly mind-altering."

"*Quite* . . . and your uncle was dating an undergraduate at the time . . . a young woman who lived in a sorority house. . . ."

"And after we left the party, somehow we imagined it would be a good idea to go see her. . . ."

"At about three in the morning. . . ."

"Then I called up at her window to come down and talk to me. . . ."

"He *screamed* at her window, and threatened to spank her if she refused."

"Oh my God!" Teresa drained her wine glass and wiped her mouth. "And . . . and *did* she come down?"

Dylan shook his head. "It wasn't *her* window. We went to the wrong house . . . which I realized just before the campus police arrived."

"So we escaped . . . but made the error of telling some friends of our adventure."

"And before long, everyone on campus had heard how we went to every house on sorority row and asked if any of the girls needed a good paddling."

Teresa laughed as Beth came out the kitchen door, a bottle in hand, followed by Lisa and Mandy. Beth walked over and filled Teresa's glass.

"Are you OK, honey? You look kind of flushed."

"I am all right." Teresa smiled at Lisa. "Only I have just heard the Guinness and champagne story."

"Oh, *man*. I missed it!" Lisa frowned when Michael crooked a finger.

"Come here, young lady." She baby-stepped toward him, a hand over her bottom. "I have the idea that *you* told her that story . . . or at least of its existence."

"Nuh *uh*, Michael . . . I mean, I um . . . I might have said *something* about Guinness and champagne, but um. . . ."

"She told me it was a Paul Bunyan story," Teresa said.

"Yeah . . . just a legend, you know?"

Michael smiled and reached for Lisa's hand. She puffed a breath and leaned over so he could kiss her cheek.

"I would rather you circulated no more *legends* about your employer and your professor . . . even amongst the family . . . all right?"

"Yes, sir . . . I mean *no*, sir . . . and anyway I *didn't*." His eyebrows arched and Lisa whimpered. "*OK!* I won't! Geeze!"

She turned and scowled at Beth, then yelped when Michael swatted the seat of her woolen slacks. Beth grimaced and took Lisa's hand, but spoke to Michael.

"Mrs. Gates is carving the turkey so it'll be just a few more minutes."

"Thank you. Would you collect the other guests? You and I will have a chat later on." He smiled but Beth frowned and muttered oaths as she headed to the stairs.

Mandy guzzled pale golden liquid from a water glass and grabbed Lisa's arm. "What the *hell* are you guys talking about?" she whispered.

"Later . . . and don't bring *that* to the table." Lisa pointed at the glass and Mandy nodded.

Michael finished his whisky and looked at Dylan. "I believe dinner is served."

The professor chuckled. "What? No gong?"

* * *

The celebrants sidled around a long table while Michael stood at its head and smiled.

"I apologize for the tight squeeze. The room was designed for a party of eight, but we inserted both extensions into the table, so I hope everyone has enough space. It was either this or some of us would have to eat in the kitchen." He winked at Lisa.

She wrinkled her nose at him as she sat between Jill and Felicia. "I *told* you this would work, Michael . . . and I *know* who'd have to eat in the kitchen."

Dylan chuckled and shook out his napkin. "The children? There aren't any . . . so you must mean the men."

Lisa grinned. "Why? So you can talk about guy stuff?"

"Of course not. So we can eat drumsticks with our fingers."

Michael scoffed. "You know better than that, Professor Travis . . . the fingers should always be eaten separately."

The German cousins stared at each other, then joined in the others' polite laughter at the ancient joke. Everyone smiled as Mrs. Gates and her helpers brought steamy plates, platters and bowls to the table. The short, round woman fussed and whispered directions while the diners filled their plates with ham, turkey, dressing, mashed potatoes, green bean casserole, sweet potatoes with marshmallows, boiled asparagus, and a congealed fruit salad. While dishes were passed amid hungry and appreciative murmurs, Mrs. Gates filled glasses with a light rosé. Mandy bit her lip and looked across the table.

"Daddy?" she whispered.

Jack smiled. "Sure, honey . . . have some if you want."

Dylan raised his glass. "To our host and his household . . . may they live long and prosper."

Michael nodded. "And to our guests . . . who honor this house with their presence."

Delia giggled and lifted the glass over her head. "*Prost!*"

Christa squeaked in anguish, but Dylan smiled and patted her hand.

"*Prost*, indeed." He sipped and then leaned over and whispered. "No more wine for you two, understand?" Christa nodded and set her glass down, then blushed when Dylan laughed as if she had said something funny.

Platters and bowls emptied, disappeared and reappeared full, while table chatter rose and fell. Michael introduced Mrs. Gates, and she smiled as she introduced her nieces, the two helpers, and

then asked if everyone would prefer their dessert later. They all agreed, then leaned back and patted very full stomachs.

Jill sighed and fanned herself with a napkin. Lisa patted her arm. "You OK?"

"Yeah . . . but I probably shouldn't have had that second helping of green bean casserole."

"It had heavy cream in it. You're not lactose intolerant, are you?"

The woman shook her head. "It could have been the wine, too."

Lisa giggled. "You didn't *drink* any."

"A little . . . for the toast. I really can't handle alcohol, honey."

"You want to lie down?"

"Maybe I better."

"OK . . . can you make it upstairs?"

"I think so."

Lisa quietly helped her around the end of the table. Dylan raised his eyebrows, then nodded and smiled when Lisa glared at him. He continued his conversation with Christa about the evils of turkey farming, and twitched when a phone rang.

"Sorry, everyone . . . I meant to turn that off."

He grabbed the cell phone from an inside pocket of his tweed jacket and aimed a thumb at the switch. Cold shivers lanced up his spine when he read the ID screen.

"Dylan? Are you all right?"

"Yeah, Mike . . . but I have to take this. Excuse me."

Michael nodded. Dylan scowled as he walked out of the room. "Hello?"

"Hi, Dylan . . . it's me."

He swallowed hard. "What's wrong, Gwen? Why are you calling from the hospital?"

"My, um . . . I left my cell phone in the car and all the payphones are busy so the doctor said I could use this one."

"Whoa . . . let's start over." He sighed and trudged up the stairs. "Why are you at the hospital? Are you all right?"

"Uh huh . . . more or less . . . but the Jetta is like *totaled,* and I really, really wish I'd of come to see *you* instead of staying in Boston and. . . ."

"Shh . . . it's OK, Princess." Jill swung her legs over and sat up on the chaise when he pushed open the study door. "Sorry, I didn't know you were. . . ."

"What's wrong, Dylan?"

"Just a second, Gwen."

Jill stood and waved him in. He cupped a hand over the microphone.

"Are you OK?"

"I'm fine but *you* look like hell . . . sit down and talk to her."

He sat in the desk chair and Jill walked behind him to open the cooler. She poured beer into a wine glass and set it in front of him. He patted her arm and smiled.

"Gwen? So . . . what happened to the Jetta?"

"It . . . it got smushed . . . the airbag popped and *everything*." She swallowed and took a breath. "I was um . . . on my way home from the church this evening and . . . we served over seven hundred meals today . . . isn't that great?"

"Yes . . . I'm very proud of you, but would you *please* tell me what happened? Are you in the emergency room?"

"Yeah . . . they took x-rays and gave me this stupid neck-brace but I'm really OK, and I . . . I'm sorry if I interrupted your dinner."

"Gwen, *please* . . . how did it *happen?*" He grimaced when he heard her sobs, and then took a deep breath. "Gwendolyn! Stop that this *instant* and tell me before I get angry."

"*Dylan* . . . don't . . . don't *yell* at me! I . . . I was in a big pile-up on the turnpike, OK?"

"I didn't mean to yell . . . I'm sorry . . . but it's *killing* me that you're hurt and I'm not there to make it all go away."

"I know . . . but I don't want to think about it 'cause it was so *horrible*. I mean . . . the road was all slippery from the sleet, and there must have been a hundred cars crunched together and knocked around . . . and I think they're *still* getting people out and . . . and I just didn't want you to worry if you saw it on the news."

"You did exactly right to call me because I probably would have. I love you, you know that, don't you?"

"Uh huh . . . I love you, too."

"Are they going to release you soon?"

"They . . . they already did but I don't know how I'm gonna get *home*. I can't get hold of Deb or Aunt Phoebe or *any*body!"

"Take a taxi . . . it's OK."

"Yeah, but . . . I don't have any *money*. My purse is still in the car so I don't have my credit cards or my keys or *anything*."

Her sobs burned his ear and tears pooled in his eyes as he scrabbled for his wallet.

"Shh . . . it's OK . . . I've got the limo service number right here. I'll call and have them pick you up. Commonwealth General, right? Gwen?"

"Uh . . . uh huh . . . but how will I *pay* for it?"

"They can bill my account . . . and when you sign, add thirty percent for the driver, OK?"

"Oh . . . OK. I will. Thanks."

He smiled. "Go home, Princess . . . you've had a busy day. Is the house key still under that rock in the garden?"

She chuckled. "Uh huh . . . and aren't you sorry you scolded me for putting it there?"

"I am *never* sorry for scolding you . . . but I doubt if I'll ever scold you again for *that*."

"Then I guess I'll take what I can get. Tell them I'll be at the emergency room exit . . . and, um . . . can I take a couple of people home?"

"Well sure, if they live close to. . . ."

"About eleven?"

Dylan frowned. "Eleven *what*?"

"People! The church van got caught in the pile-up so they need to get home, too."

"They all live in your neighborhood?"

"Uh huh . . . within a couple miles. That's OK, isn't it?"

"Yes . . . I'll order a stretch car . . . and you *call* me when you get home, all right?"

"I will. Dylan?"

"Hmm?"

"Thank you . . . you take really good care of me."

"And the immediate parish, it seems."

She grunted. "Everybody will chip in to pay for the limo so don't be . . ."

"Stop that! They will do no such thing. You conned me fair and square so I'll foot the bill . . . and *you* will pay the interest."

"But I *didn't* con you, and . . . what do you mean *interest*?"

He grinned. "No good deed goes unpunished . . . now we'd better clear this line. Get your people together and I'll have a car there as soon as I can."

"But I didn't *mean* to . . ."

"Hush, Princess . . . and hang up. Call me when you get home."

"*Dylan,* I . . ."

The phone queeped when he switched it off. Jill lay back on the chaise and smiled as she hugged her stomach.

"Sounds like you got a problem, Professor."

"Uh huh . . . looks like you do, too."

She shook her head. "I told you I'm *fine.*"

"Yes, well . . . I'm sure there's some enema equipment in Mr. Swayne's bathroom and. . . ."

Her face turned bright red. "Don't even *think* about . . ."

The study door opened and Lisa peeked in. "Hi . . . sorry to bother you guys. Is everything OK?"

"Yeah, we're *fine.*" Jill grimaced. "Maybe I should go on home, though."

Dylan shook his head. "We are *not* fine, Lisa. Would you look around and see if you have any . . ."

"Hey, I *told* you not to . . ."

"*Hush,* Jill! You need a dose of Pepto and that's all there is to it, so *chill.*" He winked at Lisa and she smiled.

"I'll get some. Be right back."

Teresa leaned around the door. "Do you need anything, Uncle Dylan?"

"No thanks . . . come in, sweetie."

Jill glared at Dylan, and Teresa frowned as she tiptoed over and sat on his lap. He patted her bottom while he thumbed the phone's keypad.

"Hello . . . Professor Travis here . . . I need a car . . . a big one . . . as soon as you can. I have an account with you. Yes, I'll hold."

"What's wrong, Uncle Dylan?"

"Nothing, sweetie . . . but Gwen had an accident and her car is out of commission."

"Gwen in Boston?" He nodded. "Is she all right?"

"I think so . . . but I have to get her home from the emergency room."

"The emergency room of the hospital?" He nodded and she handed him the glass when he reached for it. "Why is she *there* if she is all right?"

Dylan smiled and drained the beer. "Would you turn on CNN?"

Teresa stood, grabbed the remote from the desktop and flicked buttons. Lisa walked in, gave Jill a tiny cup of pink liquid and the woman leaned back and drank.

"Yuck!"

"Yeah, I know . . . but it's good for you."

Jill scowled and wiped her lip. "You sound just like Dylan."

"Hey! You don't gotta be *nasty*." Lisa grinned and took the empty cup.

"OK, OK. Thanks . . . that'll help."

Teresa gasped and turned to Dylan. "I think I have found it . . . a very bad accident on the Boston freeway."

"Yes . . . and Gwen was *in* that mess." Dylan held up a finger and pressed the phone to his ear. "What? Oh . . . hi, Jeff." He pointed and Teresa muted the TV. "Yeah, I need a *big* car . . . room for a dozen . . . and I need it quick at the hospital . . . Commonwealth General, emergency room. Yes, I know it's Thanksgiving, but I'd consider it a personal favor . . . just a run to Wellesley and a few drop-offs." He smiled. "The white wedding special? No, I don't think anybody will mind if it hasn't been cleaned up. Sure. Thanks, Jeff. Gwen McKenna . . . she'll meet you at the ER exit door. I appreciate it. Call me at this number if you have any problems."

He switched off the phone and emptied the beer bottle into his glass. Teresa leaned against the desk and took his hand.

"You will send a *wedding* car to pick her up?"

"That's all they have right now. She left her purse behind so she doesn't have any money for a taxi . . . and she connived a ride for her friends from church." He grinned and winked.

Jill chuckled. "Your armor's pretty shiny today, Professor."

"Just call me Sir Galahad."

Teresa sat on the desktop. "So what *will* you do?"

"Hm? I just *did* it, sweetie."

"Well yes, but . . . will you *go* to Boston?"

"Do you think I should?"

"No, I . . . I was merely thinking . . . what *you* might be thinking."

Her tummy gurgled with a surfeit of holiday food and Teresa bit her lip as she waited for Dylan to quit rubbing his eyes.

"I *should* go, I suppose."

"Did she *ask* you to do this, Uncle Dylan?"

"Well . . . no . . . she didn't."

"And she was not much hurt from this accident?"

"They put a neck-brace on . . . but only as a precaution, I think."

Lisa shrugged. "So you don't *need* to go running off in the middle of the holiday weekend, right?"

He scowled. "Maybe not . . . and I get the feeling you two would rather I *didn't*. Why is that?"

Teresa glanced at Lisa and then looked at him. "Be . . . because we are worried that . . . that you will make such a decision whilst you are drunk."

"*What?* I'm not anywhere *near*. . . ."

"Hi!" Beth leaned around the doorjamb and smiled. "Everything OK? There's pumpkin pie and ice cream for anybody who wants it." She gaped when Lisa frowned at her, and then strode over to the desk. "What's wrong? Something about the phone call?"

Dylan sighed. "Ms. Trelawny, it really isn't. . . ."

"Would you knock it off? My name is *Beth* . . . so unbundle your professor shorts and tell me what's going on, OK?"

Lisa, Teresa and Jill held their breath while Dylan stared at the woman, and then sighed when he smiled.

"All right . . . Beth. I have a friend in Boston who was in an accident, and my friends *here* are trying to help me sort out what I should do about it."

She smirked and walked to the cooler, twisted the top off a beer bottle and turned to him. "And none of these *friends* brought you a whisky to help you think?"

Teresa snapped to her feet. "I will get this."

"Thanks, sweetie."

She trotted out the door and Lisa followed. "I know where to find the bottle."

"OK, but the decanter was almost empty and I better tell Michael what's going on."

"Yes, perhaps. . . ." Teresa stopped at the bottom of the stairs. "Do you think he will go to Boston?"

"Do *you* think he should?"

Teresa bit her lip. "He *said* she is not injured . . . and he promised to take me Christmas shopping this weekend."

They went into the living room and Lisa knelt to pull a green bottle from a shelf in the sideboard. "So you *don't* want him to go."

"I don't wish to appear selfish . . . but if it is not *necessary. . . .*"

"Yeah . . . but you know how he feels about her. The way he went on that night during the storms?"

"But we *made* him tell us."

"I know . . . but should he be running off in the middle of the semester and do God knows what with her? He's *our* professor and he should take care of us . . . not some floozy in Boston, right?"

"Um . . . yes. I thought I would be happy that he has a girlfriend, but not if she is a . . . what did you say?"

"*Floozy* . . . and that's *gotta* be what she is. He said she *conned* him into renting that limo."

"Yes, and it is not *right* that she uses this accident to take him away from me . . . *us.*"

Lisa shook her head and then smiled as Michael and Felicia walked into the living room. "Hi . . . you want a whisky?" She popped the cork from a Glenlivet bottle.

He nodded, covered his mouth and turned as he burped. "Pardon me . . . yes, that would be splendid. Would you care for one, Felicia?"

The woman shook her head. "I'm driving. Is Dylan all right?"

Teresa held a small glass while Lisa poured, and then handed it to Michael. "His girlfriend was in a car crash . . . but he thinks she will be all right."

"*Gwen?* I'd better go see him. Is he in the study?" Teresa nodded and Felicia ran to the stairs.

Michael took Lisa's hand. "Is there anything I can do?"

"I think he's got it covered, Mike."

He glowered and Lisa bit her lip. "Young lady, Professor Travis is the only person in the *world* who is allowed to call me that and you *know* it."

"Yes, sir . . . sorry, sir."

He sighed, sipped and set the glass on the lamp table. The cousins ambled in from the dining room, fell onto the sofa and moaned.

"I cannot eat pie and ice cream now," Delia said.

Christa nodded. "I think I will not eat *anything* for a week!"

"Then you have learnt the true meaning of the American Thanksgiving holiday." Michael raised his glass and winked.

The girls chuckled and rubbed their bellies. Lisa handed Teresa a glass with two ounces of whisky in it.

"Here . . . that's for Dylan." She turned to Michael. "You want me to help Mrs. Gates?"

"No . . . but I believe these young ladies would like a glass of port to aid their digestions."

"Yes, sir . . . I'll see to it at *once, sir.*"

"Thank you." He smiled. "And put another log on the fire, would you? And a bit of Mozart on the stereo?"

"Of *course,* sir . . . right away, sir . . . you're spoiled *rotten,* sir." She grinned and Michael winked.

"You would know all about *that,* wouldn't you?"

Lisa scowled and opened the sideboard. Teresa giggled, pulled an oak slab from the pile on the hearth and dropped it onto the fire. Delia and Christa smiled when Lisa put three-ounce glasses of amber liquid on the coffee table in front of them. Mandy came in, sat on the far end of the sofa and bit her lip as she stared at her sister. Lisa rolled her eyes, poured a glass of port for her, and then went to the corner to slip a CD into the stereo. Rich orchestration filled the room and Michael nodded.

"Very splendid, my dear. An excellent backdrop for my tales of life at Oxford."

"Yeah?" Lisa winked. "You guys enjoy the port . . . and it's OK to doze off if he gets boring."

Christa smiled and picked up her glass. "He will not bore us . . . we like the way his voice is sounding."

"Where did Dad and Greg go?"

Mandy pointed. "Looking at Greg's truck."

"Like they haven't *seen* it a thousand times."

"Big boys and their toys." Michael sipped whisky and smiled.

Teresa took Dylan's glass and headed for the stairs. Lisa skipped past her and peered out the foyer window.

"Oh, *sure* . . . now they've got the hood up on *Dylan's* truck. We've lost them for good."

"Still . . . I am glad he bought it."

Lisa nodded and followed Teresa. "The Firebird wouldn't be much good in the snow, that's for sure. He didn't trade it in on the Blazer, did he?"

"Of *course* not. He would rather part with his right leg, I think."

Beth sat on the end of the chaise while she chatted with Jill and Felicia. They looked up when Lisa and Teresa entered. Dylan leaned forward in the desk chair, peered at the computer screen and mouse-clicked. Teresa set the whisky glass beside the keyboard and he smiled.

"You are looking at the airlines, Uncle Dylan?"

"Thanks, sweetie. Yeah . . . I could get out tonight if I wanted."

Teresa crossed her arms and perched on the desk edge. Lisa pouted and ignored Beth's glare as she went to the credenza and filled two glasses with merlot. She handed one to Teresa and leaned beside her against the desk.

"The weather's supposed to get worse, Dylan."

"Oh? Who told you that, Lisa?"

"Um . . . the Weather Channel."

"I see."

"Yes and . . ." Teresa gulped wine. "In any case, how will you drive to the airport if you have had so much whisky?"

He scowled and turned the chair to face them. "There are other ways to get to the airport."

"Sure but . . . with all the turkey you ate you're gonna be *asleep* in a half hour and . . ."

"Lisa, are you drunk?"

"No!"

"Then why are you so *impertinent*? You could at least call me *Professor* Dylan when you presume to tell me how to conduct my business."

Lisa stared at the carpet. "I'm *sorry,* but . . . geeze!"

"*Geeze* nothing, young lady. I think you have had far more to drink than . . ."

"Do not scold *her,* Uncle Dylan!" Wine sloshed when Teresa slammed down her glass. "She is merely saying what we *all* feel . . . that you should not go to Boston!"

Beth fluttered her lips as she grabbed a stack of paper napkins from the credenza and dabbed the spilt wine. Dylan frowned and shook his head.

"Do you mean I shouldn't go *tonight,* or that I shouldn't go at *all?*"

Green eyes burned as Teresa blinked back a tear. "You . . . you *promised* you would take me shopping this weekend."

"Yes, but that was before Gwen got hurt in the. . . ."

"But you said she is *not* hurt . . . so why must you abandon us during this time?"

"*Abandon*? During *what* time?"

"During the *holiday*! This is very unfair to me and . . . and in any case this last-minute flight is *most* expensive so you do not need to . . ."

His frown deepened and butterflies awakened in Teresa's tummy. "How I deal with this affair is none of your concern, young lady."

Lisa sneered. "Affair, huh? *That's* a good word."

"Yes . . . and with this *floozy*."

He jerked to his feet. "*What* did you say?"

"*Nothing*, I . . . I don't *know*, Uncle Dylan!"

"What do you *mean* you don't know?"

"I . . . I only *heard* this word and . . . and . . ."

"And you don't think it *sounds* insulting? You have pushed me as far as you're going to, little girl."

"No, *please?*" She wailed and stumbled as he dragged her across the room.

"That goes for you too, missy." Beth grabbed Lisa's arm and pulled her around the desk. "Put that glass down now."

"Beth, *don't!*"

Jill rolled off the chaise as Dylan sat at its foot and tossed Teresa across his lap. Felicia stood and chewed a knuckle.

"Dylan?"

He looked at his sister. "If you don't want to see this you'd better leave."

Teresa squirmed as he lifted her blue woolen skirt and black slip. "*Please* not in front of *everybody!*"

"Quiet, girl! Everyone in this room knows I discipline you so be *still.*"

Felicia whimpered and ran to the door. Beth chuckled when the woman shut it and snapped the lock. Teresa twisted and gazed at Dylan with tearful eyes.

"I . . . I am sorry *honestly!* I did not *mean* to be insulting."

"Oh *really?* Did you merely mean to be officious and impudent and *jealous?*"

"I am *not* jealous so *please* do not . . . I *said* I am sorry and . . . *no*! Not my *panties!*"

He held her waist as he pulled blue silk tap pants down her

bottom. Pale round cheeks turned pink with embarrassment, and the cleft narrowed to a thin line when she clenched. Her spine stiffened and she trembled as she lay rigid across his thighs. He raised his arm, smacked hard, and she wailed in pain and anger, then he took a breath and slapped again.

"How *dare* you insult a person you never even *met*? What were you *thinking*, Teresa Luisa?"

"But I *owee*! I did not *mean* it! Ow! Not so *ow*! *Hard*! Aauu!"

Lisa nibbled her lip and rubbed her bottom as she watched his arm rise and fall. Teresa's mounds flattened and quivered while he spanked, and she clutched the chaise leg to push her back straight. He palmed her tummy with his left hand and raised her hips.

"Put your head *down*, young lady . . . *and* your feet. Bend *over* so I can spank you *properly*."

"Oh God *please* do not make me . . . aieee! Ow! Ow! Owee!"

Sharp, serious claps echoed, and an obstinate rage filled her heart as she felt every eye in the room on her behind. He pressed his left elbow into her back and she squealed a wordless negative, pushed up even harder and thrust out her legs. Dylan growled and smacked her thigh.

"All *right*, Teresa . . . if that's how you *want* it."

"No Uncle Dylan!"

He leaned left, raised his right leg and clamped it across her knees. She whimpered and her rage dissolved in a pool of self-pity as she bent and shut her eyes against a flood of sorrow. Her cheeks parted and cool air rushed into the shameful cleft. His hand clapped the base of her open behind and she screeched as a spark of lightening shot through tender flesh and ignited moist, itchy fire between her thighs. He crossed his ankles to clasp quivery legs in a firm but gentle hold while he peppered her bottom with quick, sharp swats.

"You *know* better than to defy me when I correct you!" She babbled in German as his palm stung tender flesh. "The very idea! Acting like a *spoiled, willful* child in front of our *friends*."

"*Ich* . . . I . . . *ow* . . . I am *sorry*! I *will* be good . . . I *promise*!"

"I certainly *hope* so. Stand up, Teresa."

She moaned and shook as he reached beneath her bosom to help her, and together they stood. Her skirt fell to conceal her red bottom, and salty remorse wetted his tie while she leaned against

his chest, wrapped in his long arms, safe and loved and cleansed of guilt. His rapid, steady heartbeat throbbed against her face and she longed to remain just as she was forever, but Beth's voice rang out like a gunshot in a schoolyard.

"You ready for *this* one, Professor?"

Lisa squeaked. "Beth, no!"

Dylan sighed and patted Teresa's back as he whispered in her ear. "Pull your panties up, sweetie." She nodded and bent to retrieve the underwear that had fallen to her ankles. He turned to Beth. "It isn't my place . . . not really a matter of *college* discipline."

"Yeah, but she was egging Teresa *on.*"

"Jesus *Christ,* Beth! What are you *doing?*"

"Making sure you get what you deserve." She grabbed Lisa's arm and Dylan backed away as the woman hauled her to the chaise. "You acted just as rotten as she did and if *he* won't then *I* will."

Lisa jerked and wriggled from Beth's grasp. "No you *won't* . . . and . . . and it's none of your damn business, anyway!"

Dylan snatched Lisa's hand and spun her around. "*What* did you say, young lady?"

"I . . . well it *isn't.*" Her voice quavered and she stared at the carpet to avoid his icy glare.

"Regardless . . . your language *is* my business and I've heard *more* than enough profanity from you."

"But Dyl . . . *Professor*! Don't *do* that!"

She stamped her foot and grabbed her trouser waist, but he slapped her fingers away and unfastened the button and zipper.

"Now bend over Ms. Trelawny's lap this *instant,* Lisa Marie."

Beth smirked and waved a hand. "Go ahead . . . you're already warmed up. You want a hairbrush?"

"For Christ's . . . crying out *loud,* Beth, why are you being such a . . . ?"

"*Hush,* girl." He looked at his red palm. "If there's one handy."

Teresa whimpered and chewed a fingertip as warm, guilty moisture wetted the cotton gusset of her panties. Jill and Felicia leaned on a chair back and stared at Dylan. Beth rummaged in a desk drawer, found a short, thick strap and held it up.

"No hairbrush. Will this do?"

"Beth!"

Lisa squealed as Dylan nodded, sat on the chaise and drew the girl across his thighs. She fought back tears while he pulled snug trousers to her knees and then whined when he tugged down white bikini panties. Beth handed him the black leather strap. It was a foot long and an inch and a half wide, made of two pieces of a belt glued together, finished sides out. It clacked when he swished it against the chair leg, and he smiled as Beth backed away.

"Thank you. Are you ready, Lisa?"

She pouted and raised a fist above the carpet, then braced her palms on the floor and puffed a breath. "I *guess* so . . . but this isn't *even* fair!"

"Neither is inciting your classmate to throw a tantrum."

"But I didn't *do* anything *owee*! Geeze, Dylan, that *ouch*! Really *stings*! That's *enough!*"

He held tight to her slim waist and flicked his wrist. The strap curled and clapped soft, elastic cheeks. Wide, pink stripes blossomed on pale flesh while Lisa kicked.

"Not to mention your atrocious *language* . . . I know *Michael* would love to hear it."

"No! *Ow*! Not so *ouch*! *Hard!*"

"Or perhaps your *father?* Hmm?"

Tears sprang to her eyes and she quivered as leather stung her bottom. "No *please?* I'm *sorry!*"

"As well you *should* be." He fanned her cheeks with a dozen more quick, short smacks, dropped the strap, then stood and took Lisa with him. "Do you think you can behave like a *lady* now?"

"Yuh-yes, sir." She leaned against him while he pulled up her panties and slacks.

"Very well, then." He kissed her forehead and crooked a finger. "Come here, Teresa." The girl shuffled over and he stepped back to hold them both by the arm. "I don't know what got into you two . . . but I hope I've heard the last of it." They nodded and he hugged them. "All right . . . you're forgiven. Now go clean up."

They scurried out the door and across the hall into Michael's bedroom. Dylan sighed and picked up the whisky glass. Beth patted his arm and bent to retrieve the strap.

"You've got a lot of self-control, Dylan."

He sipped and winked. "You would have blistered her purple?"

"I would have been tempted."

"Don't think I wasn't . . . but what would I do the next time they throw a jealous fit?"

Beth chuckled and opened the desk drawer. Felicia walked over and Dylan put an arm around her.

"Do you think there'll *be* a next time?"

"I won't rule out the possibility. They don't like sharing me with *any*one, Fel."

"You think a lot of yourself, don't you?"

He laughed and squeezed her shoulder. "Do you remember when you were twelve and wanted me to take you to Six Flags one weekend . . . and I couldn't because I went to Vegas with Angela?"

She gaped and slapped his chest. "I wasn't *jealous,* I just . . ."

"You just became such a holy terror that Angela never came to the house after that."

"It wasn't my fault you couldn't keep a girlfriend . . . and besides, these girls aren't twelve."

"Sometimes they act like it." He kissed her cheek. "Why don't you start saying our goodbyes? It's getting late."

"Sure. Do you want some pie and ice cream before we leave?"

"No . . . but you go ahead."

Beth led her to the door. "You can take a pie home if you want . . . we have six and we'll never eat them all."

Jill ambled over and leaned next to Dylan. "Pity you have to work so hard on a holiday."

"Oh, great!" He grinned and kissed her cheek. "Another brat heard from."

"So what *are* you going to do . . . about Gwen, I mean?"

He sighed. "I don't know . . . but I'll wait to hear she got home safely before I do *any*thing. Why? What do you think I should do?"

"I'm sure you'll do whatever is best, sir."

"Do I not have *enough* smart-alecks to deal with?"

She grinned. "OK . . . I guess I should point out that you've *never* gone to see her unless you planned ahead of time . . . so it's kinda strange you're even thinking about it."

"Yes . . . but she never crashed her car before."

"You didn't rush out there when she had the emergency appendectomy."

"No . . . but she asked me not to."

Jill shrugged. "Then I guess she'll have to tell you what to do, huh?"

His eyes narrowed. "You *are* a brat, aren't you?"

"Don't *even* go looking for that strap!"

* * *

Lisa switched on the light in Michael's bathroom and shut the door behind them. Teresa sneered at her reflection and dabbed her eyes with a tissue.

"Are you all right, Lisa?"

"Yeah . . . I guess so. Are you?"

"Yes . . . but I was not spanked with a *strap*."

"It wasn't so bad." She dropped her trousers and turned as she pulled her panties down. "See? No welts. He was pretty ticked off at you, though."

"Yes." Teresa grimaced as she bared her bottom and looked over her shoulder. "I was not very smart . . . to act so defiantly."

"Nope . . . those hand prints are gonna take a while to fade."

"Very likely . . . is it all right if I use the toilet?"

"Sure . . . go ahead."

Teresa winced as she sat. "Do you think he *will* go?"

"I don't know. Maybe he'll at least think about it."

"What *is* a floozy, in any case?"

Lisa giggled. "It's definitely an insult . . . and I *sure* didn't mean for you to repeat it."

"I am not certain why I did this."

"Well . . . it got his attention and. . . ." Lisa turned at the sound of a knock.

"Lisa, it's Greg. You OK?"

"Yeah . . . but don't come in. Teresa's on the potty."

"*Lisa.*"

Greg cleared his throat. "I won't . . . just wanted to know if you're all right. I um . . . heard the commotion in the study."

"You did, huh? Did anyone *else?*"

Teresa flushed and then bumped Lisa out of the way to get to the sink. Greg's answer was lost in the rush of water and Lisa opened the door.

"What?"

"I said . . . Mandy was with me but I kicked her downstairs when she started giggling."

"That little *creep*." Lisa scowled as she ran a comb through her hair.

"You *kicked* her?"

He chuckled. "Not *literally*, Teresa . . . but I gave her a firm shove."

Lisa scowled. "You should of given her a firm *licking* with your belt."

"I figured I'd better check with you on that first. So . . . what was it all about?"

"I'll tell you later. We better get downstairs."

"Do you um . . . need cold cream?"

"From you?" Lisa stood on tiptoe to kiss him. "Always . . . but not right now."

"OK. Well, listen . . . I'd better be going. I have to open the store early for the Friday rush so I need to get some sleep."

She pouted. "You have to leave *now?*"

"Pretty soon."

"So I can just do my *own* cold cream, huh?"

He frowned and hugged her. Lisa yelped when he squeezed her bottom.

"Keep up *that* attitude and I'll use my belt on *you*."

"Don't be harsh. Can I come over after the company leaves?"

"Yeah, sure . . . I'll leave the door unlocked in case I fall asleep."

"OK." She kissed him and grinned. "I promise not to keep you up *too* late."

"Uh huh . . . I just *bet*." He winked and pushed her ahead of him.

The three traipsed downstairs and the goodbye chatter among the other guests quieted. Dylan held out a hand to Teresa.

"Are you ready to go, sweetie?" He nodded toward Michael.

"Yes, Uncle Dylan." She took his hand in her left and held out her right. "Thank you for a wonderful dinner, Mr. Swayne."

He squeezed the hand. "You are more than welcome . . . and I hope you will come again soon."

Felicia carried a pie to the door and Beth opened it. "Thanks for everything . . . good night."

Beth smiled as Dylan and his troupe filed out into the shivery

autumn mist. Lisa hugged her father and kissed his cheek, then hugged Mandy.

"How come you got a lickin'?"

"Shh . . . don't be so nosy. I'll call you later, OK?"

"OK."

Mandy walked away and Lisa looked around. Greg shook Michael's hand and turned to her.

"Thank you for the party. I had a nice time."

Lisa giggled. "That's *very* good . . . I'll be sure to tell your folks how polite you were. Did Jill leave?"

He nodded. "Right after you um . . . were finished in the study."

"Oh . . . then I guess I'll be over sooner than I thought."

Beth shut the door and walked over to pat Lisa's shoulder. "The boss wants a word with us as soon as Greg leaves."

"Oh, geeze. *Now*?"

"Don't start, missy." She winked at Greg. "Good night."

"Good night, Ms. Trelawny. Thank you for the party. I had a. . . ."

She laughed. "Go *home*, mister . . . and don't mess up that pretty truck on any lampposts."

"I won't." He kissed Lisa and went out the door.

Michael leaned back in an armchair and loosened his tie. Lisa dragged a hassock over and sat next to him. Beth kicked off her shoes and curled up in the other chair.

"What's up?" Lisa said.

. "I thought the dinner went well, don't you?" He arched his eyebrows and Lisa nodded.

"Well, yeah . . . we've got lots of leftovers, though."

He shook his head. "I sent most of it home with Mrs. Gates . . . except the ham. I'm rather fond of grilled ham and cheese sandwiches. Would you like to tell me now?"

Butterflies awakened in her tummy and she looked at Beth. "Um . . . tell you *what*?"

"You *know* what. I understand Dylan was obliged to punish you and I should like to know why."

"Geeze, Beth, why'd you have to . . .?"

"Lisa! Stop this nonsense and *tell* me."

His blue eyes bored into her soul and she hung her head. "I'm *sorry*, Michael."

"That is *not* an answer, young lady. What did you do to so infu-

riate a guest in my house that he had to spank you like a naughty child?"

Tears ran down her cheeks and she leaned against his knee. "He . . . he wasn't *infuriated* . . . he just . . . didn't like something I said."

He sighed and pulled the girl onto his lap. "Must I drag the story out of you word by word?"

"Nuh-no, sir . . . I. . . ." She wiped her eyes and leaned on his shoulder. "We . . . um . . . don't want him to run off to Boston so . . . so we *told* him that and . . . and he didn't like it."

"*We?*"

"Me and Teresa."

Beth shook her head. "Tell him the rest."

Lisa glared at her. "*OK* . . . we . . . kinda got in his face about it."

"And . . .?"

"*Geeze,* Beth!"

"You cussed at him, didn't you?"

"Nuh *uh* . . . I cussed at *you,* 'cause you were being such a bi . . . *witch*!" She quivered and glanced at Michael's stony gaze. "But I didn't *mean* to! Sir!"

"I am *very* put out with you, Lisa."

"I *said* I was sorry!"

"That hardly suffices, does it?"

"But I already *got* punished . . . with that nasty little strap Beth made! So . . . so you don't *need* to punish me anymore . . . and anyway, you *never* spank me after *he* does . . . that was part of the deal for me going to his school, *remember?*"

"I remember no such clause in our contract. If I have refrained from disciplining you after you were punished at college it has been due to the fact that Professor Travis does such a thorough job of it."

"And he *did* . . . you wanna *see?*"

"In a moment . . . but this has nothing whatever to do with school, so even if we *had* the sort of agreement you mentioned it would not affect your conduct this evening. You put your nose into the private business of a guest in this house and that is *completely* unacceptable. The fact that he called you to task *himself* in no way exonerates your behavior. You are a member of *my* household and in this house are answerable to *me* and to no one else. If you had offended someone

that badly while at your *father's* home, I would expect no less from your father than what I intend to do."

"You just . . . you don't *understand*! I . . . I was only trying to help Teresa! *She* was a guest here *too* and . . ."

"Don't *tell* me I don't understand. Go to your room and I will be there shortly." He pushed her up and she stamped a foot as new tears streamed from her eyes.

"But *Michael!*"

"*Now,* Lisa."

"Oh *geeze!*"

She stalked through the kitchen door and he blew a long breath. Beth leaned over and patted his hand.

"You want a whisky?"

"No . . . I've had enough for today. But tell me this . . . can these two beautiful girls *possibly* be so enamored of Travis that they go off their heads at the mere *thought* of another woman in his life?"

She chuckled. "I don't know if *enamored* is the right word . . . *territorial,* definitely. He's been swatting their bare fannies for what? Almost six months now . . . and that's a lot of intimacy for girls their age."

"I see what you mean." He winked. "What do you suppose would happen if I went to LA and visited Samantha?"

"You mean Sam the *Slut?*" She twisted out of her chair and plunked into his lap. "You'd find out how territorial *this* little girl can be, you dirty old man."

"I dare say I *would.*" He kissed her lips. "And we *still* need to have a chat about your spreading gossip, don't we?"

"Nuh *uh,* Michael." She grinned and winked.

He sighed, set her on her feet and stood. "I must go and see to Lisa."

"You want any help?"

"No . . . why don't you check the doors and turn down the bed? Oh . . . and lay out the hairbrush, will you?"

"I will *not.* You can get your *own* damn hairbrush if you think you need it."

Michael scowled and swatted the seat of her skirt. "Is there a mysterious chemical in roast turkey that turns sensible young ladies into impudent *hussies*?"

Beth sneered. "Chemical? We don't need no stinking chemical!"

He chuckled and shook his head. "Apparently *not*. Now go!"

"Yes *sir*."

She kissed him and walked toward the foyer. He took a deep breath and headed for Lisa's room at the back of the house.

* * *

Lisa sat at her dresser and pouted as she toyed with her cell phone. She left the bedroom door open so she could hear Michael's approach while she debated whether to risk a call to Greg. Finally she shut off the phone and dropped it into her purse, then clasped her hands in her lap and waited. Footfalls shushed the hallway carpet and he stepped into the doorway. His eyebrows arched and a storm of butterflies gathered in her tummy as she stood. He held out a hand and walked toward her.

"Come along. Let's have a look at the professor's handiwork."

"No, please, I . . . I said I won't do it anymore and . . . and anyway . . ."

He took her arm, led her to the bed and sat down. "Anyway *what*?"

"I . . . I don't *know*, but you're not being *reasonable*."

"Is that so? Remove your slacks and shoes, young lady."

"But I don't *want* you to!"

"*Now*, Lisa Marie."

The horrible in-trouble name echoed in her ears as she kicked off low-heeled pumps and bent to slide her trousers down. She bit her lip and turned away from him when she saw telltale dampness at the front of her panties. Her bottom tingled with remembered sting, and quivered in anticipation of more, and the tingle lit a spark between puffy lower lips. She tossed the pants into the closet and then whimpered as he pulled her across his knees. He caressed her bottom and cleared his throat.

"Raise your hips so I can take down your knickers."

Lisa whimpered and arched her back. His knuckles grazed sensitized flesh as he pulled down her underpants and the spark between her thighs flickered and blazed.

"Michael, *please?*"

"Hush." Fingertips stroked smooth skin and he shook his head. "Your bottom is white as a baby's. Are you *certain* he used a strap?"

"Well *duh!* Ow!" His hand clapped and she kicked the duvet. "I mean I was *there* . . . ask Beth if you don't believe me."

"I will take your word . . . but you *know* I detest that hideous catch-phrase. However, it doesn't appear that Dylan was *quite* as thorough as he usually is."

"Uh huh he was and it really, really *hurt*."

"No doubt it did . . . and I'm afraid *this* will also, at least for a time."

His arm rose and fell, and Lisa squeaked as his palm landed across her shadowy cleft. Bright pain surged across her cheeks and poured between her thighs as he concentrated quick sharp slaps at the base of her behind, only millimeters from her most secret passageways. His thigh muscles, tight as anchor cable, burned against her belly and tickled close-cropped hair above her vagina. On and on he slapped, as her pulse quickened and her anus throbbed. Fiery moisture bathed her labia while heat raged through her bottom. Lightening flashed from the hard bud of her clitoris and Lisa shrieked as climactic, boulder-sized marshmallows crashed, one after another, into her soul.

Michael smiled and caressed the little maid's red cheeks while her dampness seeped through his trousers. She quivered and moaned as tiny aftershocks twitched her hips. He turned her over and she wept into his collar.

"Jesus, Michael!" she whispered. "Huh . . . how could you . . .? Did you *mean* to . . .?"

"Shh . . . did you learn your lesson, young lady?"

"Um . . . uh huh. I'll keep my nose out of Dylan's business from now on, I promise!"

"Very well, then. Would you care for cold cream?"

"Yeah . . . but . . . I kinda promised Greg *he* could do it."

"*Did* you? That's going to be problematic since you are grounded for the evening."

She leaned back and blinked to focus on his eyes. "That's *mean*, Michael! What time is it?"

He glanced at the clock radio. "Almost ten."

"Well *shoot* . . . he's probably crashed already." She cuddled into his shoulder and then gave him a quick, sideways glance. "So I gotta sleep *alone* tonight . . . and that's *really* mean."

"You poor, pitiful child." He chuckled and Lisa yelped when he squeezed her cheek. "Would you like to sleep in my bed?"

– 43 –

"With you and Beth?" He nodded. "OK . . . long as *she* doesn't mind."

"I doubt that very much. You're very good at comforting her, and she'll need quite a bit of that . . . after we discuss the Guinness and champagne issue."

She whimpered and hugged his neck. "But *I* didn't tell anybody!"

"But she told *you* . . . and no doubt the more scandalous version."

"So . . . so you're only gonna spank *her* for that?" She grinned when he nodded.

"Then I'll rub lotion on *both* your tragically injured bottoms."

"Well it *is* . . . you were way harsh with me."

"Was I?" He smiled and kissed her pout. "Then you might like to watch someone *else* treated a bit harshly."

"Yeah . . . I hardly ever get to see Beth get a lickin' anymore . . . and she got a *big* kick out of it when Dylan used that icky little strap on me."

"Shall I use that one, then?"

Lisa nodded. "Except it's kinda dinky for *her* big butt."

"You think size matters?"

She giggled and shook her head. "I *know* better. You'll make her squeal."

"Indeed . . . but try not to gloat *too* blatantly, will you?"

"Who, *me?*" She kissed him hard and licked his tongue, then rolled off his lap and yanked open her pajama drawer.

CHAPTER 3
TOO WARM A WELCOME

MONDAY DAWNED FAIR and cold, with mare's tail clouds in the western sky, a sign of early snow. Felicia made coffee in the kitchen of the two-bedroom apartment she shared with Teresa. Theirs was a new unit in a complex at the far end of Main Street, three miles from Dylan's place on the top floor of a six-story former hotel downtown. Felicia carried a steamy cup to Teresa's bedroom door and knocked.

"Time to get up, honey."

"I *am* up, Fel . . . but you cannot come in!"

"Are you all right?"

"I have Christmas presents out and you must not see!"

"Well aren't *you* the early bird? I'm making oatmeal . . . you want some?"

"Yes, please . . . I will be there in a few minutes."

Felicia smiled and went back to the kitchen. She took a round carton from the cupboard and bent her knees to stretch thigh muscles that were sore from a marathon, two-day shopping trip. Teresa had dragged her and Dylan through stores in three towns, as well as two malls in Des Moines. The phone rang and Felicia glanced at the ID screen as she took it from the holder.

"Morning, Dylan."

"Good morning. Did you sleep well?"

"I guess so . . . when I wasn't dreaming I was still at the mall."

He laughed. "I had a few of those myself. Is Teresa up?"

"Uh huh . . . she's in her room wrapping presents. So is your trip all set?"

"I think I covered everything. The TA will take my Tuesday class at the U, and the girls all know that RBC is cancelled this week."

"Will you be OK to teach Thursday morning? That's cutting it close if you don't get into Des Moines until eight-thirty."

"Jennifer's on stand-by for that one, too . . . in case I'm delayed."

"Well, yeah . . . but you'll be pretty tired."

"It's only a survey course . . . I can teach it in my sleep."

"As long as your students don't *learn* that way. Oh . . . here's Teresa." Felicia handed her the phone. "It's Uncle Dylan."

"Hi."

"Good morning, sweetie. Fel said you were up early wrapping presents."

"Yes . . . I must send six to Germany and the post can be very slow. Will you go to Boston today?"

"My flight leaves at eleven-thirty so I need to get on the road soon."

Teresa pouted and leaned against the counter. "I will miss you, Uncle Dylan."

"I'll miss you, too . . . but it's only a couple of days."

"Yes, but you must be careful. Flying is very dangerous this time of the year."

"I'll instruct the pilot to be extra cautious."

"Now you are teasing."

"A little . . . I want you to worry about your university classes and not about me, all right?"

"All right." She grinned. "Perhaps I will skip my university classes altogether . . . then I truly *will* have something to worry about."

"You're teasing *me* now . . . you'd better be, anyway."

"Well . . . perhaps."

"I *could* stop by to discuss academic expectations on the way to the airport."

"No! I mean . . . no *sir.* This sort of *discussion* is not at all necessary." She smiled when he laughed.

"OK . . . you have my cell number if you need me."

"Yes . . . goodbye, Uncle Dylan. I love you."

"Love you too, sweetie. See you soon."

Dylan put the phone down and swiveled at the waist to crack his back. He checked his wallet and ticket, then grabbed a key ring and rolled a suitcase into the hallway.

Teresa sighed and sat at the table. She ate oatmeal and listened to her stepmother's chatter only enough to make noncommittal noises at appropriate times. Felicia went to take a shower and Teresa got ready for school. She listened even less to her Statistics professor, came home right after class and shut herself in her room. Internet friends in Germany and elsewhere kept her busy with news and gossip through most of the day, and then she switched screen names. As *orphangirl* she browsed adult sites to read stories and look at pictures, and then lurked in a chatroom to watch the interactions between dominants and submissives. Felicia knocked on her door at midnight and opened it.

"Honey, aren't you going to bed?"

She turned so that her body blocked the computer screen. "Yes, Fel . . . very soon. I only need to download a few more things for a homework project."

"OK . . . don't stay up too late."

"No . . . goodnight."

Felicia smiled, blew her a kiss and closed the door. Teresa puffed a breath and stared at the screen, but the type blurred to nonsense. She thought about Uncle Dylan, so far away, likely in the arms of that *woman,* and her eyes filled with tears.

* * *

Gwen McKenna fluttered her lips, glared at the mantel clock, and paced from foyer to living room, then through the kitchen and back to the foyer again. She primped boy-short brunette hair in a small oval mirror next to the coat rack and smiled as she pictured Dylan when he checked his hair in that same mirror before they went out. He always grumbled because she hung it at her eye level, ten inches lower than his, and Dylan had to crouch to see the top of his head and make sure the cowlick he hated so much had not misbehaved. A twinge shot down her spine when she turned her

head to admire the half-carat diamond studs in her earlobes, a birthday present from Dylan. She rubbed her neck with both hands as she sauntered to the bedroom to put on the white padded brace the doctor told her to wear for ten days after the accident.

"Oh, *that's* attractive," she muttered. "Cute skirt, killer sweater, spike heels . . . and a roll of toilet paper under my chin. Geeze!"

She sighed and looked at her watch, then opened a bottle and shook a pill into her hand. The tablet caught in her throat when she tried to swallow. She hurried to the bathroom basin to wash it down with tap water, but foul chemical tang already cloyed her mouth.

"Blecch!" She grimaced as she ran to the kitchen.

Ice clinked when she held a lowball glass under the dispenser, and crackled as she poured cranberry juice over it. Sweetness drove away the bitter taste and she licked her lips, then stomped a spike heel on the tile.

"Where *is* he? He said before three and it's *four-thirty*." She yanked open a cabinet, poured vodka over the drink and stirred it with her finger. Her eyes widened when she sipped so she added more juice and then carried the glass to the spare bedroom that doubled as her home office. A stack of bills lay beside the computer and she glared at it as she settled into the desk chair. The phone rang and she grabbed her headset.

"Hello?"

"Hi, Princess. Sorry I'm late."

"Where *are* you?"

"We just left Logan. Portland's fogged in so we got stacked up behind the flights they diverted here."

"Didn't you tell them who you *are* . . . and that there's a *princess* waiting for you?"

Dylan laughed. "I don't like to pull rank on the common folk. How are you feeling?"

"OK, I guess. I slept until nine and then took a nap after lunch . . . must be these muscle relaxers. I managed to make the bed but I didn't pick up anything for supper."

"That's all right. We'll go out if you're up to it."

She grinned. "I was hoping you'd say that."

"I'm sure you were. I'll be there in about half an hour."

"Did you rent a car?"

"No, I didn't bother for such a short visit. They brought *your* rental, didn't they?"

"Uh huh . . . some Ford POS."

"Gwen! Never look a gift car in the manifold."

"It's not a *gift* if I paid for it with my insurance."

"OK, OK . . . it'll get us to the restaurant tonight and the dealer tomorrow, won't it?"

"Yeah, I guess so. Who's driving the town car?"

"Mel . . . why?"

"Tell him I said to hurry!"

"I will. 'Bye, Princess."

The phone clicked and Gwen sighed as she set it down, then picked up her drink and wandered into the living room. She removed the neck brace and sat in a recliner, switched on the TV and surfed the cable channels while she sipped. Buffy and Xander's double *entendres* held her attention until a commercial break and she started to click the changer, but her bright green eyes widened and she leaned forward as a car ad rolled across the screen.

"Ooh . . . I want one of *those.*"

Ice rattled her teeth as she sat back and drained the drink while she envied the professional driver on the closed course. Her eyelids drooped and she managed to put the glass on the lamp table before they shut. Dust clouds billowed behind her as she raced across the salt flats in her flashy new Pontiac, and she growled when someone rang a bell that told her she had to stop. The bell rang again and she opened her eyes.

"Oh, shit! He's *here.*" Her heart pounded as she stood and waited for the room to straighten out, then hobbled down three stairs to the foyer. "Just a second, Dylan!"

"Are you OK?"

"Yeah, yeah . . . just a sec!"

She scowled at the mirror and wiped away a smudge of mascara while she wished her eyes weren't *quite* so bloodshot, then forced a smile and unlatched the door. He grinned as she snatched his tie, dragged him inside and slammed the door. Strong arms circled her back and she tugged on his neck. Their lips met and she thrust her tongue into his mouth. Her feet left the floor and firm breasts tingled as they mashed his chest.

"I miffed oo fo *muff!*"

Dylan cupped her bottom in both hands and she wrapped hard, slender legs around his waist. He leaned back and winked.

"Don't talk with your mouth full, Kitty Eyes."

They resumed the kiss and their tongues played while her head spun. She trembled with desire as she rubbed against his hard belly. He kneaded plump rear cheeks and felt their electric warmth through the smooth wool. Gwen panted and pressed her eyes to his collar.

"Let's go to bed," she whispered.

He laughed and carried her up the steps into the living room. "Do you mind if I get my luggage in from the porch first?"

"What do you need with luggage?" She unwrapped her legs when he sat on the sofa.

"There might be a get-well present in it, you never know."

She squealed, twisted off his lap and stifled a moan as she went to open the door and roll his bag into the foyer. Her eyes widened and she took a step back when she turned to look at him. He stood by the recliner, his eyebrows arched, the neck brace in his hand, and his expression awakened nervous butterflies in her tummy.

"Aren't you supposed to be *wearing* this, young lady?"

"Yeah, I . . . I was but, um . . . I had to . . . I took it off so I could kiss you, *that's* all. Don't *look* at me like that 'cause I didn't do anything *bad*."

He shook his head and walked down the short flight. "Then why are you acting so guilty, hmm? Here . . . put this on."

"OK, but I've been *good* . . . and anyway I want another kiss before you make me put that stupid horse collar around my neck."

"All right, but only a little one. Stand on the step so you don't have to lean back so far."

"We could just go to bed and then I wouldn't have to lean back at *all*."

"Gwendolyn?"

"*OK*, already . . . but not *Gwendolyn* 'cause I don't *wanna* be in trouble."

She held tight to him for an all-too-brief kiss and then pouted as she wrapped the brace and secured the Velcro at the back. He nodded, put an arm around her shoulders, and carried the suitcase into the living room.

"What sort of muscle relaxant did they give you?"

"I don't know . . . something that starts with a Z. Can I have my present now?"

He sat on the sofa and she cuddled next to him while he unzipped a side compartment in the roll-on. "May I have my present now?"

"Oh, um . . . I didn't get you anything, unless you mean you want to. . . ." She grinned when he cupped her chin and squeezed.

"You *know* what I mean."

"OK . . . *may* I have my present now?"

"Is it Zanaflex?"

"Huh? Oh . . . the pills? Yeah, I think so. Why?"

"Because it says right on the label not to take them with alcohol."

"But I *didn't,* and anyway . . ."

"Shh." He pressed a finger to her lips and she pouted hard. "Don't make matters worse by fibbing about it. There's more than just cranberry juice in that glass."

"But I . . . I only had a *little* bit of vodka."

"Is that why it took you so long to answer the door?"

"I guess." She blinked and held tight to his arm. "I just *forgot,* that's all, and . . . anyway you were so *late* and . . . so you're not gonna, um . . . *do* anything, I mean . . ."

"You mean, like spank your naughty little fanny?"

"Don't say that."

Her hands trembled and she closed her eyes while shame and delight heated her face. Those awful words, spoken so calmly in his deep voice, echoed in her head. Her bottom clenched and tingled with anticipation.

The embarrassment she always suffered when he pulled her over his lap and took down her panties made her want to crawl into a hole, even as it sparked quivery fire between her thighs. Her reflexive struggles to escape his powerful grasp were useless at best, and prompted stern reprimands in his strict-professor tone, which heaped shameful tinder on the blaze at the core of her being. He never hurried to spank her, and examined every detail of her bare, disgraceful behind while she whined and complained at the indignity. Then his hand, so soft and gentle when he caressed, so rigid and harsh when he spanked, swatted tender flesh, and her

humiliation vaporized in a shower of nasty, glorious sting that dripped like lava into her vagina and turned the blaze to an inferno.

She gasped when he kissed her red, damp forehead.

"I should do more than say it, young lady . . . but I don't want to aggravate your injury."

A sigh escaped her lips, part relief, part disappointment. "OK . . . that's a good idea, but it's not real serious . . . the doctor said only muscle spasms."

"I hope that's all . . . but no more liquor while you're taking the Zanaflex."

"No, sir. Can . . . *may* I have my present now? Please?"

"I spoil you atrociously, you know." He pulled out a flat jeweler's box and put it into her hand.

"A princess is *supposed* to get spoiled . . . it comes with the job." She licked her lips, lifted the top and her eyes opened wide. "Oh, it's *beautiful*. Thank you!"

Lamplight glinted on eighteen-karat gold as she held up the cat-shaped amulet by its slender chain and threw her arms around him.

"You're welcome . . . and see? He's even got your eyes."

She grinned and struggled to open the clasp. "Don't be silly . . . only *girl* kitties have green eyes."

He laughed and showed her how to undo the safety catch. "Then *she's* got your eyes . . . except hers are little emeralds."

"*Dylan!*" She banged her thigh with a fist.

"What's wrong?"

"I wanna wear it *now* and I *can't* 'cause you said I have to have this . . ."

"Oh for Pete's sake! You may remove the collar to put it on . . . you don't need to pitch a fit."

"OK!"

Velcro shrieked as she tore off the brace and turned her back so he could drape the delicate chain at her collarbone. She fingered the charm, twisted around to grab his shoulders and kiss him, then ran to the foyer and admired her gift in the mirror. He leaned back and nodded.

"It looks good on you."

"Nuh *uh* . . . it looks *gorgeous*." She grinned. "And I bet it looks even better on bare skin. Where are we going for dinner? Can I wear something with cleavage?"

"I don't know why not. Are you hungry?"

She hurried over to sit on his lap. "Not really but I wanna show off. Let's go someplace nice and I'll wear my little black dress."

He smiled and hugged her. "How about Denny's?"

"Don't *tease* . . . let's go to Bullfinches."

"I thought you didn't like our waiter last time."

"Yeah, but if we get him again my magic kitty will take care of his snotty attitude. She'll stare him down with her emerald eyes."

"All right, then. Do we need reservations on a Monday night?"

"I doubt it . . . but call anyway. I'll get dressed."

"Is this suit all right, if I put on a clean shirt?"

"Yeah, sure. I don't know *why* you have to dress up to fly, though."

He kissed her and pushed her off his lap as he stood. "To intimidate officious security guards."

"Oh, I see . . . and *not* to impress cute flight attendants, huh?"

"The merest shadow of such an idea hadn't even begun to speculate about crossing my mind."

Gwen laughed and hugged him. "You are *so* weird. Come on . . . you can unpack while I get ready."

"Put your neck brace on."

"*Dylan.*"

"Don't whine, Princess."

She did as he said, then stalked ahead of him to the bedroom. He hoisted his case onto the queen-sized bed while Gwen kicked off her shoes and dropped her skirt to the floor.

"Can I take this stupid thing off to get my sweater over my head? *Sir?*"

"Yes you may, and quit being so grumpy." He winked. "Nice undies, by the way."

"Humph!" A smile battled with her pout as she turned and palmed the seat of her baby-blue boy-leg panties. "You like these?"

"Very much." He unzipped the case, unfolded a garment bag and hung it in the closet, and then hugged her. "Micro-fiber?" His hands roamed over tight, smooth mounds and she sighed.

"Uh huh . . . and I even got them on sale. Aren't I a good girl?"

"Yes . . . except when you're naughty. Good thing you've got such a sweet little fanny for me to spank when *that* happens."

– 53 –

She wriggled and puffed a petulant breath. "Nuh *uh* . . . I'm *always* good so you don't *ever* have to spank it . . . just only fondle it . . . mmm . . . like that. Ooh! You gotta stop so I can fix my makeup."

"OK, good girl . . . put superfluous paint on your pretty face while I finish unpacking. Is there any Glenfarclas left?"

"That Scotch you bought? Sure . . . who would drink it?"

"I don't know . . . gremlins? Your other boyfriend?"

He grinned and backed away when she slapped his chest.

"You are just *impossible*."

She snatched a robe from a hook in the closet and headed to the bathroom. He cleared his throat.

"Aren't you forgetting something?"

"Oh, *geeze!*" She grabbed the neck brace and stuck her tongue out at him, then squealed and stepped backward as he raised an open hand. "Did you take a *bossy* pill or what?"

"I'll *show* you bossy in a minute. Put it on."

"There . . . it's *on*, OK?"

"That's better."

She slammed the bathroom door behind her. Dylan chuckled and unwrapped one of four laundered dress shirts, shrugged out of his jacket and tie, and put on the fresh one, then emptied his suitcase into the bureau drawer she kept open for him. He went to the kitchen and drank a half-liter bottle of cold water to quench his airliner dehydration, then poured two ounces of amber malt into a glass. Rich, mellow whisky warmed his tongue and tickled his palate when he sipped, and he looked around for the phone book. He found it in her office, sat in the desk chair and opened the book to the restaurant section. His eyes narrowed as he reached for the phone and saw the bold print at the top of a department store bill.

"Unbelievable." He picked up the headset and dialed Bullfinches, but sighed and switched off the phone after the first ring.

Gwen hummed as she dug black lace panties, dark self-gartered stockings and a black strapless bra from her lingerie drawer. Her face glowed with light, fresh foundation and only a touch of blusher, her lips sparkled with gloss, and a wisp of taupe shadow highlighted her eyelids. She grinned at the mirror as she toyed with the golden charm and then turned when Dylan walked in. He leaned against the doorframe, his shirt open at the collar, sleeves

rolled to his elbows, and his arms crossed at his chest. She swallowed hard when she saw the flinty gleam in his eyes.

"Whuh—what's the matter?"

"Sit down, Princess . . . we need to talk."

"But you . . . we don't . . . I didn't *do* anything! Why are you *looking* at me like that?"

"Come here." He took her hand and led her to the bed. They sat and he hugged her shoulders. "We've had this discussion before, but apparently it's time for another one."

"Oh, *God.*"

Her chin quivered as she uttered the prayer, and icy, guilty butterflies careened in her tummy. He was all serious and she did not want to be serious, not *now.* His arm felt so strong, so warm, so good, and she only wanted to dress up and go out and have fun, but there he was with his *stern* face on and it wasn't *fair.*

"What did I tell you about those store cards, young lady?"

"Um . . . what store cards?"

"Don't play games with me . . . specifically, your over-limit Macy's card."

"Nuh *uh!* I mean . . . it was but I called them when I got the statement and they raised my limit so it's OK!" Her lips trembled in a desperate smile.

"It's *OK* that you spent a few thousand dollars more than you were supposed to, as long as they gave you more *credit?*"

"It wasn't *thousands,* only a few hundred and . . . and anyway. . . ." She took a deep breath and glared at him. "Why were you snooping in my mail in the *first* place?"

"Do *not* take that tone with me, Gwendolyn."

"But I . . ." Anxious fingers clutched velour robe at her bosom while the awful name resounded in her ears.

"If you didn't want me to see it you shouldn't have left it lying around. We have *talked* about this and you agreed to curb your spending on nonessentials, didn't you?"

"Yuh-yes, but . . . but I *had* to have new clothes 'cause . . . because I. . . ."

He sighed and cupped her chin. "You have three *closets* full of clothes so why do you . . .?"

"But not *winter* clothes!"

"*What?*"

– 55 –

"I . . . I mean I *didn't* have any, but now I do 'cause. . . ."

"Because you bought out the petites department at Macy's!"

"*No!* I . . . I gave away all my old ones and I truly, honestly didn't have a *thing* to wear!"

Dylan turned and coughed to cover a smile. "You, um . . . you gave them away?"

"Uh huh . . . last month . . . to the closet at church, 'cause they didn't have hardly *anything* in small sizes, and anyway it's tax deductible when I give to the church and. . . ."

"All right, all right . . . I know better than to argue with you about *that* subject . . . but I simply fail to understand how you continually run up debt when you make as much money as you do."

"I don't make all *that* much . . . after taxes."

He sighed and shook his head. "Between your insurance company salary and the Treasury Department retainer you gross almost ninety thousand, so why in the name of all that's reasonable . . . ?"

"*Over* ninety . . . I just got a raise." She grimaced at the stupid remark. "I mean, *yeah* but . . . house payments and property taxes . . . and. . . ." Her lip stuck out half an inch as she pouted. "Don't be mad at me, OK? Let's just forget it and go to dinner."

"Perhaps . . . after I correct you for disobeying me."

Her mouth dropped open and fear gripped her throat as she stared into his eyes. "But . . . but you *said* you wouldn't spank me 'cause I'm already *hurt.*"

"And I meant it. Now stand up and let's take off your clothes."

"What . . . what are you gonna *do?*" She trembled as he pulled her to her feet and untied her belt.

"Punish my naughty little princess."

"But *Dylan!*"

"Hush that squealing." He pushed the robe down quivery arms and tossed it onto the bed, then reached behind her to unclasp the bra.

"Dylan, *please?*"

"Please what?"

"Ju-just tell me what you're gonna *do?*"

Baby-blue lace fell from round breasts and Gwen shivered as cool air caressed hard, cherry-red nipples. His thumbs slipped into her panties' waistband and hot, frightful tingles bathed her bottom cheeks when he pushed the garment down her legs and left her naked except for the hideous collar at her neck.

"Lift your feet."

"*Dylan.*"

She stepped out of the underwear and he stood, blue panties in hand, to lead her to the corner. Embarrassment burned her cheeks, fore and aft, when he patted her behind and leaned close to her ear.

"I have to make *sure* you think about how naughty you've been and remember to *mind* me in the future."

"But how . . . what are you . . .?" Horrid, squirmy, thrilling realization burst upon her and she threw her arms around his neck. "Not the *plug!* Don't make me wear it to *dinner!*"

"Shh." He patted her back, unwrapped her hands and turned her to the corner. "You were a bad girl and you need a lesson in obedience, so wait here while I get everything ready."

"No *please?*" Hot, humiliated tears dripped from her eyes as she clenched her bottom to still the throb in her anus and between her lower lips.

"*Behave* yourself."

Dozens of harsh, rebellious words raced through her mind but could not pass the fearful, excited lump in her throat. She could only whimper, lean against the wall, and wait for him to take the awful, lascivious toy from its hiding place. He kept it in a steel box in her hope chest, along with the other icky, nasty tools he used to make her squirm, and just the sound of the key in the latch made her heart pound and caused a quivery ache inside her bottom. The box lid snapped shut and he went into the bathroom to bring towels and a tube of K-Y Jelly and set them on the nightstand. She turned when he put a warm hand on her arm, and stared up at him with sad, pitiable eyes.

"*Please* don't make me have the plug, OK? I *promise* I'll be good and not ever. . . ."

"Shh . . . come along."

Frantic butterflies zoomed around her tummy as he pulled her to the bedside, sat, and draped a white towel over his lap before he tugged her wriggly nakedness across his thighs. She squeezed her rear cheeks hard and stared at the white plug. It was made of soft rubber, three and a half inches long, a cone that tapered from a rounded tip and bulged to an inch in diameter at its widest part, then narrowed to a short, quarter-inch neck above the base. The base was flat, designed to keep the plug from slipping all the way

inside a girl's anus, flexible so it folded a bit, but rigid enough to be a constant reminder that she had the device securely lodged between her cheeks.

He patted the tight, smooth mounds and reached over to pull a pillow under her head. "Here . . . now keep your neck still and straight while I put the plug in your bottom hole."

"Why do you have to say that? It's embarrassing enough you're gonna *do* it so you don't need to. . . ."

"Hush that *whining* . . . and open your legs so I can see inside."

"But I don't *want* to and it's not *fair* and you're just being *mean!*" She clutched the pillow to her face and parted her thighs an inch. "Dylan?"

"Wider than that."

"Can . . . can I have a spanking *instead?* I'll be real good and not wiggle or whine or *anything*, but *please* don't look inside my bottom and . . . and put that icky *thing* in me, OK?"

He leaned over and kissed her ear. "You say you won't wiggle but I *know* you. As soon as your fanny starts to sting, you'll squirm and kick and jerk your head around and that's *not* good for your neck."

"Nuh uh I *won't*, honest!"

"Stop arguing and relax. You're having the plug in your bottom and that's all there is to it. Now open your legs, please."

His calm, reasonable tone rankled, and sparked a desperate defiance.

"You . . . you'd just rather spank your *teenagers!* It's no *fun* with a thirty-eight year old when you've got all those moist *young* fannies to *owee!*"

A hard hand squeezed her bottom and tears pooled in her eyes. His face reddened with indignation.

"That is absolute *nonsense* and I can't believe you're jealous of *schoolgirls*. You're worse than they are."

"Am *not!* You . . . you don't think my bottom is *cute* enough to spank and . . . and anyway I don't *deserve* to get the plug just 'cause I spent a little money on clothes!"

"Oh, you *don't?*"

"*No!*"

"And you think your adorable tushy is too *old* for me to spank?"

"No, *you* think that! You only wanna spank your so-called *niece*

and her Barbie-doll *friends* . . . with their baby-fat bottoms and *ouch!*"

The sharp crack of his palm on white, tender flesh echoed through the room.

"That is *enough*, Gwendolyn! This nonsense stops! Right! *Now!*"

"Ow! *Ow!* Aiee!"

"Get up and lie on the bed, young lady!"

She rubbed sting from her behind as she rolled off his lap and stood on quaky knees before him. His eyes burned shame into her soul and she whimpered as she looked away.

"I . . . I didn't *mean* it," she whispered.

"Obviously you *did* . . . now lie down like I told you."

"Whuh . . . what are you gonna *do?*"

"Lie *down!*"

"OK, *OK* . . . sir!"

Her nipples tingled when she stretched out on the satin duvet and lifted her hips to offer him her bottom. He shook his head and slipped a folded pillow beneath her to raise the plump behind even higher. She parted her thighs and felt the cool air between her cheeks.

"I . . . I'm sorry I lipped off, *honest.* I didn't *mean* it, I just. . . ."

"You are my one and only princess . . . but I am *not* going to take anymore of that drivel from you, understand?"

"Yes, sir. Are . . . are you gonna spank me?"

He sat on the bedside and caressed her neck. Tight muscles jerked beneath his fingers as he rubbed.

"What I *ought* to do is bend you over your own desk and paddle your fanny purple, since you think that's what I enjoy doing *most,* but your neck is in no condition to. . . ."

"*No!* I really and truly didn't *mean* it about those girls and. . . ."

"*Hush*, Gwen! At first I was tempted to blame this outburst on the drug you're taking. . . ."

"Yeah! That's *it!* I'm too stoned to know what I'm saying!"

"Except Zanaflex isn't a psychotropic, even in combination with alcohol and. . . ."

"Uh huh it *must* be! Why *else* would I say such . . .?"

"You *said* it because you *meant* it . . . and since I punished my *so-called* niece and one of her *Barbie-doll* friends for being

jealous of *you,* it's only fair that you receive no less of my attention to your jealous little fanny."

She huffed and winced as she turned to look at him. "You *did?*" He nodded. "Why were they jealous of *me?*"

His lips curled in a half smile. "Don't play the innocent. They can tell how much in love with you I am, even if they hadn't pried it out of me."

"Mmm . . . that's nice to hear. Did you paddle them?"

He shook his head. "I hand spanked Teresa . . . but I used a strap on Lisa's *baby-fat* bottom."

"*Dylan!* I *said* I was sorry . . . don't keep throwing that *back* at me." She pouted and wriggled her behind. "So . . . so do I gotta get the *strap*? And not even over your *knees*? That's kinda mean, don't you think?" She simpered and reached over to take his hand.

"No . . . not the strap. That *would* be mean . . . on top of the ginger treat I'm going to put inside your bottom hole."

The words hung in the air for horrid, achy seconds, like sparks from a Fourth of July aerial bomb, before their full import registered in her mind. *Ginger treat . . .* his nasty euphemism for hot, itchy torment in her anus, a ghastly, insistent burn that baked every nerve in her body. Her mouth gaped with inexpressible protests as her eyes pleaded. She yanked her hand but he held it firmly and wrapped an arm around her shoulders to keep her still.

"No *please,*" she squeaked.

"You'll squirm, I know . . . but you'll keep your neck still and your fanny open for me, won't you?"

"*Dylan!* That . . . that's not *even* necessary! I'll be *good* now, I *swear,* and I won't say *anything* while you put the plug in me, OK? But not . . . not with *ginger,* for God's sake!"

He leaned down and kissed her moist, trembling lips. "You *will* be a good girl for me . . . and stay just like this while I get it ready, hmm?"

"But I . . . I *can't* just lie here and watch you . . . do that horrible *thing!*"

"Yes you *can* . . . and you'd *better* . . . or I may change my mind about the strap."

"*No!* I mean *yes!* Spank me with the strap, OK? I . . . I was *bad* . . . just like those girls so . . . so I should only just get the *strap,* OK? *Dylan?*"

"That's *enough*, young lady! Lie still and keep your bottom up. If you're so sure I've been neglecting your sweet little tushy in favor of my schoolgirls, then it's up to me to prove you wrong."

"You're not *listening* to me! I *said* I was wrong and . . . and it doesn't *matter* what you do to *them* just don't . . . don't put that *stuff* in my butt!"

"Shh . . . I told you to keep *still*." He reached down and pulled a corner of the duvet over her legs as she whined and clenched her rear cheeks. "No . . . relax and open your bottom. You *said* you'd be a good girl, and if you're *not* I will be very irritated."

"*God*, Dylan! This is just . . . just . . . . *horrible!*"

She sobbed into her hands when he opened the metal box once more and removed a small plastic jar. Terrified eyes peeked between her fingers and she sobbed louder when he sprinkled yellow-brown powder into his palm. Her heart throbbed and a hot blush bathed her from forehead to ankles. The tiny rosebud between her cheeks pulsed with dreadful anticipation while he dribbled K-Y into the powder and used the tip of the plug as a pestle to compound the hellish mixture.

"Quit wiggling, Princess . . . you know better than that."

"But you *can't* just. . . ."

"And stop all this *arguing* . . . or I'll go to the grocery for a fresh root and you may wear a plug of *that* instead!"

"*Nooo!*"

Tears dripped from her eyes as she covered them with both hands. Why oh *why* did she show him that nasty web story? He might have found it anyway, but how could she have been so *stupid* as to bring it to his attention? It described how a Victorian girl who was exceptionally bad, in the eyes of a father, headmaster or magistrate, had a *fig*, a finger-sized piece of peeled ginger root, thrust into her bottom before punishment. Anal irritation overcame the girl's natural urge to clench her buttocks when bent and presented naked, so a cane or birch rod could strike her most sensitive and intimate flesh.

Even though Dylan told her the story was pure nonsense, she should have *known* he would take it too seriously, but at least this time it *wasn't* fresh ginger like he used before. The minutes he spent whittling a gnarled root with a pocketknife while he made her wait in horrified silence, naked and bottom up on the bed,

were the longest and most dreadful of her life. He wore latex gloves to protect his fingers from the caustic juice that oozed from the hard pulp, his face calm, intent, as if it were balsa for a model plane he trimmed and not an evil, insidious plug that would heat the tender membrane of her anus and the sensitive flesh inside her cleft. She dared not speak because he had already spanked her for arguing with him when he said she had to go to the doctor for a physical, and even her plaintive whines were met with a steely blue glare that said more clearly than words that she was skating on thin ice. When finally he snugged her waist under his arm and told her to open her bottom, she complied at once. The awful reality of the nasty plug was preferable to the horror of its expectation, and she squealed only a little when he slid the devilish bit of pulp past her quivery ring. It was as long and round as his index finger, with a deep groove in the middle so her sphincter would clamp down and hold half of it inside and half out of her rectum. And it wasn't as bad as she expected . . . at first. She trembled and took long, shaky breaths while she pushed her bottom up, cheeks parted to avoid contact with the horrible tool, but it was no use. Peppery irritation seeped past porous membrane and lighted bright, nasty fires in her most sensitive nerve endings. High-pitched wails scratched her throat as she fought to expel the intruder. Dylan scolded, pressed the plug back in and then spanked her. He didn't swat hard but she closed her bottom instinctively and wailed louder when the wet ginger inflamed her tender cleft. She had no choice except to open for him, and his fingers stung the crowns, the soft under curve, the exposed insides of her cheeks, and yet she scarcely felt the spanks for the terrible heat that emanated from her anus and spread across her body in shuddery waves.

"Don't close your bottom, Gwen."

"*Huh?*"

His smooth, deep voice jerked her into the moment and she stared at the plug he held in his hand. Its whiteness was discolored by a thick coat of jelly and ginger powder that glistened in the lamplight like the skin of a primordial serpent.

"You heard me."

"Dylan *please!* I don't *want* you to . . . I *hate* this . . . why do you gotta . . .?"

"Hush and open your fanny for me."

Shame flowed over her like hot syrup as she spread her thighs. Strong fingers pushed her cheeks even farther apart and tears wetted the duvet while he inspected her most secret recesses. Guilty moisture glistened on lower lips and betrayed her true emotions to his watchful eyes. He stroked her tight, puckered opening with a thumb and drew breathless kitten wails from her throat.

"Shh . . . you've been very naughty and now you have to pay for it."

"But I said I was *sorry!*"

"Relax your bottom and be still while I put the plug in your little hole."

"God *nooo!*"

She gasped when the tip nudged her tiny portal and fired lewd impulses up her spine that burst in her brain as naughty, squirmy images. He pressed, slowly, inexorably, and the plug slid through the tight ring. It felt cool inside her, but she knew not to be deceived, and moaned in anticipation of the spicy heat to follow. The bulge drew nearer and her anus stretched and tingled around it. Dylan pushed it home and she wailed when the plug's base nestled against her anus. She held her breath and gritted her teeth as the herbal zest worked its awful magic inside her bottom. Warm tingle became hot itch that turned to sharp, nagging burn. Her knees parted and she thrust her hips high to open her cheeks in a futile attempt to push the fire away. Heat prickled her thighs and swept up her spine, and the moistness between her vaginal lips simmered and roiled.

"Please take it *out!* It's horrible!"

He gazed into the furrow and patted a quivery buttock. "Be quiet and relax."

"I . . . I *can't* relax! You don't know how muh-much it *hurts!*"

"Yes I do . . . but it's perfectly harmless and you *know* that. Now stop all this whining or I'll have to spank you."

"You said you wouldn't!"

"It's a male's prerogative to change his mind."

"Nuh *uh!* That's a *female* prerogative and . . . and just take it *out!*"

His palm clapped the wriggly crown of her right cheek and she squealed. "*Especially* since you were so rude about the other girls who *also* need my guidance."

"Then put this crap in *their* bottoms!"

"All right . . . that *does* it!"

"No *please!*"

"Keep very still while I give you the spanking you so richly deserve."

She groaned and squeezed her eyes shut when he put his left hand gently on the back of her head. A crisp swat fell on her left cheek and his fingertips stung the hypersensitive inner flesh. She clenched her bottom on instinct, then yelped and opened it again when the fire in her anus blazed hotter.

"Not inside!"

"That's what the fig is *for* . . . don't you remember? It's to make a naughty girl keep her fanny *open* so she can be punished more effectively." He swatted the damp inner surface of her right cheek and she jerked a hand back to cover. "Gwendolyn! You know better than that!"

"But I . . . it's *nasty* to get spanked this way!"

Her arm trembled as she drew her hand away, then she wailed when his fingertips smacked once more into her open cleft.

"Then perhaps you will learn! Your! Lesson!"

"Yow! Haiee! Yeek! *Yes!* I *won't* buy any more clothes and I *won't* say nothing about those girls or . . . or *anything* but just *stop!*"

"You've been *much* too naughty for only a half-dozen spanks . . . but at least you have your fanny open nice and wide for me."

"*Jesus,* Dylan! Like I have a *choice? Ow! Owee! Owitch!*"

Three quick swats stung her bottom and he shook his head as he once more raised his arm. "It can't be all *that* uncomfortable if you can still! Manage! To be! *Impertinent!*"

"*No!* Ow! *Hi!* I'm! *Sorreee!*"

Hard fingers fanned the ginger blaze and she squealed incomprehensible apologies and pleas for mercy even as she opened her bottom wider to escape the terrible heat. The plug, of its own volition, stretched her burning ring and slid upward but Dylan thumbed it back in place and she screeched.

"Shh . . . it's all right. I won't spank you anymore."

"Ahee! Oooh thank *God!*" He let go of her head and she turned her wet face to look at him. "I . . . I really *am* sorry, honest!"

"I know. Are you ready for me to take the plug out?"

"Uh . . . uh huh . . . *please?*"

"All right. Put your head down and be still."

"OK."

Waves of dull, achy sting bathed her bottom as he slipped the awful device from her tightness and wrapped it in a towel. He grabbed tissue to clean his hands and then took more from the box to wipe slippery yellowness from her cleft. She opened her mouth to protest the childish cleansing but then closed it and shuddered at the exquisite agony when he dabbed feminine dew from her swollen labia. The plug's departure damped the inferno in her rectum only a few degrees, and she kept her bottom spread wide as sweat beaded her forehead. She whimpered when he lifted her gently, set her on her feet and hugged her.

"You're a good girl now."

"Thuh-thank you . . . Dylan?"

"Hmm?"

She leaned against his hard chest, her feet wide apart to open her cleft. "My bottom really, really burns!"

"I know it does . . . and it *will* for a while. You need to get dressed."

"*Nooo!* We don't gotta go *out,* do we?"

"But you wanted to go show off your magic kitty."

"*Huh!* I don't think she *is* magic."

"Oh?"

"*Nuh* uh . . . if she was she would of kept you from setting my bottom on fire! *Geeze!*"

He grabbed her hand when she reached back to rub. "Don't do that . . . you know it only makes it worse." She pouted as he kissed her fingers. "I'm afraid your kitty isn't trained to protect you from the consequences of naughty behavior."

"Yeah well . . . I'll have to work with her on that."

"If you think it will do any good." He leaned down and kissed her mouth. "We really should put *some* sort of clothes on you."

"OK." She hugged him, and then looked up and grinned through her tears. "You are just *evil,* aren't you?"

"*Excuse* me?"

"You're hard as a *rock* from doing all those horrible things to my poor little bottom!"

His shoulders rose in a quick shrug before he kissed her again. "It's your own fault for having such an *adorable* poor little bottom."

– 65 –

"Nuh *uh* . . . it's a *hot* poor little bottom."

"Then I should wash the ginger out, don't you think?"

"Um . . . yeah. So . . . you're not gonna . . . make me go to dinner with . . . with. . . ."

"A firestorm in your fanny? No . . . I didn't make the reservation."

"How come?"

"Because I had the feeling you wouldn't feel up to going out. I'll call for Chinese later . . . or would you rather have Thai?"

"Not *Thai* . . . they put too much spice in everything."

"OK, not Thai. Are you ready for me to douse the fire?"

She nodded and walked bowlegged as he led her to the bathroom. "Um . . . I can wash my own *bottom*, you know."

"*Can* you?" He left her leaning against the doorway and went to get her robe.

"Dylan?" Her forehead furrowed. "Why are you smiling like that?"

"No idea what you're talking about. Here . . . slip this on."

"What do you *mean* . . . you're gonna douse the fire?" She trembled and hugged the soft velour as he opened a cabinet. "*No, Dylan!*"

"Don't tell me *no*, Gwen."

"But I . . . I don't *deserve* an enema! Not on top of everything *else!*"

"Shh." He dropped the bag and hose next to the basin and wrapped her in his arms. "This isn't punishment . . . but it's the best way I know to get all the stuff *out* of you that I put *into* you."

"Yeah but . . . I mean *no* . . . that's just . . . it's still *icky* when you make me bend over and put . . . *things* in my butt!"

He sighed and shook his head. "So you would rather have the fire in there for . . . what . . . another two or three hours? Isn't that how long it lasted when I used the fresh root?"

"Uh huh but . . . *dammit*, you *know* how much I hate . . . nooo!"

She quivered and yelped as he swatted her velour-covered seat a dozen times, then moaned while he hugged her.

"Now . . . what were you saying?"

"I . . . I'm sorry I cussed but . . . *geeze!* It . . . it feels like I got a hot curling wand up my ass . . . *bottom* so . . . so you don't gotta be so *strict* with me!"

"And *you* don't have to be so petulant when I try to help you."

– 66 –

He kissed her pouty lips and turned her toward the basin. "Now lean forward and rest your elbows on the counter like a good girl."

"Oh, *God!*"

Water splashed and he wetted a hand towel while she groaned and rested her forehead on the cool Formica. He lifted her robe hem, tucked the material into the belt, and the nagging burn subsided as he swabbed her cleft with cool water. She squealed when he gently dabbed her red, swollen anus.

"Feels a bit inflamed there?"

"Well, *geeze* . . . what do *you* think?"

"I *think* you had better watch your tone of voice, young lady."

She grunted and stamped a bare foot but kept her legs spread. "Um . . . Dylan?"

"Hm?"

"I . . . I'm all better now. You don't have to do anything *else.*"

He smiled at her reflection in the mirror and patted her hip. "No? Don't you think the *inside* of your bottom hole is just as inflamed as the *outside?*"

"Well . . . yeah but . . . it'll go away."

"Eventually, yes . . . but I'd rather not have dinner with a fidgety five-year-old, even if it *is* only fried rice at the kitchen bar."

"But I don't *want* an enema!"

"*Really* . . . I would never have guessed. Now stop fussing and straighten up. I'll leave the towel inside your cheeks to keep you cool while I prepare the bag." Green eyes flashed fire as she stood and turned to him. "Close your legs a bit . . . so the towel stays where it's supposed to."

"Do you stay awake nights just *thinking* of ways to embarrass me?"

He smiled, pulled her robe hem from its belt and let it fall over her nakedness. "No . . . I improvise."

"Nuh *uh!* I bet you got a whole *notebook* full of nasty ideas somewhere and when I find it I'm gonna throw it in the fireplace!"

"Don't be silly . . . your sexy naughtiness is my sole inspiration."

"Yeah right." She smiled when he kissed her, and then leaned her shoulder against the wall. "Except you got that icky *ginger* idea off the web."

The clear plastic bag bulged as he filled it.

"True . . . but I would never have noticed it if you hadn't shown it to me."

She sniffled and squeezed her cheeks around the moist cloth. "You'd think I'd *know* better by now."

"Let's get you cleaned out so you can sit more comfortably . . . kneel on the bathmat."

"Oh, *God!*"

He held her arm as she sank to her knees, then he hung the plastic bag on a towel hook. "The water's a bit cooler than usual but I'll rub your tummy so you won't cramp."

"You're just *too* kind." She leaned forward, legs spread and bottom uppermost, and cradled her head on her hands.

"Sweet of you to say so." He lifted the robe skirt, furled it across her back and plucked the moist towel from her cleft.

"Sarcasm is wasted on you, isn't it?" New blush painted her face when his eyes once more inspected her open behind.

"Not always . . . why? Was your comment *supposed* to be sarcastic?"

"Well duh . . . *eesh!*"

The slender nozzle penetrated her hot, slippery vent and she gasped as icy wetness chilled the embers inside her bottom. She squeaked and bowed her back to lift her behind while his hand massaged her belly. As the bitter heat in her rectum cooled, a warm, quivery glow grew between vaginal lips and she put her hand on his to urge it closer to the glow.

"*What* are you doing, Gwen?"

"But . . . *well* . . . you *said* this wasn't puh-punishment so . . . you gotta be *nice* to me."

"I'm *always* nice to you."

"Uh huh sure . . . what planet do *you* live on? *Ooh* Dylan!"

His finger slipped between wet, steamy folds of flesh and caressed the hard, needy bud within. Bright electric sparks shot up his arm and he held her tight when she squealed and pushed her bottom higher. Water flowed and stilled the ginger heat even as lascivious fire burned her vagina. She spread her thighs wide and soft petals unfolded to his wanton fingers. He circled and stroked, pressed and flicked, and orgasmic screams echoed against the tiles.

She sobbed, shuddered, and fell limp as a rag-doll against his forearm. Her body trembled with quick, shivery aftershocks, and

she drew her knees together. Sweat-moist inner cheeks touched the chilly hose and she wailed.

"Shh . . . it's all right . . . remember you have a nozzle in your fanny."

"Guh-*God!* You just . . . I can't . . . *Jee*sus!"

He smiled and massaged her distended belly. "Feeling a bit inarticulate, are we? That's OK . . . the bag's almost empty."

Her eyes struggled to focus as she turned her head. "I . . . I'll inarticulate *you* in a minute! *God,* you're mean!"

"Oh? Who was it put my hand on her naughty parts, hmm?"

"Yeah but you . . . you're the one who made them naughty to *begin* with!"

"There's just no pleasing some people." He chuckled, twisted the valve to shut off the flow and then slipped the nozzle from her bottom. "Come on . . . I'll help you stand up."

"I . . . I think all my bones melted . . . and my butt's numb!"

"*Is* it? Well I'm sure you'll get the feeling back once you sit on the potty."

"*Dylan!*" She moaned when he lifted her upper body. Quivery muscles fought to clench against the flood inside her bottom. "It . . . it's a *toilet,* for God's sake! Haven't you embarrassed me *enough* for one night?"

"I don't know . . . have I?" He slipped his hands beneath her armpits and raised her to her feet. "You still seem a bit feisty."

"Yeah well . . . *that's* not gonna go away . . . but *you* better, and *quick,* 'cause I gotta go to the *toilet* and I mean right *now!*"

He laughed. "And you'd rather I didn't watch?"

She groaned and glared at him as she hobbled to the commode. "*Go!*"

"Very well . . . call me if you need anything."

Her exasperated grunt followed him out the door. The latch clicked and she whimpered as tepid water gushed from her anus and splashed into the bowl. The flow further cooled gingery embers but sparked new heat in her vagina and she whimpered as tiny orgasms flickered through her exhausted body.

Six flushes, a dozen little climaxes and several yards of tissue later she felt able to stand at the basin and wash her hands and face. The door opened and he leaned in, a bright smile on his lips. He wore a dark gray sweat suit instead of his shirt and trousers.

"Feeling better, Princess?"

"As *if!* You totally *destroyed* me, you know."

"I'll take that as a *yes*. The food will be here soon." He walked over and hugged her from behind. "Why don't you bend over so I can wash your bottom?"

"You're not *listening* to me!"

He shrugged and pushed on her back. "You said I had to be *nice* to you . . . I recall that quite distinctly. Now stop being so fussy and *bend*."

"Oh geeze!" She did as he said, and then squeaked when he put a small plastic tube on the counter. "What's *that?*"

"Something to take away the burn."

"*Cooling* gel? This is for hemorrhoids! I don't have *those,* do I?"

"No . . . but it should soothe whatever irritation you *do* have."

She pouted while he lifted her robe. "I wonder what the Preparation H people would say if they knew their stuff was being used to cool off a girl's fanny after it got filled up with a ginger plug."

He chuckled and wetted a washcloth in the basin. "Somehow I doubt that information would make its way into their advertising."

"Ya *think?*" She grinned at his reflection in the mirror and then shut her eyes as he bathed her cleft and anointed her hot, tender anus with cool, clear slipperiness.

Goose bumps rose on her arms and legs when he took her to the bedroom and removed her robe. She sighed as he seated her on his lap and pulled white cotton panties up her legs, then he made her stand so he could dress her in a yellow sweat suit.

"So . . . you gonna peel the banana later?"

"*Sooner* rather than later, I expect."

He kissed her long and hard, and she whined when the doorbell rang and he grabbed a money clip from the dresser as he went to answer it. She hugged herself and followed him into the kitchen.

"What do you want to drink?" He took cartons from a plastic bag on the bar.

"Vodka on the rocks . . . and you can skip the rocks." She smiled when he shook his head.

"Diet Pepsi it is. You want chopsticks or a fork?"

"Um . . . maybe a spoon. I'm still kinda jittery."

Silverware clattered as he pulled utensils from a drawer, then he went to get a throw pillow from the sofa and laid it, with great ostentation, on a barstool.

"Your throne, my Princess."

"When do I get head chopping off privileges, anyway?"

He laughed and kissed her lips. "When you get big. Moo goo gai pan or mu-shu pork?"

"Yes, please."

They ate and talked, and she wriggled only a little while they discussed the car she wanted. She piled the dishes in the sink and Dylan stacked the leftovers in the refrigerator, then they sat on the sofa and she cuddled beneath his arm. He leaned down to kiss her and her fingers twined in the hair at the back of his head. Their tongues met, danced and played, and his hands roamed her soft body. She shifted around to sit on his lap and his hardness burned her fanny even through thick fleece.

"Something tells me it's time for you to peel the banana."

He took a deep breath. "I believe you're right."

She held tight to his arm as they walked to the bedroom. He tugged off his sweatshirt and dropped it on the hope chest, then did the same with hers. Pants and underwear followed, and he tossed back the duvet. Her heart pounded when he stacked two pillows in the middle of the bed.

"Um . . . what's *this* for?"

"To raise your cute little behind. Now lie down."

"But . . . not for a *spanking*, OK? 'cause I was a *good* girl! You *said* so." She stared at his erection as she wriggled on top of the pillows.

"Did I?"

"Uh huh . . . I remember *that* quite distinctly and I was."

"All right . . . if you're sure." He chuckled and patted her tight cheeks. "And a *good* girl doesn't whine when her lover takes her bottom, does she?"

"Oh God *no* . . . I mean *yes* . . . I mean . . . *Dylan!*"

Her heart pounded with primal fear and her throat burned with silent, desperate screams while her eyes pleaded to be spared the awful, delightful helplessness she always felt when he impaled her behind with his hardness. How *could* he do that to a good girl? It was *wrong* . . . it was *naughty* . . . it was . . . *forbidden* . . . and as with the fruit in the Garden, it tempted her like no other.

"Open your tushy for me, good girl."

"But . . . but it still *burns* . . . from the *ginger* and. . . ."

"I doubt very much if it *burns* . . . but it may be more than usually sensitive to erotic stimulation."

"Nuh *uh!* You . . . you just *can't* do that to me!"

The shadowy divide widened like the gates of Paradise when he gently pushed her legs apart. Her eyes glowed with womanly desire even as she sucked a fingertip in the coy, gamin way that melted his heart. His hands trembled as he opened the nightstand drawer to get the lubricant, and then lay beside her and flipped the top off the tube. He coated the fingers of his left hand with slipperiness and palmed her cleft. She grabbed his neck as fingers tested and probed her tender vent. He pressed his lips to hers and their tongues battled while he caressed and she squirmed. A fingertip stroked, prodded, slipped in, and Gwen squealed as he once more invaded her tightness. Dylan leaned back.

"I want you, Princess. I want your naughty, squirmy little bottom, and I shall have it."

"*Please?*"

"Please what? Please make love to your bottom?"

"I can't . . . say that . . . but . . . let me put stuff on your . . . your. . . ."

He nodded and filled her palm with jelly, then lay on his back while she bit her lip and reached down to wrap her fingers around his stiffness. Her warm hand bathed him in soft, wet fire that tingled every nerve. He shut his eyes and moaned.

"Cuh-careful. He . . . he's kind of um. . . ."

"Sensitive?"

"Yeah."

"So is my fanny, *remember?*"

"Of course it is." He looked at her and smiled. "I'll be careful, too. I love you far too much to hurt you."

She sighed and let go of him, then moaned when he rolled over and covered her with his body. His shaft lay lengthwise along her cleft and tingled the inner surfaces with damp, slippery heat. He dug his knees into the duvet and used his feet to spread her legs wide. She squirmed as he took her wrists in a soft, firm grasp, pulled her arms over her head and held them there with one hand. Helpless beneath him, powerless but to accept, she surrendered to her desire, arched her back and gave herself to him.

He reached down and guided the purple tip to her sweet, rubbery vent. They gasped at the same instant as the tight ring opened and he slipped inside.

"Are you OK?"

"Uh huh." She licked dry lips and let the pain wash over her, through her, to vanish in a haze of longing. "I . . . I *want* you."

"*That's* my good girl."

The shaft slid like a hot knife into a warm, oily sheath, but slowly, as in a dream, and his belly pressed her bottom, his manhood thrust inside to the hilt. He kissed her neck and inner muscles rippled to squeeze him tighter. She squealed when he pulled out a little and then pushed, sparking fire in her feminine core. The flames leapt higher, fanned by his strong, slow rhythm, and heat flashed through her vagina like a lightening bolt.

Sweat beaded his forehead as he lunged into her depths, her grip on his organ like a round vice of steamy molasses. Each wriggle, every clench of the beloved bottom sent shock waves up his spine that crashed between his ears like foam rubber bricks. The crisis approached and his manhood swelled and lengthened. He heard her scream as if from under water, and then bellowed when his passion burst and filled her.

Deep, shuddery spasms racked his body and he moaned as he released her hands. She reached back to grab his buttocks and held tight while she milked him for every drop. He rolled onto his side and took her with him, his member still snug in her behind, and hugged her close. She whimpered as his shaft retreated, and he groaned when she clutched him.

"No not *yet*."

"Shh . . . turn over and stop whining. You know the laws of nature as well as I do."

She twisted around and cuddled into his chest. "Doesn't mean I gotta *like* them."

He kissed her and caressed her tingly bottom. "But you *do* have to obey them."

"Or what? I get arrested by the nature police?"

"Possibly . . . but more likely *this* happens." His hand clapped warm rear cheeks and she whimpered.

"Nooo, you have to be *nice* to me now and . . . *Dylan*."

Warm fingers slipped inside her cleft and between quivery

lower lips. She hugged his neck while he toyed with the hard, wet bud at her core. Waves of heat swept over her and she clung to him as she once more climbed the summit. He held tight as delirious tremors rocked her body, then he lay on his back and pulled her on top of him while she shuddered and panted.

"What were you saying, Princess?"

"*Jesus!* You . . . you're gonna *kill* me if you keep doing that."

She grabbed his ears with tremulous fingers and clapped her lips to his. He kneaded quivery buttocks with both hands while they kissed. Long minutes later she sighed and rested her head on his shoulder.

"I love you, Kitty Eyes," he whispered.

"I love you, too. Are you going to sleep?"

"The thought *had* occurred to me."

"But I wanna cuddle some more."

"So do I, but it's been a *very* long day."

"I could make coffee . . . and anyway I wanna talk about what we're gonna do tomorrow."

He sighed and kissed her lips. "All right. No coffee . . . but go get a washcloth while I straighten the bed."

"But I don't *wanna* get up . . . *ow!* OK, I'm going!"

Moist new sting bathed sore bottom flesh and she rolled to her feet. Her knees quaked as she stumbled to the bathroom. Dylan smiled while he rearranged the covers and climbed beneath them. She wetted a hand towel, then went back to the bedroom and giggled as she squeezed warm water drops onto his closed eyes. He blinked, scowled and grabbed her arm to tug her into bed.

"Are you just *not* going to be satisfied until I blister your impudent tushy?"

"You're too *tired* to blister anybody's tushy."

She snuggled next to him and he moaned as she bathed his penis with the towel, then she wriggled over to straddle his loins. Her wet sex gently rubbed his spent member, and he gasped as she teased his nipples with her teeth and tongue.

"You *know* that drives me crazy, don't you?"

"Yeah . . . but *you* know how much I love your nipples . . . they're so soft and hard and bumpy."

He chuckled and took the towel from her. "Soft *and* hard, huh?"

"Yep . . . and bumpy and . . . *oooh* . . . Dylan!"

"Shh . . . I'm only washing off the lubricant."

"Well, you could *warn* me before you go playing inside my fanny."

"Right . . . the same way you warned *me* before you nibbled my naked nipples."

Her tongue traced circles around his aureole while he stroked the towel up and down her tingly cleft.

"Mmm . . . this is pretty much perfect."

"Yes . . . pretty much. Come here." He raised her chin and their lips met in a long kiss. "I love you, Princess . . . but I have *got* to get some sleep if we're going to buy a car tomorrow."

"But I'm not sleepy at *all* and. . . ." She grimaced when he lifted his hand over her widespread bottom. "OK! *Geeze,* you're grumpy."

"You'll *think* grumpy in a minute. Now give me a kiss and I'll tuck you in."

"OK." She held the kiss as long as she could, then whined when he rolled her onto her side. "Where are you going?"

"To the bathroom . . . and then to *sleep* . . . unless you want me to bring the hairbrush and help *you* get some rest."

"Grumpy and *mean!*"

He gave her bottom a quick squeeze, twisted out of bed and snugged the duvet to her chin. She hugged herself and listened to his water splash, then to the hum of an electric toothbrush. Her eyelids drooped and she jerked when he crawled into bed and turned her over. His warm stomach pressed her bottom and long arms enveloped her. Soft darkness closed in and she dreamt of ginger snap cookies until he nudged her awake at six-thirty the next morning.

CHAPTER 4
MEMORIES AND FEVER DREAMS

RAINDROPS CLICKED WINDOWPANES and Gwen burrowed deeper into her duvet cocoon. Dylan tied the belt of a long burgundy terrycloth robe and sat on the edge of the bed, his hair wet and slick and his cheeks agleam with aftershave. He smiled and tugged the comforter down far enough to see her eyes.

"Rise and shine, sleepy head."

"*Nuh* uh . . . you're shiny enough for both of us. How come you're up so early?"

"I'm still on Midwest time. If I make breakfast will you get your little bottom out of bed and eat it?"

"Sure . . . cook something that takes a while, OK?"

"Eggs Benedict with Hollandaise from scratch?"

"Yeah. Sounds perfect."

He laughed and yanked off the covers. "You wish! Now *move* it. Take a shower and get your blood pumping."

"*No!*" She grunted and tried to crawl under the duvet but he wrapped an arm around her waist and picked her up. "*Dylan!*"

"Come on, sweet cheeks . . . we're burning daylight."

"But there *isn't* any daylight! It's raining cats and frogs . . . *dogs!* Put me *down!*"

She squealed as he carried her, naked and draped under his arm like a potato sack, into the bath and set her on her feet in the

shower stall. He leaned over and she gave him a perfunctory kiss as she glared at him.

"Well, good morning to you *too*, Princess."

"I *hate* mornings."

"Get wet, young lady."

He twisted the knob to turn the water on and backed out the door. Her scream followed him down the hall to the kitchen. His lips fluttered as he shook his head and searched the refrigerator and cupboards.

"What *does* she eat?" he muttered, and stalked back to the bedroom.

The shower roared while he dressed in a striped cotton shirt and blue wool slacks. Gwen grumbled and yawned as she finger combed wet hair, slicked moisturizer on her face and brushed her teeth.

"Gwen?"

"What?"

"I have to go out . . . anything you need? Besides food?"

She slipped into her robe and opened the door. "I've *got* food. I mean . . . there's eggs and cheese and stuff."

He hugged her and smiled. "The eggs expired a month ago and I'm pretty sure cheddar isn't supposed to be green, so unless you want reheated mu-shu pork for breakfast . . . is that bagel place still open in the strip mall?"

"No . . . it's a Vietnamese take-out now."

"Too bad. I'll go to the grocery. Where are the car keys?"

"On the hall table . . . but don't get bagels . . . theirs aren't very good."

"All right." He rubbed her bottom and reawakened sting and pleasure from the night before. "Get dressed . . . and don't forget your neck brace. Do you need to call work?"

"Um . . . not until nine-thirty or so . . . this new VP . . . Calvin . . . he never comes in before ten, then works 'til like midnight, so nobody bothers to show up early anymore."

"How long did you tell him you'd be out?"

"I said probably all week."

Dylan smirked. "A week off for muscle spasms?"

"*Yes*, 'cause it was a *horrible* accident and I gotta wear that stupid neck thing and *Calvin* didn't care so why are you being such a . . . ?"

"OK, OK . . . just checking. I'll go get breakfast. You want to come along?" He laughed when she scowled.

"Yeah right . . . a *grocery* store . . . first thing in the morning?"

"I love the way you say *grocery* store in the same tone most people say *concentration* camp."

"Well they're icky and boring and I *hate* them."

"I may as well pick up lunch too, but I'll try not to be gone too long."

"Take your time. Did you make coffee?"

"Yes . . . *that* you have plenty of."

She stepped into fuzzy green slippers and held onto his arm as they walked to the hall closet. "I *like* shopping at Starbucks."

"Of course . . . because it's ridiculously overpriced." He pulled a leather coat from its hanger and shrugged it on.

"Oh, hush and go get some food. I'm *starved*."

"And spoiled rotten, as well. Good thing I love you so much."

"Uh huh." She stood on tiptoe to kiss him. "I love you, too . . . 'specially when you spoil me rotten."

"I can imagine. Now get dressed and don't forget the. . . ."

"Neck brace . . . I know, I know."

He swatted her fanny, kissed her grin and went out the door into the garage. She ambled to the kitchen and poured a twenty-ounce mug of coffee, took it to the office and booted up her computer. Her bottom tingled as she wriggled on the leather seat, and her eyes gleamed while she scanned a zip disk full of bank records she brought home from the office. Her job as underwriting analyst gave her free access to files from businesses that applied for insurance policies, and put her in a unique position to carry out covert investigations for the Treasury Department. Dylan's father, a specialist in financial forensics, had honed the keen eye she already possessed so that she could spot an irregularity in a spreadsheet from ten feet away. She clicked file after file, frowned as she sipped coffee, and then smiled.

"*There* they are." She giggled as she highlighted entries and dragged them onto her hard drive.

Wipers sluiced sheets of water from the windshield as Dylan drove the rented Taurus slowly through a winter downpour. Haze fogged the glass and he leaned forward to switch on the defroster. The shoulder harness shifted and he thumbed it to a

more comfortable position, then patted his breast pocket and grunted.

"Well, *drat!*" He made a U-turn five blocks from the house and headed back, then sighed when he got to the garage and found the roll-down door still open. "Wonder what *else* I forgot."

He went inside and stopped in the hallway outside Gwen's office. She hunched close to the computer screen, a hand on the mouse, while she clicked and dragged line after line of cells. He scowled, folded his arms and leaned against the doorjamb.

"*That's* a good position for someone with a broken neck."

She squealed and whirled. "*Jesus!* Don't sneak up on me like that!"

"*What* do you think you're doing, young lady?"

"I . . . I'm just. . . ." Her heart pounded with adrenaline as she jerked to her feet and fisted her hips. "What do think *you're* doing, huh?"

"Don't take that tone with *me*. You're supposed to be dressed . . . you're supposed to have the brace on . . . and you are *not* supposed to be working with your head inside the monitor."

"But . . . but *Dylan!*"

"Come on. *Now*, Gwendolyn."

"Oh, shit! I mean *shoot!* I mean . . . what are you *doing* here?"

"I *said* come on."

He took her hand and led her to the bedroom. She whimpered as he untied her robe and dropped it onto the bed. He scolded her the whole time he put her underwear on, dressed her in the yellow sweat suit, pulled thick wool socks onto her feet and then wrapped the brace around her neck. She whined and muttered excuses, but each alibi was met with more scolding. Finally he sighed, sat on the bed and took her on his lap.

"Princess, I'm *very* disappointed with you."

"I said I was *sorry!* Please don't be mad, OK?"

"I'm not mad . . . but you know I have to do something about this."

"Nuh *uh* . . . 'cause . . . 'cause you already *yelled* at me and I feel just *awful* so you don't have to . . . *do* anything!"

She hugged him and wept into his neck. He kissed her forehead and patted her bottom.

"Go turn off your computer while I get my wallet. One thing I *do* have to do is get you something to eat."

"OK." She leaned back and wiped her eyes. "You came back 'cause you forgot your wallet?" He nodded and she sniffled while her mind raced. "Um . . . that . . . that's probably why I did it."

"Hm? *What's* why?"

"Low blood sugar. I was delirious so . . . so you *can't* puh-punish me for. . . ."

He smiled and shook his head. "You're delirious if you think I *buy* that nonsense. Now go sit in the recliner and I'll put the afghan on you, then I'll run get something for breakfast and you can come with me later to stock up."

"Ew! I don't *wanna* go to the. . . ."

"Do you want to go to the grocery with the plug in your bottom?"

"*No!* I'll just stay in the chair all day, I *promise,* and I'll keep the stupid brace on and I won't complain or *anything* just don't. . . ."

"All right, all right . . . go do what I told you."

"OK." She trembled as she stood. "Dylan?"

"Hm?"

"Are you sure you're not mad at me?"

He chuckled and got up to hug her. "Furious . . . but that's probably *my* low blood sugar."

They kissed while he rubbed her bottom and calmed the scary butterflies his scolding had awakened in her tummy. All too soon he pushed her toward the office and retrieved his wallet from his suit coat pocket. She saved her file and shut down the computer, then he led her to the living room, put her in the chair and tucked the knitted blanket around her. He gave her a kiss and left the house.

Gwen surfed the morning news shows and gasped when she stumbled on a filmed interview with a caption that read Corporal Punishment in Schools. A doe-eyed teenage girl spoke into the reporter's microphone while she twisted her hands at her waist and glanced from side to side.

"So yeah um . . . like if you get more than three detentions? Um, you have a choice? So um . . . either you get suspended or like, um . . . you can take licks? With a paddle?"

An off-camera reporter turned the mike around. "And *did* you take the licks?"

The girl stared at the floor and nodded. "It . . . it hurts, you

know? But it's like so embarrassing? I mean *shoot!* Just . . . just bending *over* for Mr. . . . um . . . for the principal? Showing him your backside? That's just . . . well, it's *yucky,* never *mind* that he's gonna whop your bee hind with that big old board!"

"Yes, I can imagine. Do you think you *learned* anything from the experience?"

"*Shoot* yeah! Don't get caught *doing* stuff no more."

The camera shifted to the reporter. "And there you have it. Many states, especially in the South, *still* allow corporal punishment in public schools, despite numerous studies and piles of research that appear to show that it is not just ineffective, but counterproductive. What did Miss X learn from being spanked at school? Only to avoid being caught the next time. From a small town in northern Alabama, I'm Misty Caldwell."

Gwen pointed the remote and muted the talking heads that came on next. "God, I wish I had that on tape!"

Gingery warmth tingled her anus and she leaned back. Her hand trembled as she cupped the front of her pants and squeezed tender labia, moist already from Dylan's scolding. A picture gelled in her mind of the nervous schoolgirl in tight jeans, her eyes wide with fear and shame as she bent and looked back at the rural principal standing behind her, fat, bald, a perpetual sneer on his lips, the paddle in his hand. Bright quivers surged up her tummy and the image wavered. The principal disappeared and Sister Mary Bernard stood in his place, her wimple starched, ironed, immaculate, the ubiquitous eighteen-inch ruler in her long fingers, her brown eyes hard as agates, her back straight as a decking plank. Twelve-year-old Gwen, in a rumpled wool skirt and white blouse, quivered before the terrible specter, neck bowed by the weight of childish sins, while she prayed silently that the sister would take her to the cloakroom and not punish her in front of the other girls.

The cloakroom held a dark, awful secret, shared by most of the students, voiced by none. A correction in class meant four or five ruler swats on the seat of the skirt while the girl bent over the desk, more ignominious than painful, but a trip to the cloakroom was another matter. Already in disgrace, the girl was led into a large closet and the massive door shut behind her. The smell of wet rubber boots and damp wool permeated the atmosphere, along with profound silence. An oak kneeler sat in one

corner, shiny, polished, ready for the penitent. The girl knelt . . .
Gwen knelt . . . and leaned forward, hands folded in supplication,
while warm fingers lifted her skirt and quiet yet stern
admonitions grated her ears, and then the hard ruler swatted soft
bottom, protected only by thin cotton panties.

She felt the cushion on her knees and squeezed her eyes tight as
she slipped a hand inside her sweat pants, beneath her panties, and
slid a finger between wet, squirmy nether lips. She moaned, pulled
the brace from her neck, and the sister faded from her vision.
Dylan stood behind her, his mouth twisted in the ironic half-smile
she loved and feared so much, and in his hand the short, nasty
leather paddle he used for her schoolgirl spankings. He could be
so *horrid* then, to make her bend and grasp her knees so the skirt
rode up and bared her thighs even before he lifted it, and then to
scold her when she looked back at him, when all she wanted was
to feel his hard thighs beneath her tummy, his arm around her
waist, while she lay on his lap. Yet her stupid, willful libido
betrayed her every time, and bathed her vagina in naughty essence
as soon as he slipped cotton schoolgirl underpants down her
bottom, just as it did now while she remembered the leathery sting
and the warm, gentle hand he kept on her back to steady and reassure
her throughout the awful ordeal.

Her finger caressed the wet node at her core, hot and quivery
already with the memory of ginger sting and his wanton stiffness
the night before. Fiery, shuddery bolts of ecstasy lanced up her
bosom and exploded behind her eyelids. Womanly wetness
drenched her fingers and she screamed as she bounced in the chair.
She panted and stared at the hallway, her ears attuned to his footfall.
There was none so she swallowed the dryness in her mouth,
wriggled to her feet and ran to the bedroom. The yellow sweat suit
flew at the hamper, followed by her wet panties, and she scrambled
into worn blue jeans, a tee shirt and a green cashmere sweater.
She washed her hands at the basin, fluffed her hair, and then shook
a Zanaflex into her hand and took it to the living room.

The garage door motor hummed as she swallowed the pill with
a gulp of tepid coffee. She gasped and hurried to clamp the brace
around her neck as she sat and pulled the afghan over her lap.
Dylan smiled and carried two plastic bags past her.

"You changed clothes," he yelled from the kitchen.

"Yeah um. . . ." She rose and followed him. "I feel a little better now. What did you get?"

"The usual . . . milk, bread, eggs, oatmeal, raisins . . . non-green cheddar." He grinned when she slapped his arm, and then turned to hug her. "You *do* seem a lot perkier. Would you like an omelet?"

"Sure. Is it still raining?"

"A little . . . not like earlier. Would you whip the eggs, please?"

"Why? Were they naughty?"

Dylan laughed and swatted her bottom. "All right . . . *whisk* them to a medium froth while I grate the cheese."

She grinned. "Long as you don't *cut* the cheese."

He moaned and shook his head. "I'll pretend I didn't hear that . . . now get *busy.*"

"Yes, *sir.*"

They chatted and cooked, and then sat side-by-side at the kitchen bar. Gwen finished her omelet, then held onto the crook of his arm and nibbled whole wheat toast while she stared into space.

"That was really good. Must be time for a nap, huh?"

"Not if we want to buy a car today. Or would you rather wait?"

"Nuh uh . . . I just feel a little woozy."

"The Zanaflex, probably. Maybe a *little* nap wouldn't hurt you."

She bit her lip and looked up into his eyes. "Yeah but . . . I think we *both* need a nap . . . a *naked* nap."

He chuckled and kissed the top of her head. "When we get back from the dealer."

"*Nuh* uh . . . I wanna get naked *now.*"

"Gwendolyn?"

"Nooo!" She leaned back and pouted hard. "Don't *call* me that."

"Then don't be impertinent. You're already in trouble for that prank this morning."

"But I don't *wanna* be in trouble and . . . and anyway I found the kickbacks they've been stashing, so *there!*"

"*What* kickbacks?"

"At this cement company . . . mostly commercial jobs, but they deposit a lot of cash."

"And *you* think there's something nefarious in that, I take it."

"Well, yeah . . . there's a bunch of deposits, all between ninety-nine fifty and ninety-nine ninety, and all at different bank branches to get in under the radar."

"But why are you even *looking* at them?"

"I look at *everybody* . . . that's what I *do*. And who pays for twenty truckloads of cement with cash?"

He sighed. "You *know* I'm not thrilled about all this cloak and dagger. Due diligence is one thing, but I think your boss has delusions of MI5 running through his head."

"Nuh *uh* . . . Randy is very level-headed . . . and also a lot nicer than most of the brass in Washington . . . *plus* he came up with this insurance cover so I don't have to sit in a stuffy Department office and crunch numbers all day."

"Yes, well . . . I'm not sure *this* is what Dad had in mind when he trained you."

She giggled. "I'm not sure *either* . . . 'cause Randy said, flat out, that I was too young and pretty to be a good expert witness . . . not for a while, anyway."

"Oh *did* he? He told you that over dinner and cocktails, I suppose."

Her forehead furrowed and then she smiled. "Yeah . . . and I drank vodka martinis . . . shaken, not stirred."

Dylan stood and laughed as he pulled her off the barstool. "All right, Ms. Bond, I've had *enough* of your silliness for one morning."

Gwen squealed as he scooped her up and carried her to the bedroom. She held tight to his neck while nasty, wonderful butterflies race through her tummy.

"So we're gonna take a nap now?"

"No . . . we're going to discuss your taking the week off to snoop in someone's bank accounts." He sat on the bed and hugged her while she sputtered.

"But it's my *job* . . . you *know* that!"

"All I know is that you disobeyed me and put your health at risk by working with a sore neck, and that does *not* make me happy."

"Dylan, *please!* I . . . my neck doesn't hurt at *all,* so I didn't *really* put my. . . ." He smiled and she clapped a hand over her mouth. "Oh my *God.*"

"I'm *very* happy to hear that . . . but I want to make sure you're in A-one condition . . . before I blister your bottom."

"What? *Nooo!*" She squirmed and sucked a fingertip as he unfastened her jeans.

"I *told* you I would have to do something about your little escapade, so stand up while I take your pants down."

"But I don't want you to!"

"On your feet . . . there." He opened her fly and pushed the jeans down. "Gwen, *where* are your panties?"

"I . . . um . . . I forgot."

"Didn't I put underpants on you earlier?"

"Yeah, but . . . when I changed clothes I . . . I just *forgot*, that's all!"

"Oh *really?* What have you been *doing* while I was gone?"

"Nuh-*nothing*, honest!" Hot, guilty blush covered her face and spread down her spine to redden her bare bottom.

"I *see* . . . then stand right here and while I get the thermometer."

"Not the thermometer!"

"Hush! I don't know what you've been up to, but you're acting very strangely."

"Nuh *uh,* I just . . . don't take my *temp*, OK?"

He put a finger on her lips and shook his head. "I told you to *hush.*"

She stamped a foot and pouted, but kept her mouth shut. Her knees quivered with fear and excitement as he turned toward the bathroom. She yearned to pull her pants up and run out the door, to jump in the car and escape the horrid embarrassment he planned for her. But her feet, so warm in woolen socks, refused to budge, like blocks of ice, frozen in place. Her hands trembled as she tugged the tee shirt hem down to cover her sex, and sneered at the futile gesture of modesty. His back was turned to her as he rummaged in a cabinet, and she yearned to shout at him, to threaten dire, awful consequences if he even came *near* her with the childish thermometer.

His heels thumped and she whimpered as he paced toward her, that scary, ironic smile on his lips, those nasty *things* in his hands. She pouted as hard as she could, but he ignored her and put the *things* on the nightstand.

"Come on, Princess."

"Puh-please not *Vaseline,*" she whined.

He sat on the bedside and draped her across his thighs. She rested her forehead on folded hands and squeezed her eyes shut as a warm hand patted bare roundness.

"You were a bad girl to make me worry like that." Latex

snapped when he tugged on a glove. "Now keep still so I can lubricate your little hole."

"But that's icky."

He popped the lid off the plastic jar and she squeaked. No sound in the universe, she thought, could be as nasty and horrible as *that* one. Her bottom cheeks clenched to guard the tender orifice within.

"Relax, Gwen."

"I don't *want* you to!"

His gloved hand swatted hard across her cleft and she yelped. "Don't be ridiculous. Bend your back and lift your fanny . . . that's better."

Strong fingers parted her buttocks and thick goo daubed her anus. His touch sparked fire in ginger-stung nerves and reheated her tingly vagina. He pushed his fingertip through the tight ring and she squealed.

"*Dylan.*"

"Stop *whining,* young lady. You've been stubborn, willful and bratty all morning, and that ceases as of now . . . so keep still while I put the thermometer in."

"But I *hate* it when you. . . ."

"Hush that this *instant.*"

She moaned as he leaned over to pick up the glass rod. He coated it with pale green slipperiness and once more spread her cheeks. Her sensitive hole puckered as he circled the opening with the tip, and she whimpered when it slid into her. He smirked and pushed it halfway in, then backed it out, slowly, and then down again.

"Why do you have to *do* that? Just . . . just put it *in,* for Christ's sakes!"

"You aren't making any good-girl points with that attitude. You know I have to make sure it's positioned right so I get an accurate reading."

"Nuh *uh,* you just . . . oooh!" *You just love to torment my innocent bottom and make me all naughty and wet down there 'cause you're evil!* The words burned through her mind and she congratulated herself that she didn't say them out loud. She heard the hard edge in his voice, and knew she had pushed him as far as she dared.

Finally he left the thermometer deep inside her rectum while he

admired her tender pink cheeks, framed by wrinkled jeans below and the soft sweater above. He patted her back and she sighed.

"Just a few minutes, Princess."

"You . . . you already *know* I don't have a fever, right?"

"I won't be sure until I take the thermometer out . . . and a fever *could* explain your naughty behavior."

"Nuh *uh* . . . you *said* it was the muscle pills and . . . and low blood sugar." She squeaked when he patted her bottom and made the thermometer jiggle and shoot quivery tingles through her.

"No, *you* said that."

"So . . . so when you find out I *don't have a fever, can we go look at cars?"*

"Yes. Right after your spanking."

"But I don't deserve a spanking! I'm being *good* and . . . and not wiggling or *anything!"*

"Not at this precise instant, no . . . but you *were* naughty this morning and this is what happens to naughty girls."

"That was like *hours* ago . . . and you already *hollered* at me so you don't *need* to. . . ."

"That's enough. Now unclench your cheeks and I'll take out the thermometer."

"Oh, *geeze!"*

He spread her bottom once more, a wholly unnecessary procedure from her point of view, slipped the little rod out of her tightness and held it toward the light.

"Hmm . . . a bit *low,* actually. That's a good indication."

"Yeah? Of what?"

"That you need your fanny warmed."

"No I *don't.* You're just being a . . . *ew!"* She huffed and squirmed as he plucked tissue from the box on the nightstand and wiped Vaseline from her furrow. "I *hate* when you do that!"

"Stop fussing." He tossed the rubber glove and the wadded tissue at the trash basket, and then snugged her waist with his left arm. "You were a bad girl to try to work when I told you to rest."

"I . . . I'm *sorry,* Dylan, please don't . . . *ow!"*

His palm landed on her bareness, just hard enough to jiggle the cheeks. He slapped again, with no more force than he would clap her back for a job well done. She sighed and bit her lip as she wriggled her hips and reveled in the hardness of his thighs, the

smoothness of his hand on her bottom. Ten, twenty, thirty swats, more like caresses than spanks, warmed and excited her.

"See what happens when you're naughty?"

"Mmm . . . yes, sir. I won't be naughty any more." She grinned and turned her head toward him as the gentle slaps continued. "Thank you for the good-girl spanking."

He arched his eyebrows and she gasped. "I hate to disappoint you . . . but this is a *warm-up*."

"Not a . . . *ouch!* Warm-up! You can't *blister* me just 'cause I. . . ."

"Worked without your neck brace? Fibbed to me and your boss about how bad your injury is?"

"No *owee!* I *didn't* eek! *Dylan!* Not so *ow* hard!"

"Your fanny is nice and pink and all the little nerves are wide awake . . . so quit that squawking while I teach you a lesson!"

"But I don't *owee* . . . *need* a lesson! Ow! I won't do it anymore I . . . *eesh!* Promise!"

Bright burn replaced the gentle warmth in her bottom as he stepped up the pace, and she whined wordless protests at the injustice. How could he be so mean to her? And how could she not recognize a warm-up when she felt it? Now he was going to spank her until she was red and sore and there was nothing she could do about it except kick and complain!

He smiled and showered sting droplets, first on one cheek, then the other, over and over again, each swat a micro-dyne harder than the one before. Her squeaks and squeals intensified as her bottom darkened from blush-pink to rosy red. She kicked and wriggled, and he snugged her waist tighter beneath his arm. The deep, amber cleft narrowed and spread as she clenched and relaxed. Redness turned to crimson, and the musky scent of her arousal tickled his nostrils. He bent his wrist and used only his fingers to pepper the scarlet mounds with quick, noisy spanks.

An achy blaze swathed her bottom and she no longer felt the individual swats, only the continual shock that flowed through her hips and jolted the shuddery node between her labia. She pounded the duvet with fists and toes while she begged him to stop, but the fire only leapt higher, consuming her in its awful heat. Hot, steely fingers clapped the base of her cleft and poured fuel on the conflagration at the center of her being. She pushed with all her strength, up and into the hand that scorched her

soul, and screamed as searing white waves of passion crashed through her.

He held tight and squeezed her cheeks while she twisted and howled, and then finally collapsed, panting. She moaned as he gently lifted and turned her over. Tremulous fingers grabbed his neck, and he kissed her wet, quivery lips. Her tongue invaded his mouth, searched, probed, retreated, then thrust again. He patted her sore bottom and she pulled away, only to smother his face with damp, frantic kisses.

"*Gaahd,* what did you *do* to me?"

"You mean, besides spank your impudent behind?"

He chuckled and she glared at him as she yanked off the neck brace and threw it to the floor.

"That wasn't a *spanking* that was a . . . I don't know, but you nearly turned me inside *out.*" She licked her lips and then grinned. "So do I get *lotion* now, you mean old bully?"

"Is *that* any way to ask, you impertinent little minx?"

"Umm . . . maybe not?" She slid her bottom away from his belly and reached for his fly. "But I bet if I ask *him* real nice I'll get *lots* of lotion."

Dylan gasped as she unzipped his pants. His organ, already aroused, sprang to attention when she put a hand inside his shorts.

"Gwendolyn!"

"Nuh *uh!* I *can't* be in trouble anymore 'cause you blistered me *purple,* so now I get to play."

He leaned backward and coughed as she squirmed around to kneel on the bed. She squeezed his erection and he moaned when she bent and took the fat, warm cap between her lips.

"Young lady, this is *not* getting us to the duh-dealership."

She turned her head to look at him. Her eyes sparkled while she bathed his stiffness with her tongue. "Oo uh '*ere?*"

"To the *dealership,* and don't be smart-alecky or I'll. . . ."

"No you won't." She wrapped both hands around his penis, took the tip in her mouth again and licked.

Dylan gasped, lay flat on the bed and reached out to fondle her red bottom. Her velvety tongue flicked, teased and caressed while her hands stroked. She brought him to the boiling point, then relaxed her grasp. He moaned as the quivers subsided, and swallowed hard as she resumed the delightful torment. Once more she

brought him to the brink with her hands, her tongue, her sharp little teeth, only to stop and watch his face as he shuddered and took deep breaths. She began again, more slowly, with only her wet lips around the hot corona, and moved her head in gentle arcs. The crisis approached again and she stopped. He growled, deep in his throat, and clutched her bottom hard. She squealed and gripped him tighter in reflex, and then giggled and dodged as his semen spouted. He groaned and shuddered while she squeezed, and hot cream splashed his shirt and pants.

"You. . . ." He took a deep breath and pulled her down to lie beside him. "Are a *brat*."

"Yeah . . . but that's why you love me, huh?"

He nodded and kissed her, long and soft. "Among other reasons."

She wriggled into his side and rubbed his chest. "I like hearing that . . . 'cause I love you, too . . . even when you're so mean to me."

"Yes . . . you suffer terribly, I know." He kissed her again and raised his head. "What a mess."

"Oh, don't be a grinch. Tell me how much you liked that."

He laughed and hugged her. "It was truly wonderful, Kitty Eyes."

"See? Was that so hard?"

"I don't recall *ever* being that hard."

"*Dylan*." She pouted and slapped his arm. "That *wasn't* what I meant."

"I know. Now get undressed."

She grinned. "We get a naked nap now?"

"No, we get a naked *shower* now . . . and *you* get to send these clothes to the laundry."

"But I already *had* a shower! And what about my lotion? You can't just. . . ."

"Shh." He quieted her with his lips and then patted her behind. "I'll massage your fanny with lavender soap."

"Yeah, OK . . . but I want *lots* of it 'cause you blistered me *purple*."

"Yes, you mentioned that . . . but it's pure hyperbole. Now get going."

"Huh!" She twisted to look at her bottom. "I don't know what color *hyperbole* is but it's not *this*."

He laughed and pulled her off the bed as he rose. "Go!"

She dodged a swat he aimed at her bottom and stumbled to the bathroom, hobbled by the jeans at her ankles. He grimaced as he doffed wet, sticky clothes, emptied the pockets and then rolled the pants into a ball. Gwen pouted while she stood naked before the mirror and inspected the horrid, delicious redness his cruel, lovely hand painted on her behind. He smiled when he walked in, then shook his head and scooped her clothes from the floor and tossed them into the hamper along with his own.

"Hey! I was gonna wear that."

"No . . . I want you in a dress when we talk to the dealer."

"How come?"

"You'll be the good cop today."

Gwen giggled. "OK. The dutiful housewife bit, huh?"

"It's worked before."

"Yay! I get to whine and flutter my eyelashes and beg my honey to buy me the car."

He chuckled and turned on the shower spray. "Just don't get *too* wrapped up in the part and forget to tell the dealer what a jerk I can be if I don't get my way."

"Nope. I know the drill."

She stepped into the stall. He grabbed a plastic bottle from the cabinet and followed. Steam rose and water splashed as he held her in his arms and reached around to spread sweet, flowery gel over wet, crimson cheeks. She moaned and flicked his nipple with her tongue until he turned her around. Foamy, slippery fingers caressed the insides of her cleft, then deep between her lower lips. She squealed when, for the third time that morning, hot, blissful shudders crashed over her like a tidal wave.

* * *

The alarm buzzed at four o'clock Thursday morning and she grumbled as she slapped the snooze bar. Dylan awakened her ten minutes later and she rolled out of bed to hug him when he asked if she would rather he phone for a car.

"*Nuh* uh . . . I said I'd take you to the airport and I will." She cuddled, naked, into his robe and shut her eyes.

"Princess?"

"Hmm?"

"It would be much safer if you were awake enough to drive."

"Hush and go make coffee."

He smiled and kissed her pout. "Already did. Should I set up the IV pole and pump it in?"

"You should quit being such a smart-ass at four in the . . . *ow!*"

She rubbed warm sting from her chilly bottom and clutched handfuls of terrycloth as he walked her to the bathroom. He waited while she put on her robe and used the toilet, then they went to the kitchen.

"You're sure you're all right to go to work today?" He blew steam off his coffee and sipped.

"Yeah, I suppose. Might as well since you're *abandoning* me."

He sighed and buttered a slice of toast. "Do you *need* a sore fanny this early in the morning?"

"No!"

"Then behave yourself and try to control the histrionics, little drama princess."

"You said I couldn't make a scene at the *airport* . . . you never said nothing about having a tantrum *here.*"

"I'll do more than just say it . . . and watch your double negatives."

"Are you back in professor mode *already?*"

"I never leave it, as far as I can tell."

She giggled and peered at him over the rim of her cup. "You said some pretty unprofessorly stuff last night while I had my. . . ."

"All right, all right." He scowled and then smiled. "No man can be held accountable for what he says when a girl's naughty finger is in his . . . fundament."

"Oh, geeze!" She leaned over to kiss him. "*That* wasn't what you were calling it."

"Could we change the subject, please? This is hardly suitable conversation for the breakfast table."

"You are *such* a hypocrite." She gasped and leaned back when he glared.

"Would you like to drive your shiny new car with a pillow under *your* fundament, young lady?"

"*No,* sir . . . not at *all,* sir." She grinned. "Maybe next time, sir."

"Very well, then." He smiled and squeezed her hand. "Do you want to shower before we go?"

"I'll do it when I get back. But . . . Dylan?"

"Hmm?"

"Thanks for helping me with the car. That salesman didn't know what *hit* him. First you stormed out because he wouldn't come down any more . . . then you handed him a credit card to pay for it and I thought his eyes were gonna pop out."

Dylan smirked and nodded. "I don't enjoy doing that to people, but I knew he had more wiggle room on the price. Which reminds me. . . ."

"I know, I know . . . I'll put in for the loan on my life policy today and mail you the check as soon as it comes, I *promise*."

"All right. I'd better get presentable."

Gwen carefully backed the Grand Prix out of the garage and drove to the airport. The traffic into Logan was lighter than usual, but they arrived at the concourse less than an hour before the flight. Their goodbyes were brief and made through the car window.

"Call me when you get there, OK?"

He smiled and kissed her. "I will. If your neck bothers you at work I want you to go home."

"Yes, sir. Dylan?"

"Hmm?"

"Do you love me?"

"More than life itself." He kissed her again and stepped back. "I have to go."

"I love you, too. Don't forget to call, OK?"

"I won't." He waved and she wiped a tear as the car rolled away.

CHAPTER 5
GREEN EYES FLASHING

THE JET TOOK off on time and Dylan slept through most of the two-hour flight, his chair pushed back, a smile on his lips as he dreamt of the wonderfully bad girl-woman he left in Boston. They landed in Des Moines a few minutes early and he drove straight to campus, had a triple espresso in the café, and led his American Lit class discussion. All went well until a young woman in the back row, a tall, green-eyed blonde with round glasses and too much blusher, asked if Dylan thought Twain was a racist.

"No . . . why? Because he used racial epithets?"

"Well, yeah!" She went on to read a passage from Huckleberry Finn that contained several instances of a particular word, then flipped pages and began another.

Dylan held up a hand. "We got it, Ms. . . ." He glanced at his roll-sheet. "Tolliver. You needn't belabor the obvious."

"OK, so how come he can say that and we can't?"

He looked at his three black students but none showed any inclination to speak. "Why would you want to, given its connotations?"

She sneered. "I didn't say I wanted to, but what about academic freedom?"

"That would depend on the context. If you say it, or write it, in an effort to make a point, you are free to do so. If you shout the word in order to hurt someone, that's another matter entirely."

"So . . . you're saying my intention . . . what I'm thinking . . . is how people decide what I can and can't say? Like some kinda thought police?"

"No, I'm saying that's how people decide what sort of person you are. You put your thoughts out there for people to see, whether you speak the words or write them, and people judge you by what you say and write, and the power to judge you is also part of academic freedom."

"Yeah, but . . . if I just wrote it, like on the chalkboard, in big block letters, with no context at all, how could people know what I was thinking? And besides . . . they say it."

Dylan puffed a breath. "Could you be more specific?"

She glared at him. "Black people do. They call each other that all the time."

"Really? All of them? All the time?" He raised his eyebrows and nodded to a young man in the first row. "Mr. Jackson? Is that accurate?"

"Hell no! If my dad heard me say that he'd smack me across the mouth."

"Indeed?" Dylan looked at Ms. Tolliver and shrugged.

"Well, I've heard them say it."

"As have I . . . but again you must consider the context. One theory is that such usage is an attempt to co-opt the word . . . the insulted stealing it, in a manner of speaking, from the insulter . . . much in the same way queer has been co-opted by homosexuals."

"So . . . if the word is already co-opted, then it's pretty much meaningless as a slur, anyway, so I ought to be able. . . ."

"It hasn't lost its ability to hurt . . . and I really think we should move on to. . . ."

She slapped the desktop. "Don't interrupt me when I'm making a point!"

The hair at the back of Dylan's neck stood on end. "Young lady, you have made your point, spurious as it may be, and if I hear any further impudence from you. . . ." He coughed and twisted away to hide his embarrassment, then turned back to the class. "Excuse me. I believe everyone here has an opinion on the subject, but this is a literature class and I think the matter is more suited to Sociology or Political Science. Also I see we're short on time, so are there any questions about next week's assignment?" A bell rang and Dylan

sighed. "I'll stay a few minutes in case there are . . . otherwise have a good weekend."

Notebooks rustled, books slammed and the students headed for the door. Dylan leaned against his desk and waited, but apart from a few nods and goodbyes, his pupils were done with him. He packed his briefcase and switched off the lights as he left. Crisp autumn air chilled him as he walked toward the parking lot, and hurried footfalls made him turn. He smiled at the young woman who ran along the asphalt path.

"Ms. Tolliver?"

"Brandi . . . with an I."

"Yes, I know. Is there something I can do for you?"

She bit her lip and fell into step at his side. "Are you mad at me, Professor?"

"Of course not. Why would I be?"

"I did kinda push your buttons."

"Oh? In pursuit of academic discourse . . . or were you merely bored?"

"No! I like your class. I just wanted to see what you'd do."

He sighed, stopped and looked at her. "Not that it's any excuse, but I doubt if I would have reacted as harshly if I weren't so travel weary."

"Really? I pulled the same stuff on my Sociology professor and he called me a lot worse than impudent."

Dylan chuckled. "So I can look forward to more gratuitous controversies?"

"No way . . . next time you'd probably paddle my bottom." Dylan swallowed and a hot blush bathed his face. Brandi grinned. "You don't remember me, do you?"

He shook his head. "We've met before? I mean, before this class?"

"Uh huh. Try Brandi Hargrove."

"What? You're Kate's little . . . when did you . . .? Oh for crying out loud!"

She laughed as he hugged her. "When did I grow up?"

"When did you become a blonde? You had the prettiest brown hair . . . when it was combed. Why didn't you tell me?"

"Tell you what? That I color my hair? Come on, Professor!"

"That you're Kate's little sister!" He frowned and held her arms as he looked into her eyes. "And why did you change your name?"

"I was married . . . for about three months, right after high school. Katey says I just did it to annoy her . . . and she could be right. The guy really was a loser. I filed for divorce when they hauled him away for grand theft auto."

"As well you should have."

"Uh huh. So are you going to?"

"Going to what?"

"Paddle my bottom . . . like you did Katey's."

"Did she tell you that?"

"She didn't have to . . . I used to sneak down to the basement and listen at the den door when you came over to give her lessons."

"I see. Does Kate know you're aware of her, um . . . past discipline issues?"

"Yeah . . . but she won't talk about it. I asked her a few times and she told me to mind my own business."

"An excellent policy in most cases."

She laughed and squeezed his arm. "Is that your way of telling me to mind my own business?"

He smiled. "I suppose so. This isn't a topic I should even be discussing with a student."

"You discuss it with the students at your other school."

His eyebrows arched. "My other school?"

"Oh, quit being so evasive. I know all about Red Blossom College."

"Do you, now?"

"See? There you go again. I stayed at Kate and Vick's house this summer. They talk about all sorts of stuff in their bedroom, you know."

"I didn't know . . . but I see a pattern emerging."

She grinned. "What? That I'm a sneak?" He nodded. "Don't have to be . . . the walls in their place are like paper thin. So? How do you get away with that?"

"Get away with what?"

"You know . . . paddling those girls' bare butts."

Dylan rubbed his forehead, pulled her to a nearby bench and they sat. "First of all, they aren't girls . . . they're young women of legal age, and as such they have consented to accept whatever discipline I see fit to employ."

"Like Katey did when you tutored her?"

"Exactly. Now my question to you is . . . what possible use do you have for this information? Is it something you intend to broadcast to the whole community?"

She pouted and leaned on his arm. "Is that what you think? That I just want to gossip?"

He patted her knee, then yanked his hand back. "Honestly, Brandi, I don't know what to think."

"Well, I won't. I just don't wanna be ignored anymore."

"Ignored by whom?"

"By you, that's whom!" She bit her lip and leaned back. "I've had a major crush on you since I was eight, and I was so jealous of Katey I couldn't stand it, and you didn't pay any attention to me at all."

Dylan coughed to cover a chuckle. "I'm confused. Aren't you the same girl I brought bags of candy for when I came to your house? And listened to raptly when I had coffee with your mom and Kate while you rattled on about cartoon shows I'd never seen and toys I'd never heard of?"

"You always brought sugar-free candy and you only pretended to listen."

"Then how would I remember what you rattled about?"

She sighed and nodded. "I guess . . . but anyway. . . ."

"Just out of curiosity, what would you have preferred I do? In response to this crush of which I was unaware?"

"I don't know. Maybe I'm being silly." She stood and shouldered her pack. "Sorry I bothered you, Professor."

"Brandi! Sit down. Please."

"Why?"

"Because I asked you to." She sneered and he scowled. "I said sit down, young lady." He nodded when she bit her lip and plopped onto the bench. "That's better. Now. Is this crush still active? And if so, will it interfere with your ability to learn in my class?"

"Um . . . it's kinda still there, but . . . I won't let it interfere."

"Are you sure?"

Brandi shrugged. "I'm a big girl . . . and like you said . . . what can I do about it?"

"That's the question, isn't it?" He squinched his right eye. "As I recall, your papers have been good so far . . . but good isn't exceptional. Would you like to write exceptional papers from now on . . . for this and your other classes?"

She nodded and a smile brightened her face. "You'll tutor me?"

"Not formally . . . but as my schedule allows I'm willing to help you with your work . . . but only off-campus and unofficially. Understand?"

"Uh huh . . . and if I unofficially do a lousy job?"

He smirked. "In that case I would have to give you incentive to do a better one, wouldn't I?"

Brandi grinned and leaned toward him, her lips puckered, and then frowned when he held up a hand. "OK, Professor. Can I tell Katey?"

"This can't be a secret, but she may have some hard questions for you . . . especially if you brag about it."

"Why would I do that?"

Dylan stood. "I want you to think about your feelings and hers before you even mention it, all right?"

"Um . . . yeah. I guess she sorta had a crush on you too, huh?"

"I have to go . . . but I'll call you with a time for our first meeting."

"OK . . . um . . . thanks, Professor. I know you're busy so. . . ."

"I'm not blowing you off . . . I really will help you, but please be patient."

"All right. I gotta go, too . . . I'm late for lunch with some people."

"Goodbye, Brandi."

"See ya, Professor."

She waved and trotted toward the student union building. Dylan watched her plump, round bottom wriggle beneath tight, low-cut jeans. He walked to the Blazer, then sat with the engine running and the heater on high while he shivered off the chill. His chest rose and fell as he leaned against the headrest and took long breaths to still the nervous tension. There had always been girls, young women, in his classes who wanted more from him than academic attention, but this one was different, and he considered whether he had gone too far, with the adjunct professorship in addition to his duties at Red Blossom College. He growled, shook his head and yanked on the safety harness.

"You knew the job was dangerous when you took it," he muttered and threw the shifter into drive.

The traffic light turned red and he stopped at the parking lot

exit. He glanced toward the bus stop, then smiled, made a left turn and pulled to the curb twenty feet from the Plexiglas shelter. A servo hummed as he rolled down the passenger-side window.

"Teresa!"

She stared straight ahead. He scowled, shouted her name again and honked the horn. The other five students at the stop looked at him, then at her, and she sighed and ambled to the truck. He smiled.

"What's the matter, sweetie? Hop in and I'll drive you home."

"Very well." She climbed inside and slammed the door.

Dylan opened his mouth, then shut it and drove away. Two blocks later he tried again.

"Is everything all right?"

"Fine."

"I missed you."

"Oh?"

He blinked and shook his head. "There's a bug crawling on your jacket."

Teresa gasped and looked down, then glared at him. "Very humorous, Uncle Dylan." She stared ahead once more.

"Are you going to tell me what's wrong? Did something happen at school?"

"Perhaps."

"What do I have to do to get more than one-word answers out of you?"

She turned to him and pouted. "Who was that girl?"

"What girl?"

"The one you were so deeply in conversation with that you chose to ignore me."

"But I never . . . how could I ignore you if I didn't know you were there?"

"I passed by only five meters away but you were so intent on this girl that you. . . ."

"Wait, wait . . . the girl I was talking to on the bench just now?" Teresa nodded. "That was Kate's little sister."

"Kate?"

"The policewoman . . . you remember. Why didn't you just come over and say hello?"

She licked her lips. "Be . . . because you . . . seemed so engrossed that. . . ."

"Sweetie, she's in my class . . . we were talking about school-work. Why are you so upset?"

"Because I. . . ." Tears welled in her eyes and she leaned over to grab his arm. "I missed you too, Uncle Dylan!" She wept on his coat sleeve while he patted her knee.

"OK . . . it's all right. I'm sorry I didn't see you . . . and I'm sorry you thought I was ignoring you. Feel better now?"

"Yes." She sat up and dug in her purse for a Kleenex. "I . . . I am sorry also, but to see you and . . . and be not able to speak to you, or to welcome you home, I merely. . . ."

"Shh. Don't worry about it. How's Fel? Is she OK?"

"Yes. She helped me send the packages to Germany and. . . ."

Dylan jumped when his phone rang. "Blast!" He dug it out of his coat pocket and scowled at the caller ID. "Oh boy." The phone beeped when he thumbed a contact and he forced a smile into his voice. "Hi, Princess!"

"Did you forget something, mister?"

He made a right turn and stopped between two driveways. "Yes, um . . . it appears I did. Sorry. Did you make it to work all right?"

"Don't change the subject. You said you'd call."

"I know. It slipped my mind. Forgive me?"

"Huh! I don't get forgiven that easy."

"No . . . not usually. What can I do to make it up to you?"

"Umm . . . get on the next plane back to Boston?"

Dylan laughed. "You know I would if I could. How's your neck?"

"It's fi . . . um . . . it's pretty bad. I think you need to massage it."

"Oh, really? It seemed so much better the past couple of days."

She giggled. "You mean the past couple of nights. I'm gonna hate waking up tomorrow without a big warm hairy arm around me."

"The arm will miss you, too. I'd better get going. I'm in the car taking Teresa home."

"OK. I'd say, call me later, but then I'd just have to forgive you all over again."

"No you won't. I'll call you later."

"Uh huh. I might not be here . . . I think my other boyfriend's taking me out dancing tonight."

He grinned. "Don't stay out too late, now."

"God, you're aggravating!"

"Bye, Princess. I love you."

"I love you, too . . . bye."

Teresa frowned as he shut off the phone and put it away. "That was Gwen?"

He nodded as he swerved the truck around and turned onto the boulevard. "I was supposed to call when I got in but it slipped my mind."

"Yes . . . so you said." She pouted and watched Dylan rub his neck. "She is a princess?"

"Hm?" He glanced at her and smiled. "Just a pet name . . . same as I call you sweetie."

She scoffed and crossed her arms. "That is not a name. You might call anyone this."

"But I don't. Have you ever heard me call anyone else that?"

"I do not remember . . . perhaps. In any case, I am not with you always, so how will I know?"

"Sweetie, what's bothering you?"

"Nothing."

"Is it Gwen?"

"Of course not." She pointed as he pulled in front of the apartments. "You can let me out at the mailboxes."

"All right. I'll park and be up in a minute."

She looked at him and shook her head. "You should go home and rest. You seem very tired."

"I do? So I shouldn't take you and Fel out to lunch?"

"Perhaps another time."

The door handle clicked and she jumped out. Dylan puffed a breath and shook his head as he drove away.

Felicia sat at the kitchen bar and typed on a laptop computer. She looked up when the front door slammed.

"Hi, honey! How was school?"

"It was all right." Teresa dropped her book bag on the tiled floor and opened a cabinet. "Would you like a glass of wine?"

"Um . . . it's a little early, isn't it? I was thinking more about lunch."

"Yes, well . . . I am thinking about a glass of merlot."

Utensils clinked as Teresa fumbled in a drawer. Felicia scowled, saved her file and closed the computer lid.

"Is something wrong, sweetie?"

Teresa slammed the corkscrew on the counter and glared at her stepmother. "Do not call me that!"

"Call you what? What's the matter with you?"

"Nothing! I am fine!" She ripped foil from a bottle and stabbed the corkscrew at its top. "Au! Damn it!"

"Teresa, stop that!" Felicia hurried around the bar. "Let me see . . . no, don't put it in your mouth! Here." She led the girl to the sink, turned on the cold water and dowsed the injured thumb beneath the stream.

"Owee! That stings, Fel!"

"OK, OK . . . let me have a look." She examined the wound while Teresa pouted. "It's not that bad but I'll put some iodine on it and . . . Teresa? For heaven's sake, it's just a scratch. Why are you crying?"

"I . . . I am not!" She sobbed and leaned on Felicia's bosom.

"Come on. Let's sit in the living room."

"No . . . I . . . I am OK, honestly!"

"You're not either, now come on."

Felicia wrapped a paper towel around Teresa's thumb as she guided her to the sofa. They sat and Teresa leaned away from the woman.

"Truly I am fine."

"If you were you wouldn't keep saying that. Now tell me what's wrong."

She blew a petulant breath and wiped her eyes with the towel. "Uncle Dylan hates me."

"What? That's just ridic. . . ." Felecia bit her lip and hugged the girl. "Tell me what happened, honey. Why do you all of a sudden think he hates you?"

"Be . . . because he . . . he would rather be with them."

"Uh . . . which them are you talking about?"

"The . . . the girls in his class at university and . . . and that Gwen person."

"But, honey. . . ." She took a deep breath. "I thought you were all past that thing with Gwen . . . and you know he doesn't think twice about girls in his classes."

"Yes he does! He . . . he was flirting with one only this morning and. . . ."

"Whoa, wait a minute. This morning?" Teresa nodded. "Where did you see him this morning?"

"On . . . on campus and . . . she had her head on his arm whilst they were talking and . . . he merely ignored me and then . . . when he drove me home he told me to be quiet so . . . so he could talk on the mobile . . . to her."

Felicia wrinkled her forehead. "To who? The girl he was talking to on campus?"

"No . . . to Gwen! So you see? He does not care for me at all!"

"Teresa, you can't possibly. . . ." She leaned back and took a deep breath. "Let's slow down, OK? Dylan gave you a ride home?"

"Yes. He . . . he came to the bus stop and made me get in the car."

"He what? OK . . . never mind. So he brought you home . . . why didn't he come up and say hello?"

"I . . . I do not know. Perhaps he was in a hurry to go home and call Gwen."

"But you said he just talked to her."

Teresa stared at the crumpled paper around her thumb while she bit her lip. Felicia's eyes narrowed and she cupped the girl's chin in her palm.

"Look at me, Teresa. Were you so mad that you told him to go home?"

"Nooo, only . . . he . . . he was very tired and he wanted to go, so . . . so . . . I said he did not need to take us to lunch and. . . ."

The woman's full lips compressed to a thin line. "That is so not acceptable. He loves you more than anyone and you're treating him like a . . . a leper because he has a girlfriend!"

"But . . . but also he . . . he was flirting with that . . . that. . . ."

"Stop it! He would never flirt with a student . . . but I know they flirt with him, and it's all he can do to keep them at arm's length, so you just . . . ooh! I ought to blister your ass for even thinking that!"

Teresa gasped and wriggled away. "You . . . you have no right to speak to me this way! You are not my real mother!"

Felicia jumped to her feet and grabbed Teresa's arm. "That does it!" She dragged the girl down the hallway and into the bathroom. "Ever since I married your Papa I've wondered what

I'd do if I ever heard those words come out of your mouth and now I know!"

"Please, Fel! I . . . I didn't mean to say this, only . . . ouch!"

"Oh hush! I have to take the towel off so I can put a Band-aid on."

"Th-thank you. You . . . you are not angry with me, are you?"

"Yes, I'm angry with you!" She snugged a plastic strip around the wounded thumb and glared. "I don't have Dylan's self-control and obviously neither do you or your female hormones wouldn't have driven you to . . . to this weird jealous rage you're on."

"But Fel, I. . . ."

"No buts, young lady!" She grabbed a wooden hairbrush from the basin counter and Teresa sobbed as the woman waved it in her face. "If you want to argue with someone, argue with Dylan! Oh, that's right . . . you told him to go home! So you'll have to deal with me. Now come on!"

Teresa wailed and struggled to break free of the woman's grip, but Felicia pushed her into the bedroom, sat on the bedside and yanked the girl across her lap.

"Please, Fel! How can you do this to me?"

"Because I have to! You've been acting like a spoiled little brat for the past . . . I don't know how long, and if he isn't here to paddle your butt I'll just take care of it myself!"

"Noooo!"

Felicia held tight to the squirmy waist while Teresa kicked and grabbed at the woman's wrist. She squeaked when Felicia swatted the hand away and clutched her harder. Never in her thirty-one years had the woman given a spanking, but she was more than familiar with the procedure. William Travis doted on his only daughter and rarely even said no to her, but after he fell victim to the ravages of age Dylan took charge of his sister's discipline. He made up for their father's lapse, and by the time she graduated college she knew only too well the sting and embarrassment of a spanked bottom, the shame of the scolding that went with it, and the incentive it gave her to not incur her brother's displeasure.

"Quit that wiggling this instant, Teresa Luisa!"

Those horrible words, so often heard from Dylan's lips and now from Felicia's, burned Teresa's soul like acid. She moaned and pressed her hands to her ears, then shrieked when Felicia lifted her long woolen skirt. A deep, frightful knot gripped her tummy,

unlike anything she had ever felt. How could she do this? It was not right . . . it was not fair . . . it was not . . . proper for Fel to spank her! Only Uncle Dylan could do so and he was not there to protect her from this base humiliation. Why had she sent him away? It seemed so stupid now, but Fel was being most unreasonable and she had to stop!

"Please, Fel! I . . . I am sorry! Please let me go!"

"When I'm done with you, young lady, and not before! Now keep still."

The words again! The nasty, scolding words, in the same cadence, the same inflection as Dylan's, brought new tears to Teresa's eyes. The hairbrush popped tight boy-leg briefs, a dull, flat sound to her ears, but a sharp, lively pain to her firm right buttock.

"Ow! Fel!" She yanked a hand back to rub away the insult, then gasped when Felicia grabbed her wrist and snugged it hard against her hip.

The hairbrush struck again, on the left cheek, and Teresa bit back a screech. She covered her eyes with her free hand and clenched her teeth while hardwood painted bitter sting across her bottom. The sting grew to a burn, but she kept silent as Felicia fanned her behind with short, quick strokes. When redness glowed beneath pale blue micro-fiber the woman rested her forearm on Teresa's thighs and took a deep breath.

"Do you think you can behave now, young lady?"

"Yes! And . . . and stop calling me that!"

Felicia huffed and slipped her fingers into the panties' waistband. The doorbell rang but she ignored both it and Teresa's anguished wail as she pulled the pants down.

"Quit telling me what to do! I tried to be nice and not spank you bare, but I guess I'll have to."

"Jesus Christ, Fel, that is auu! Noo! Aiee! Pleeease!"

Crisp, clean smacks of wood on flesh echoed through the room, counter-pointed by Teresa's squeals. Flame scorched her behind and hot tears streamed from her eyes. She yanked and twisted, but the woman held her close and bounced the heavy brush from one rubbery mound to the other. A movement caught her eye and Felicia jerked her head toward the door.

Dylan stood in the hallway, two plastic bags and a key ring in

his hand, his eyes wide, brows arched. Felicia bit her lip and let go of Teresa's wrist. The girl scrambled to her feet and howled while she rubbed fiery sting with both hands and stamped her feet in a dance of pain. Dylan set the bags down and crossed his arms. Felicia dropped the hairbrush behind her.

"Hi . . . I . . . um. . . ."

Teresa whirled and swiped tears from her eyes, then ran to her uncle. He hugged her while she rubbed her bottom and wept into his chest.

"Fel?"

"But Dylan, she . . . she was just a . . . and . . . and anyway you said I could. . . ."

"All right . . . slow down. I know you must have had your reasons."

"Uncle Dylan!" Teresa scowled and stomped the carpet. "Whuh . . . why must you take her side! She has been most cruel to me and . . . and. . . ."

He put a finger over her lips and kissed her damp forehead. "I'll hear both sides of this . . . but I want you to think very carefully about what you tell me, because the way you were acting earlier leads me to believe you asked for this."

"I did not! And . . . and she is not allowed to punish me! Only you are and you . . . you were not . . . not here so. . . ." Her voice trailed off as her argument fizzled, and she buried her face once more in his shirt.

"Sweetie, I never said she couldn't punish you." The woman smirked and crossed her arms, then bit her lip when he looked at her. "But I did ask her to discuss it with me first."

"Dylan!"

"If possible." He took a breath and patted Teresa's back. "Go stand in the corner."

"No! I hate standing in the corner! It is not fair to make me ouch!"

The light tap of his fingers stung like a whip stroke on her sore behind, and new tears slipped from her eyes as she trudged across the room. He plucked tissues from a box on the bureau and pressed them into her hand.

"Lift your skirt."

"Please do not make me! That is so horrible!"

He furled the woolen skirt to her waist and twisted it in front so she could hold it with one hand. "I want Fel to see what she did to you while she tells me why she did it. All right?" She looked up at him, a huffy pout on her wet lips. "Do you really want a heavy skirt over your tushy right now?"

"It . . . it hurts."

"I'm sure it does . . . so we'll let it cool off, hmm?"

"But Uncle Dylan, I. . . ."

"Shh." He kissed her and ignored her petulant grunt as he turned away.

Felicia stood to face him, fists clenched on her wide hips. He shook his head and waved a hand.

"Sit down, Fel. I'm not going to yell at you."

She sat and rubbed her thighs with both palms. The tight denim was still damp with Teresa's perspiration and her own. Her heart pounded with exertion and nervous tension, and she jerked when he sat beside her and put an arm around her shoulders.

"Whuh . . . what's in the bags?"

"Lunch from Kwang's."

"Beef and pea pods?"

He nodded. "Fel?"

"Huh?"

"Don't make me play Twenty Questions."

"She . . . she just . . . I'm sorry, Dylan!"

"Stop it, Fel! I'm not looking for an apology . . . I want to know what happened."

"You said you weren't going to yell at me!"

"All right, all right." He squeezed her shoulder. "Start at the beginning. What happened after I dropped her off?"

"She, um . . . she was already in a snit . . . when she came in . . . and then she tried to open a wine bottle and cut her thumb and, um . . . then she started crying and told me you hated her and. . . ."

"I did not, Fel! I only said. . . ."

"Teresa! Hush and face the corner. I'll listen to you in a minute." The girl glared at him for an instant, then turned away from his steely gaze. "Go on, Fel."

"So, um . . . I tried to talk to her, but all I got was that same old stuff about Gwen and how she's stealing you away from us . . . her." She glanced at his eyes and then took a deep breath. "And . . . I mean

. . . you already spanked her once for that sh . . . stuff, but then, um . . . she said you were flirting with a student and . . . and I guess I sorta lost it."

He nodded and stared at his niece's red bottom. Teresa ached to hurl a furious denial of Felicia's accusation, but the lie stuck in her throat and all she could do was stamp her foot and reach back to rub fire from her tender behind, in defiance of Dylan's corner time rule. He opened his mouth, then shook his head and turned to his sister.

"Why didn't you call me?"

"Be . . . because I knew you were tired and I didn't think you'd want to . . . to deal with this after the plane ride and your class and everything, and . . . and I just felt like I ought to do something so you didn't. . . ." His lips curled in a quick half-smile that irritated her. She jerked to her feet and glared at him. "So you didn't have to be so damned in control all the time!"

He stared at her for a second, his mouth open. "What?"

"Well you are! And . . . and if you don't trust me to discipline my own daughter when she insults you then. . . ."

"I am not your daughter!"

Dylan stood and glared. "Hush, girl!"

"See?" Felicia's finger quivered as she pointed. "She even said I'm not her real mom!"

"And you aren't, Fel . . . Gerhard never intended that."

Felicia sneered. "So what do you suppose he intends when you move out to Boston with Gwen, huh? Am I supposed to call and ask your permission to breathe?"

He covered his mouth and coughed as his mind raced. "Not you too."

"Well? If you have to call the woman when Teresa's right there in the car with you, maybe I'm starting to see her point!"

"Gwen called me because I forgot to call and tell her I landed safely!"

"See? You're not Superman!"

Teresa shuddered and leaned against the wall as her two favorite people in the world squared off. Felicia's face was flushed, angry. Dylan's jaw muscle twitched for a few seconds then he shook his head and took a deep breath.

"I won't have it, Felicia."

"Won't have what?"

"You two thinking I would run off and leave you when I brought you here to be a family." He held out a hand but Felicia took a half-step back.

"Dylan!" Her eyes clouded with tears.

"I know the adjustment has been hard on you, but we are not going to fall apart over misperceptions and stress. Now come here and hug me."

"But . . . you just . . . oh, Dylan!" She leaned into his arms and swiped her eyes.

"You haven't screamed at me like that in a long time, honey."

Felicia bit her lip and nodded. "I know. Not since. . . ." She gasped and leaned backward. "You're not thinking about. . . ."

"Not since you were fifteen and considered it your inalienable right to go skating in Malibu with your friends."

"Yeah, but . . . you . . . I didn't. . . ."

"And what did I say would happen if you ever did it again?"

"God, Dylan! You can't be serious!"

"I tried to be reasonable about your spanking Teresa, but that wasn't good enough."

"But you . . . you had that stupid look on your face and I didn't think you were even listening and . . . and you even said how stressed out I am and . . . Dylan, no!"

He held her arms and nodded. "If you're that stressed out I'd better un-stress you . . . before things get any worse."

"No, please?" She threw her arms around his neck and sobbed. "I . . . I'm not a little girl anymore so you can't . . . I'm sorry I screamed at you, OK? Don't . . . just don't! Please?"

She held onto him like a life ring in a tempest while her stomach writhed in knots. Her buttocks clenched with remembered pain, but his strong, steady arms, tight against her ribs, supported and reassured her, as he always had done. Long ago scenes of his hard hand as it punished her, through adolescence, college, and almost to the day she married Gerhard, flickered through her mind in a kaleidoscope of foggy images, and in the fog she saw his warm, soft eyes when he forgave her whatever trespass she had committed.

"Take your jeans down, Fel."

The kaleidoscope shattered in a million jagged shards and

Felicia squealed. She clapped a hand over her mouth at the childish sound and wriggled from his grasp.

"No! This isn't right! I'm too big . . . too old to get spanked so you just. . . ."

"Felicia!" He grabbed her arm and she wailed as he pulled her close to him. "Do you want me to get Dad's belt?"

"Dylan, that's . . . nooo! You . . . I'm not . . . you can't possibly . . . !"

"Pull your jeans down, young lady. You may not be a little girl, but you're acting like one, so do what I said."

The phrases, at once so familiar and so foreign, spoken without rancor, assumed the tone of a litany, a purification ritual, a chance to start over. Her fingers trembled as she unzipped her pants and stared into his eyes. There were wrinkles at the corners of his lids she never noticed before, wrinkles like their father's, but finer, less pronounced. A tear rolled down her cheek.

"Dylan?"

"What, honey?"

"Not . . . not too hard, OK? I really am sorry."

Teresa chewed a fingertip as Felicia tugged down tight denim. A white band surrounded her hips, and the slender panty thong disappeared between high, rounded cheeks. Dylan sat on the bed-side and pulled her across his lap. Teresa knew well his distaste for thong underwear and her bottom flinched in sympathy as he regarded his sister's nearly naked behind.

"I'm sorry, too, Fel . . . now lift up a little."

"Dylan, no . . . my ass . . . my bottom's already bare so why do you have to . . . ?"

He swatted her hand away when she reached back to grab. "Stop that! I haven't spanked you with panties on since you were twelve."

"But they don't cover anything!"

"Then why does it matter if I pull them down?"

"Be . . . because it's embarrassing."

"I'm sure Teresa felt the same when you removed her under-wear." He thumbed the waistband and pulled.

The thong curled upward from between the cheeks and Teresa covered her mouth to hide a smile. Dylan looked at her and she turned her face to the wall. Felicia clenched Stair-Master-toned gluteals to hold the thin strip of material in her cleft, then whim-

pered when he yanked it free and pushed the tiny garment a few inches down her thighs.

"God, Dylan, you're just being a. . . ."

"Hush, Fel . . . I'm being your big brother and reminding you how a grownup girl is supposed to act."

She scoffed. "How can I act grown up if you treat me like a owee!"

His palm clapped firm roundness with quick, light swats that shocked more than they hurt. She pushed up on her elbows and stared at the counterpane until he nudged her shoulder and made her lie down. Her bottom lifted and she squeezed hard to close the wide furrow. He raised his arm higher and slapped harder, and Felicia gasped as prickly heat grew in her bottom.

"Will I ever! Ever! Ever! Hear! You! Scream! At! Me! Again?"

"No! Ow! Ow! Jesus! Dylan! No! That's enough! Ouch!"

He smacked hard, straight across the thin crevice. She yelped and reached back to rub, then sniffled and scowled as she twisted to look up at him. His arm tightened around her waist when he leaned back to grab the hairbrush. Her heart pounded and she pushed away from him with hands and knees.

"Be still, Felicia!" He curled his forearm beneath her belly and held her tight to his ribs.

"Not the hairbrush! You already spanked me, for Christ's sakes, so just let me go!"

"When I'm done with you, young lady, and not before. Now keep still."

Teresa's mouth fell open and her bottom flinched at the all too familiar words, then she leaned her shoulder against the wall and watched hard, nasty wood smack Felicia's big, grownup fanny.

"All this nonsense! About Gwen! Stops! Right! Now!" Sharp claps rang out, bright and clear, and her behind jerked down and up with each crisp swat. "We will! Be! A family! Is! That! Clear?" He rested the hairbrush on a sore, red cheek and waited.

Felicia gasped, kicked and wiped her eyes as she nodded. "Dylan?"

"What?"

"I . . . I'm sorry, OK?"

"Are you? Are you sorry you screamed at me?" He lifted the brush three inches and popped bare, achy flesh. She whined and

– 113 –

nodded. "Are you sorry you thought I was about to abandon you?" He popped again and she squealed.

"Yes."

"And are you sorry you spanked Teresa without talking to me?"

She clenched against the pop that never came and turned to look at him, then swallowed and wiped a tear as he loosened his grip and let her go. "Yeah . . . I'm sorry for that, too."

Teresa chewed her lip as Felicia wriggled to her feet, yanked up her underwear and held out her arms, then she dropped her skirt, and ran to hug her. Dylan took a deep breath, stood, and wrapped his arms around them while they embraced.

"I love you, honey," Felicia whispered. She leaned back and smiled.

"I love you, too, Fel, but. . . ."

Dylan frowned. "But what, sweetie?"

"If you will insist on spanking me . . . you must learn other scolding besides Uncle Dylan's."

Felicia coughed, swiped a tear and then laughed. "OK . . . but I'm not going to make a habit of it."

Teresa grinned. "I am happy to hear this."

"So am I." Dylan kissed them both on the cheek and patted their bottoms. "Who wants lotion?"

"Me!" they both said.

"All right. Lie down, Teresa. Fel's going to take care of you this time."

"But Uncle Dy. . . ."

She noted his quick change of expression when she hesitated, so she turned and fell onto the bed. He nodded and smiled, then looked at Felicia.

"Put some sweatpants on and I'll get the lotion."

"OK."

He walked out and grabbed the bags from the floor. Felicia kicked off her loafers and pushed the jeans to her ankles. She bent to pull them off and her wide buttocks rounded. Teresa looked at the bright red ovals on Felicia's cheeks and grimaced as she reached back to rub acetate lining over the marks on her own behind. The woman smiled at her and dug fleecy pants from a bureau drawer.

"You don't mind if I put your lotion on, do you?"

– 114 –

"It is only right you should comfort me after such a hard spanking . . . except. . . ."

Felicia pulled on the sweatpants, sat on the bed and yelped, then leaned on her elbow as she stroked Teresa's hair. "Except . . . Uncle Dylan usually does this?"

"Yes but . . . he also. . . ." Felicia frowned and shook her head. "Forgives me," she whispered.

"Oh! Oh, God . . . yes . . . yes of course I forgive you."

The bed jiggled when Dylan sat on the opposite side and handed a bottle to Felicia. She smiled.

"Good choice."

He nodded and loosened his tie. "I thought Bvlgari was more suitable for a milestone occasion than plain Jergen's."

"Uncle Dylan! It is not proper to celebrate her spanking me."

"That isn't what I meant." He leaned over and kissed Teresa's pout. "One can acknowledge without celebrating . . . but I'll get the Jergen's if you prefer."

"Never mind." Felicia tipped the bottle and filled her palm as Dylan lifted Teresa's skirt. "The Body Milk is perfect."

Teresa's panties clung to her thigh tops in a pale blue roll, and she sighed when he pulled them down to her knees. His knuckles grazed sensitive skin and she bit her lip when she felt his eyes on her tender red bottom. Felicia smeared light, silky lotion between her palms and then caressed the sore, plump mounds. Dylan tugged low-heeled pumps from her feet, dropped them to the floor and Teresa bent her knees so he could remove her underpants. She moaned, deep in her throat, and spread her thighs, then gasped and put them together when she felt cool air on her moist vagina. A blush darkened her face and she peered at Felicia from the corner of her eye. The woman glanced at her and smiled.

"Feeling better, honey?"

"Yuh . . . yes, thank you. It . . . it is not nearly so sore now."

"That's good."

Dylan stood and shrugged out of his jacket. "I'll go try to salvage lunch."

"Hey!" Felicia glared at him. "Don't I get lotion?"

He walked around the bed and leaned down to kiss her forehead. "Your daughter can do that. Where do you keep the casserole dishes?"

"You spanked me . . . you oughta take care of me."

"Not while you're wearing that ridiculous undergarment."

"Dylan!"

Teresa patted the woman's arm. "I will do it . . . and you need not remove your undergarment."

"I'll see about the food." He kissed her again and walked away.

"Why is he so weird about thongs?" Felicia shook her head and concentrated on the red bottom.

Teresa giggled and cleared her throat. "They are an abomination . . . they neither conceal nor expose, and the ambiguity is quite intolerable," she said in a gruff lower register.

Felicia laughed and stroked a slippery cheek. "You've got it memorized, huh?"

"I have heard it often enough."

"Well, it's still weird. Personally, I think he just can't understand how a girl can go around all day with a strip of material in her crack."

"But I do not even feel this . . . so long as the panties are of good quality." Teresa sighed. "That is much better, Fel. Shall I do yours now?"

"Sure, yeah."

She handed Teresa the bottle, stood and slipped down the sweatpants, then lay on the bed. Teresa pulled her skirt down, knelt beside the almost bare bottom and shook her head.

"He was very strict with you, Fel."

"Always has been. Pretty red, huh?"

"Yes . . . more so than mine, I think. I will be gentle with the lotion."

"Thanks . . . but it looks worse than it feels. I've got a lot more padding than you do."

Teresa swiped a lotiony palm across the round cheeks. "I am sorry that I . . . made so much trouble for you."

"It's OK." Felicia smiled. "I already forgave you . . . remember?"

"But I never said I was sorry." She bit her lip. "And I think you would not have had your tantrum if I did not have one first . . . so it is also my fault you were punished."

"Well . . . not entirely. I've been kind of on edge ever since we moved here . . . haven't really felt comfortable . . . and him run-

ning off to Boston didn't help. So I probably would have said something sooner or later."

"To . . . to make him angry?"

"Not that angry . . . not on purpose . . . I just needed to let him know how I felt."

"He was not at all pleased to know this."

"That's an understatement." Felicia chuckled. "The thing is, he tends to overanalyze the issue when you talk to him, and it can take a while to make him to see your point . . . so I kind of short-cutted the process."

Teresa blinked and frowned. "You took this spanking . . . merely to avoid truly talking to him?"

"I really didn't mean to scream at him, and I sure didn't want him to spank me . . . but now that it's over and done with, and we've cleared the air, I think we're both OK that it happened." She winked. "So it's kinda like you helped us get past it."

"Really?" Teresa grinned. "Then you should be thanking me . . . instead of forgiving me."

"Sure thing . . . so the next time I have a problem with Dylan, I can just blister your butt and everything will be OK, right?"

"I do not think so!"

Felicia laughed. "Neither do I, honey . . . I'm teasing. So . . . do you feel better about what happened?"

"Yes." Teresa puffed a breath. "As you say . . . the air is somewhat clearer now."

"That's good. We'll leave the spanking to Dylan, same as always."

Teresa poured more lotion into her palm. "He . . . he used to spank you often?"

"Uh huh . . . more often than necessary, as far as I'm concerned. He probably has a different opinion."

"Most probably . . . he is very headstrong in these matters."

"Yeah, that's a good word for what he is." She wriggled as the soft hand soothed her behind. "Actually that's what he called me, the last time he spanked me."

"Oh? When was this?"

"While we were planning the wedding. I wanted six bride's maids, and your Papa thought that was about six too many, so we kinda argued about it."

"You mean . . . six besides me?"

"Uh huh . . . I thought a twelve-year-old maid of honor should have a court . . . and I got pretty insistent about it."

"But there were only twenty guests . . . the wedding party would have been as large as the congregation!"

"A point Dylan and your father both made . . . but new brides aren't the most reasonable animals on the planet." Felicia smiled. "And I hope I remember that when you decide to get married."

Teresa grinned. "So Papa could not change your mind?"

"Oh, he tried . . . but I think he was as nervous as I was, so he asked Dylan to deal with me."

"And he did this by spanking you?"

"Yep . . . that's when he called me headstrong . . . and a few other things that weren't as nice. But after I settled down your Papa said my fanny was his responsibility from then on."

"What? So he . . . then . . . after you were married . . .?"

Felicia nodded. "He was a quick study . . . and took his responsibility real seriously."

"I did not know that Papa . . . he did this a lot?"

"Not that much . . . and not as hard as Dylan, but he managed to get his point across."

"But I never heard you even argue with him." Teresa grinned. "Perhaps this is the reason?"

"Oh we argued . . . but not when you were around. And he didn't spank me unless I got really stubborn." She sighed and blinked. "I remember once when he. . . ."

"Are you girls ready to eat? I zapped everything but it won't stay hot for long."

They looked at Dylan and nodded. Teresa wiped her hands with a tissue while Felicia pulled up her pants, then they followed him to the kitchen. Steam rose from crockery bowls and the table was laid for three. They sat and loaded their plates with shrimp fried rice, beef and pea pods, and kung pao chicken.

"This is great, Dylan . . . thanks."

"You're welcome, Fel. Oh . . . I forgot drinks."

"I will get them, Uncle Dylan. Would you like soda or water?"

"How about the merlot?" Teresa glanced at her thumb and Dylan shook his head. "I'll open it, sweetie."

Felicia nodded. "Sounds good to me, too."

"All right . . . Teresa?"

"Yes, please . . . if I may?"

He smiled and kissed her as he stood. "Of course."

Teresa crunched a pea pod and watched him open the bottle. Her bottom tingled when she wriggled on the chair, her lotiony cheeks sliding against warm acetate. His shirtsleeves were rolled to the elbows, and tight forearm muscles bulged when he tugged out the cork. Warm purple flowed into goblets and he brought them to the table. The women raised their glasses when he did.

"To our family."

Felicia smiled. "Our family."

"Yes." Teresa swallowed the lump in her throat. "Our family."

CHAPTER 6
WARM BEER AND HOT BOTTOMS

THE NEXT FRIDAY Teresa left chemistry class and trudged through two inches of new snow toward the bus stop. She shivered and hugged a light jacket to her neck while she cursed the changeable Midwest weather. When she left the apartment that morning the sun shone brightly in a hazy sky and the air was crisp but calm. Now flurries swirled around her and the wind bit like cold teeth. She pushed open the door of the business technology building and stamped slush from her shoes on the mat inside the airlock.

"Hey, Teresa!"

Lisa came through the opposite door and smiled as she buttoned a brown leather coat. Two slender, late-teen blondes stopped when Lisa did and zipped thick ski jackets to the neck.

"Hello, Lisa . . . hi, Britney . . . hi, Ashley. The weather has turned most awful."

Ashley scoffed. "It didn't *turn* anything . . . it's been nasty ever since Halloween."

"Perhaps . . . compared with California . . . but it was nice this morning."

Britney shrugged. "So are you done for the day?"

Teresa nodded. "I only came in to warm up before I wait for the bus."

"We're gonna get a beer at Suds . . . you wanna go?"

"I do not think Unc . . . I do not think I should."

"Oh, come on." Lisa wrapped an arm around Teresa's waist and pushed open the door. "A little anti-freeze won't hurt . . . then I'll drive you home so you don't have to stand in the cold."

The girls huddled around Teresa as they slipped and slid across the parking lot, then through an alley to the back door of a dingy wood frame building a hundred yards from the edge of campus. They entered and wrinkled their noses at the smells of stale beer, cigarette smoke and industrial-strength disinfectant. The bar was an enclosed rectangle in the center of the room; three pool tables sat on the right; electronic dartboards lined the left-hand wall, and a Wurlitzer jukebox sparkled and gleamed beside them. Eight small tables with mismatched wooden chairs were scattered around, and televisions, all four on different channels, blinked silently from ceiling brackets in the corners.

Two grizzled men in shabby coats sat at the far end of the bar, empty pint glasses in front of them. They turned bleary eyes on the girls for a moment then continued a heated conversation. A tall young man with a shock of unruly brown hair and a wide grin tossed a towel onto the bar and swabbed the battered oak.

"Hey, ladies."

"Hey, Stick." Britney climbed onto a stool. "The usual, I guess."

"Uh huh." He watched Teresa as the girls sat at the bar.

Britney followed his gaze. "She's OK. Show him your school ID."

"My school ID?"

"Yes, your *school* ID."

Teresa dug a laminated card from her purse. Stick glanced at it and flipped two glasses in the air, caught them and set them under a tap.

"What's yours, Teresa?"

"Um . . . do you have only beer?"

"There's wine if you want . . . rosé, burgundy and. . . ." He bent to look under the bar. "Chablis. Miller Lite for you, Lisa?"

"Sure." She patted Teresa's hand. "I don't recommend the wine."

"Oh? Why is this?"

Stick frowned and tossed coasters on the bar, then set three foamy glasses on them. "Hey, now. . . ." He bent and picked up a gallon jug. "It's imported, you know . . . all the way from California."

Teresa laughed. "Yes . . . it says so right on the label."

He snapped his fingers and grinned. "I bet I know what you'd like." The lid clanked as he opened a cooler, pulled out a green bottle and snapped off the cap with the side-mounted opener. He put the bottle and a glass in front of Teresa and folded his arms. "There you go . . . best German beer I ever tasted."

"Thank you. I like Beck's."

"Good deal."

"How much, Stick?" Ashley opened her purse but he waved a hand.

"I'll run a tab. So are you guys partying tonight, or getting fortified to hit the books?"

"Just celebrating the end of another week," Britney said.

Lisa nodded. "We can't stay long."

"Long as you like . . . you sure brighten up the landscape." A glass shattered and he cringed. "'Scuse me, ladies." He turned and raised his arms. "That's *it,* guys! Both of you go home and sleep it off."

"Come on, man . . . it was an accident, ya know?"

"I mean it, Louie . . . take a hike. The college kids are coming in and they don't need to hear you fight over baseball games that happened before they were born. You too, Gus . . . on your way . . . I'll see you tomorrow."

"'K, Stick . . . see ya."

They stood and held onto each other as they weaved to the door. Six young men entered as Louie and Gus left, and shouted hellos and beer orders at Stick while they gathered around a pool table. He filled glasses with graceful efficiency, took bills and made change, and then grabbed a broom and dustpan to sweep glass shards from the warped wooden floor.

Teresa poured beer into her glass and leaned toward Lisa. "Is Stick truly his *name?*"

"I kinda doubt it . . . but I've never heard anybody call him anything else."

Ashley wiped foam from her lips. "I'll bet it's really Steve."

"Or Sylvester." Britney laughed when they looked at her. "*What? If my* name was Sylvester I'd rather be called *anything* but that."

"Even *Stick?*" Ashley drained her glass and set it down.

Lisa nodded. "Kinda makes sense, though . . . the guy with the beer stick?"

"*What* beer stick?" Teresa sipped and frowned.

"That's what they call the handle on the tap. So what *are* you guys doing tonight?"

Britney shrugged. "Probably just hang with Jimmy and his crew until they head to their gig. What about you?"

"I need to start my MIS project or I'm *never* gonna get it done."

Ashley grinned. "You're *such* a girl scout." She leaned back when Lisa glared. "Hey, I'm just saying . . . I oughta probably catch up on my Bio. Finals aren't that far off and I'm about four chapters behind."

"I bet Teresa's all caught up." Britney leaned over and winked. "No slackers in Professor Uncle's family, huh?"

Teresa wrinkled her nose, then looked up when Stick set full glasses on the bar in front of the other girls.

"You don't like the Beck's or what?" His lower lip protruded and Teresa smiled.

"It's good, only . . . a bit too cold."

He smacked a palm to his forehead. "Should be *cellar* temp, right? I'll get some from the basement."

"That's OK, I will. . . ."

"Be right back." He ducked under a gap in the bar's facing and trotted to a door behind them.

Lisa giggled. "What did you *do* to him, Teresa? Flash your boobs when we came in?"

Front and back doors opened at the same time and the cross draft chilled them as more customers tramped inside. Teresa hugged herself and shook her head.

"It seems he is nice to everyone. He does not care that I am underage?"

"This is what they used to call a speakeasy." Britney finished her first beer and lifted the second. "Everybody on campus knows they'll serve you if you're not twenty-one . . . but if you get busted you're supposed to say you got loaded at a kegger someplace."

"A *speakeasy?*"

"Yeah . . . like from Prohibition."

Bottles clinked as Stick shoved a carton through the opening. "Here you go . . . cellar temperature." Foam dribbled from the neck as he uncapped a bottle. He grinned, filled a glass and then set it on a coaster.

"Thank you, Stick. That was very kind."

"All part of the service." He winked and glided away to fill more orders.

Teresa slurped foam and smiled. Lisa shook her head.

"I think he's got a crush on you."

"Looks like." Britney winked. "And he's *cute*."

"Yes . . . and I cannot *wait* to tell Uncle Dylan that my new lover is the bartender at a speakeasy."

The girls laughed and drank. The noise level increased as more students clamored in. Britney and Ashley watched the young men and scored each one that entered. Teresa finished her second beer and then started on the first when it had warmed. Lisa turned to her.

"So are you studying tonight or what?"

"Later, perhaps. I must have dinner with Felicia and her boyfriend first."

"Yeah? Not Uncle Dylan?"

"Him also." She glanced at her watch. "We will leave soon? It is almost four-thirty."

"Sure . . . drink up and keep an eye on Stick or he'll bring another round. Oh, and don't say anything when he tells us how much the bill is, OK?"

Teresa frowned. "He will charge us a hand and a foot?"

Lisa chuckled. "Arm and a leg . . . no. You'll see." She turned to Ashley. "You guys want a ride home or you wanna stay and party?"

"We *always* wanna stay and party . . . but I guess we better not."

"OK. I'll get the tab."

Britney laughed. "Last of the big spenders, huh?"

"Absolutely." Lisa grinned and guzzled beer. "You guys leave a tip, OK?"

Ashley nodded and opened her purse as Stick cruised to a halt in front of them.

"'Nother one, ladies?"

"No thanks . . . we gotta go. How much do we owe you?"

He fisted his chin and looked at the ceiling, then nodded. "Five bucks."

"OK." Lisa put a five on the bar as Teresa gaped. "Thanks, Stick . . . see you later."

Stool legs scraped and Britney dropped four folded singles beside the five.

"Anytime." He grinned and gathered glasses. "Hey, Terry . . .

– 125 –

come back when you can stay longer. I'll keep my Beck's warm for you."

Teresa blinked. "Oh . . . oh, yes . . . of course. Thank you, Stick . . . it was nice to meet you."

"Same here . . . 'bye."

They went out the back door and kept close as they hurried across campus. Teresa's teeth chattered and she turned to see Lisa grinning at her.

"What?"

"You didn't know who he was talking to, did you?"

Teresa laughed and hugged Lisa's arm. "No one calls me *Terry*."

"Except your new boyfriend," Britney said. "What was he was gonna keep warm for you?"

"The *beer* . . . but I know what you *think* you heard." She stuck out her tongue and Britney laughed. "Besides . . . he seems the sort who will flirt with *any* new girl who comes to his bar."

"Maybe . . . but he never called me *Brit*. He ever call you *Ash*, Ash?"

"Nuh uh . . . he called me a *brat* a couple weeks ago when I threw my cue stick on the floor, but I don't think *that* counts."

"No way . . . but calling her *Terry* . . . I mean, it's practically a marriage proposal."

Lisa thumbed a key holder and the Land Rover lights flashed. "You guys quit picking on Terry . . . I mean Teresa . . . and get in."

Teresa yanked open the front passenger door. "All of you should quit picking on me or . . . or I will tell Stick that he makes your panties wet!"

Ashley howled a laugh as she climbed in the back. Lisa giggled and revved the engine as Britney leaned forward between the seats and slapped Teresa's shoulder.

"That's good, Terry. We oughta have a pajama party and invite him over."

"Yeah," Ashley said. "And tell him to bring plenty of warm German beer . . . or warm *something*, anyway."

"Yeah, for his warm German girlfriend!"

"OK, OK . . . you guys settle down." Lisa shifted into drive and nudged the truck across the parking lot. "Let's try to act like we didn't just come from a bar, OK?"

Britney chuckled and clicked on her safety harness. "Yes, Aunty Lisa. We'll be good."

The cousins laughed as Lisa glared at them in the rearview mirror.

"Don't make me stop this car and deal with you two." She winked at Teresa and nodded at her purse while Ashley and Britney giggled and slapped each other's hands. "Would you get the Tic Tacs?" Teresa unzipped the leather bag. "And get my hairbrush while you're at it," she added in a loud, stern tone.

"Oh, *gosh*, Aunty Lisa! Not the *hairbrush*."

Teresa blushed and bit her lip as she sprinkled mints into Lisa's palm, then popped three into her own mouth. Britney coughed and shook her head.

"I think you've been hanging around Uncle Professor way too long, Lisa."

"Nope . . . that was pure *Dad* . . . he never took us anywhere without a hairbrush in the car."

"Us?"

"Me and my sister." Lisa pumped the brake and twisted the wheel. "You'll have to tell me which one's your apartment."

"Keep following the driveway around . . . it's the third building on the left."

"OK . . . not too far from Delia and Christa's, huh? And Jimmy lives next door?"

"Yeah . . . for the time being."

Ashley laughed. "One more complaint about the loud music and he's evicted."

"They didn't know he was a musician when they rented to him?"

"Nah . . . he's got a day job. Some warehouse, I think."

"Here you go."

"Thanks for the ride, Lisa."

"Yeah . . . and thanks for not using the hairbrush on us, 'K?"

The girls giggled as they jumped out and slid up the walk toward the door. Lisa thumbed the window down and yelled.

"You two behave yourselves."

Britney turned, grinned and lifted a middle finger. Teresa shook her head, leaned back and sighed while Lisa circled a cul de sac and headed for the street.

"This was fun, Lisa."

"You didn't mind us teasing you about Stick?"

"Of course not! It was merely play." She blew into her hand, sniffed, and shook another mint from the box. "He always charges so little for the beer?"

Lisa nodded. "You were right that he flirts with everybody . . . well, the *cute* everybodies." She grinned and nosed the truck into Teresa's apartment complex. "And you gotta admit we're cute . . . so he wants to make sure we come back."

Teresa laughed and handed Lisa the mints. "You will go and see Greg now?"

"No . . . he's closing tonight so I'll just go home. Michael has some store stuff he wants me to do . . . so it looks like Drudge City for Lisa." She pulled into a space and stopped.

"Perhaps myself also." Teresa sighed.

"So what's Felicia's boyfriend like?"

"Well . . . he is Uncle Dylan's age, but looks older. He is a department head at university."

"Yeah? Is he Dylan's *boss?*"

"No . . . he is in mathematics."

"Ew! Major boring, huh?"

Teresa shrugged. "Not so much. He can be amusing if he does not *try* to be. And also he has a strange accent."

"*What?*" Lisa slapped a hand across her mouth. "Sorry. What kind of strange accent?"

"He is Scottish . . . from Edinburgh . . . and sometimes I cannot even understand the words he uses."

"Some Scottish accents are cool . . . like Sean Connery's."

"Yes . . . but *he* is trained to speak so that people will understand him no matter what sort of accent he is using."

"I guess so . . . maybe you just need to get used to this guy. What's his name?"

"Haimish McFrazier . . . but his friends call him *Mac.*"

Lisa laughed. "I'll bet! Well anyway . . . nobody would ever suspect he's anything *but* Scottish."

"I think not. I had better go in. Thank you for the ride, Lisa . . . and the beer."

"No problem . . . you can pick up the tab next time."

Teresa grinned. "Are you sure I can *afford* this?"

"You might have to break open your piggy bank." Lisa winked and Teresa opened the door. "See ya!"

"Goodbye, Lisa."

Tires slithered when the truck rolled back. Lisa waved and then stopped at the parking lot exit to move the seat an inch forward. Snow billowed like ash from a paper fire and she turned the wipers on high as she peered to her left. Headlamps gleamed yellow through the whiteness, and she waited while four cars crept past before she pulled onto the boulevard.

Teresa kicked off her wet shoes inside the front door and shouted a hello, then followed a warm, beefy aroma to the kitchen. Felicia smiled and shut the oven door.

"Hi, honey."

"Hi . . . what smells so good?"

"Pot roast. We're having company tonight, remember?"

"Of course. What time will they be here?"

"Around six-thirty . . . you want a snack to hold you until we eat?"

"No thank you."

"Why don't you get out of those wet clothes?"

"Yes. This is a good idea."

"Still snowing pretty hard?"

Teresa nodded. "Fel?"

"Hm?"

"If this weather continues to be bad and . . . and Mac has trouble to go home. . . ."

The woman watched Teresa bite her lip. "Then what, honey?"

"It is all right with me . . . I mean . . . he does not need to sleep on the sofa . . . if you would rather he will sleep with you."

Felicia choked back a happy sob and held out her arms. "Come here, you!"

"Fel!" Teresa giggled while the woman hugged her hard. "I must go and change these wet clothes, you know."

"Not until I give you a big smooch and tell you how glad I am to hear you say that." Teresa lifted her chin and returned the sisterly kiss, then backed away. "And I won't even ask if that means you're starting to *like* Mac . . . but I think I'll open a bottle of wine to celebrate."

"It is not a large deal, you know . . . only I *would* like a glass of wine."

"Then you shall have it! What have you been eating, anyway?"

"What? Oh . . . merely breath mints. My mouth stays so dry in this weather."

"Yeah, mine too. Go change and I'll get the wine."

Teresa hurried to her room and threw her damp skirt and stockings into the hamper, then rifled her closet for wool slacks and a light sweater to go over her blouse. She puffed breath into her hand and grimaced at the faint smell of alcohol. A Sonicare hummed as she brushed her teeth.

Felicia smiled as she opened a merlot bottle and half-filled two goblets, and then put six pecan sandies on a plate. She set the glasses and the plate on the breakfast bar and settled onto a stool. Teresa skipped in and sat beside her.

"Thank you, Fel." She raised her glass and waited.

"Sure." The woman lifted her goblet in salute and they sipped. "You're in a good mood . . . or maybe I shouldn't say anything."

"Why?"

"Don't want to jinx it." She grinned and nibbled a cookie. "But . . . um . . . you sorta caught me off-guard, you know?"

Teresa shrugged. "It is only that I have not been very kind about Mac . . . and I think you care for him very much. I merely did not want you to think I was being a surly teenager."

The woman laughed and wrapped an arm around the girl's shoulder. "No, honey . . . I think you're growing up nicely."

"So . . . you will invite Mac to stay?"

"Uh . . . I'm not sure. He may have other plans."

"Perhaps. I know I have made him uncomfortable in the past."

"Well, don't worry about that. Whatever happened to change your mind, I'll just go with the flow and I'm sure he will, too."

"Yes. Have you completed this article you are writing?"

The two chatted, drank, and ate cookies until a timer buzzed, and Felicia got up to work on dinner. Teresa poured more wine and went to switch on the TV. She sat in the living room and watched Buffy and Spike's amorous badinage while warmth glowed inside and out. The doorbell rang at six-forty and she jumped from her chair.

"I will get it, Fel!" She opened the door and grinned. "Hi, Uncle Dylan . . . you are tardy!"

"Is that so?" His left eye squinted in an amused sneer as he

hugged her and swatted the seat of her trousers. "I prefer to think of it as stylishly late."

"You will have to discuss *that* with your hostess."

He kissed her cheek and shut the door. "I thought *you* were my hostess."

"No . . . only the beautiful but lowly scullery maid, waiting for a strong, handsome stranger to come and carry her away from this awful drudgery."

Dylan laughed as he took her hand and led her to the kitchen. "You've been reading bodice-rippers again, haven't you?"

"They are called historical romances, and you need not be such a literature snob . . . but it *is* my week to do the washing up."

Felicia dried her hands and hugged him. "Hi! Did you have any trouble on the streets?"

"Not much . . . the snow's just about stopped, but I'm glad I bought that truck. Mac's not here yet?"

"No . . . he said he might be a little late if his faculty meeting ran long."

"Who schedules a faculty meeting for Friday afternoon?"

"Dylan!"

He grinned when she slapped his arm with a tea towel, then he opened a cabinet. "I guess *he* did, huh?"

"Yes, and he *had* to. Those budget cuts have caused a major rebellion in the ranks."

A bottle gurgled as he poured whisky. "Then I'll save some of this for him. He may need it."

"I'm sure he'll appreciate that."

Teresa went to retrieve her wine glass and sat next to Dylan at the bar. He took a deep breath.

"What smells so good?"

"Guadalajara pot roast . . . more or less."

Dylan smiled. "Not *quite* like Rosa used to make."

"Nope. I started doing it without the jalapeños when I lived in Hamburg."

Teresa nodded. "I liked the peppers but Papa thought they were too strange with beef."

"And I'm sure Mac would feel the same." Felicia turned the oven heat down and picked up her glass.

"I detect a hint of cumin, though."

"Of course . . . I didn't want *you* to hate it."

The doorbell rang and Teresa slid off her stool, but Felicia waved her back.

"I'll get it." She fluffed her hair as she walked down the hall.

Dylan stood and patted Teresa's arm. "You OK, sweetie?"

"Certainly. Why do you ask?"

"Just checking. Let me see your hands."

"Uncle Dylan!" Teresa scowled while inspected her palms. "What are you *looking* for?"

"I don't know . . . a joy buzzer . . . sneezing powder. You don't plan on putting a whoopee cushion in Mac's chair, do you?"

"You are being *most* strange. Why would I *do* this?"

He shrugged. "You just seem in a feisty mood so I wondered what was going on."

"I merely have decided to be an adult about Mac and Fel . . . as you *told* me to do."

"Oh? Then I shouldn't jinx it, I suppose."

Teresa giggled. "That is what Fel said."

Felicia walked in, both hands wrapped around Dr. McFrazier's arm. He stood six-one but his neck bent so he looked shorter, and had a shock of curly red hair with a bald spot at the back of his head like a tonsured monk. A handlebar mustache, red streaked with gray, covered his upper lip and curled to waxed points at the ends. Steel eyeglass frames held thick lenses that magnified the wrinkles at the corners of his lids. He smiled and held out a hand. Dylan nodded and rounded the bar to shake it.

"Good evening, Professor."

The man grunted and squeezed Dylan's palm. "That's enough of *that,* now! I've had professors aplenty today and need nay more of them, d'ye ken?"

Dylan laughed and flexed his fingers as he let go of the hand. "Fel said you had a rebellion in the department."

"A *riot* is more like. There be naught worse than faculty without travel money."

Felicia stepped to a cabinet. "Do you want a whisky, Mac?"

"Do people in Hell want . . .?" He glanced at Teresa and cleared his throat. "Aye . . . a small one, if ye don't mind."

"Uh huh . . . I'll get you a *small* one."

Teresa grinned. "Hello, Mac."

– 132 –

"Good evening, Teresa. How are you?"

"I am well. And you?"

"Very well, thank you." He took a glass from Felicia, sipped and closed his eyes. "And getting better all the time."

"Come and sit down, Mac." Teresa patted the stool next to her.

The man looked at Dylan, who raised his eyebrows and held out a palm toward the bar. Felicia smiled.

"Dinner's just about ready. Dylan, would you open the cabernet?"

He nodded and took a bottle from her. "How were the streets, Mac?"

"Not so bad . . . they're just bringing the plows out." He settled onto the stool and Teresa raised her glass.

"To the end of a bad week?"

Mac chuckled. "Aye, it was that . . . for me, at any rate. You've had one as well?"

Teresa shook her head. "Not really . . . but *one* of my professors. . . ." She grinned. "I mean one of my *instructors* . . . was very grumpy in class."

"Oh, aye? Who was that?"

"An English teacher . . . he was *most* put out when two of his students were very late to class."

"Teresa!" Dylan uncorked the wine bottle and scowled.

She giggled. "Well you *were*."

"Possibly . . . but that is *exactly* what is meant by telling tales out of school."

Felicia filled salad plates from a bowl and looked at Teresa. "Honey, you want to set these on the table for me?"

"All right." She drained her glass and scooted around the bar.

Dylan leaned on his elbow and talked to Mac while Felicia loaded a silver dish with beef, potatoes, onions and carrots, then opened the oven and slid hot rolls into a wicker basket. She poured gravy from a saucepan into a china boat and set the ladle beside it.

"I think we're ready."

The men carried the food to the table and Teresa poured the cabernet. Mac held Felicia's chair and then kissed her before he sat down.

"This looks grand, lass."

"Yes it does, Fel." Dylan lifted his wine glass. "To the chef."

She grinned and they clinked glasses. "We'll see what you say *after* you taste it."

Teresa sipped wine then gasped and clapped a hand to her cheek. "Felicia!"

"What is it? Did I forget something?"

"Yes! Where is the haggis?"

Dylan set his glass down and his shoulders trembled with laughter as he tried to swallow a mouthful of wine. Mac grinned while Felicia scowled and shook a finger.

"I'll give *you* haggis in a minute, missy!"

"But how will Mac survive without this?" Teresa blinked wide, innocent eyes and Felicia laughed.

Mac picked up his salad fork and shook his head. "Have ye ever *tried* haggis?" The girl shook her head and speared a grape tomato. "It's possibly the vilest foodstuff known to civilized man." He winked. "Almost as bad as the bratwurst."

"How can you say . . .?" Teresa blushed when Dylan held up a hand.

"That's enough, sweetie . . . I refuse to be party to an international food fight." He smiled and handed the roll basket to Mac. "Fel says you have the townhouse on the market. Any luck?"

"Could be . . . but I had to hire a lawyer because it's part of Rebecca's estate trust."

Felicia nodded. "The guy who's looking at it is a corporate attorney so Mac figures he'll play hardball."

Mac sighed. "It's difficult enough to part with. Rebecca loved the place, but I suppose it's time to move on."

"Um . . . Dylan, would you slice the roast?" Felicia bit her lip and her eyes pleaded with him.

He nodded and picked up a carving knife and fork. "What's your new article about, Fel?"

"Oh, uh . . . it's a piece on children of divorce. Fascinating stuff . . . in a depressing sort of way."

Teresa listened while they ate and chatted, and almost spit out a mouthful of roasted onion when Dylan began to describe Red Blossom College to Mac. She sighed with relief and refilled her wine glass when he talked only in vague generalities about his students and the curriculum. Mac pushed his plate away and reached out to take Felicia's hand.

"An excellent dinner, lass . . . *more* than excellent."

"Thanks . . . I'm glad you liked it."

"Have you ever tried cooking chili peppers in with the beef?"

"*What?*"

"Oh, aye . . . gives the meat a real zest. Not that there was ought wrong with *this* one, d'ye ken."

Felicia smirked and shrugged. "I'll have to try that . . . with jalapeños, maybe?"

Dylan and Teresa laughed, and Mac leaned toward Felicia.

"What's the matter with the two hyenas here?"

She smiled and kissed him. "Culinary culture shock, I think. You want dessert? We have cake and ice cream."

Teresa wiped her eyes with a napkin. "I will get it."

"Can ye wait a bit, lass?" Mac sat up straight and clasped Felicia's hand in both of his. "I, uh . . . have somewhat to ask of your uncle and it concerns you as well."

"Mac? What are you doing?"

"It's all right, Felicia. I know we were going to wait, but now seems a good time." She gaped and Mac turned to Dylan. "Dr. Travis, I need to ask you a very important question."

"Oh, *God*." Felicia closed her eyes.

Teresa whimpered. "Are you OK?"

"Quiet, Teresa." Dylan nodded. "Ask anything you like, Dr. McFrazier."

"Felicia and I have . . . become very close, these months past and. . . ."

"Mac, please!"

Dylan smiled and shook his head. "Hush, Fel. Let him talk."

"I know this is old fashioned of me. . . ."

"You're damn *right* it is!"

Mac shot her a glance then looked at Dylan. "But as her eldest male relative, I feel I should ask. . . ."

"Oh for Christ's sakes!"

"Shut *up*, Fel," Dylan whispered.

"For your permission to. . . ."

"That's it . . . I'm *out* of here."

She yanked her hand away from Mac and slapped her napkin on the table. Her chair rocked backward as she jerked to her feet and stormed away. Dylan sighed and looked at Mac.

"Yes . . . marry her . . . *please*. Now go get her and don't take any guff."

Mac grinned and twirled out of his chair. Dylan picked up his wine glass, then set it down and went to the bar to get his whisky. Teresa watched him and grimaced as Felicia's bedroom door slammed.

"What was *that* about?"

"Tradition, sweetie. Your father did the same thing."

The door slammed a second time and Dylan smirked when Teresa winced.

"Papa asked *you* if he could marry Fel?"

"Well . . . yes."

"Did he not ask *her*?"

"Of course he did. She already said yes to Mac, the same as she said yes to your Papa before he called me. It's only a formality, but it's important to some people."

"It seems very silly to me."

"I suppose it would."

"And it certainly has put her panties in a knot."

He smiled and sipped. "Yes . . . and Mac's gone to straighten them out."

Teresa gasped. "He will not s-spank her . . . *will* he?"

"From what I've seen, it won't be the first time."

"And . . . and you will *allow* this?"

"I know her pretty well, sweetie . . . if she doesn't think she should be spanked, she won't *get* spanked."

Muffled claps of flesh on flesh followed by high-pitched squeals echoed down the hall and brought a blush to Teresa's face. Dylan chuckled and poured whisky into his and Mac's glasses, then set them on the table and sat next to Teresa. She bit her lip and slurped wine.

"Could . . . could you have said no? When Mac asked you?"

"Why would I?"

"Well . . . they have known each other so short a time and, um. . . ."

"Longer than she knew your Papa before they got married. You still don't like him?"

"I . . . I was *beginning* to . . . as her *boyfriend*, but now they will. . . ." She huffed and wiped her lips. "And what is to become of *me* when they are married?"

Well . . . let's see." Dylan stared into amber malt. "I suppose all the *usual* things that happen with a new stepfather . . . he will thoroughly cow his wife so she can't protect you from his abuse, and then he'll send you to work twelve-hour days at his boot-blacking factory in the slums of London."

She gaped at him. He smirked over the rim of his glass and winked. Teresa grunted and banged a fist on the tabletop.

"That is not *funny*, Uncle Dylan. I am *not* Oliver Twist!"

"David Copperfield."

"Who*ever!* If anyone abuses me it is *you.*"

He cocked his head and raised an eyebrow. "Really?"

The corners of her mouth curled upward a little and she leaned on his arm. "Yes! To tease me so when you see that I am upset."

Dylan held out his glass. She smiled, lifted hers and they clinked.

"I'm sorry, sweetie . . . but you shouldn't take this so seriously. It's not the end of the world."

He stood as Mac led Felicia to the table. Her eyes glistened in the lamplight and she winced when she sat.

"Sorry, Dylan . . . sorry, Teresa. I'm better now."

"Good." Dylan patted her arm and cleared his throat. "As I was saying, um . . . it's all right with me if you want to get married. You have my blessings, for whatever they're worth."

Felicia nodded and then turned to pout at Mac. "But it's *such* a crock of. . . ."

"Nay, lass . . . you promised." Mac kissed the back of her hand.

"Fel, it was a sincere and touching gesture even if it was old fashioned." Dylan smiled. "Mac wants only the best for you, as I'm sure he's told you many times and in many ways."

"*Too* many, if you ask me." She scowled and shifted her bottom.

"Yes, well . . . what he just said to *me,* in no uncertain terms, is that he will take care of you as well as Dad or Gerhard or I ever did. That means a lot to me, to him . . . and I hope to you."

"Are you talking about him asking permission or . . . something else?"

Dylan shrugged. "Both, perhaps."

"Well I just hope you guys got all this tradition crap out of your systems . . . and I need more wine . . . a *lot* more wine."

She drained her glass and Dylan emptied the cabernet bottle into it, then he went to the kitchen and brought the merlot.

"So? Do you have a date in mind, Fel?"

"We're thinking January sometime . . . on the slopes at Telluride."

Mac grinned when Dylan gaped at him. "She wants a white wedding."

Dylan laughed. "Yes . . . well . . . if you need me, I'll be in the bar near the fireplace."

"You are *such* a wimp. You won't ski because you hate to try anything new."

"Not true. Only last week I installed a whole new anti-virus program on my computer."

"Oh, for crying out loud." She giggled and leaned over to kiss his cheek.

Teresa cleared her throat. "Fel?"

"What, honey?"

"Where . . . where will you live?"

"Well, we're looking at a house in that new subdivision out by the old brewery. You'll love it, I know you will."

"Are you sure it is not near the old boot-blacking factory?"

"What? No, it's . . . what's the matter, honey?"

"I have to move *again*? What a bunch of shit!"

"Teresa," Dylan hissed. "*Behave* yourself."

"I do not *have* to! I . . . I had to leave my friends in Hamburg and . . . and now I must have a new stepfather and he is not even my *real* stepfather. This truly *sucks*."

She jumped up and stomped out. Felicia leaned over and grabbed Dylan's arm.

"*Do* something, for Christ's sakes."

"She's all right . . . let's give her a few minutes."

A door slammed. Mac puffed his cheeks and blew a long breath.

"I apologize for this, but I thought she had . . . that she was more. . . ."

"I know." Dylan leaned back and rubbed his chin. "I thought the same thing . . . but I should have known it was too good to last."

Felicia nodded. "Do you think she was upset because he spanked me?"

Dylan smirked. "She couldn't have found it *too* shocking . . . not

in *this* household. She's only reacting to change like any normal teenager."

"I should have waited." Mac squeezed Felicia's arm. "Sorry, lass."

"No . . . I doubt if it matters *how* we told her."

"She's right, Mac. Her tantrum was primed and ready to go off, regardless of whether you told her now or six weeks from now."

"Do you think we ought to postpone the wedding, Dylan?"

"You can't put the toothpaste back in the tube, Fel. She'll have to deal with it."

"I suppose." Felicia sighed and gathered plates. "This is all *your* fault, Mac."

He leaned back and gaped. "*My* fault? But you said. . . ."

"For being so damned *charming*." She kissed him and carried the plates into the kitchen.

Dylan snorted. "Can't argue with logic like that."

The man sneered. "Nay . . . I'm sure ye *know* I've had to beat the lasses off with a stick me whole life."

"If *that's* your idea of a good time. . . ." Dylan winked and raised his glass.

Mac laughed and they drank.

* * *

Teresa lay on the bed and kicked the duvet as she wept. Her tummy roiled with too much wine and beef, and her forehead burned with alcohol and righteous indignation. She punched her pillow, rolled to her feet, and grabbed boots and a hooded parka from the closet. The door latch clicked and she bit her lip as she tiptoed down the hall. Water roared in the kitchen sink and covered the sound of the deadbolt's snap when she opened the front door, tramped downstairs, and stepped into the night.

Nippy, eager wind swept clumps of snow from bare branches. Stars shone in a clear sky like cold candles in the blackness, and she snuggled her hood tight over her ears as she slogged across the rutted parking lot to the boulevard sidewalk. Cars sprayed gritty brown slush when they passed, and she quick marched five blocks to another complex.

No one answered her knock on Delia and Christa's apartment door. She swiped a tear, then went back outside and wandered the

lane in search of Britney and Ashley's place, but the buildings were too similar and she tried wrong ones twice before she found a folded sheet of printer paper taped over the number on an upstairs door. It crinkled when she lifted a corner and read:

> Hi, Jill! If you're reading this we aren't here but we're on our way HONEST! We just went out to McGuffy's to hear Jimmy's band and we'll take a cab home but if the weather is still sucky we might be a TINY bit late so don't call the professor, OK? We'll call you on the cell but the place is way out in the boonies so we maybe can't get a signal. See you soon! B & A

Teresa sighed and stomped downstairs. She leaned on the entryway wall, dug a phone from her purse and pressed a speed key, then pushed her hood back and listened to three rings.

"Hey, Teresa!"

"Hey, Lisa. Um . . . are you busy?"

"No . . . well, yeah . . . I'm reading résumés, if you can believe *that*. What's up?"

"Oh . . . nothing. What résumés are you reading?"

"Michael's gonna hire an operations manager for the stores and he wants me to help pick one. All the day-to-day stuff is getting to him and Beth, so it's probably a good idea." Lisa cleared her throat. "So, um . . . what's going on? You sound kinda down."

"Yes . . . a little." She took a deep breath. "I do not like to ask . . . but could I come to your house?"

"Um . . . sure. Like . . . right now?"

Teresa nodded. "I . . . I need someplace to stay."

"Oh *man*. Where *are* you?"

"At Britney and Ashley's apartment . . . but they are gone out and will not be back until late. I do not know where Delia and Christa are."

"So you . . . uh . . . ran away from home?"

"Well . . . I suppose you could say this. It . . . it has been a very bad evening."

"Did Dylan . . .? Oh, never mind. Sure, come on over. You remember how to get here?"

"Yes, I know the way. It will take me some time to walk there, however."

"Oh . . . yeah . . . I'll come get you."

"I do not like to impose even more, Lisa."

"Don't be silly. It's ice cold freezing so stay put and I'll be there in fifteen minutes."

"Thank you. I will watch for you from the front door."

Lisa thumbed off her phone and rubbed her eyes. She stacked résumés in a pile on the kitchen table and went through the door into the living room. A Vivaldi concerto played on the stereo and Michael looked up from his book.

He smiled as she sat on the chair arm. "Have you decided on a candidate?"

"I've got it narrowed down but . . . um . . . I gotta go get Teresa. She's gonna help me with that MIS project tomorrow so . . . she'll stay over and we'll get an early start in the morning."

"I see." He set his book on the lamp table. "She knows a lot about management systems, does she?"

"Uh huh . . . she's good with that stuff . . . took a course in Germany, ya know?"

He nodded. "Do you want me to drive you?"

"No, that's OK. It's not snowing anymore."

"Very well . . . but I *would* like your hiring recommendation this weekend if possible."

"Sure." She stood up. "I'll be back in a half hour or so. Do you need anything while I'm out?"

"Nothing I can think of. Shall I retire to the study so you girls can have your pajama party down here?"

"*Michael!*" She grinned and kissed his smirk. "It takes at least *three* girls to be a pajama party."

"Oh dear." He frowned and shook his head.

"What's the matter?"

"Beth will be here around nine . . . so you will have your quorum."

Lisa giggled. "Then you better keep her busy so she won't want to party with us. I gotta go."

"Take your cell phone and be *very* careful."

"Yes, sir . . . I will, sir. See you later, sir."

He sighed and picked up his book as she trotted away.

* * *

Lisa circled the cul de sac and stopped at the end of the walk. Teresa ran and jumped inside. She shivered and Lisa patted her arm.

"You OK?"

"Yes. Thank you *so* much for this, Lisa."

"No problem." She drove off. "Oh, by the way . . . you know all about management information systems."

"What?"

"That's our cover story for Michael. You're helping me with my MIS project tomorrow."

Teresa nodded. "Do you *need* this help?"

"Um . . . not really, but . . . why? Do you know about MIS stuff?"

"A little . . . that which I learnt in a course at university last year."

Lisa grinned. "That's great! So I *didn't* lie."

"No, but . . . I wish you did not feel you *have* to lie for me." Teresa sniffled and wiped her nose on her sleeve.

"Hey, now . . . it's none of his business . . . and I wouldn't be much of a friend if I couldn't make up a little fib when you're in trouble."

"Perhaps . . . but if you bring *yourself* into trouble I will feel badly."

"Yeah well . . . I couldn't tell him you ran away from home or he'd be on the phone to Dylan . . . and the fib's all gone *anyway* so . . . um . . . what's it all about?"

"Well. . . ." Teresa wriggled around in her seat to face Lisa. "You will think I am being foolish . . . and perhaps I *am.*"

"You *know* I won't think that. Is this about that woman in Boston? Did you say something about *her* that made him mad?"

"It was not that . . . except . . . Mac *did* spank Felicia because he was being old fashioned and. . . ."

"Whoa . . . hang on. This is about *Fel?*"

Teresa sighed. "I am sorry. I should start at the beginning."

"OK, yeah . . . but let's wait 'til we get home and warm . . . maybe have some wine."

"Yes . . . I am sorry to be such a bother, only. . . ."

"Cut it out . . . Terry." Lisa grinned when the girl frowned. "No more *I'm sorrys,* OK?"

"Huh! Very well . . . but you must cut out the *Terrys,* also!"

"Oh, OK. You don't *look* like a Terry, anyway."

"I should *hope* not." A slow smile curved her lips. "You are teasing to distract me, yes?"

Lisa nodded. "Is it working?" She thumbed a switch on the dashboard to open the garage, drove past a Pontiac in the driveway and parked next to a Mercedes. "Beth's here."

"Is this a problem, do you think?"

"Nah. She'll be with Michael and we'll just . . . oh *man*."

"What's the matter?"

"I didn't even *think* about where you're going to sleep."

"The sofa will be all right."

"No . . . I'll put you in one of the guest rooms. I don't suppose you brought any PJs."

"Pajamas?" Teresa shook head.

"Then I may have to tell a couple more little fibs. You OK with that?"

"Um . . . I suppose, but . . . does Michael have Uncle Dylan's fib detector radar?"

The garage door rolled back down and Lisa laughed as she got out of the car. "Yeah . . . but it's not nearly as fine-tuned." She went to a shelf at the back of the garage, picked up a small nylon bag, shook the dust from it and fluffed it out. "Here . . . this is your suit-case. We'll have to wing it with pajamas and stuff."

"All right, but . . . now I am nervous . . . that I have put you in this situation."

"Don't worry, OK? It's only a sleepover. Come on."

They entered through the utility room and Lisa peeked through the kitchen door, and then went to look into the living room.

"I'm back, Michael . . . hi, Beth. Do you need anything?"

He shook his head. "Did you have any trouble on the roads?"

"Nope . . . piece of cake. Is it OK if I open a bottle of wine?"

"Surely." He looked at Beth. "Would you care for some, my dear?"

Beth nodded and stood. "I'll get it." She winked at Michael and walked past Lisa into the kitchen. "Hi, Teresa. How's it going?"

"I am well, Ms. Trelawny. How are you?"

"Hey, now . . . if we're gonna have a pajama party you oughta call me Beth."

Lisa grimaced and took a bottle from the cabinet. "So, um . . . I thought you'd hang with Michael."

"What? I'm not invited?"

"It's not really a *party*, Beth . . . we're just gonna talk and . . . and then go to bed so we can get to work early."

"Yeah?" Beth grunted as she uncorked the bottle. "Is that your bag, Teresa?" The girl nodded. "You travel pretty light."

"Oh, um . . . she forgot to bring pajamas. Could she borrow your sweats to sleep in?"

"Sure. You know where I keep them, don't you?"

"Uh huh . . . thanks."

Beth filled three glasses, handed off two, and then raised her own. "Here's to plain speaking and clear understanding." She sipped and then smirked as the girls looked at each other. "What's the matter?"

Teresa shook her head and drank. "Nothing . . . Beth. This is very good."

"Yeah, um . . . thanks for opening it." Lisa sidled toward the rear door. "We'll just hang out in my room for a while."

"OK. Don't forget your bag, Teresa. The one I got in London to bring home the clothes I bought at Harrod's."

"Um . . . maybe it just *looks* like. . . ."

"Knock it off, Lisa. Dylan called Michael . . . they were on the phone when I came in." Teresa set her glass on the counter and backed away. "Hey . . . don't do that. Nobody's mad at you . . . well, nobody *here*."

"He . . . my uncle was very angry?"

"I'm sure he was *less* angry when he found out you were all right." Beth picked up the glass and handed it to her. "And it's OK if you stay here tonight . . . so you guys can talk. Michael and I are gonna watch a movie upstairs."

"Beth?"

"Hm?"

"How much trouble am *I* in?"

The woman smiled and wrapped an arm around Lisa's shoulder. "That depends on how well you tell him your story. I'd go with a 'lying to help out a friend is no crime' defense . . . but you'll probably get a lickin' anyway."

"But I *didn't* lie . . . she *does* know MIS."

"Suit yourself . . . but that *wasn't* the reason you went to get her, and you *know* how much good it does to argue with him."

"Well *geeze*, Beth!" She took a swallow of wine. "Did he say he wants to see me *now* or what?"

– 144 –

"No . . . obviously there's a problem and you two need to talk about it. Just don't stay up all night, OK?"

"OK. Um . . . thanks."

"Sure . . . here." She gave Lisa the bottle and went out the door.

Teresa bit her lip and watched Beth leave, then grabbed a paper towel and wiped her eyes. "I . . . I am so *sorry!*"

Lisa shook her head. "I *told* you to cut that out. Now come on."

They walked the back hallway to Lisa's room and she shut the door behind them. Teresa sat on the desk chair and shivered. Lisa pulled her terrycloth bathrobe from a hook in the closet.

"Here . . . take off your coat and put this on."

"All right." The thick robe warmed her and she sat next to Lisa on the bed.

"Better?"

"Yes . . . thank you, Lisa. I am so . . . I mean . . . I do not *mean* to be. . . ."

"Shh. You said you'd start at the beginning."

Teresa took a deep breath and told her what happened. Lisa nodded.

"But they're not moving out of town, are they?"

"No . . . only to another house and . . . and they will want *me* to live there as well and . . . and I have only just *moved* . . . so it seems like. . . ."

Lisa got up to grab a box from her desk. "Like it's mega unfair to bounce you around like this, huh? Here."

"Thank you." Teresa snatched Kleenex and blew her nose. "I . . . I am glad you understand. I believe you are the only one who does so."

"Well . . . I'm glad you told me and everything . . . but I kinda think Dylan would understand . . . if you talked to him."

"But I *did* this! I . . . I *told* him this is unfair and . . . and. . . ." She wept on Lisa's shoulder while the girl hugged her.

"OK, OK . . . it's all right, but . . . did you *tell* him? Or did you scream at him and run out of the house? I'm just asking 'cause that's probably what I would of done if they dumped something like that on *me*."

Teresa wiped her eyes. "So . . . so you do not think I was unreasonable to run away?"

"I didn't say *that* . . . but I understand why you'd want to. So . . . you feel any better?"

"Yes . . . very much so. It is good to talk about these things."

"Yeah. You wanna call him? Tell him you're OK?"

"Well I. . . ." Teresa finished her wine and Lisa refilled the glass. "Thank you. I do not think I am ready for him to yell at me . . . or . . . or anything."

"Don't you think if he was gonna yell . . . or anything . . . he'd be over here already?"

"Perhaps . . . I do not know. But. . . ." She took a drink and shook her head. "I promised never to run away again, and I think he will be very angry with me now."

"You did this before?" Teresa nodded. "Recently?" Another nod. "Do I have to guess what he did the *last* time?"

Teresa pouted. "I believe you have guessed already. And . . . and the other time I ran away it was because of Mac also."

"Yeah, well . . . I see why you don't want to talk to him. It'll probably take more than a couple hours for him to chill out if this isn't the first time."

"Very likely . . . and it makes me feel even more stupid that I did this."

"He was pretty mad the other time?"

"Yes . . . and he spanked me very hard." She sniffled and grabbed more Kleenex. "I do not know how I will face him now."

"I doubt if you'll be facing him for very long." Teresa gasped. "Sorry . . . that was kinda lame."

"Indeed . . . and how long will you be facing *Michael,* because you fibbed to protect me?"

"Not very. Should I open another bottle?"

"No . . . I am a little bit drunken. Perhaps some water?"

"Sure. I'll get it."

Beth leaned against the counter when Lisa entered the kitchen. A popcorn bag bounced in the microwave.

"Is Teresa OK?"

"Yeah, I think so. Better, anyhow. What movie are you guys watching?"

"The second half of *Lord of the Rings* . . . second *third,* I guess."

Lisa took two half-liter water bottles from the refrigerator. "I thought he hated those movies."

"It's sort of a love hate thing. He hates what they did to the story, but he loves to tell me all the stuff that's different from the books. You want me to bring you those sweats?"

"That's OK . . . I can get them. I'll put her in the corner bed-room."

Beth chuckled. "The one furthest from Michael's room?"

"I know how loud you guys can be. Are you going to bed when the movie's over?"

"Maybe before. I'm starting to fade and he is too . . . and he's seen the thing already. Why?"

"I um . . . I kinda wanted to talk to him."

"Get it over with so you don't have to worry about it tomorrow?"

"Uh huh. What do you think he'll do?"

Steam rose as Beth opened the bag and poured popcorn into a bowl. "Well, he *sort* of understands why you did it . . . but you know how he is about lying."

"Yeah, but I couldn't just. . . ." Lisa took a deep breath. "So, um . . . should I bring him the whip?"

"He's not *that* mad . . . but if it's contrition you want, you could take him my hairbrush."

"Eww!"

"Whatever . . . just try not to argue with him."

Lisa sighed. "I won't. So where's your hairbrush?"

"In my purse . . . on the lamp table out front."

"I'll um . . . take care of Teresa and be there in a few, OK?"

Beth hugged the girl and then picked up the popcorn bowl. "I'll tell him you're on your way . . . so he can limber up his arm."

"You don't gotta be so witchy." She stuck out her tongue, grabbed the water bottles and went to her room.

Teresa lay on the bed, her back against the headboard, and stared out the window. A full moon lighted the snow and bare trees like an Ansel Adams photograph. She smiled when Lisa handed her the water.

"You will go to bed soon?"

"Pretty soon . . . you tired?"

"Yes. I may not sleep . . . but with the beer and the wine, I would like to lie down."

"Sure. Um . . . I have to talk to Michael, so . . . just ignore any um . . . noises in the study, OK?"

Teresa grimaced. "Where he will punish you?"

"Maybe . . . anyway I don't want to worry about it all night."

"I understand." She sipped water and then twisted around to put her feet on the floor. "You will find this sweat suit of Beth's?"

"Yeah, sure. I'll get you a toothbrush, too."

Lisa held out a hand. Teresa took it and they went upstairs. Chaotic battle sounds poured from the open study door as Lisa rummaged through a dresser drawer in the bedroom down the hall.

"You want the jersey or this tee shirt?"

"The shirt, I think."

"OK. They're kinda big for you, but mine would be too tight. Go change and I'll find a toothbrush."

Teresa nodded, crossed to the bedroom nearest the stairs and closed the door. She dropped her clothes on the duvet that covered a queen-size bed and pulled on the gray sweat pants. They were three inches too long so she pulled up the waistband and tied the cotton string at her ribs, then tugged the huge tee shirt over her head. She sat on the bedside and inhaled the scent of spiced apples that came from a bowl of potpourri on the bureau. Lisa tapped the door and entered.

"Here you go." She handed Teresa a slender box that read Colgate and sat next to her. "You're gonna be OK. Don't worry about stuff tonight."

"But . . . what about *you?*"

"What do you mean?"

"You are in very much trouble with Michael and this is *my* fault."

"Hey, come on . . . it's no biggy. It'll be over in a few minutes. Now get up and I'll turn the covers down." She stood, pulled Teresa to her feet and folded back the duvet and sheet.

"Lisa?"

"Hm?"

"I will go with you . . . to talk to Michael."

"*Why?*"

"So . . . so to explain that this is not your fault."

"Just get in bed, OK?"

Teresa stamped her foot. "No! I . . . I must go *with* you."

"Listen . . . he's not gonna care *whose* fault it is. I lied and that's all that matters to him. If you go in there and argue about it he's liable to get mad at *you.*"

"He *should* be mad at me!"

"Geeze, Teresa! Do you *want* him to spank you?"

"I . . . I . . . *yes.*"

"Are you *that* drunk?" Lisa sighed and hugged the girl while she wept. "OK, OK . . . I think I understand. But Michael's not Greg . . . when *he* spanks the guilt out of you, you don't sit too well for a while."

"This is very different than when Greg spanked me, I know . . . the guilt is *much* worse."

"Sure but . . . I hope you're not counting on Dylan to go easy on you tomorrow, even if you've got bruises on your butt."

"I . . . I do not know what I am counting on . . . only that I cannot let you take the blame for this *alone.*"

"All righty, then . . . but don't say I didn't warn you."

The girls hugged long and hard, then took deep breaths and went into the hall. Lisa stopped and snapped her fingers.

"Hang on a minute."

She ran down to the foyer and opened Beth's purse, then grimaced and tromped back upstairs. Teresa bit a knuckle as she eyed the heavy brush.

"He will use *this* to spank us?"

Lisa shrugged. "I never got a *hand* spanking for lying, and there *are* worse things. You having second thoughts?"

Teresa shook her head and Lisa peeked into the study. Beth sat in a wing chair next to the chaise where Michael lay, his legs stretched and ankles crossed. She glanced at Lisa and nudged his shoulder. He looked up, thumbed the remote and the battle noise ceased. A tense stillness filled the room as he stood and beckoned to Lisa. She bit her lip and tiptoed toward him. Teresa chewed a fingertip and followed. Michael nodded to her.

"Good evening, Teresa."

"Good evening, sir," she whispered.

"Did you call home after you arrived?" Teresa shook her head. "Your uncle was most anxious to speak with you."

"I . . . I will call him in the morning, sir . . . but . . . I wish you to understand that Lisa is *not* at fault for . . . for any problems which *I* have caused."

"No?" He turned and his steady blue eyes bored into Lisa's soul. "And yet you believed it necessary to fabricate a story to hide the *real* issue, didn't you?"

She swallowed dryness. "Yeh-yes, sir . . . and I know better and I won't ever do it again."

"Indeed you *do* know better, so I'm sure you understand why I am cross with you."

"Yes, sir, and. . . ." She held out the brush. "And I know I deserve this."

"At the very *least*." He folded his arms and looked at Teresa. "You appear to be dressed for bed. Has Lisa seen to your needs for tonight?"

"Very much so . . . she has been most kind and helpful to me, sir."

"I'm quite sure. You may run along, then, if you like."

"Nuh-no, sir."

Michael scowled. "I will rephrase . . . go to *bed*, Miss Wagner."

"But I . . . you must not *punish* her when she is not the one who. . . ."

He fisted his hips. "I can't *believe* I'm hearing this sort of impudence, young lady! Shall I call your uncle right *now* and have him come and collect you?"

"No! Please! I . . . I meant . . . you must not punish *only* her! She . . . she made up this story to protect *me* and it is not . . . not *fair* that she will be punished alone!" Teresa sniffled and rubbed her nose.

Beth sighed and went to the desk. She looked at Michael, her eyebrows arched, as she plucked tissues and gave them to Teresa. Lisa's knees trembled and butterflies zoomed around her tummy. Michael took deep breaths as he scratched his chin with a thumbnail, then he crooked a finger at Lisa. She slogged toward him on leaden feet and quivered when he clasped her arms with warm hands.

"I really shouldn't, you know . . . spank *her*, I mean."

"She'll feel worse if you don't."

"Do you think so?"

Lisa nodded. "Anyway . . . Dylan spanks both of us so why shouldn't you?"

"Because she isn't my. . . ." He puffed his cheeks and nodded. "She *would* no doubt take it badly if you are punished for something she did . . . so I will do as she asks and deal with Dylan later."

"OK, but . . . um . . . *she's* gonna have to deal with him later, too."

"Of course."

"So . . . so maybe you could let us *both* off . . . just this once . . . and then you won't have to deal with *anybody*."

His forehead wrinkled and he suppressed a smile as she gazed up at him with wide, pleading eyes. "Give me the hairbrush and remove your jeans."

"Well *geeze*, Michael!"

"Lisa Marie!"

"OK, *OK* . . . sir!" She kicked off her loafers and unfastened her pants.

Michael looked at Beth and pointed the brush at a chair. Teresa shivered as the woman led her to it and made her sit. Her bottom tingled against the cushion and she reached down to tug out a fold in the loose cotton fleece. Lisa rolled her jeans and dropped them onto the desk, and then he took her arm and led her to the chaise. Her toes curled inside pink anklets, and red micro-fiber panties swelled over plump bottom cheeks as he sat at the end of the chaise and draped her across his lap.

"I'm quite disappointed with you, Lisa."

"Yes, sir."

He thumbed the waistband of French cut underpants and slipped them down. Her bottom clenched and goose bumps rose on pale flesh. She clutched the chaise leg with both hands and twisted her ankles.

"It was very foolish of you to cover up for Teresa."

"Yes sir and I'm really, really *ow!*"

A sharp splat echoed when wood collided with soft skin. Michael held her waist and swatted her behind in a slow, measured cadence while she squirmed, grimaced, and choked back squeals. He used only his wrist to pop the brush down one cheek and then up the other, painting a rosy glow across the smooth mounds. Heat grew as he lifted the brush higher and spanked quicker.

"And you know how very! Very! Wicked! It! Is! To! Lie! To! Me!"

She howled as he emphasized his point with hard smacks at the crowns of her cheeks, then shortened his stroke and pelted the under curve with quick claps that spanned her cleft.

"Ow ow oweeee! Yesss! I'm sorreee! Michael! *Please!* Not! Right! *There!* Yoweee!"

He leaned back and swatted sting around the cheeks' outer surfaces while Lisa kicked, screeched and pounded her fists on the floor. Flame

blazed across her bottom and salty wetness squeezed from her tight shut eyelids as bright pain grenades burst inside her head.

The hairbrush clunked when it hit the carpet and she sobbed into her hands as he stroked fiery red mounds. Her ears rang with a wavy siren blast that shrieked from her bottom and up her spine. She heard his voice but not what he said, so she turned her head and swiped away a veil of tears to look at him.

"Whuh . . . what?"

"I said . . . do you think you will ever fib to me again?"

"Nuh-no sir, not . . . not *ever* I promise! And I . . . I'm sorry!"

"Do you recall making exactly the same promise the *last* time I punished you for fibbing?"

"Yesss! But I *won't* I swear to *God* so . . . so don't spank me anymore *please?*" She wailed and grabbed his pants cuff as he slid the panties off her feet. "Michael, noooo!"

Teresa whimpered, drew up her knees and tucked them beneath her chin, then bit a knuckle as she watched Lisa squirm and kick. Her own bottom throbbed in sympathy with Lisa's crimson pain, and she twitched and looked up when Beth stroked her hair.

"You sure you want to stay?" the woman whispered.

"I . . . he. . . ." She swallowed the taste of copper coins and nodded. "I *must.*"

Beth sighed, sat on the chair arm and put a hand on Teresa's shoulder. Lisa squealed as Michael twisted her around so her legs straddled his left thigh, then crossed her ankles behind his calf and pressed them against the chaise. Her cleft yawned and she reached back with both hands to cover herself, but he growled a *no* and swatted the hands away.

"*Please* not like *that!*"

"*Just* like this, young lady! You *will* keep your promise from now on, won't you?"

He bent her waist, held it tight against his side and slapped the tender flesh between her cheeks with his fingers. Lisa shrieked as he opened her intimate secrets, not to caress but to punish, and shame drenched her soul even as moisture bathed the naked slit that rubbed against his muscular thigh. Painful humiliation battled the lascivious glow in her lower belly, like an Orc mob against a tall, glorious Elf. Fingertips flicked soft fire around her puckered anus and the glow grew to a yearning throb. Hurt turned to shame-

less lust and she squeezed her thighs tight around his leg to open wet, wanton petals against him.

Dampness seeped through his trouser leg and he loosed his grip. Lisa wailed in anguish and disappointment as he lifted her to sit on his lap. Plump breasts heaved and her body trembled with unreleased passion while he whispered meaningless words of comfort. Moisture boiled between her thighs and hot tears drenched his shirt.

"*Michael!*"

"Shh . . . you were a very bad girl and I had to spank you very hard . . . but it's over now and you're forgiven."

"Yeah but . . . *geeze*, Michael!"

"Lisa? Did you hear what I said?"

She whimpered and swiped a hand across her face. "Yeah . . . *yes,* sir. Thank you, sir. I won't do it anymore . . . sir."

"That's a *bit* better. Now go stand in the corner while I tend to Teresa."

"*OK.*" She pouted and lifted her chin so he could kiss her, then stood and stomped away.

"Lisa?"

"*What?*" She turned. "Sir?"

"Hands at your sides . . . where I can see them."

"Oh for crying out. . . ." He glared and she bit her lip. "Yes, sir."

"And no rubbing, young lady . . . of *any* sort."

A hoarse grunt scratched her throat and she clenched her fists as she stared at the bookshelf next to the TV. He stood and brushed his trousers, then turned and took three steps toward the chair where Teresa sat curled in a fetal ball.

Fear of Michael and embarrassment for Lisa burned and twisted in her tummy. She gazed at her knees to avoid his blue eyes, so like and yet so different from Uncle Dylan's. They glowed with such attractive warmth, how could they be the eyes of a man who would expose a girl to the awful shame Lisa had endured? Would he place *her* in such a posture? Was this the price of loyalty? Could he not only spank her bottom red and sore, but also open it wide for all to see the most intimate details? This was *not* what she bargained for, with her regrettable gesture of friendship, and she raised her head to look across the room at Lisa. The girl peeked over her shoulder and her eyelid flinched. Teresa took a deep

breath and then gasped and looked at Michael when Beth patted her arm.

"Come along." He held out a hand to her, the same hand he used to spank Lisa so shamefully.

Her arms quivered and her thighs ached as Teresa uncurled. Beth rubbed a palm on the girl's back, pushed her forward and leaned toward her ear.

"You said you needed to do this."

"But I did not *know* he would. . . ."

"Hush, Teresa . . . and give me your hand."

His soft tone smoothed the command to an entreaty, and she reached out to grasp long, warm fingers. Her cold feet scraped the carpet as she followed him to the chaise. The waistband cord loosened and her pants slid down her hips. She grabbed them, but he nudged her hands away and reached beneath the tee shirt's hem to untie the string. A frightened, embarrassed moan escaped her lips as fleece fell to her ankles, and a deep blush prickled her face when he sat and drew her across his lap.

She rested her palms on the floor and gritted her teeth as she looked toward the corner, desperate for reassurance, but she saw only Lisa's red bottom and the back of her blonde head. Michael swept the shirt up, snugged his forearm across her waist and stroked her pink, lace-trimmed knickers. She whimpered and twisted her neck to look at him.

"Muh . . . Mr. Swayne *please* do not. . . ."

He shook his head and his lips shushed. "You know I have to spank you, and rather hard, or you will continue to blame yourself for Lisa's misbehavior."

"Yes sir, but. . . ."

"The matter of your unexcused absence from home is entirely between you and your uncle . . . but should he happen to see your bare behind tomorrow, I trust you will explain why it is marked and a bit tender."

Tears pooled in her eyes as his calm, reasonable voice embarrassed, frightened, and assured her all at the same time. "But . . . but he *will* see my . . . my behind . . . you *know* he will and. . . ."

"Yes, I'm sure you're correct . . . because you've been selfish and inconsiderate of your family's feelings and deserve whatever

chastisement he thinks necessary . . . in addition to what you are about to receive."

"I . . . I *know* this but. . . ." She wailed and squeezed her eyelids shut when he slipped her panties down. "*Please* do not spank inside my . . . my bottom!"

The tears flowed and dripped to the carpet as she hung her head. He tapped warm, elastic cheeks with the hairbrush and looked at Lisa.

"No, my dear . . . that sort of punishment is reserved for *very* naughty girls . . . those who fib *and* break a promise to me." Lisa turned to glare, but he pointed the brush at her and she jerked back to the corner. "However, since you have acknowledged your culpability in the fib, you *will* answer for it. Are you ready?"

Relief and dread tightened like hands at her throat and she could only nod. Wood popped her right buttock and the sting surprised more than it hurt. She wriggled against his thighs and waited an interminable two seconds before the brush stung again, high on the crest of her left cheek. Pain forced a choking sob and she stared at the carpet while hard flatness bounced from one smooth mound to the other. Quicker and quicker fell the spanks, each in a different spot, until the separate stings blazed in a single fierce heat. Hoarse squeaks and squeals rasped her throat and she kicked against the twisted pants that fettered her ankles. The heat raged across her behind and she stiffened her spine and screeched.

"Naauuueee! *Enough!* It *hurts!*"

"Bend right *over,* young lady, and stop all this squirming!"

He leaned his elbow on her back to push her head toward the floor and never broke the harsh rhythm he played on her sore flesh. New tears wetted the carpet and she slapped the chair leg with both hands as she yelled wordless pleas. The heat grew to a firestorm that engulfed her and closed her senses to all but the flame that scorched her behind. Yet in that flame a brighter light glimmered, deep in her loins, and she reached for it with frantic longing, as a spent swimmer reaches for a bit of flotsam in a storm tossed sea. Amid the shock, amid the hurt, she clung to the achy, quivery tingle at the center of her being, and the flames subsided.

She blinked and swiped wetness from her eyes, vaguely aware of the silence that replaced the sharp splats on tender

skin. Her waist felt cold and damp, bereft of the strong arm that held it so tightly for so long. The painful wail in her ears diminished and she wept tears of gratitude as he lifted her shoulders, set her on her knees at his side and dabbed her face with tissue. The shirt hem fell and she rubbed her bottom with both hands. She held her legs tight together to quell the achy tingle at their apex, but he put his long arms around her and the tingle intensified.

"You're a good girl, Teresa . . . and you took your punishment well. May I kiss you?"

Her mouth opened and then shut as she nodded. He pressed warm lips to hers for the briefest of moments and she longed to caress their softness with her tongue. A vagrant notion flickered across her mind. How odd that he would ask to kiss her. He did not ask to take her pants down, or ask if he might spank her until she cried like a baby, but he was British, after all, and British gentlemen seemed always to have a strange sense of honor.

The stray thoughts vanished and she whimpered when he leaned forward to pull up her panties. His fingers grazed sweat-moist flesh and heightened the naughty tingle. She held his arms as he helped her to stand, and then she looked down. The cotton pants were nowhere to be seen.

"Looking for these?" Beth held up a ball of fleece and smiled. "I was afraid you were going to break a leg with all that kicking so I pulled them off."

"Oh! I . . . I do not remember. Thank you."

Michael smiled, took the ball and gave it to Teresa. "Would you like to go to bed now?"

"Yes . . . I. . . ." She wiped her face with the pants.

"Here . . . we have lots of tissue." He pressed a dozen into her hand and she leaned on his chest while she blew her nose.

"Th-thank you, Mr. Swayne." She looked up at him. "Must I . . . s-stand in the corner?"

"Not this time." He turned his head. "Come here, please, Lisa."

She grumbled and stalked over to him, her hands clasped in front of the cropped triangle of hair above her sex. He wrapped an arm around her shoulders.

"*What?*" She whimpered when his brow wrinkled. "Sir?"

"You both are forgiven for your deception, and I know it won't

happen again. Am I correct?" The girls nodded. "Good . . . then off to bed with you. Lisa, will you make sure Teresa finds the lotion?"

"Michael! Aren't you gonna . . .?"

He kissed her lips and smiled. "I'm afraid I'm all in, and more than ready to retire . . . and Dylan will no doubt be here early, so I suggest you get to sleep immediately. All right?"

Teresa nodded and backed away. Lisa scowled as she stood on tiptoe to kiss him again.

"Good *night,* Michael."

"Good night, my dear."

"'Night, Beth."

"'Night, honey . . . g'night, Teresa."

Lisa picked up her clothes and led Teresa out. She went into the bathroom next to the study and grabbed a lotion bottle, then followed Teresa to the bedroom, shut and locked the door behind them.

"*God,* what a jerk!"

Teresa gasped and cowered by the closet as Lisa threw the bottle at the bed. It bounced and clattered against the vinyl slats that covered the window.

"Lisa, do not be angry, please? I *know* he punished you very harshly but. . . ."

The girl turned and shook her head. "*That's* not why I'm mad. He just . . . ooh!" Her heels thudded the carpet as she stomped over to pick up the bottle. "I mean . . . you *saw* what he did to me!"

"It . . . was *most* horrifying . . . that he would spank you in . . . in such a way."

"*Huh?* Well, *yeah* but. . . ." She crawled onto the bed and patted the sheet. "Come on . . . take your panties off and lie down."

"Why?"

"So I don't get lotion on them. They're silk, right? Might stain."

"You will put lotion on my behind?"

Lisa gave her a crooked smile as she picked up a pillow and tucked it between her bottom and her heels, and then knelt back. "Sure . . . unless there's something that hurts worse . . . then I'll start with *that.*"

"But . . . I could do this myself."

"Yeah, but I do it better. I'll show you . . . then you can do me."

Teresa bit her lip, dropped the sweat pants on the lamp table and

thumbed her panties to the floor. The sharp burn in her cheeks had softened to a throbbing ache. She turned at the bedside and lifted the shirt to look at her reflection in the bureau mirror. Her bottom was hot pink from chink bone to under curve, with red oval splotches where the brush bit hard. She moaned, climbed onto the bed and tugged a pillow beneath her chin.

"He is very strict, your boss."

"Uh huh . . . and a *mean* bastard, besides." Lisa scowled as she filled her palm with lotion and cupped her other hand on top to warm it. "I bet he's already got Beth in bed with his big old *thing* in her butt!"

"Lisa?" Teresa stared at the girl then shut her eyes as soft hands spread slickness over her bottom. "I . . . I have never heard you speak this way. I thought you *loved* him."

"I *do* . . . I just don't *like* him very much right now. Here. Lift up and I'll put this under you."

She raised her hips and Lisa slipped a pillow beneath her. "But he has spanked you so *often* . . . are you angry that he . . . exposed you that way?"

"You really don't know, do you?"

"Know *what?*"

"How *close* I was!" She sighed and squirted more lotion into her hand while Teresa gave her a quizzical look. "To getting *off* . . . guess not, huh?"

"To getting off of *what?*"

"OK, um . . . you saw how he had me . . . spraddled on his leg like that?" Lisa leaned forward to slide her hands down and then back up the red cheeks. Her thumbs slicked just inside the cleft and Teresa quivered at the unaccustomed sensation. "You *know* what that felt like . . . with my 'gina right *on* his leg?"

"With your China . . .? Oh . . . your *vagina* . . . yes."

"Why? What do you call it?"

"Um . . . *pussy.* I think this is a cute word."

"Yeah? I always thought it was kinda crude . . . but I only ever heard it from the tough girls at school. Beth laughs at me 'cause I won't say it."

"It is the same in German, you know."

"Really? *Meine* pussy?"

Teresa smiled. "No . . . *Muschi* . . . this is a common name for cats, and also means vagina."

"That's weird." Lisa grinned. "But no weirder than in English, huh?"

"I should say *not*. English slang is very confusing to a foreigner, but *this* at least makes sense." She sighed as Lisa massaged away the pain. "And *that* is feeling much better."

"Thanks . . . so anyway I was *almost* at the top and he just *quit* . . . like he *knew* I was about to . . . you know . . . and he wouldn't *let* me."

"He . . . so in such a position. . . ." Teresa swallowed. "You nearly had a . . . climax?"

"Uh huh . . . I really thought you knew. And *then* he told me not to *rub* anything. I mean geeze! Is that cruel or *what?*"

"I . . . I do not know . . . if you say, but . . . do you . . . have you *had* these? While he spanks you?"

"Don't *you?* Sometimes?"

"Never!"

Lisa slid two fingers between the cheeks. "You got pretty close a few minutes ago . . . didn't you?"

"No! What are you *doing?*"

"I could see it in your face . . . now just hush and relax." She leaned her forearm on Teresa's back as her soft fingers caressed the deep furrow. "You're about ready to explode so I'll help you get there."

Teresa gasped and twisted, but found no strength to pull away. Rampant butterflies coursed through her tummy, and guilty, horrific pleasure drained her will.

"Lisa, *please!* This . . . this is not *proper!*"

"I said to *hush*. You know you need this . . . and if *I* don't, you'll have to do it yourself and *that's* no fun."

"*No* . . . I do not!"

"Whatever." She leaned harder on Teresa's back and stroked coral lips. "Just pretend I'm your boyfriend."

The warm, forbidden touch fed Teresa's desire even as it filled her heart with guilty dread. The bright light reappeared and her longing increased. She squeezed her thighs tighter together to fight the lust that threatened to overwhelm her, but the lotiony fingers slipped nearer still to the needy, hidden bud.

"But . . . but you are a *girl* and . . . and. . . ."

"And you've never *been* with a girl, right? It's OK . . . I'm not going to kiss you . . . just make you feel better . . . so quit wiggling or I'll have to spank you."

"You . . . you must not suh . . . suh . . . *say* that!"

Lisa grinned in triumph as she found the electrified node deep inside the wetness. "I know," she whispered. "You *hate* the thought of getting spanked, don't you?" Teresa wailed and nodded her head in tiny arcs as a horrible, nasty, delightful fingertip traced light circles around her clitoris. "Having somebody see your bare heinie . . . while you're helpless across his lap . . . his big old arm holding you so tight and his big hard hand just spanking and spanking and spanking until your pussy is so wet you can't hardly stand it?"

"*Nooooooo!*" Fiery blue lightening flashed through her vagina and up her bosom, then exploded in her head like a cannon shell full of sweet red jelly. Every muscle in her body twitched as she jerked away from Lisa, twisted and curled up like a ball. She lay on her side for a dozen seconds while the spasms subsided, then she growled, reached out with both arms and yanked Lisa down to lie beside her.

"You . . . you are . . . very, very *bad!*"

Lisa grimaced and stretched her legs, then grinned. "I bet you say that to *all* the girls."

"But I never . . . I do not *do* such things!"

"OK, OK! I was *kidding.*" She winked. "But if you're mad you oughta spank me."

"You . . . I. . . ." Teresa sighed, pulled the tee shirt over her slippery bottom and rolled onto her back. "I am *not* mad with you . . . but . . . perhaps with myself."

"Why?"

"Be . . . because I could have *stopped* you."

"Nuh *uh!*" She put her elbow on the bed and propped her chin with her hand. "I can be real persuasive . . . people say that all the time . . . and anyway, why *would* you? Didn't it feel good?"

Teresa blew a breath through pouty lips. "That is not the point! It . . . it was *wrong.*"

"If it was so *wrong* then you better spank me. I'll go get the hairbrush."

"Are you *insane?* You were spanked so hard already!"

"Then I guess you gotta use your hand." She crawled across Teresa's thighs and bent her back to raise her bottom. "Well?"

Her plump cheeks, still swollen and angry red, glowed in the

lamplight. She winked and a smile curled the corners of her mouth. Teresa pushed up on her elbows and stared into blue eyes that sparkled with mischief and innocence. She clucked her tongue.

"I am very tempted, you know . . . but I think you might *enjoy* a spanking."

"No way! Well . . . not very *much*." Lisa frowned. "So I don't get lotion *either?*"

"Well . . . *that* is only fair . . . and your bottom most definitely *needs* it."

"You're telling *me*."

"But this is not a good position."

"OK!" She twisted around, grabbed a pillow and flopped on her tummy.

Teresa reached for the lotion, folded her legs and sat up, then opened the bottle and filled her palm. Warm, giddy tingles flowed through her behind as it pressed the mattress, and the remains of her anger at Lisa's wicked, wanton familiarity evaporated. She rubbed her palms together and then massaged the hot, bruised cheeks.

"Is this all right? I am not pressing too hard?"

"You're doing great."

"Um . . . thank you. He . . . Michael will do this for you? After he has spanked you?"

"Sure . . . when he's not being a jerk." She turned her head and blinked. "Can I ask a personal question?"

"Well. . . ." Teresa chuckled. "I do not think you could *be* more personal than to . . . what is your question?"

"Does *Dylan* ever . . . you know . . . do what I did?"

A blush warmed her face and she shook her head. "He . . . he would *never* um . . . Lisa!" She swatted the girl's bottom softly and Lisa squealed through her grin. "He is my *uncle,* you know!"

"Well, yeah . . . sort of. I mean . . . you're not *really* related . . . like *blood* related."

"Perhaps . . . but in any case he . . . he would not even *think* of such a thing."

"But I bet *you* do."

"That . . . that is *ridiculous*."

"Is it? I bet you don't feel any different than *I* do . . . when he pulls your panties down and puts his hand on your heinie."

Teresa shook her head, licked her lips and swallowed hard. "But you . . . you are a very bad girl and I am *not* . . . so do not say such nonsense."

"Okie dokie . . . I got my answer."

"What do you *mean?*" She huffed when Lisa shrugged. "You . . . you think that I . . . have *that* sort of feelings when . . . when he touches me . . . and this is not so!"

"Yeah? Didn't he ever, like . . . maybe by accident . . . make you feel, you know . . . the way I did . . . after he spanked you?"

"I . . . well . . . he. . . ." She bit her lip and squeezed more lotion into hand.

"Michael says it's perfectly natural." Lisa moaned and parted her thighs as Teresa spread cool slickness over tingly ache.

"Why . . . why did he say *that?*"

"'Cause it happens to me."

"You . . . you will, um . . . *get off* when he puts lotion on you?"

Lisa nodded and shut her eyes. Teresa leaned forward and her fingers slipped inside the hot damp crevice.

"Uh huh . . . sometimes even *while* he's spanking me."

"As he did tonight?"

"Well . . . he never did it like *that* before . . . but . . . yeah . . . if I wasn't *too* naughty and he spanks me over his lap I . . . I'll have one."

"Have you ever . . . do you do this . . . when *Dylan* spanks you?"

Her eyes popped wide and Lisa shook her head. "Nuh *uh* . . . no way . . . and even if I *did* I wouldn't tell you."

"You would *not?* Why?"

"Are you kidding? The way you feel about that Boston woman?" She grinned. "You're so jealous about Dylan I might as well tell you I *slept* with him."

"I am not *that* jealous! Am I?" She smiled a wicked smile and squeezed a soft cheek. "Am I?"

Lisa whimpered. "OK, OK, you're *not.* Don't be mean."

"So . . . *did* you?"

"Did I what?"

"You *know* what. When *he* spanked you?"

"Um . . . no. I got close a few times . . . not *while* he was spanking me. He hardly ever uses his hand, and those paddles just *burn* too much. But after . . . when he puts lotion on . . . except he *knows* how easy a girl can get off with all that stimu-

Lisa reached out to squeeze Teresa's arm. "Don't be so *literal*. It's a *game*."

"And . . . and this will please you? That I do this?"

"Uh huh . . . very much. So would you?"

"This will, um . . . get you *off?*"

"Yeah . . . if you don't quit before I get there."

Her eyes focused on Lisa's milky red flesh, her smooth, open cleft, and the pink, moist nether lips, and remembered the giddy, forbidden pleasure of playing with the neighbor children. Lisa's pale blue eyes pleaded for the same release Teresa had, and her sense of fairness overcame her reluctance to touch another woman so intimately.

"I . . . I will do my best . . . but . . . you must tell me how."

"OK . . . um . . . just do what you'd like your boyfriend to do to *you*."

"But . . . no boyfriend has ever *done* this."

"*Imagine*, OK? Just put your finger in and shut your eyes, and try to feel what you think *I'm* feeling."

Teresa nodded and pressed the tip of her index finger against the soft ring. It pulsed, warm and insistent, and Lisa spread her legs wider. The tiny vent relaxed and the finger slipped into velvety tightness. Electric sparks tingled through her hand, up her arm and down her spine as her second knuckle passed the sphincter. She closed her eyes and imagined that a finger probed her own bottom. At first it was Anna-Lena's little digit, as she lay on her tummy on the old blanket beneath the bushes where they played their naughty games. She thrust deep into Lisa's rectum, heard the girl moan, and the sound shifted the image to that day not long since when Uncle Dylan put his big finger inside both their bottoms to prepare them for an enema.

Now she truly *felt* the finger; her own inside Lisa became Dylan's inside *her*. She clenched her cheeks and lay on her side. Lisa's tightness clutched and quivered, and she drew her finger up and out of the channel, and then thrust once more into hot, slippery depths. Lisa reached out and took Teresa's free hand.

"Yeah . . . you got it . . . just like that."

"All right." She licked her lips and closed her eyes. "This . . . does not hurt?"

"Nuh uh . . . keep going."

Lisa bowed her back even more to open the way and watched

the play of emotion on Teresa's face while she enjoyed the gentle sodomy. The soft finger delved, retreated, then pressed toward her vaginal canal. Lisa moaned with pleasure and closed her eyes as Teresa's empathic instinct took command and led her to the most sensual and sensitive spots inside Lisa's sensual, sensitive bottom. The finger twisted, curled and plunged, as it sought the naughtiest nerve endings, caressed them, and fired delicious lightening straight between wet, frustrated nether lips.

Teresa's mind whirled. The heat in Lisa's bottom bathed her arm and tingled all the way to her taut nipples, while Dylan's phantom finger stroked her tender anus. Soft, erotic moans filled her ears, and she rubbed her thighs together to fan the achy, tingly spark that flickered in her vagina. Lisa's hips wriggled and bounced, but Teresa followed every contortion since she *knew* which way the bottom would move. She quickened and deepened her thrusts as the heat inside them both flashed incandescent, and the girls screeched at the same moment when explosions rocked their bellies and blasted them with shuddery fire.

A groan escaped Lisa's lips as the finger slipped out. "Unbelievable," she whispered.

"Whuh . . . what is?"

Lisa pulled the pillow from beneath her hips and rolled onto her side. "You, uh . . . you never *did* that before?"

"*No*. I . . . I only did as you *said*."

"Then I'm a pretty good teacher, huh?" She grinned and lifted an arm. "So are you gonna hug your teacher? I *should* get a hug."

Teresa smiled. "For such a good teacher, I think a hug is appropriate."

They embraced and Teresa sighed as Lisa squeezed her hard.

"So? What? You got a third hand or something?"

"A *what?*"

The girl giggled and leaned back. "I just wanna know how *you* got off when I knew right where both your hands were."

"Oh, um. . . ." She blushed and turned away. "I . . . I did not know you were aware that I, um. . . ."

"Came like a freight train?"

"Lisa! I did *not!*" She snorted and then smiled. "Well . . . not so much as when you *made* me do this."

"So I'm still the bad guy, huh?" Lisa swatted Teresa's bottom

and she squealed. "You aren't as demure and innocent as everybody thinks . . . *are* you?"

"Huh! People may think as they like, you know."

"Yeah, well . . . *I* never got off just doing it to somebody else, and you *know* how naughty I am."

Teresa pouted. "You . . . you will not *tell* this to anyone, will you?"

"Oh for crying out loud! I don't kiss and tell." Lisa chuckled. "Except we *didn't,* did we?"

"No, but we. . . ." Teresa sighed and rolled onto her back. "That is *all* we did not do." She took Lisa's hand, squeezed it and grinned. "So I *cannot* be naughtier than you . . . if you have kissed girls before?"

"I can't say . . . that'd be telling." She laughed when Teresa scowled. "Now get up so I can fix the bed."

"All right." Teresa rolled to her feet and leaned on the lamp table to steady herself. "Lisa?"

"Hm?"

"Where . . . where will you sleep?"

"In my room, I guess. Why?"

"It is only . . . well. . . ."

"Um . . . I could sleep here if you want." She straightened the duvet and took Teresa's hand. "I don't like sleeping in strange beds either . . . not without company, anyway."

"You will not mind this?"

"Not a bit . . . but I *usually* get a goodnight kiss from whoever I'm sleeping with."

Teresa blinked, then smiled and nodded.

* * *

Birchwood embers glowed red in the fireplace and cast a ruddy glow on Dylan's face. His phone beeped when he shut it off, then he dropped it into his pocket, sipped coffee and stared at nothing while his tension drained. Felicia waited as long as she could.

"Well? Where is she?"

He blinked. "Sorry . . . at Mike's house . . . or she's headed there. Lisa just went to get her."

"From *where?*"

"I don't know, honey . . . but she can't be *too* far away. Mike

said if they don't show up in half an hour he'll call me. Is there more coffee?"

Felicia half rose from the sofa but Mac patted her shoulder and she sat back down.

"I'll get it." He walked to the kitchen and Felicia sighed.

"Are you going to bring her back?"

Dylan shook his head. "She'll be OK at Mike's."

"What did he say when you told him she took off?"

He smirked. "That he thought something didn't smell quite right. Apparently Lisa spun him quite a yarn."

"So what *are* you going to do?"

"Deal with her tomorrow. Since I got the answering machines at both student apartments I may have my hands full tonight anyway." He held out his cup so Mac could fill it. "Thanks."

The man nodded. "How do ye keep track of all those lasses?"

"It isn't easy. Friday nights are the worst. Sometimes I think I should chain them to their beds on weekends."

Felicia chuckled. "They're not *that* bad."

"Maybe not . . . but Delia and Christa were late to class Wednesday so I grounded them."

"Is that *all* you did?" She grimaced when he scowled. "You're um . . . taking it pretty well . . . that they aren't there, I mean."

"I said they could go to the library but to be home by ten." He glanced at his watch. "I'll check their apartment on my way past . . . if you two can stand me a while longer."

"Not a problem." She got up and dropped a split log onto the embers. "So, um . . . what do you want *me* to do . . . about Teresa?"

"Mostly don't worry . . . she'll get over this."

"I know, but . . . well . . . to be honest, I'm sort of worried about *you.*"

Dylan blinked and set down his cup. "Me?"

"Well, yeah . . . I mean . . . you hit the ceiling last time she ran away. Are you repressing or . . . just deciding what shade of scarlet to blister her fanny?"

He chuckled. "Neither. I think I understand her better . . . since we've been so close the past few months. She's impulsive but not out of control, so I don't intend to be *too* tough on her."

"Wait a minute." Felicia grinned. "Who are you and what have you done with my brother?"

"What?" He smiled. "I sound too reasonable?"

"You're not even gonna spank her?"

"I never said *that* . . . but I plan to talk more than spank."

She sat down and cuddled Mac's arm. "Did you get all that, honey?"

"Oh, aye." His eyebrows bristled as he frowned. "Talk more than spank . . . but only if ye learn to control that impulsiveness . . . otherwise, blister your fanny."

Dylan laughed when Felicia growled and swatted Mac's thigh. "There you go, Fel . . . he was paying attention."

"Uh huh . . . and heard what he *wanted* to hear."

Mac smiled and kissed her. "I heard ye mention dessert as well . . . or was that merely being impulsive?"

"Oh, shoot . . . I forgot all about it." She jumped to her feet. "You want some, Dylan?"

"Sure . . . big cake, small ice cream."

* * *

Michael shut the bedroom door, snaked off his tie and threw it at a wooden valet. Beth twined her fingers at the back of his neck and frowned.

"Are you gonna be mean to *me*, Michael?"

His eyebrows dipped. "I beg your pardon?"

"Why did you *do* that to her?"

"What *are* you on about? You know very *well* why. Shall I send you to fetch the brush for *your* impertinent bottom?"

"No! Not until you tell me why you *tortured* her that way." She grunted when he scowled. "Well you *did*. You mushed her pussy right on your leg and spanked her 'til she was about two wiggles from coming and then you just *quit* . . . and wouldn't even give her any lotion!"

"And you think that was mean?"

"Well *duh* . . . ow! *Yeah*, it was mean." She pouted and rubbed her trouser seat.

"So you would have preferred that I embarrass her by allowing her to climax in front of her friend?"

"Couldn't be any worse than spanking her wide open crack in front of her friend."

"You think not?"

"Jesus, Michael! It embarrasses *me* when you do that even if nobody's watching!"

"Then the procedure served its purpose." He unzipped her pants' side vent and pushed them down. "Any further embarrassment would have been superfluous."

"Yeah but . . . she was so *frustrated.*"

She moaned when he slipped a hand inside her panties and cupped her damp vagina. He kissed her, soft and quick, on the lips.

"Then I imagine she will remember this lesson the next time she thinks to deceive me."

"You just . . . better not be planning to frustrate *me,* you . . . you *ogre.*"

His finger slid between plump labia and Beth quivered as she clung to his neck. "Is there any reason I *should?* Have *you* been a bad girl? Apart from calling me names?"

"Nuh . . . *nuh* uh! But . . . but you already got so *hard* whuh-while you were spanking Teresa . . . I'm scared you're gonna come in your shorts before you even . . . even . . . oh *God.*"

The finger thrust up and into her vagina. She wriggled and clamped her thighs on his hand as pleasure waves swept through her belly. His lips brushed her ear and he whispered.

"So you are determined to have your bottom spanked, are you?"

"Nuh-*no* . . . just . . . keep . . . doing . . . *that.*"

"Only a *very* bad girl would accuse her employer of having lascivious thoughts while he merely carried out necessary discipline."

"Bullsh . . . *baloney!* You . . . you were practically *drooling* over that cute little huh-*heinie!*"

"Ah! *Now* I see . . . you are projecting your *own* lasciviousness onto *me,* and that's very, *very* wicked."

"Michael *noooo.*"

He drew his finger from her hot core and then pushed her panties and trousers down. She pouted while he stripped her naked, then he sneered and winked.

"Now shall you *feel* the terrible wroth of my indignation."

She gasped and then laughed when he sat on the bedside and yanked her across his lap. "I am *never* gonna let you watch that movie *agaouch!*"

His hand clapped sting into firm, mature buttocks and Beth

squealed as she punched the counterpane. The heat from his palm fed the blaze his finger lighted deep inside, and she pressed her *mons* against his thigh to stoke the fire. The harder he spanked the higher she climbed toward the summit, and then he stopped, stood, and set her on her feet. She grabbed handfuls of his shirt and glowered, but he cupped her chin and shook his head.

"Go stand in the corner . . . and *no* rubbing!"

"Don't even *think* about . . . *no!*"

He wrapped his left arm tight around her, held her close and slapped her thighs as she danced. "Do! What! I! Said! This! *Instant!*"

"Ow! Ow! Owee! Okaaaay!" Beth swiped an angry tear as she trudged to the corner by the door. "You're *such* an asshole," she whispered.

"*What* did you say?"

She grunted and stomped a bare foot on the carpet. "Nothing! Sir!"

"Yes, well . . . if I hear any *more* of that nothing I *will* get the hairbrush."

He gritted his teeth to suppress a smile as he undressed and watched her pink bottom squirm. She whimpered when he turned her and hugged her hard, his erection pressed against her thigh, and then led her out of the corner. They stood naked beside the bed, their clothes scattered about the floor. He palmed her tingly cheeks in both hands and slipped his fingers into the moist furrow to caress her anus.

"Are you all finished with your tantrum?"

"Um . . . yeah . . . I *guess* so."

"Then lie down so I can take care of you."

She sat on the bedside, rolled onto her tummy, and then grinned at him over her shoulder. He shook his head and twirled his finger in a circle.

"No lotion?" She frowned, turned over and rested her head against the pillows.

"Later, perhaps . . . if you're a good girl." He took a foil packet from the nightstand drawer and then stretched out beside her.

"I'm never anything *else*." She grabbed the packet and ripped it open. "So I don't know *why* you have to spank me all the time."

His hips quivered as she smoothed latex over his erection. Her

long, soft fingers curled about him, squeezed and tantalized, and drew guttural moans from deep in his chest. Sweet fire pulsed through his loins and he licked dryness from his lips.

"There are, um . . . countless reasons, I'm sure . . . but at the moment I can't seem to think of any."

She lay back and he rolled on top of her. "That's what I figured . . . all the blood rushed out of your brain and wound up down *there* . . . so you might as well screw *my* brains out too!"

"Young lady, you do *not* use that sort of language in my *bed!*"

He lunged and she squealed as hot stiffness lanced deep into tight wetness. She lifted her feet, crossed her ankles over his back and drew him further into the smooth channel. Soft, shuddery slickness boiled around his organ and he grunted as she opened her mouth and forced her tongue between his teeth. He lifted his hips to slide up and out, then groaned with pleasure when he rippled special tummy muscles. She whimpered when he thrust home, and quivered in delight as his testicles settled between open cheeks and pulsed against her sensitive vent.

Their tongues danced as he pushed with his toes to rock them in slow, gentle arcs. His penis slid deep, retreated, slicked in once more, a bit faster, a bit deeper, and he squeezed his eyelids hard as the fire in her core burned his belly and blazed through his head. Loud, sweet thunder roared in his ears and his heart throbbed to a primal rhythm as drum-tight bellies beat the ancient tattoo.

Beth gasped and her head jerked from side to side as the hot sword prodded her higher and higher toward the peak. His hard chest mashed her nipples, striking sparks that cascaded between her thighs to heighten the conflagration. The sword grew hotter, longer, harder, and she screeched as squashy fireballs pelted her like summer hail. Massive, shuddery tremors jolted her as his hips jerked quick and hard to pump his essence into her.

Timeless minutes passed as they clung together in the sweaty afterglow. He raised his head and kissed her lips. She kissed back, soft and slow, and then moaned as she unwrapped achy legs. He rolled off and she groaned when his warmth slipped away, but he pulled her to him and kissed her again.

"I suppose I must admit you're a good girl *some* of the time."

She grinned and leaned up on her elbow. "Yeah? Does that mean I gotta admit you're not an ogre *all* the time?"

"Certainly you do . . . if you want any lotion on your tragically abused behind."

"Well it *is* . . . 'specially *now* . . . after you screwed my . . . *no!* Kidding! I'm *kidding!*"

She laughed and wriggled away from his upraised arm to grab a bottle from the nightstand.

CHAPTER 7
THE PRICE OF FLIGHT

TERESA JUMPED WHEN the clock radio blared. She blinked and then shut her eyes tight to recapture the trail of a dream that involved an Italian villa, a steamy bathroom and Dylan. Lisa moaned, coughed and rolled over to shut off the radio, then wriggled back under the covers and smiled at Teresa.

"'Morning."

"Good morning. What is the time?"

"Six o'clock. You can go back to sleep if you want, but I gotta fix breakfast."

"No . . . I will get up also. Uncle Dylan will be here soon and I must get ready."

Lisa stroked a hand over the girl's sleep tousled hair. "You feel OK? You had kind of a rough night."

"My stomach is upset . . . from the wine, I think . . . but nothing more."

"Yeah, but . . . you were yammering and thrashing around like you were having bad dreams. I woke you up once and you cussed at me in German . . . I *guess* that's what you were doing, anyway."

"I am sorry to disturb you like this."

"No problem . . . but next time we sleep together I'm bringing a German dictionary to bed." She grinned, kissed Teresa's cheek, then tossed off the quilt and shivered as she pulled on her clothes.

"You wanna use my bathroom? Then you won't have to worry about running into Beth or Michael wandering around up here."

"Yes . . . thank you . . . Lisa?"

"Hm?"

"I . . . I think I had *many* dreams last night."

"Uh huh . . . sure seemed like it."

"But . . . did I dream that we . . . that you and I . . . that we . . .?"

Lisa giggled as she shook out Teresa's trousers. "Were unbelievably naughty together? Yep . . . just a dream . . . didn't happen . . . now go take a cold shower before you decide we oughta do it *again*."

Teresa gaped, blushed, and then rolled off the bed. "*Now* I remember! You were unbelievably naughty, not I!" She grabbed for the pants but Lisa yanked them away. "Give that to me or . . . or. . . ."

"You'll spank me?" She backed against the closet as Teresa glowered and stalked toward her. "OK, OK . . . here! *Geeze,* you're grumpy in the morning."

"*Thank* you." Teresa turned on her heel.

"Hey, come on . . . I'm sorry. I won't tease you anymore. Why don't you just put the sweatpants on and get dressed after you shower?"

"All right. I think perhaps I *am* grumpy . . . but as you said, I had a rough night."

"It's OK. You'll feel better after you get cleaned up and have some breakfast. Don't forget your toothbrush."

They went downstairs and Teresa showered while Lisa dug in a bureau drawer, threw her clothes into the closet and pulled on a robe. The hairdryer roared and Lisa opened the bathroom door. Teresa gasped and turned as she shut off the dryer, her arms crossed to shield her nudity. Lisa rolled her eyes and grinned.

"I found some clean panties for you. Is it OK if I shower while you primp?"

She didn't wait for an answer, and Teresa switched the dryer on to finish her hair. Lisa hung her robe on a hook and stepped into the stall. Water spurted and splashed, and Teresa brushed her teeth then opened the mirrored cabinet to inspect an array of tubes and bottles.

"Lisa?"

The water shut off and the stall door opened. "Huh?"

"May I use your lip gloss?"

"No problem." Lisa shivered as she dried herself. "Anything you want . . . Beth gave me a bunch of stuff I hardly ever use."

"You do not need makeup."

"I will someday."

Teresa wrapped herself in a towel, smoothed on tan eye shadow and a touch of blusher, and then glossed her lips. Lisa grinned at the mirror.

"Who are you getting beautiful for? As if I didn't know."

"Oh, yes . . . you are so smart. I must be beautiful when I go to the bar and flirt with Stick."

Lisa laughed and draped the towel over her shoulders. "Yeah right. Try the eyeliner . . . it'll make those big green eyes *huge* . . . and sad . . . so Uncle Dylan will take pity on you." Teresa bit her lip. "Oh, *God* . . . just call me Ms. Sensitive. I'm sorry, OK? That was really stupid."

"No . . . it is *I* who is being stupid." Teresa sniffled and grabbed a washcloth.

"Don't wipe it off . . . you look great." She took the cloth from Teresa's hand and hugged her. "Forget I said anything and go get dressed while I dry my hair."

"He . . . he will be *furious* with me."

"No he won't. He's had all night to cool off . . . now go on."

The bedroom air chilled her and Teresa's teeth chattered as she put on her bra, blouse and sweater. She draped her parka over her shoulders and searched the clutter atop the bureau. A cloud of steam followed Lisa when she stepped out of the bathroom.

"What are you looking for?"

"You said you have panties for me?"

"Yeah . . . right here."

Lisa grabbed a garment from the bed and held it up. The pink gingham drawers had frilled, elasticized legs and a happy red teddy bear motif in the pattern. Teresa gaped, then swallowed, and then laughed.

"*This* is what you found for me to wear?"

"Well, sure! You've got hairbrush tracks on your butt and you *don't* wanna be wearing tight panties."

"But . . . where did you *get* these, in any case?" Teresa took the drawers and held them to her waist. Lisa giggled.

"Beth . . . she got me some new baby doll pajamas to replace the ones she ripped to shreds."

"She ripped . . . *why?*"

"It's a long story . . . but I bet they'll be comfortable. Put 'em on."

Teresa stepped into the pants, tugged them to her waist and grimaced as she adjusted the elastic around her upper thighs, then pulled her slacks on.

"This is not so bad . . . certainly they are not tight." She turned to the bureau mirror and smoothed the seat of her trousers. "It *feels* like I am wearing a balloon, but the panties do not show . . . do you think?"

"Nope . . . not at all. I gotta start breakfast."

"I will help."

* * *

Dylan pulled into Michael's driveway at ten o'clock. He rubbed his eyes and took a deep breath before he stepped out of the truck into slushy snow. The sun shone low but bright, and snowmelt dripped from the eaves. He rang the bell and scraped his shoes on a bristly porch mat. Lisa opened the door and nodded.

"Good morning, Professor."

He smiled. "Good morning. May I come in?"

"Certainly, sir." She stepped back and then shut the door behind him.

"How are you, Lisa?"

"I am well. Thank you for asking, sir."

"I see . . . and I can look forward to this cold shoulder for the duration of my visit?"

Lisa pouted and crossed her arms. "Are you mad at her?"

"No . . . is Michael mad at *you?*"

"Nope . . . not anymore." She grimaced. "So, um . . . are *you* mad at me?"

He reached out and she gave him her hand. "If I had reason to be, I'm sure he took care of it."

"Yeah, he . . . we had a talk."

Dylan smiled. "Did you?"

"Uh huh . . . a pretty loud one, too. You wanna see?"

She turned halfway round and pushed out her skirt-clad bottom. He chuckled.

"Thanks, anyway . . . I assume he convinced you that honesty is the best policy." She nodded and Dylan glanced toward the office door. "Is he in?"

"Upstairs . . . getting ready to go to the gym. You want me to get him?"

"No, that's all right . . . where is . . .?"

Footfalls pounded the stairs and they turned.

"Good morning, Dylan."

"Good morning, Mike. You're looking dapper as usual."

They shook hands as Dylan inspected the man's thick blue sweat suit. Michael laughed.

"I'll give you my tailor's card . . . absolutely the finest in town. Would you care for coffee?"

"No thanks . . . I've disrupted your routine enough for one weekend."

"Not at all . . . I was glad of her company. Routines are meant to be broken on occasion."

"Nice of you to say, but . . . where is she, anyway?"

Lisa pointed a thumb over her shoulder. "In my room . . . starting my MIS project."

Michael smirked. "Shouldn't *you* be doing that?"

"She's only *helping* . . . don't be a fussbudget." Lisa covered her bottom with both hands when he frowned. "So, um . . . you want me to get her?"

"If you would be so kind."

She turned and trotted to the kitchen door. Michael shook his head.

"Is everything all right, Dylan?"

"I think so. She needed to blow off steam, and I hope she did . . . but I'm sorry I put you in the middle of it."

"Nonsense. What's a friend for, if not to help out in a crisis?" He set his gym bag on the lamp table. "I should tell you, though . . . she *insisted* I punish her as well . . . for her part in Lisa's deception."

Dylan smiled. "That doesn't surprise me. She has a lot of integrity."

"Indeed . . . and possibly a tender bottom . . . so. . . ."

"It's all right . . . I'm not out for blood. Did she tell you *why* she ran off?"

"I didn't ask . . . but Lisa told me Teresa's version this morning after breakfast."

"And . . . ?"

"There were minor variances, but in the main it was as you said last evening . . . Felicia's wedding plans have made her feel put out . . . literally. Unsure of her footing, that sort of thing."

"Well, at least she didn't paint her step-family as insensitive ogres." He scowled when Michael choked a laugh. "*What? Did she?*"

"No, no . . . nothing of the kind. I was thinking of something else entirely . . . sorry."

The kitchen door swung open and Teresa walked toward them, her parka draped over her arm, lower lip clutched beneath her top teeth. Dylan smiled and held out a hand.

"Good morning, sweetie."

"Good morning, Uncle Dylan."

Teresa stopped and looked at Lisa, but the girl pushed her forward. She stumbled the last ten feet and sobbed as he wrapped his arms around her.

"Shh . . . it's all right. Let's go home."

"Yes . . . OK."

"Did you thank Mr. Swayne for his hospitality?"

She shook her head, swiped wetness from her cheeks and turned. "Th-thank you for . . . for the hospitality, Mr. Swayne."

"You are most welcome . . . at any time."

Dylan led her toward the door and she jerked around.

"Thank you, Lisa."

"Sure . . . thanks for getting me started on the project."

Michael held the door for them and they walked to the truck. Teresa stared out the window as Dylan drove along wet streets, then he stopped for a red light and she glanced over to find him looking at her.

"How do you feel, sweetie? Did you sleep well?"

"Somewhat. Do I look terrible?"

"Not at all . . . radiant, in fact. Did you do something different with your hair?"

"Only a bit of. . . ." She twisted in her seat. "Uncle Dylan, I . . . I am *sorry.*"

"Shh . . . it's all right." He patted her hand but she jerked it away.

"Stop *saying* that! Why are you torturing me this way?"

"What?" He scowled, made a right turn and parked at the curb on a quiet street. "Is *that* what you think I'm doing?"

"Well . . . *yes* . . . because you told me . . . the last time when I ran away . . . that you . . . you would. . . ."

"All right, yes . . . and I'm glad you remember, but . . . uh . . . I'm prepared to believe you *didn't* run away."

"But I . . . I. . . ."

"You went for a walk to think things over, and you got side-tracked and wound up spending the night with a friend." She gaped at him and he smiled. "I *would* have appreciated a call to tell me that . . . but since I knew where you were. . . ."

"So . . . so you truly are *not* angry with me?"

He shook his head and patted her knee. "Just concerned. Do you feel up to talking about things?"

She nodded. "So long as you mean to talk and not . . . not *discuss*."

"Hm?"

"I have noticed that when you *discuss* matters with me, it often means that I say very little but cry a large amount."

"Really?" He smirked and turned the wheel. "I wasn't aware I had redefined the word . . . but I *do* want to talk. We'll go to my apartment."

"I . . . I must change my clothes."

"That can wait, can't it?"

"Yes . . . I suppose." She watched his eyes for a minute as he steered through the hectic Saturday morning traffic. "Uncle Dylan?"

"Hm?"

"Are you *sure* I am not in trouble?"

"Yes . . . why?"

"You said you did not worry for me, only . . . you look very tired . . . as if you did not sleep enough."

He chuckled and turned a corner, parked in the garage behind his building and shut off the engine. "You're very observant. Come on . . . we'll make coffee. Maybe that will smooth out some of the wrinkles."

She leaned against the counter in his kitchen while Dylan filled a coffee maker. He thumbed a switch to start the machine and leaned next to her.

"Would you be upset if I tell you I didn't lose any sleep worrying about *you?*"

"No . . . why would I?"

"Just checking." He put an arm around her and kissed her cheek. "It was your classmates' fault . . . that I got so little sleep."

"Why? *Which* classmates?"

"Almost all of them . . . the ones at RBC. There was a full moon last night, wasn't there?" Teresa nodded. "That could explain it."

"But what happened?"

"First it was Delia and Christa . . . I went by their apartment to see if they were home yet and. . . ." He stopped and turned when the coffee maker hissed steam.

"But . . . did you not ground them?"

"Yes . . . but I said they could go to the library, which I assume they did. They had piles of photocopies . . . but I don't know how much of it was actual research."

Dylan filled two mugs and nodded toward the door. Teresa went ahead of him and sat on the living room sofa. He stopped at the bar and doctored one mug with whisky, then looked up when Teresa coughed.

"Might I have a little also?"

He chuckled. "You think my coffee is too strong as it is."

"Yes . . . the liquor will tame it somewhat." She smiled when he dribbled whisky into her cup and brought it to her. "So . . . what about the girls? Did they stay out too late?"

"No . . . they were home when I told them to be . . . but so were their friends."

"Oh? What friends?"

"Two boys . . . young men, I suppose. I think I've seen them on campus, but they were in a hurry to leave so I can't be sure."

She sipped hot, spiked coffee. "Did you shout at the boys? To make them leave?"

"I didn't have to . . . Christa pushed them out the door as soon as she opened it for me."

"Yes . . . I think she *would* do so. It is not allowed to have guests when one is grounded."

"True . . . they must have planned to kick the boys out before Jill came over at midnight to check on them."

"Then . . . you have extended their grounding?"

He smiled and shook his head. Her face flushed with embarrassment for her friends as she wriggled her bottom on the cushion. Dylan sipped coffee and leaned back.

"They tried to tell me the boys were only there to study."

"This is not an excuse, I know, so . . . did you punish them?" He nodded. "Very hard?"

"Hard enough . . . I hope. They *acted* very sorry, anyway. Then I checked on the other girls, since I was right there . . . and they weren't home."

"Yes . . . I saw the note they left for Jill."

"Oh? Well, I called her and told her not to bother with curfew check then I waited for them. They weren't late, after all . . . but they *had* been drinking."

"Oh my God."

She bit her lip and cuddled closer to him. Queasy butterflies flicked through her tummy, reminders of her own excess of alcohol the previous night. Lisa had given her a dose of Pepto before their breakfast of pancakes and sausage links, and she felt fine until that moment.

He sipped coffee and cleared his throat. "Do you know their friend? The one in the band they went to see?"

"No . . . only I have heard of him. He . . . he gave the beer to them?"

His eyebrows curved inward. "How did you know it was beer?"

Her mouth opened and stayed that way for a long, tense second while her mind raced. "I didn't . . . only I thought perhaps it was . . . but they were not late coming home?"

"No . . . Britney said they left the dance club and went to a kegger at some frat house." He wrapped an arm around her and Teresa shuddered. "Are the girls accustomed to drinking beer?"

"I am not sure, only . . . it is very difficult for them . . . to know that I am allowed to drink alcohol and they are not . . . when we are almost of the same age."

"Yes, I suppose it would be . . . even if you only drink at home." He smiled and cuddled her close. "You do only drink at home, don't you?"

"Um . . . Lisa gave me a glass of wine at her house."

"As long as there was adult supervision." He chuckled when she stared at him. "I *meant* Mr. Swayne . . . not Lisa."

"Oh, yes . . . then . . . you were very upset with them?"

"Probably more than I should have been . . . they weren't *drunk,* but I could smell the beer."

"So . . . you punished them?" He nodded. "Very strictly?"

"I suppose . . . a fairly hard spanking and then an enema."

Teresa cringed. "That . . . that is *horrible!* How could you be so harsh if they were not even drunk?"

"So they'd learn a lesson . . . but perhaps I *did* overreact. It was late, I was tired . . . and already upset about everything *else* that happened last night."

"You . . . you mean about me?"

She hated the thought of his big, warm hand on the California girls' bottoms, as he parted their cheeks to probe their nasty little holes, and then to push a nozzle inside and fill them with water. Even if their behinds *were* sore from a spanking, such intimate attention from *him* was better than they deserved, merely for returning to Suds for more cheap beer!

He shrugged. "Yes . . . and about Delia and Christa . . . they put up quite a fuss when I used their own hairbrush on them. Altogether it was a rough night."

"And I suppose you made them feel *better,* after you punished them so strictly?"

"What?" He stared at her, surprised at the bitterness in her voice. "What's the matter, sweetie?"

"*Nothing* . . . only . . . you rubbed lotion on their . . . on *them*, didn't you?"

"Well, yes . . . don't I always? After I spank you girls?"

His blithe tone galled her and she jerked away from him. "Not *we* girls! If you were *this* upset that you had no sleep then . . . then you are blaming *me* for causing the trouble and . . . and it is not *fair* because you already have *said* I am not to blame!"

"What are you *talking* about? I'm *not* angry with you, so why don't you . . .?"

"Yes you *are* and it is *awful* to . . . to torment me this way!"

"Oh, for crying out loud! Are you mad because I *didn't* spank you?"

"No! That is *ridiculous!* And . . . and besides, you have all those *other* girls to spank so you are *much* too busy to be bothered with . . . Uncle *Dylan!*"

She kicked and squealed as he twisted her over his lap. Dylan bit his under lip to suppress a chuckle, astounded at his own blindness. He snugged the girl's waist tight beneath his left arm and cleared his throat.

"Young lady, *you* are being ridiculous . . . to think you can speak to me that way!"

"Don't *do* this!"

He swatted her trouser seat. "Hush! You were a very bad girl to run away from me and I intend to see that it never happens again!"

"But you *said* you are not angry!"

"Apparently I said a great *many* foolish things this morning, but I am thinking much! More! Clearly! Now!"

She squeaked at each hard thump of his palm on her wool-covered seat, and then squealed when he opened the fly and tugged her trousers down. His jaw dropped when he saw the pajama pants.

"Young lady, you . . . you know better than to. . . ." He coughed to cover a laugh, shook his head and patted the gingham drawers. "Sweetie?"

"*What?*"

"Where on *earth* did you get these panties?"

She twisted her neck to pout at him, and then scowled to suppress a smile when she saw the amusement in his face. "I . . . I did not wish to wear the ones I wore yesterday so . . . Lisa gave them to me."

"Well they um . . . they're adorable . . . and that doesn't make my job any easier, you know."

Hope and disappointment battled in her heart. "You . . . you will not spank me? Because I have adorable underpants?"

He took a deep breath. "If your adorableness could stop me spanking you, you never *would* be spanked. Now lift up so I can pull down your panties, knickers . . . what*ever* these things are."

"But I . . . I do not *deserve* a spanking because. . . ." Conflicted emotions whirled in her mind as she raised her hips. The soft drawers slid down sensitive cheeks and he left them in a puffy bundle at her thigh tops. "Because you already *forgave* me for running away!"

"Did I? I don't recall that."

"Yes you . . . you said I did *not* run away and . . . and we would *talk* about it and not. . . ."

"Oh we *will* talk about it . . . after we *discuss* your attitude toward the other girls."

Her eyes widened as his arm rose. "*What* attitude? *Ouch!*"

She whimpered as he fanned warmth into her bottom and re-

lighted hairbrush sting. The heat grew with each swat, glowed, tingled, and fed the quivery ache between her thighs. He rested his palm on her behind after a dozen sharp claps.

"The *attitude* that somehow *you* are less important to me because I have other! Naughty! Disobedient! Wayward! Little! Girls! To! Correct!"

"Ow! Ouch! Ach! Aauu! Unc! Ull! Dy! Lan!"

His arm rose and fell in short, quick arcs as he avoided the light blue bruises at her cheeks' summits and swatted the soft flesh around them. Tears of remorse and relief flowed from her eyes while she squirmed against his thighs. Guilt drained away with the tears, and the aching need within her blazed as he slapped the tender base of her bottom, so, so near the moistness at the center of her desire. Mad, fiery lightening flashed, echoed, rolled over her, and she wailed into her hands while hot tremors rocked her soul.

Dylan bit his lip and held her close as she jerked and squeaked through the climax. He knew that someday he would have to deal with this occurrence, but the shock of the event and his own excitement in its wake took him by surprise. Gently he lifted his hand from her damp, electrified bottom, and took deep, even breaths while he stared across the room. The pounding in his chest stilled, and his erection lessened as he concentrated on a spot just above the bar mirror.

She whined her embarrassment when he stretched the waistband, raised the childish panties and concealed the source of her humiliation and delight. Eyes closed, she stiffened her spine as he turned her over and seated her on his lap. His thigh muscles burned her bottom and she clasped her hands beneath her chin while she quivered in his arms.

"It's all right, sweetie . . . now you're forgiven."

The soft pardon scorched her ears like a rebuke, and painful tears dripped down her face. Her lips trembled with apologies that burst forth as sobs. He stroked her hair and hugged her tighter, but still she fought to shut him out, to deny his existence. The awful conversation with Lisa the night before played over and over in her mind. *Michael says it's perfectly natural . . . haven't you ever . . . you know . . . ?* Then the horrible image of the girl's fingers, as they filled her with guilty pleasure, flashed behind her closed lids, only to be replaced by the shameful, wondrous picture of his hand as it spanked her to ecstasy.

Dylan cleared his throat. "Sweetie? Are you OK?"

She leaned into his shoulder and salty remorse wetted his shirt. "Uncle *Dylan.*" The squeak rasped her throat like sandpaper.

"Shh . . . I know you're embarrassed but it really *is* all right."

"No it is *not* and . . . and . . . must I also stand in the *corner?*"

He shook his head and cupped her chin. "Do you want to go freshen up?" She nodded and closed her lips tight when he kissed them. "There's no hurry. Take your time."

Her knees trembled as she struggled to stand and tug up her slacks. Dampness inside the knickers chilled her thighs and she bit her lip while she stumbled to the guestroom bath. She closed and locked the door, kicked off her boots and dropped wrinkled trousers to the floor, then pushed wet gingham down and off and slung the panties at the hamper. Her bottom ached and tingled when she sat on the toilet, and quick, quivery aftershocks flicked through her tummy as her water streamed.

How could he *do* this? To make her climax right on his lap was so . . . improper . . . so humiliating . . . and so *frustrating,* because . . . because. . . . She wiped the wetness between her thighs with tissue and washed at the basin, then pulled the stool from beneath the vanity, sat and folded her arms, and rested her head on the counter. Once again Lisa's voice echoed in her mind. *Didn't he ever . . . maybe by accident . . . make you feel the way I did . . .?* And he could *not* have meant to do this, could he? But he showed no regret, as if it *were* only natural, a mere byproduct of his firm hand punishing her sore bottom. So it must be *her* fault, *her* wickedness that allowed her to reap such pleasure from the seeds of pain. She snatched Kleenex to wipe away the remains of wet makeup as she stared at the mirror.

"He is your *uncle,* you bad girl," she grumbled at her reflection. "How *can* you have such thoughts of him? How can you enjoy so much his hand on you, as if he were merely a *man* . . . such as Michael?" She gasped and rubbed her forehead. "But he is *not* my uncle, is he? How did Lisa say? He is not blood related . . . no more than Michael . . . and *he* put that feeling into me, with his nasty hairbrush. Dylan only used his hand to . . . to. . . ."

She closed her eyes and rested her chin in a palm as steamy, forbidden images wafted through her mind. Knuckles rapped the door and she jerked around.

"Sweetie? Are you OK? I know I said not to hurry but it's been half an hour."

"I . . . I am all right, Dy . . . Uncle Dylan. I will be only a minute."

"I'm making sandwiches. Do you want pickle on your ham and Swiss?"

"Yes . . . if you have the sweet kind." She splashed water on her face and finger combed her hair, and then put on her trousers and boots.

Dylan held the chair for her as she sat at the kitchen table. She smiled and lifted the top of her sandwich. He snapped his fingers. "Forgot the potato salad."

"You made potato salad?"

He smiled and pulled a tub from the refrigerator. "The deli did . . . and it's not too bad. You want to try some?"

Teresa nodded and he spooned salad onto her plate. "Uncle Dylan?"

"Hm?"

"Can . . . may we talk about . . . about Felicia now?"

"Sure. Why don't you talk and I'll listen?"

"Um . . . I hope you will not be upset by what I will say."

"I'm all out of *upset* for this weekend . . . so say whatever you like."

"OK . . . I . . . I know I can trust you." He smiled and chewed as he nodded. "I do not wish to live with Fel . . . with her and Mac . . . after they are married."

She bit her lip and watched his face. His eyelids flickered, but then he swallowed and reached for his water glass.

"Go on. I'm listening."

"You . . . you do not mind . . . that I feel this way?"

"Sweetie, you feel how you feel . . . I understand that. But can you tell me why?"

"It is not that I *hate* them, only . . . I think I will be in their way." She took a deep breath. "They . . . they will want a new life together and . . . they do not need a *stranger* to live with them." He frowned but took a bite of his sandwich. Teresa huffed. "Well I *am*. I . . . I am not related to *either* of them!"

He swiped his lips with a napkin and waited a dozen seconds. "Fel *did* adopt you . . . so you're *legally* related."

"Yes, but . . . but that is not *truly* related!"

"Shh . . . I'm not arguing with you. It just seemed like you wanted me to say something."

She sipped water and nodded. "I suppose I did. I am so used to you *telling* me what to do that I . . . I. . . ."

"Then why don't you tell me what *you* want to do?"

"Only I am not sure I *know!*"

"OK, OK . . . let's look at your options. We'll assume for the moment that you *don't* live with them. You could go back to Germany and stay with Aunt Gerta." He chuckled when she sneered and chomped into her sandwich. "I guess we can cross *that* one off. There's the house in Hamburg. It's a bit large for one person, but it's yours."

"I would not like to live there on my own."

He winked. "I could ask Professor Bender to keep an eye on you. I'm sure he wouldn't mind."

"Uncle Dylan! Do not *tease* like this." A slow smile lighted her face. "You are very bad . . . now be serious."

"All right . . . how about an apartment here? The one the Swedish girls stayed in is available."

Her eyes widened and her jaw dropped. "You . . . you *mean* this? That I shall have my own apartment?" He nodded and she clapped her hands, then frowned and poked her salad with a fork. "Except . . . I will be alone *there* also."

"Well . . . yes . . . but the other girls are practically next door. What's the matter, sweetie? I thought you'd be thrilled."

She sighed and leaned back. "Do you want to know what I *truly* would like?"

"Very much."

"To live with *you.*"

"Oh boy. You um . . . why don't you let me think about it, hm?"

"That is what you told me the *last* time I asked you!"

He blew a breath and nodded. "I suppose it was . . . but under the circumstances I'll have to give it *serious* consideration . . . when I'm not quite so tired."

She pouted, blinked, and then sighed. "Very well . . . if you *promise.*"

"Promise." He smiled and leaned over to kiss her. "Now eat your sandwich."

CHAPTER 8
UNDER NEW MANAGEMENT

MICHAEL PUSHED OPEN the kitchen door and Lisa smiled. Papers rustled as she pulled a manila folder from a pile on the table and handed it to him.

"How was your workout?"

"Simply splendid, my dear . . . I feel quite the new man. What's this?"

"My choice for the ops manager."

"Thank you." He sat next to her and opened the folder. "Excellent . . . Jenkins was in my top three, as well."

"Yeah? Are you going to interview all of them or just the top three?"

"Actually, I thought I would phone them and whoever is home gets the job."

Lisa gaped. "What?"

He grinned and patted her arm. "I'm joking. I'll phone the top three and whoever seems most anxious for the position is the person I'll hire."

"You don't even want to meet them?"

"No reason to, really. I've checked references on those I thought likely candidates, and their résumés speak for themselves. We will meet the person when he or she begins work."

"But . . . what if she . . . or he . . . is mean and ugly? Or . . . or psychotic or something?"

"I doubt if any psychotics would have the credentials of these candidates. And I believe that as an equal opportunity employer we are required to hire the ugly as well as the attractive."

"Michael!" She squeezed his arm. "I didn't mean ugly ugly just . . . you know . . . bad-tempered."

"Ah! As head of operations I would expect the person not to be a creampuff . . . a certain amount of temper is necessary, otherwise suppliers might walk all over him. And that's not really something we could determine in an interview, since everyone would be on his best behavior. What made you decide on Jenkins?"

"Um . . . she's got an MBA in accounting, and she worked at her last job for nearly ten years."

"So you suspect that she has good people skills . . . to remain with one firm for so long?"

"Uh huh . . . and she went to college in California, so Beth will get along with her."

He laughed. "I'm not sure about that issue, but you were correct on the other points."

"Well, at least they'll have something in common." She grinned when he kissed her cheek. "Did you get any lunch?"

"Yes . . . did you?" He sighed when she shook her head. "Am I working you too hard?"

"Nuh uh. I just wanted to get this done so I can go out and play tonight."

"Then you really should eat something."

"I will." She licked her lips. "So, um . . . I'm not grounded or anything?"

"Of course not." He frowned. "You mean, about last evening?" She nodded and he shook his head. "You paid in full for your poor judgment. Have you heard from Teresa?"

"No, but she'll probably call later . . . after, um . . . after the dust settles."

She got up and went to the refrigerator. Michael crossed his arms and leaned back.

"I truly don't believe she was in any grave danger. Dylan seemed remarkably calm about the matter."

"Yeah . . . almost too calm and that kinda worries me. Did you know she ran away before?"

"He didn't mention it. I take it there were, um . . . repercussions?"

The door clicked when she put a pre-packaged teriyaki rice bowl into the microwave. "Yeah . . . and it wasn't that long ago . . . since they moved here."

"I see. Then you think it odd that he wasn't more upset?"

"Uh huh . . . I mean, as strict as he is with me. Once he even. . . ." Michael raised his eyebrows and leaned forward. Lisa bit her lip and went to sit on his lap. "Um . . . so what do you want for Christmas?"

He laughed and patted her back. "Only the joy of having you with me, my dear."

"Are you sure you don't want a new hairbrush?"

"Hm? I believe there are several in the house . . . but if you have something special in mind. . . ."

"It's just . . . I mean . . . the one you spanked me with last night must not of worked very well, so I thought maybe. . . ."

"Lisa, what are you on about?"

"Well you . . . um . . . had to do that other icky thing to me so . . . so I figured there must be something wrong with the hairbrush."

His left eyebrow arched and awakened quivery butterflies in her tummy. She wrapped an arm around his neck and waited a dozen long, scary seconds before he cleared his throat.

"You know we usually don't discuss these issues once the correction is over." She nodded and chewed the tip of her pinky finger. "But I must say this is a novel way to broach the subject, so obviously we need to make an exception. Would you care to tell me what's bothering you?"

Her bottom wriggled on hard leg muscles. Faded hairbrush marks tingled and sparked a glow between her thighs. "Well . . . I mean . . . you just . . . embarrassed me half to death and then . . . then you wouldn't even . . . even. . . ." She hugged his neck and whimpered as he stroked her hip.

"Let you finish what you started?"

"You mean what you started! Didn't you know what that would do to me?"

"Of course I did." He unwrapped her arms and she leaned back to frown at him. "But I wanted you to remember the experience, and it seems you will do."

"Geeze, Michael! I . . . I remember every single time you gave me a lickin' so . . . so why didn't you just . . . ?"

He pressed a finger to her lips. "Shh . . . calm down. If you want to discuss this we will . . . but reasonably. Now . . . what is it you want? Should I apologize for punishing you so harshly?"

"No, I just . . . I mean. . . ."

"Do you want me to finish what you say I started? Hm?"

"Well . . . yeah . . . kinda."

Michael smiled and kissed her lips. She sighed and kissed back as she held onto his neck. He squeezed her bottom and the kiss ended.

"That's an extremely impertinent request, you know."

"Uh huh . . . maybe. . . ." She leaned back and gazed into his eyes. "And if I'm impertinent I probably need a . . . a spanking, huh?"

"Undoubtedly!" He chuckled and pushed her off his lap.

"But just a little one, right? 'cause . . . I mean. . . ." She twisted her fingers at her waist and twitched when the microwave timer dinged.

"Your lunch is ready."

"Yeah . . . I'll eat later . . . so . . . um. . . ."

He smirked and nodded. "Go to my room this instant, young lady."

"Your room?"

"You heard me . . . switches should be cut, and I will be up shortly."

"Not switches! You said you'd. . . ."

"I have said very little at all. Now do as you're told."

"But I thought you were just gonna. . . ." She squealed when he stood and swatted the seat of her skirt. "God, Michael! Why are you being so mean?"

His arm rose and Lisa ran from the kitchen. Her heart pounded as she tramped the stairs, and butterflies dashed madly around her tummy. How could he? It was just a suggestion. God, how dumb was that? She only wanted to give him an excuse to pull down her panties and now he was going to whip her with switches! And he didn't even like sticks. She stomped into his room, sat on the bedside and slapped the duvet with both hands. The mattress jiggled and sent warm vibrations through her tender behind. She squeezed her thighs tight and gasped at the thrill that coursed through her breasts. How could he be so horrible? Would he make her undress?

Take off all her clothes so she would be completely exposed and vulnerable? The awful possibility played in her head, and a picture of her own nakedness blazed across her mind's eye. The warm tingle in her vagina grew hotter as she envisioned the terrible scene, and she slipped a hand beneath her skirt to still the quivery fire.

"Lisa?" She jumped to her feet and stared at Michael, who leaned against the doorframe. "What, may I ask, are you doing?"

"Nuh . . . nothing . . . sir!"

"I had the impression you wished me to do that."

"But I wasn't . . . I mean . . . you . . . and the switches and. . . ." She blinked, scowled, and then stamped her foot. "You didn't get any switches!"

"Didn't I?" He smiled and walked toward her. "Perhaps I never intended to."

"Then why . . .?" She slapped his chest as he wrapped her in his arms. "That's just . . . that's even meaner!"

"I see!" He laughed, sat on the bed and tugged her across his lap. "Not cutting switches for your naughty bottom is worse than actually doing so?"

"Yes it is and . . . and you lied to me!"

He flipped the skirt up and slapped her quivery mounds, snug inside blue boy-leg briefs. "So you wish to add disrespect to impertinence, young lady?"

She kicked the duvet and turned to glare at him. "Well you did."

"I said that switches should be cut . . . not that I would cut them, or indeed that they would be cut at all."

"But that's just . . . whadayacallit . . . sophistry!"

He laughed. "I suppose I have Dylan to thank for that addition to your vocabulary."

"Well anyway it was really mean to scare me like that and you don't gotta ow! Geeze! Not so owee! Hard!"

His hand clapped and Lisa yelped as the heat rose inside her panties. Her fear and irritation dissolved as the familiar palm stung and then remained for a second between swats to squeeze sensitive flesh. Feminine dew seeped from the coral lips at the apex of her thighs and a blush warmed her face. The blush turned fiery when he thumbed the tight undies and slowly pulled them down her legs and off.

"Only a very naughty girl would presume to such impudence, and your sweet little behind must pay the price."

"But you said I already paid. . . ." She whimpered and turned to look at him. "You think my behind is sweet?"

He smiled and swatted bare pinkness. "Exceptionally so . . . and quite! Quite! Spankable!"

"Ow! Owitch! Michael!"

She twisted her bottom and he clamped her waist to his belly. Quick, crisp spanks rained on plump under curve. His fingertips flicked awful, delightful sting into the tenderness between her cheeks and Lisa squealed with horrified pleasure as she parted her thighs to offer herself.

A bare, wriggly hip rubbed the growing tumescence beneath his sweatpants, and a warm chill shivered up his spine as he inhaled the aroma of her excitement. Her shadowy cleft opened and shut as she bounced to the rhythm his hand played on the smooth mounds. Delicate lower lips, wet and swollen with desire, pleaded silently for attention. He nudged her spine with his elbow; she raised her bottom; and his fingers spanked delicate fire into coral dampness. Lisa shrieked his name, then moaned and gasped as horrid, achy, delirious shock washed over her.

He cupped the warm, moist groove and a finger searched her molten core for the hard bud at its center. It blossomed at his touch and electric tingles shot through his arm and into his throat. Fountains of blue-red sparks erupted between her thighs, flashed up her bosom and exploded behind her eyes. He held tight to her waist while orgasmic tremors shook her like a rag doll. She flailed her arms and kicked, then groaned and shivered as he scooped her up and sat her on his lap. Tremulous arms surrounded his neck and held him close.

"Oh God, Michael!" she whispered.

His hand squeezed the sore cheeks and she quivered through an aftershock.

"Then I am forgiven for neglecting you last evening?" He smiled and raised her chin to kiss her.

"Uh . . . uh huh . . . and um . . . I know I'm supposed to say I'm sorry for . . . whatever I did. . . but geeze! You destroyed me and now I can't even remember!"

Lisa grinned and Michael shook his head.

"It seems there was something about impertinence and uh . . . disrespect . . . but I believe we can safely put those issues aside."

She giggled and kissed his smile. "OK . . . but what about this other issue?"

"Hm?"

"This really hard one under my butt."

"Lisa!"

Her hips shifted and a hot cheek pressed his erection. He gasped and pushed her off his lap, but she swung around and straddled his thighs.

"I think he needs some attention."

"Young lady, you . . . Lisa Marie!"

She tugged the pants' waistband with one hand and slipped the other inside. He grabbed her wrist, shut his eyes and moaned as she squeezed his organ.

"Don't, Michael . . . let go. You make me feel good all the time, so why can't I? Huh?"

"Well, I . . . I rather thought you reserved that sort of attention for um . . . Greg."

He leaned back to rest his palms on the bed, and Lisa pulled the pants down to free his stiffness. Quivery heat throbbed in her hand, and she slicked her thumb across the clear fluid that moistened the fat, red tip.

"He knows how I feel about you . . . and how good you make me feel . . . and he's OK with it."

"Yes, well . . . a man might say he is, but. . . ."

"Besides . . . it's not like we're married . . . or engaged, even." She lifted her skirt and scooted forward to press his length against the wetness between her thighs.

Steamy moisture bathed his erection and he shivered. "I . . . I was sure you wanted to . . . to be a. . . ."

"A virgin?" She caressed with both hands and pressed the shaft between her lower lips. "Well . . . yeah . . . I won't put it in. Probably."

He scowled. "Lisa!"

She giggled and squeezed him. "I'm just playing. Don't you like this?"

"I . . . um . . . it's extremely . . . well . . . yes."

"Then hush and enjoy it."

Soft fingers slid up and down while hot, slick labia boiled the underside of his penis. The thick vein throbbed against her clitoris, and she closed her eyes and clenched him harder with each quivery aftershock.

"For God's sake, Lisa, you are . . . just. . . ." He gritted his teeth as ecstatic fire washed over him.

"Whuh . . . what? You . . . wanna put it someplace else? Like in my bottom?"

His eyes shot wide and he grabbed her. "Lisa! Oh Christ!"

Her jaw dropped when his hips jerked, then she grinned and pumped his thick, liquid fire against her belly. He twitched and panted while she milked him. His fingers dug into her arms, then he relaxed as he took a deep breath. She kissed his lips and smiled.

"Wow! That was pretty spectacular."

He swallowed hard and hugged her. "Spectacularly wicked, you bad girl."

"Michael? No! Please?"

She let go of his drained manhood but he held her tight and lifted her skirt to swat soft new sting into achy bare cheeks. Their bellies rubbed together as he spanked and his warm essence slicked between her tummy and the skirt's lining.

"That was the most impudent!" His hand clapped between her open cheeks and she squealed. "Naughty! Impertinent! And thoroughly lascivious thing you've ever done, young lady!" He chuckled as she reached back to caress the quivery tingles inside her bottom. "Now what have you to say for yourself?"

"Um . . . you're welcome?" She grinned and then hugged him while they kissed.

"You might at least pretend remorse, you know."

"Me? I'm not the one who got stuff all over my skirt."

He sighed and shook his head. "You had better take it off, then. I believe we both need a shower."

"OK!" She wriggled backward, stood, and groaned as hard-stretched thigh muscles spasmed.

"Are you all right, my dear?"

"Uh huh . . . just not used to that position is all."

"Well I should hope not." He pulled off his jersey and tossed it into the corner. "Whatever happened to the demure little housemaid I hired only a few years ago?"

She winked and dropped her skirt on the floor. "I think she figured out how much fun it is to be naughty."

"Yes, well . . . as long as she remembers how painful it can be at times." He kicked his track shoes away and stood to push his pants off.

Lisa, now naked, leaned against his chest and lifted her chin to pout at him. "You wouldn't hurt me, would you? Just for being naughty?"

He bent his neck and kissed her pout. "I would never hurt you for any reason under the sun." His palm smacked red bottom flesh. "Now let's have a wash, shall we?"

* * *

Greg glanced at the security monitor, saved a file and then shut down the computer in the shop office. He hurried to the sales floor and smiled at the people in the register line.

"I can help the next person here." He twisted a key into the second terminal and reached over the counter to take a pile of clothes from a young woman. "Did you find everything you were looking for?"

She nodded and brushed a wisp of hair from her eye. "And then some. These pants are on sale, right?"

"I think so but I'll make sure."

He scan-gunned the barcode tag on a pair of wool slacks as he glanced around. Cindy, his part-time sales assistant, stood next to a rack of leather coats, hand on her hip, while a red-haired teenager admired herself and a shiny black jacket in the triple mirror. Barbara, the assistant manager, bumped him when she backed away from her register to look beneath the counter.

"Sorry, Greg. Do we have any more of those small gift boxes?"

"Sure . . . in the back. How many do you want?"

"I'll get them."

"OK." He folded the slacks and nodded to the woman. "Forty percent off, right?"

The woman nodded and smiled. "I should buy another pair . . . but my Visa's too hot to touch as it is."

Greg chuckled as he folded blouses and slipped them into a bag. "Lot of that going around this time of year . . . but they'll be on sale until New Years, in case you hit the lottery."

"I'll keep it in mind . . . just in case." She grimaced when the total flashed, and then handed him a card.

"Thanks . . . could I see your ID, please?" She opened her wallet and he peered at the license. "Thank you, Ms. Gardner."

"I'm glad you check . . . not everybody does."

He swiped the credit card and smiled as he tapped the store code. "Wouldn't want anyone else maxing out your card, would we?" The POS terminal blinked and he frowned, then grinned and coughed as he reached inside the bag of clothes and rattled it noisily. "Declined, Ms. Gardner," he whispered.

"Oh! Um. . . ." She glanced past him at the people by the other register while a blush reddened her face. "Can I write a check? I have a guarantee card."

"No problem." He handed her a pen and leaned forward. "Sorry about the maxing out comment."

"That's OK . . . my husband said he was going to a friend's house but he must have gone Christmas shopping instead."

The register whirred and clicked when he fed the check to it. He smiled and handed her the receipt.

"Happy holidays, ma'am."

"Same to you. . . ." She looked at his name badge. "Greg . . . and thank you."

"Thanks for shopping with us and come back soon."

"I will."

He turned. "Next in line, please?"

Barbara smiled at him over her shoulder, but her eyes flickered toward a coat rack. Cindy stood with her arms crossed while the red-haired girl hugged a full-length shearling to her neck and pirouetted before the mirror. The street door opened and four more teenaged girls trooped inside. Greg sighed, smiled at his customer and picked up the scan gun.

Lisa waited while a battered LTD pulled out of a street space and then backed the Land Rover into the spot a block from the store. Slushy snow squished beneath her boot heels when she stepped around to the curb, and wintry fog haloed the streetlamps as she strode along the sidewalk. Foil garland glimmered around the show window and she stood for a moment to admire the red, blue and green party dresses Barbara had put on the mannequins. The woman looked over and smiled when Lisa pushed inside, and then

turned back to her customer. Lisa ambled toward the back of the shop and stopped to straighten a table full of sweaters that looked like a tornado had struck it. She, Barbara and the customer, a young woman in bellbottomed jeans and a short woolen jacket, were the only people on the sales floor.

"I like the denim skirt with this blouse, honey. . . ." Barbara said. "But if it's a dance party you might want to reconsider the boots. We've got some really nice low-heeled sling backs on sale."

"Ya think? I just can't see the skirt without my boots."

Barbara nodded and peered at the floor for a moment. "You could carry the shoes . . . and change when you want to dance."

"OK . . . let's see what you've got."

Lisa winked as Barbara led the woman to a corner shoe display. She finished a stack of sweaters, frowned at the chaos that remained, and turned toward the office. Greg's voice rumbled from behind the closed door and Lisa bit a fingertip. His words were muffled but the tone was unmistakable. It was his scolding voice . . . not as gruff and scary as Michael or Dylan or Dad's, but as deep as his normal tenor allowed, and she always knew he wasn't playing when he used it. She leaned against the wall opposite the office and peered out the short hallway at Barbara, who smiled as she rang up clothes and shoes. The young woman left the store with her bag and the office door opened at the same moment.

"Hi!" Greg said. "Be with you in a minute."

"No hurry. You OK?"

He glanced over his shoulder. Cindy sat in the guest chair, arms folded, a scowl on her face.

"Yeah . . . uh . . . maybe you want to come in."

"Um . . . you can take care of . . . whatever it is. I don't wanna micromanage."

"Thanks, but. . . ." He stepped into the hall and shut the door. "I think I need an executive opinion."

"OK . . . for whatever it's worth. What did she do now?"

"Lost her keys. I told her twice to open the second register when it got busy and I thought she was just being lazy when she didn't . . . but I finally wormed it out of her. I'll have to get NCR over here to re-key, which isn't what I had planned for the week before Christmas."

"I guess not. So . . . is that expensive?"

He shrugged. "More expensive than not having to do it . . . but it's aggravating that she didn't tell me up front."

"Yeah . . . so . . . um . . . what executive advice can I give you?"

"Well . . . I already told her the cost is coming out of her pay, but . . . I just wondered if that was enough."

Lisa nodded. "I know she's been a pain in the butt ever since you started . . . well, for Sharon, too. You want to fire her?"

"I'm tempted . . . but I don't want to look for a replacement this close to Christmas . . . and she's got good sales . . . when she tries."

A slow smile curled the corners of Lisa's mouth. "Are you asking if . . . you should spank her?" she whispered.

He coughed and covered his mouth as he glanced toward the sales floor. Barbara held up a bright red dress while two women looked at it and nodded. Greg sighed.

"I kinda think she's expecting it."

Lisa bit her lip and took his hand. "OK . . . but be sure to forgive her and make her feel better afterwards." He nodded. "But not too much better, OK?"

"Of course not. You mean . . . better in a business way, right?"

"Yeah . . . business better. Don't make the same mistake Sharon did with her."

"No . . . Darcy told me what you guys did to Sharon . . . and what Sharon did . . . or didn't do . . . to Cindy."

"Really? I thought I told you about that."

"Yeah, but you left out some of the, uh . . . steamy details." He smiled. "So? Are you gonna watch?"

"I'm not sure I need to see you spank another cute girl."

He shook his head. "She's not nearly as cute as you . . . but I think you ought to."

"You are a terrible flirt, Mr. Bentley." She covered her mouth to suppress a giggle. "And why do you think I ought to?"

"Well for one thing, Ms. Carlson . . . I don't want there to be any question about the professionalism of the sanction."

"Oh, God . . . you sound just like Darcy!"

"And B. . . ." He winked. "She'll be more embarrassed with you watching and I won't have to spank as hard to get my point across."

"Since when have you had any trouble getting your point across on a bare heinie?"

He chuckled. "Gotta save my strength for any unprofessional spanking I might have to do later."

"Oh, yeah? Well you better serious up before we go in there."

"Yes, ma'am." He glanced toward the sales floor. "I'll tell Barb I need few more minutes."

She nodded and leaned against the door. Butterflies of a different species danced in her tummy. Their wings were soft as a baby's kiss, but every bit as manic and whirly as the ones she felt when her own tender behind was in jeopardy. The smell of fresh coffee tingled her nostrils and she reached for the pot just as the office door swung open.

"Oh!" Cindy's eyes widened and she frowned. "Is Greg coming back or what?"

"Um . . . yeah. Why don't you um . . .?" Lisa glanced toward the registers and then stepped into the office as Cindy backed away. "I . . . heard you lost your keys."

The girl sneered. "So?"

"So that's . . . not good." She took a deep breath and crossed her arms. "And it's . . . kind of inconvenient for us right now."

"Us? Since when do I gotta deal with you? I thought you were like a silent partner or something . . . so why don't you just mind your own . . .?" Cindy clamped her lips tight when Greg walked in and shut the door behind him.

"You remember Ms. Carlson don't you?"

"Ms. Carlson? Huh!" She blinked at the floor when he glared. "Yeah . . . I know who she is."

"Then you should know that what goes on in this shop is her business." He went to sit behind the desk and waved Cindy to the guest chair.

She sat and clenched her fists on her knees. "Yeah but . . . I thought Swayne was like the big boss."

"Right now you're only concern is the two bosses in the room with you."

Lisa shrugged off her jacket and sat in a straight-backed chair by a filing cabinet. Cindy looked at her from the corner of her eye.

"So now I get fired?"

"Nobody wants to fire you," Lisa said. "But we're not happy that you lost your keys."

Greg cleared his throat and Cindy scowled at him.

"Yeah, but . . . I'm gonna pay for the stupid keys! How come I gotta listen to her holler at me?"

"She wasn't hollering at you . . . and there's more to this than the cost of re-keying. Customers have had to wait because you didn't tell me what was going on, and I never want anything like that to happen again, young lady."

Cindy's mouth dropped open and Lisa stifled a gasp. The few times Greg called her 'young lady' had been in jest, but the voice tone and the hard glint in his eye when he said it then made her bottom flinch.

"OK . . . I just won't lose the damn things anymore, OK? God . . . how come you're making such a big deal?"

"It is a big deal . . . but I don't think you realize that yet."

"Uh huh . . . I mean shit! Maybe a hundred and fifty bucks isn't a lot to you but it sure as hell is to me!"

"I've told you about that kind of language in the store, Cindy . . . and I don't want to hear any more of it, understand?"

She slumped and crossed her arms. "Yeah, well . . . if you'd quit picking on me I'd quit cussing."

The chair banged the wall as he jerked to his feet. "That's it! I've had it with your attitude. Stand up and bend over the desk."

Her head twitched back and forth as she looked from Greg to Lisa and back again. "What? You're not gonna . . . you gotta be kidding!"

"I think you know I'm not. Now stand up!"

"You . . . you just can't! I . . . I'm too old to get paddled and . . . and anyway it's illegal!"

"And you can mention that in your lawsuit . . . when you're not working here anymore."

She stared at him and swiped her eyes. "But you said you weren't gonna fire me!"

"I'm not. You can leave this room with a sore rear end and your job . . . or simply leave. It's up to you . . . but I'm not going to put up with your attitude or your gutter language anymore!"

"But . . . but. . . ." She turned in her chair. "You can't let him do that, Lisa!"

He picked up an eighteen-inch ruler and clapped the blotter. "Ms. Carlson already tried to talk me out of it, but my mind is made up. She will stay here while I paddle you . . . to make sure there are no improprieties."

"Impruh . . . improprieties? Are you nuts? It's a impropriety just to . . . to talk about it, for God's sake!"

"I know Sharon spanked you . . . and you know I know it. So stop all this nonsense and bend over like I told you."

Tears welled in the girl's eyes and she reached out a hand. Lisa took it and squeezed.

"I um . . . I don't like this any better than you do, Cindy . . . but I think you need it, because . . . it'll help you concentrate. I've looked at your sales and the numbers always got better right after Sharon . . . corrected you."

"Jesus! You're nuts too! I . . . I gotta get out of here!" She snatched her hand away from Lisa and stood up as she glared at Greg.

"All right." He dropped the ruler and sat down. "I'll deduct the hundred and fifty from your final paycheck."

"No . . . you . . . you said you'd take it out a little at a . . . a . . . oh, shit!"

"Cindy!"

"I mean shoot! OK! Jeesus!"

Lisa bit her lip as the girl turned and slapped her palms on the desk. He nodded and retrieved the ruler, then winked at Lisa as he walked around the desk. She stood and leaned against the wall by the window, and prickly caterpillars joined the soft butterflies in her tummy when Greg bent down behind the girl. Cindy wore a bright red crop-top sweater with long sleeves, a knee-length gray woolen skirt, tight around the hips but split to her thigh tops on both sides, and charcoal pantyhose with black, high-heeled lace up boots. He furled the skirt's back panel at her waist to expose a round, sheer-nyloned bottom a full size larger than it was the first time Lisa saw it. He slipped his thumbs into the waistband of the pantyhose and Cindy jerked her head toward him.

"God, Greg! Don't pull 'em down!"

"Hush and face forward . . . you're getting it on the bare so you remember this."

"But I will! You don't gotta show everybody my. . . ."

"I said hush!"

A hoarse groan graveled her throat and she squeezed her eyes shut. He pushed the nylon down and left it in a bunch at the base of her deep cleft. A silver dollar-sized unicorn tattoo, white with a

golden horn and tiny blue eyes, decorated the right hip just beneath her waist. He put his left palm atop the pile of woolen at the small of her back, held the ruler loose between his thumb and two fingers, and tapped it against the hard-clenched cheeks. His full lips compressed to a tight line as he pulled it back, and then yanked his arm sideways. The thin wood whipped through the air, clacked bottom flesh, and Cindy yelped.

"Hands right back on the desk and stay still."

"But it hurts!" She stamped a boot heel but returned her palms to the desktop.

"You can rub when I'm finished!"

The ruler swished, popped again and she stamped the other boot. "Huh . . . how many?"

Greg glanced at the ceiling and cleared his throat. "Twenty-five for not telling me about the keys . . . and twenty-five for cussing at me."

"But I didn't cuss at you . . . ow!"

"Don't argue with me while I'm spanking you!"

"Well geeze, you don't gotta . . . ouch!"

"I said to be! Still!"

"Ow! OKaay!"

The ruler whisked the air as swats landed in hard, slow cadence, and each clack painted a pink stripe across the wide expanse of flesh. He started at the center of her bottom and worked down, then began again at the top of her cleft. Cindy squeaked and kicked the carpet, and Lisa felt heat grow in her own behind as the separate stripes melded to a satiny, allover pink. Greg pushed the girl's back and she slumped closer to the desk, then he turned panic-stricken eyes to Lisa.

"What's the count?" he mouthed.

"Twenty-eight!" Her whisper was lost beneath Cindy's wails.

He nodded and clapped sting into plump under curve. Her wails grew louder, shriller, and Lisa glanced at the monitor, but Barbara stood with two customers, oblivious to the uproar in the office. Greg dropped the ruler on the desk and lifted Cindy by the arm.

The girl quivered while he held her close to his chest, then she looked up and wiped a tear from her eye. "I . . . I'm sorry, Greg."

"Then everything's all right. You can pull up your pantyhose."

"Um . . . OK." She lifted the skirt and tugged nylon into place, then let the skirt drop and rubbed achy bottom flesh.

"I don't want to leave you short over the holidays so I'll wait until the end of January to start deducting the payments from your check. Ten dollars a week won't be a problem, will it?"

Cindy glanced at Lisa and then shook her head. "No . . . that's OK . . . um . . . thanks."

He held out a hand and she took it. "Then everything really is all right, isn't it?"

"Yeah . . . I guess so. But. . . ."

"But what, Cindy?"

"If . . . if I ever piss you off enough to do that again, could we like do it in private?"

"I'd just as soon not have to do it again." He squeezed her hand and smiled as he let it go.

"Yeah, me too . . . but . . . um. . . ." She puffed her cheeks. "You're not gonna tell Barb I got a lickin', are you?"

"Of course not . . . do I tell you when I spank her?"

Her eyes bugged and then she sneered. "You do not! You're such a liar!"

"Hey now!" He grinned and raised a finger. "A little respect for the boss, huh?"

"Yeah, well . . . you don't . . . do you?"

He winked and shook his head. "I said I'd never tell and I won't. Now . . . weren't you supposed to clock out at six?" She nodded and he looked at his watch. "OK . . . put seven-thirty on your time sheet and leave it in the slot."

"Um . . . OK . . . thanks. I . . . I'm really sorry about the keys."

"It's past history. I'll see you at . . . what? Noon to six tomorrow?"

She nodded, glanced at Lisa, and then stood on tiptoe to kiss his cheek. "'Night, Greg . . . 'bye, Li . . . Ms. Carlson."

The office door opened and then the restroom door slammed. Lisa puffed a breath and shook her head. Greg held out his arms and she fell into them.

"So? How'd I do with my first sanction, boss?"

Her left eye squinched when she looked up at him. "Probably better than I will when I sanction you for calling me boss . . . young man!"

"Uh oh . . . guess I should close the door, then."

"Nuh uh . . . but just wait'll I get you home!"

He laughed and then did a quick check with Barbara before they left the store. They went in his pickup to D'Antonio's for dinner, then he let her out next to the Land Rover. Lisa turned the heater to high and followed the Toyota's taillights. She parked beside it in the lot next to his building and he hugged her shoulder as they climbed the stairs to his apartment. He switched on the lights and shut the door behind them.

"Do you have any wine?" She shivered and clutched her collar at her throat.

"Sure . . . OK, OK . . . I'll turn up the heat." He walked to the wall next to the bath and adjusted the thermostat, then went back to the kitchenette.

"I'll tell Michael to pay you more in the winter so you don't have to have this place like an ice box all the time."

"Don't do that. I like it cool . . . so you'll snuggle up close to me in bed."

She giggled, slipped off her jacket and hugged him from behind as he filled goblets from a two-liter jug of Chablis. "Like I wouldn't anyway. You're just cheap, so admit it."

"Excuse me? What about that fancy new bed I bought?" He turned, handed her a glass and raised his own. "And this brand new imported crystal?"

"Yeah right . . . imported from Mexico . . . six for five dollars at Pier One . . . I saw them there last week."

"And your point would be . . .?"

"Cheep cheep cheep . . . ow! Greg!" She grinned and stood on tiptoe to kiss him. "Don't smack my heinie or I'll spill fancy imported wine out of my fancy imported glass all over your fancy imported shirt."

He laughed and they drank as she rubbed her stomach against the front of his trousers.

"Lisa? What are you doing?"

"Just checking." She grinned and sat on the sofa.

"Oh that was subtle . . . seeing if I still had a woody from spanking Cindy?"

She frowned and leaned away when he sat next to her. "What do you mean still?"

"Hm?"

"You said still had a woody . . . Greg! Are you kidding or

what?" Her knees cracked as she twisted around to straddle his thighs, and she winced at the strain on her leg muscles.

"Are you OK?"

"Uh huh . . . just . . . not as limber as I used to be."

He set his glass on the end table and rubbed her thighs. "Why don't you sit down? You don't look too comfortable."

"I'm OK . . . I um . . . yeah, I think I will." She wriggled off his lap, stretched her legs and pointed her toes.

"What did you do to yourself?"

"Nothing . . . must be the cold weather . . . right here in this room!"

"Nag, nag, nag." He smiled and covered her mouth with his for a long minute. "You wanna watch a movie on my fancy imported TV . . . or just get in my fancy new bed and warm up?"

"Mmm . . . that sounds sorta nice. So did you get turned on spanking that little brat's fanny?"

"Nothing little about it."

"Yeah, she put on a few pounds . . . and am I the only girl in town without a tattoo on my butt?"

He laughed and hugged her closer. "Since I haven't seen them all I can't really say. Why? Who else has one?"

"Well, just my sister . . . but Delia and Christa were talking about it the other day at school."

"What? It's not bad enough Travis paddles them three times a week they gotta go looking for more pain in their butts?"

"Maybe not three times a week, but yeah . . . go figure. So how do you do that?"

"Get a tattoo? Well there's a place on Railroad Street that'll. . . ."

"No . . . change the subject." She grinned when he wrinkled his nose.

"Except it looks like I didn't."

"Come on . . . I know how you get when you spank a girl."

"No way . . . not gonna cop to this one." He picked up his glass and took a healthy swig. "There's a, um . . . a hormone in the male body . . . kind of an autonomic defense mechanism . . . that prevents him from getting turned on by anyone except his significant other when in her presence."

She sneered and swatted his thigh. "That's a bunch of bull!"

He raised a hand. "I swear on Gray's Anatomy . . . they call it

the . . . self-preservation hormone, and it's automatically secreted by the uh . . . duodenum . . . whenever a guy is exposed to any bare heinie that doesn't belong to his girlfriend . . . assuming she's in the room watching him."

"Wow . . . it does all that?"

"You bet . . . miracles of the human body . . . amazing, huh?"

"You're amazing!"

"Well thanks!"

"An amazing liar!"

"Hey now!" He grabbed her glass and set it down, and she laughed as she wriggled to the end of the sofa. "Come back here, young lady!"

"Nuh uh! I thought I was gonna die when you called Cindy that!"

"Oh you did, huh?"

She squealed when he lunged, picked her up and tossed her across his lap. "Don't you dare! I'm already freezing and . . . Greg!" Boot toes beat sofa cushions as she struggled to push his hands away from her pants zipper.

"Now you're gonna find out what happens to little brats who call me a liar!"

"But I didn't mean it! I was kidding! You know? What you do to me all the . . . no!"

He held tight to her waist, opened her fly and tugged the trousers down. "Don't tell me no, young lady!"

"OK, OK!" She giggled as she turned to look at him. "How 'bout if I tell you . . . um . . . how strong and masterful you were when you spanked her?"

"Hmm . . . maybe . . . but you better convince me." His hand clapped the seat of her pink cotton briefs. "Or I'll think you're just kidding to get out of a good butt warming."

"Who me?" She grimaced when he raised his arm. "I mean no . . . never! Um . . . you . . . you like totally took charge and . . . and scolded her real good and. . . ."

"Really well."

"Oh, shut up . . . ow! OK, really well! And . . . and . . . it was really me who got all hot and bothered from watching you be so stern and strict!"

He laughed and she yelped when he pulled down her panties. "That's not bad . . . but I have to spank you anyhow."

"Nuh uh . . . 'cause I'm a good. . . ."

"Ouch." His fingertips caressed blue hairbrush souvenirs. "Where'd these come from?"

"Um . . . Michael . . . last night."

"Yeah? What did you do? Or shouldn't I ask?"

"I . . . fibbed to him."

"Uh huh . . . and you think I'm gonna go easy 'cause you got marks on your butt?"

"Um . . . yeah?"

"Nope!"

"Ow!"

"Not the strong!"

"Owee!"

"Masterful!"

"Yowtch!"

"Manager! Of! Lola's! Down! Town! Bou! Tique!"

"Haiee! Greg! Not! So! Hard! Ow! Owitch!" She pouted while he rubbed her bottom, and giggled when he leaned down to kiss a red palm print.

"He was pretty mad at you, huh?"

"Yeah . . . sorta."

"What did you fib to him about?"

"Nothing, really . . . I just covered up for Teresa when she ran away from home."

"She did?" He blinked and shook his head. "How come Dylan didn't spank you?"

"It's a long story . . . you wanna hear it?"

"Sure . . . when I'm finished."

"Greg no!"

She whimpered and wriggled while he held her tight and spanked, but the slaps warmed more than they burned, and he concentrated on the sensitive flesh nearest her thigh tops. After a dozen tingly swats he pushed the panties farther down her legs and caressed the damp tenderness at the base of her behind.

"So what happened . . . hmm?"

"He just . . . I . . . I can't tell you if you keep doing that."

"Doing what?" He grinned and slid a fingertip inside the moist cleft to tease the edges of her swollen labia.

"Thuh . . . that! You . . . you're making me crazy!"

"Yeah? So you're just gonna moan and wiggle while I have my way with your naughty bits?" His finger slipped between hot flesh folds and she gasped.

"Geeze, Michael . . . I . . . I mean Greg!" She turned to look at him as he took his hand from her bottom. "Don't . . . um . . . I'm sorry . . . it was an accident."

He leaned back and folded his arms. "Yeah?"

"Uh huh . . . I . . . when you said naughty bits I kinda slipped . . . 'cause that's what he always says."

"Did he have his way with them? Is that why your legs are so stiff?"

"No, he just . . . I mean . . . you said you didn't wanna know about. . . ."

"About what?" His green eyes burned into hers, and she blinked away a tear.

"Whuh-what he does to me."

"Maybe it's time I did . . . if he's going to be right here with us!"

"But he's not and . . . owee!"

He rubbed a new handprint on her bottom. "Don't argue with me. Now . . . will you tell me the truth if I ask?"

"Um . . . yeah . . . I guess . . . ouch! Greg!"

"Try again, Lisa . . . and quit waffling."

"OK! Yes!" His hand clapped. "Owee!"

"Yes what?"

"Yeh . . . yes, sir!"

"That's better." He caressed the stinging fanny while he shifted to get comfortable. "Let's start with last night . . . did he paddle you?"

"No . . . sir . . . he um . . . it was Beth's hairbrush."

"She was there?"

"Yeah . . . sir. And . . . and Teresa . . . he spanked her, too."

"Why? Did she fib to him?"

"Nuh uh . . . ow! Nuh uh, sir . . . geeze, Greg!" She pouted and wriggled, and then looked away from his icy glare. "She um . . . she felt bad 'cause I fibbed to keep her out of trouble . . . which didn't work, anyway, so. . . ."

"OK . . . so did he make both of you feel better . . . afterwards?"

"No . . . sir . . . he was a complete jerk!"

Greg's mouth twisted in a wry smile. "Doesn't sound much like Michael. Did Beth do the honors, then?"

She shook her head. "They . . . went right to bed . . . afterwards."

"No lotion or anything . . . nobody made you feel better?"

"Um . . . nope . . . ow . . . no, sir!"

"Lisa! You said you'd tell me the truth!"

"OK! I . . . we . . . we did it ourselves, OK?"

He frowned to suppress a chuckle. "You and Teresa?"

Her eyes burned as she glared at him. "Yes, and I promised I wouldn't tell anybody so . . . ouch! Quit that! Owee!"

His palm landed twice in quick succession and then he rubbed. "All right . . . I didn't hear a thing . . . now. Let's talk about him."

"What about him? Greg!" She twisted and kicked as he swatted her bottom a dozen times.

"You can just lose the exasperated tone! Why are your legs so sore? And I want the truth!"

"OK! He . . . I . . . um . . . I was mad . . . 'cause he was so mean to me and didn't . . . didn't finish whuh-what he started so I . . . um. . . ."

"Yeah . . . so you what?"

"I got him to s-spank me again and then he . . . he touched me and. . . ."

"And that made your legs sore? I don't buy it."

She buried her face in the cushion. "I . . . I just . . . straddled his legs and rubbed his uh . . . until he . . . you know!"

"You jerked him off?"

"God, Greg! You make it sound so nasty!"

"Well it should!"

"Nooo!"

His arm rose and she reached back to cover. He grabbed her hand, held it tight to her waist and slapped fire into her fanny. After twenty hard licks he loosened his grip and rubbed the red cheeks.

"We need a few ground rules here, because you are getting way out of line!"

"I am not and . . . I just . . . all I did was help him . . . you know! Like . . . like he does me and . . . and like Darcy did to you and. . . ."

"This is not about me! And that was before I had you . . . or thought I did!"

She sobbed. "Don't say that! You do have me and . . . and I'm sorry I did it and . . . and I won't ever, ever, ever do it again so don't be mad, please?"

"All right . . . all right. I know you . . . and I know how you get when your butt's heated up . . . but I want you to listen because this is how it's going to be from now on."

"O . . . OK . . . sir." She wiped her eyes and looked at him.

"I get that I'm not the only guy in town who pulls down your panties . . . not to mention Beth, but I'm not real concerned with. . . ."

"She hasn't lately . . . ow!"

"Hush and let me talk!" He squeezed her behind and took a breath. "And I'd be stupid to think you won't get turned on when they've got you half-naked and bent over . . . but as of now, you keep your hands off of other men, understand?"

"Yes . . . sir. I promise I won't ever, ever. . . ."

"Shh! I'm not finished. If you accidentally get off while they're spanking you that's one thing . . . but you keep your thighs tight when you get lotion from anybody but me . . . and don't be giving them those big blue gosh-it-hurts-won't-you-please-touch-me-there eyes!"

"Greg, I. . . ."

"Don't tell me you don't do that because I've seen it! And no pushing them, either . . . no tweaking their noses and then looking all innocent and surprised when they whack your fanny. If you need your bottom warmed up . . . or your naughty bits taken care of afterward, you call me . . . got it?"

"But I . . . yes, sir."

"And if I can't to do it right now . . . you just keep it in your pants and wait for me."

"Yes, sir . . . I will, sir."

"Get up." He pushed her off his lap and she grabbed her trousers as they slid down. "You've been an unmitigated brat today so it's time I did something about it."

"But you already . . . no!"

Her heels skittered threadbare carpet when he towed her by the arm around the coffee table and into the alcove. He made her bend with her upper body flat atop the new four-poster and then crouched to pull a cardboard box from beneath the high bed. She pushed up with her arms but he glared and shook a finger.

"Stay right where I put you, Lisa!"

"Why are you being so . . .?"

"Down!"

She dropped onto the quilt and bit her lip as she craned her neck to watch him. Guilty, frightened butterflies flapped about her tummy as Michael's warning echoed in her head. How could she have thought Greg was OK with it? But he never seemed to mind before, and she thought he liked to hear about her harmless escapades with other people. When did he get so bossy? After all, she let him spank her even though she was his boss, technically. Why was he all of a sudden so stern and strict with her? It made no sense, and she opened her mouth to tell him that, but then he looked up and she saw the fire in his green eyes, and the words stuck in her throat. Books and videotapes clattered as he dug in the box, then he stood, Darcy Weller's ash wood paddle clutched tight in his fist.

"Greg!" The syllable whined through half an octave.

"I knew I'd need this sooner or later."

"Nuh uh! Thah . . . that's horrible! My butt's already sore and. . . ."

"Hush!" He tucked the board under his arm and pulled her panties and trousers to her knees.

Goose flesh prickled her bottom and thighs. "Please not with the. . . ."

"I told you to hush. You need to get over the idea that you can do whatever you want with whoever you want and not have to pay for it! Put your hands above your head and keep them there."

"OK, but. . . ."

"What?"

"I . . . I mean yes, sir!"

"Better . . . now bend your knees so your bottom sticks out."

He pushed his left palm on the small of her back and she moaned as her cheeks rounded and parted. Fear and guilt drenched her soul and the knuckles of her twined fingers whitened. He stretched his arm and the paddle smacked hard.

"Ow!"

"I have had enough of this nonsense from you!"

Wood flamed across her cheeks again and she squealed.

"Owee! Greg!"

"You're a spoiled little brat . . . but you're my brat!" The paddle seared her cheeks right at the base and both hands jerked back to cover. "No you don't!"

"Greg, please!"

He gathered her wrists and pressed them against her spine, then clapped red, jiggly flesh once more and she screeched.

"I don't care who they are! How rich they are! How stern! And strict! And sexy they are! You take your spanking! Keep your legs together! And keep! Your! Hands! Off! Other! Men!" His forearm swept in short arcs as he fanned intense heat into soft tissue.

"Ahee! Noweee! Yeeaagh! I will! I swear! Greg!"

Her legs twisted and flailed but she could not kick away the pain that spread through every nerve. Tears streamed from her eyes like water from a boiling cauldron and guttural moans burned her throat. Spank after nasty spank drove shockwaves through the top of her head, then down to her toes. He held her tight to the bed, his grip soft but unbreakable, and she surrendered in her restraint. Her mind blanked, washed clean of all but the most primal sensations . . . the fierce heat in her bottom, the needy fire in her belly.

"Shh . . . shh . . . it's OK, Lisa . . . open your eyes."

She blinked at him, felt his long arms around her. His hard thighs soothed her behind, throbbing with the sting of a thousand bees. He wiped a salty flood from her face with his sleeve and then let her sob into his neck. The blaze in her bottom subsided as she wept away the dregs of guilt and remorse, and searched the foggy recesses of her mind for words she knew must be there.

"I . . . I . . . I'm sorry!"

"I know . . . you were a bad, bad girl . . . but I can forgive you because I love you so very, very much."

The bright smile on his lips thrilled her and she kissed it. Smooth, quivery lightening flashed through her vagina as the kiss went on, and she moaned when he leaned back and patted her swollen cheeks.

"Should I do something about this fire in your butt?"

"God I guess!" She clenched her teeth as she stood. "Um . . . where'd my boots go?"

"Under the bed."

"When did I take them off?"

"You didn't . . . I did . . . now hold onto my shoulders so I can take off your pants."

Denim wrapped her ankles and she winced as she lifted her feet so he could remove the trousers and panties. He tossed them at the desk in the corner and helped her lie down, then pulled a folded

blanket from the foot of the bed and draped it across her naked lower half.

"I'll be right back so don't go away."

"Like I could. Can I have some wine?"

"You wanna rub alcohol on paddle rash?"

"Greg!" She started to giggle but a cough scratched her throat. "I meant to drink!"

"Oh . . . well then, sure."

"God, you are just . . . uuhh!"

"Yeah, I guess I am . . . that's probably why you love me." He leaned over to kiss her and she grabbed his shirt.

"I do love you!"

"I know . . . I love you, too. I'll be back in a sec."

"Hurry, OK?"

"OK."

She closed her eyes and listened to his sounds as he moved about the tiny apartment. Her bottom throbbed with a burn that flowed like lava between moist lower lips and she squeezed her thighs to enhance the delicious tingle. The bed shuddered and she blinked when he sat beside her and folded the blanket off her sore cheeks. She propped herself on an elbow, took the glass and guzzled cool, dry wine. He smiled and shook his head.

"Easy on that or you'll make yourself sick."

"Yes, sir." She gave him the goblet.

He set it on the nightstand and then opened a jar of Pond's. Slick, gentle fingers bathed relief across arid, scarlet mounds and she whimpered her delight into the duvet.

"Does it feel better?"

"Uh huh . . . lots better." Her thighs parted and she wriggled her bottom.

"No, Lisa."

She turned and stared at him. "No what?"

He shook his head. "That's how he does it."

"Who . . . Michael?" She gasped and grabbed his knee. "But you . . . are you still mad about . . .?"

"Hush!" He squeezed a slippery cheek and she squealed. "You've been pampered and spoiled enough for one weekend."

Sad, frustrated tears welled in her eyes. "But you . . . you already forgave me for . . . for being a brat!"

"Yes . . . and now I'm going to make love to you . . . my way."

"Whuh-what do you mean?"

"I mean . . . I don't think you're convinced of who is in charge here." He rolled her over and pulled the sweater over her head.

"But you . . . you just blistered my butt, for crying out loud!"

"Yeah . . . same as two other men do, and I won't play third string anymore. Now quit wiggling so I can undress you."

"No . . . I . . . I mean . . . what are you gonna do?" She whimpered while he removed her blouse and bra and tossed them away.

"Show you that I'm not those men." His hand pressed her mouth when she opened it. "I love you more than you can possibly imagine . . . and I want you to tell me right now . . . whether you trust me or not." He removed the hand and she sobbed.

"I do, Greg, but what are you . . .?"

"Up on all fours." He grabbed her shoulders and lifted her. "I'm going to ravish your sore, red bottom so don't move while I get ready."

Her heart jumped with fear and excitement, and her arms trembled as she stared at him. "Buh . . . but I'm cold!"

He leaned a hand on her back and gave her three quick smacks with his open palm, then yanked off his tie. "Feel warmer now?"

She squealed and reached back to rub, but stopped when he growled no. "You . . . you'll be sorry when I catch pneumonia . . . sir."

"That would be dramatic . . . unlikely, but dramatic." He threw his shirt at the desk, kicked off his loafers and shoved his trousers and shorts to the floor.

His curved, thick-capped erection bobbed and he leered as he removed his socks. She swallowed hard and clamped her thighs together. Her bottom smoldered beneath the cold cream, and its heat inflamed the delicate petals between her thighs. The tiny o-ring inside her burning cheeks pulsed and contracted in anticipation of the awful, stretchy, delirious intrusion to come. He opened the nightstand drawer and rummaged out a condom and a tube of K-Y Jelly. She slid down onto her tummy, eyes wide, expectant, fearful, but he shook his head.

"I told you to stay put!"

"But . . . my arms are sore."

"Then get on your knees with your head down so your butt sticks up."

"Why are you being so . . . ?"

The bed rattled when he jumped on it, knelt beside her and grabbed her waist. She screeched as he clapped new fire into her scorched behind.

"And no backtalk!"

"Yee-yes, sir! OK!"

He let her go and she hid her face in the quilt while he rolled the condom over his stiffness, then filled his palm with lubricant and coated the shaft.

"Spread your legs."

"You . . . you don't gotta talk to me like. . . ."

"Now, girl!" His hand crashed into her bottom and she wailed as she wriggled her knees apart. "That's better. Bend your back . . . down . . . down." He pressed her spine with his fingertips and her buttocks gaped. "I'm gonna screw you in the ass, so keep it open."

"God, Greg!"

The harsh, nasty words frightened even as they thrilled, and awakened dark, eerie moths that swarmed from her tummy into her breasts and throat. She squealed when, without warning, a slippery finger pressed her anus and slid inside. It thrust, retreated, twisted, thrust again, and ghastly, delightful sparks shot through thin membrane to ignite hot quivers deep in her vagina. Her fists clenched and her toes pounded the mattress while hard nipples mashed the duvet.

He pulled his finger from her tightness and took quick, shallow breaths as he moved around to kneel between her calves. Cold sweat dampened his forehead and he swiped it before he grasped his member and guided the fat tip to her puckered entry. Adrenaline rushes tingled his scalp and his hips quivered when he leaned forward to plunge his penis into her fiery grip. The head popped like an egg through a bottleneck and her guttural scream covered his moan of pure ecstasy.

"Put your hands behind your back!"

"Whuh-what?"

"Give me your hands, Lisa . . . now!"

"Greg?"

Her pitiful whine tugged at his heart even as a terrible thrill lanced up his chest. He reached down and grabbed the trembling wrists that inched toward him, crossed them in the middle of her

back and lifted her upper body parallel with the mattress. His hardness slipped farther in as she rose, and he pushed all the way inside her throbbing channel. He held her wrists tight with his left hand and wrapped his right forearm under her belly, then drew halfway out of her depths. She screeched when he lunged, and electric fire bathed his organ. His pelvis rubbed scarlet, steamy cheeks as he moved back, forth, back again, slowly at first, then quicker and harder as waves of ecstasy crashed behind his closed eyelids.

Harsh, glorious sting inflamed her tender hole as the hard shaft filled her to bursting. She wanted to yell at him to stop, but his savagery stunned her to silence. His strong arms held her in check while he moved her at his whim, used her to sate his passion. Her neck bowed and her hair swept the quilt as he pounded her bottom to drive her higher and higher, closer and closer to the brink. Desperate, delirious screams burned her throat while the scalding piston stroked in and out of her oily sleeve. Pain raged, spread, enveloped her body and soul like a hot glove and she gave in to its rapturous embrace. The strokes quickened, shortened, the hardness swelled, burst and sent her soaring off the brink into shuddery clouds of frenzied bliss.

He jerked his hips and yelled at the ceiling while spasms rocked his body. Her boiling sheath held him in an iron grip as semen gushed in long, delicious spurts. She jerked and shrieked out her orgasm, then dropped when he released her. He fell on her sweaty back and covered her neck with soft, panicky kisses. Long minutes later he opened his eyes.

"Lisa?" His voice crackled and he cleared his throat. "Honey? Are you OK?"

She groaned and stretched her arms out to the sides while she squeezed his diminished manhood with her bottom. "No." An aftershock flicked through her and she twitched. "You . . . you ravished me to death . . . so you might as well just bury me."

"OK." He smiled and rubbed her shoulder. "Can I have a kiss first?"

"Ha! Like you deserve one!" She grimaced as she turned her head.

Their lips met and he took her with him as he rolled onto his side. She whimpered when his penis slipped from her bottom, and then twisted around to continue the kiss. Damp arms and

legs wrapped and twined, until finally he moaned and came up for air.

"You don't feel dead."

"That's all you know! What did you do to me?"

He shrugged and kissed her. "Blistered your naughty bottom and then had my way with it."

"I guess . . . how come you're so mean tonight?"

"Not mean . . . strict . . . and you need strict, young lady."

"Nuh uh . . . you tore my heinie all up!"

"You didn't like it?"

She licked her lips and cuddled closer to him. "I didn't say that."

"So you do like it rough."

"Well . . . maybe . . . sometimes. I like it just fine when you're gentle with me . . . and it's not like I had a choice, either, you . . . you beast!"

"But I'm your beast." He hugged her hard and thrust his tongue into her mouth.

She gasped when the kiss ended. "God, Greg! What is with you?"

"Just making sure you don't have to go anyplace else to get your bottom ravished."

"Nope . . . you're the only bottom ravisher I want . . . but you could warn me next time."

"No way . . . that'd take all the fun out of it."

"Fun? You are sick and twisted and. . . ."

"And . . .?" He raised his arm and she glanced at the open hand that hovered over her sore cheeks.

"And I love you?"

"I love you, too. Now go get me a beer."

"Beast!"

She squealed and rolled off the bed as his hand bounced on painful flesh, then grabbed his bathrobe and stuck her tongue out at him as she trotted to the refrigerator.

CHAPTER 9
VICTIM'S CHOICE

WEDNESDAY AFTERNOON, THREE days before Christmas, atten-
dance at Red Blossom College fell sharply. Four students left
town for the holidays and the two who remained were annoyed
that the professor held class at all. Lisa's mind wandered and
Teresa struggled to keep her yawns in check while they wrote,
rewrote and re-rewrote essay topic sentences from a list of sub-
jects he gave them. Dylan peered over Lisa's shoulder and
pointed at her paper.

"You didn't change anything from *here* to *here*."

"I *meant* to . . . I was gonna say *most* likely, instead of *more*
likely but I guess I. . . ."

He scowled when a fist pounded the front door. "Who in the
world would . . . ?"

The door banged open, then slammed shut and boot heels shook
the hallway floor. Kate Hargrove stomped into the classroom,
stopped a foot from Dylan and glared.

"Who the *fuck* do you think you are?"

His mouth hung open for a second. "What's *wrong*, Kate? Are
you all right?"

"*No* I'm not all right! Why did you beat the shit out of Brandi?"

"*What?* I *never* . . . did somebody . . . ?" He put a hand on her
arm but she shook it off.

"Cut the *crap,* Travis! It wasn't *somebody* . . . it was *you!* What'd you *do* . . . get drunk and crazy or *what?*"

She took a pace back, her fingers loose around the nightstick handle at her belt. His lips compressed to a thin line and he jammed his fists on his hips.

"*Well?* Are you going to use that? Or do you want to talk . . . like *civilized* people?"

"Don't be so fucking *smug,* you prick!"

Lisa and Teresa exchanged astonished glances and then stared at the policewoman. Her eyes flickered towards them and she let go of the truncheon. Dylan took a deep breath and covered his mouth as he coughed.

"Girls, Kate and I need to have a chat so why don't you pack up and go home?"

They nodded and trembled while they stuffed books and papers into satchels. He pointed a hand toward the hallway and Kate muttered but preceded him to the study. The latch clicked when he shut the door behind them. She stood five-ten, almost as tall as Dylan. Her uniform trousers fit snug around long legs and high, round buttocks; her brown hair was cut short, and blue-green eyes glimmered beside a thin, upturned nose; her smooth, even features were spoiled by an angry scowl. She folded her arms, glared, and waited. He turned to face her and cleared his throat.

"The officer usually asks the questions in these situations . . . so go ahead."

"Tell me you didn't whip her butt raw last night."

"All right . . . I didn't . . . but that wasn't actually a question."

"Don't *start* that shit, you self-righteous. . . ."

He took two steps and she backed away from the finger he waved at her nose. "Kathryn Louise Hargrove, settle down right *now* and tell me what's going on! And *without* the hardboiled cop language, understand?"

"*Dammit,* Dylan, I don't have to take that kinda . . .!" She coughed and turned toward the window. "OK! Just . . . gimme a minute."

"I'll uh . . . get some water from the fridge."

"I don't want any."

"Well I do. I'll be right back."

Teresa and Lisa stood by the kitchen sink when he walked in.

"Is she *OK*, Uncle Dylan?"

"What's *with* her, Professor?"

"I don't know, exactly . . . something happened to her sister." He opened the refrigerator and took out two plastic water bottles. "You girls really *should* go home."

"But . . . but what if she *attacks* you?"

"She won't, sweetie . . . or she would have by now. I'll be all right."

"Are you *sure*, Professor? I mean, *geeze!* You can't even call the cops 'cause she *is* one."

"Which means she's trained to handle stress in emergencies . . . except perhaps when it strikes this close to home. She'll calm down and I'll get to the bottom of it."

Lisa snickered. "If I yelled the F word like *she* did, you would of got to *my* bottom pretty quick."

He smiled. "Very *quickly*, Lisa . . . but *you* aren't carrying a pistol. Now go home."

"OK."

"Yes, sir."

The girls hoisted their satchels and picked up their coats as he went back to the study and shut the door. Teresa sighed.

"I . . . I think I will use the restroom before I leave."

"Yeah? Maybe I will too." Lisa winked.

"He will be angry if we stay after he told us to go."

"Uh huh . . . you wanna hang out in the bedroom or the class-room?"

"The bedroom . . . it is closer to the front door if we must leave fast."

"Good thinking. So this Brandi is Kate's sister?"

"Yes . . . her younger sister . . . she is in his class at university and. . . ."

* * *

Kate stood by the window, just where he left her. Dylan opened a water bottle and she nodded as she took it.

"Brandi showed up at the house about two this morning and Vick let her in. She was loaded and pretty out of it so he just told her to go to bed."

– 223 –

"Where were you?"

"Asleep. I didn't hear the doorbell, so I didn't know about it until I woke him up to tell him I was leaving for roll call. We worked four fender benders this morning and then I took some personal time." Kate sipped water and went to sit on the sofa. Dylan pulled the desk chair around and sat. "She was still in bed when I got home about twelve-thirty and I was pretty pissed by the time I got her awake enough to talk to me."

"And she told you I *beat* her?"

"Well . . . she mumbled *Travis* a couple of times while she was still groggy, but she clammed up after that." She sighed and shook her head. "I kept asking her what happened and she got a little hysterical, so I put her on my lap and she just *screamed. That's* when I found out how messed up her butt was."

"And you assumed I did it?"

"Well she said your *name* . . . and she *told* me you were tutoring her and . . . and I couldn't get her to *talk* to me so. . . ." Tears filled her eyes and she slammed the water bottle on the coffee table.

"All right, all right, I um . . . so you're not on duty?"

"Huh? No . . . why?"

"I'd like a whisky and I'd rather not drink alone."

"Yeah, OK."

He took a key from the desk and opened the liquor cabinet. Amber malt sloshed into glasses as he poured. "I met with her *once.*" She took the glass he offered. "Day before yesterday at your mom's house . . . and *that* is the extent of my tutoring. But I have to admit . . . *confess,* I suppose . . . that I spanked her."

The woman glared at him. "What *with* . . . a bullwhip?"

"With my *hand* . . . on the seat of her jeans . . . because she was *determined* to make me do it and I knew she wouldn't settle down to work until I *did.*"

"My baby sister *goaded* you into spanking her . . . yeah *right.*"

His cheeks puffed as he blew a breath. "What did she *say* when she told you I was tutoring her?"

"Huh?"

"How did she *put* it? Did the way she *said* it make you angry?"

"I don't know, she . . . yeah, I guess . . . but she's got this . . . *little sister* voice she uses sometimes that just . . . she could tell me *the sky is blue* and piss me off."

"So you were already mad at *me* for tutoring her . . . because you knew I would treat *her* the same way I treated *you*."

"Ha!" She gulped the drink and shook her head. "You never smacked *my* butt with jeans on."

"You were already a hard-case when I got you so there was no reason to be subtle."

"I was *not*." Glass clicked her teeth when she drained the whisky and he reached for the bottle. "So . . . *what?* Brandi was *jealous* 'cause you spanked me?"

"Envious, yes . . . of the attention I paid you." He smiled and poured an inch of liquor into her glass.

"But she was just a little *girl*."

"Little, but precocious . . . like her big sister."

"Yeah, well . . . I remember a few times I had trouble sitting after you got done with me."

"For an hour or two, perhaps . . . that doesn't sound like the case here."

"Not hardly . . . OK, so *maybe* I jumped to conclusions. I guess I knew you couldn't of done that to her, but. . . ."

"But you were mad as hell and had to take it out on *somebody,* right?"

"*No* . . . I just . . . didn't know where else to go. Vick drove out to the cabin this morning and . . . and I don't wanna drag the *job* into my family shit . . . *stuff*."

He nodded. "And she wouldn't tell you *anything* about what happened?"

"Just kept saying how *sorry* she was she got loaded . . . and when I'd ask who did it, she'd start in again with the *I'm sorrys*."

"So she's covering for someone?"

"Must be."

"A boyfriend?"

She shook her head. "Hasn't *got* one . . . that I know of. She broke up with Tyler over the summer . . . and he's at school down in Florida so I don't think it's *him*."

"So where did you leave it with Brandi?"

"Just told her to sleep it off . . . and I'd be back."

"Then I suppose it's time for us to go talk to her."

"Whaddaya mean *us?*"

"Do you want to be good cop or bad cop?"

"I *want* to be concerned big sister,.if you don't mind."

"Hmm . . . *that* might work. I'll follow you home."

"OK." She finished the whisky and grimaced. "You got any mints?"

He held out the bowl and she popped three candies into her mouth, then he did the same, slipped on his long leather coat and opened the door. Metal snicked as he keyed the deadbolt home and they walked down the wet paving stones and through the gate.

Lisa peered out the bedroom door, then ran to the window and opened a slit in the blinds. The Blazer rolled backward down the driveway and into the street.

"Where do you s'pose he's going?"

Teresa huffed and put her jacket on. "If you were not so afraid we could have listened at the keyhole and *know* this."

"Yeah, well . . . Kate just got into that Honda and it looks like he's following her."

"Perhaps . . . so we can go home."

"Uh huh . . . who's afraid *now?*" She grinned and Teresa moaned. "Let's go after them, OK?"

"Are you *insane?* This is not our business and he will be *furious* if he sees us."

"But aren't you *dying* to know what's going on? I'll follow real far behind so he won't notice us, but we gotta *hurry*."

"I think you watch too much television."

"Let's go!"

Lisa ran out the front door and Teresa stopped to relock the deadbolt, then shut the gate behind her just as Lisa pulled the Rover to the curb and leaned over to throw open the passenger door.

"Come *on!*"

"But they are *already* too far ahead!"

"Maybe not." Lisa gunned the engine and Teresa struggled to fasten her safety harness as the truck veered left onto the boulevard. "That red Blazer sticks out like a sore thumb so I bet we can . . . *see?* That's it at the stoplight. We got him now!"

"And police films . . . I will bet you see every one that is *made*."

"Shut up and keep an eye on him."

Dylan pulled into the driveway at Kate's house and waited while the garage door rolled up. She parked in a space just large enough

for the Civic amid heaps of fishing and camping gear. He shut off the engine and followed her to the inside door.

"Any idea who's tailing us?"

"What? No!" He turned but she grabbed his arm and pulled him into the kitchen.

"Black Land Rover, late model . . . I think it was a woman at the wheel."

"Oh for crying out . . . Lisa . . . and Teresa, no doubt. I'll settle with *them* after we take care of Brandi."

Kate smirked and unbuckled her belt. "They're just looking out for you, Professor . . . probably think I lured you here to use a rubber hose on you."

"No telling *what* they think." He shrugged off his leather coat and hung it on a peg next to the door.

"Or *if.*" She dropped her hat and gun belt on the counter, pushed into the living room and stopped.

Brandi lay on the sofa beneath an afghan, her tousled blonde hair sprayed over a throw pillow. She pointed the remote at the TV to shut it off, and then grimaced as she sat up.

"Hi, Katey . . . I borrowed some sweats, OK?"

"Sure . . . look who's here."

The girl blinked and focused on Dylan as he rounded the couch and sat beside her.

"Kate tells me you had a bad night."

"Oh, *God.*" She moaned and fell sideways onto the pillow. "Why'd you have to bring *him?*"

"The suspect is allowed to confront his accuser. Let's have a look at the evidence."

"*What?* What are you *doing?*"

He pulled her legs up onto the sofa and tossed the afghan aside. She grunted, wriggled and grabbed the sweatpants' waistband with both hands as he pushed her shoulder to keep her on her tummy.

"It seems my name came up during the interview and. . . ."

"Huh? What are you *talking* about? I never said. . . ."

"Be *still,* Brandi! And let go of your pants so I can have a look."

"*Katey,* tell him to . . . *no!*"

She kicked and twisted as he wrestled her pants down. Blue and purple welts covered her bottom and thighs, and the crowns of the cheeks were crusty with dry, shallow abrasions. Dylan gritted his

teeth, gently snugged the fleece back into place and stood up. Brandi kicked again and scowled at him.

Kate sat on the sofa arm and grabbed the girl's hand. "Just *chill,* OK? Are you ready to tell me what the hell *happened?*"

"*Nothing.*"

The woman snorted and turned to Dylan. "Your turn."

Brandi glared as he sat on the coffee table and leaned toward her. "Let's start with what *didn't* happen, all right?"

"I don't gotta *talk* to you and you got no *right* pulling my pants down and. . . ."

"Hey! I told you to chill and you *do* gotta talk to him so just knock it off!"

"But *Katey,* he. . . ."

Dylan held up a hand. "That's enough! *Both* of you! Kate, could I get a cup of coffee, please?"

"Um, yeah . . . I'll have to make some so. . . ."

"Thanks . . . take your time."

"Oh . . . OK . . . sure."

The door swung as Kate went into the kitchen and Dylan smiled.

"I thought she'd *never* leave."

"Huh?"

"How do you feel? Is it still very painful?"

"Um . . . not that much. Sorta aches but not as bad as. . . ." She cleared her throat and looked away from him.

"Did you know your sister was a total *brat* a little while ago?"

"Ha! *That* doesn't surprise me."

"Stormed into my classroom . . . shouting expletives . . . accusing me of the foulest deeds imaginable . . . right in front of my students!"

She squirmed and grimaced as she shifted to lean against the sofa arm. "Yeah? So . . . what did you do?"

"What *could* I do? I pulled out my trusty Taser, shocked her senseless and went on with the lesson. Perked up my students no end, let me tell you!" He grinned and patted her hand.

Her lips trembled as she suppressed a smile. "You *did* not. She'd *never* let you get close enough to use a Taser on her."

"No . . . probably not . . . even if I *owned* such a device. But she *did* accuse me of beating you last night."

"That's *bullshit!* I didn't even *see*. . . ."

"Brandi! Being hurt is no excuse for bad language."

"Well *geeze,* Professor! I mean . . . didn't you *tell* her you didn't do it?"

"Yes . . . when she calmed down enough to *listen.* I hoped that's what *you* were waiting for . . . someone calm enough to hear what you have to say without throwing a fit."

She chewed a pinky finger and stared at his knees. "Well . . . kinda. I really fu . . . *messed* up last night."

"I see. So you think it's *your* fault you were brutally beaten?"

"Yeah . . . sorta."

"I thought you were smarter than that."

"Whadaya mean? I *told* the guy to. . . ." She turned away and cupped a hand over her eyes.

"Brandi . . . blaming the victim is way out of style. A mistake in judgment shouldn't cost you the injuries you've suffered. Can you tell me what kind of drugs you took?"

"I . . . I *didn't!*" A tear rolled down her cheek as she looked at him. "I only had a . . . a few beers . . . and a couple shots of tequila."

"Who was with you?"

"Uh . . . some people."

"*Please,* Brandi. Were you at a party?" She nodded. "You *knew* these people?"

"Some of them . . . most of them, I guess. It was a bunch from high school . . . home on break."

"Any old boyfriends?"

"Um . . . yeah . . . kinda."

He looked up when Kate peeked around the kitchen door and he waved her in. She handed him a steamy mug and then sat in an armchair behind him. He sipped coffee and watched Brandi over the cup's rim.

"Was Tyler there?"

"*Tyler?*" The girl scowled at her sister. "That is *so* over with."

Kate folded her arms, and Dylan nodded as he set down the mug.

"But you saw *someone* there . . . someone you thought you could trust, and you started talking . . . and the more you drank the easier it got to talk about things . . . hopes . . . dreams . . . what you wanted, what you needed. . . ."

– 229 –

Brandi swallowed and nodded. "Travis."

He glanced over his shoulder when Kate gasped.

"Travis *Hunter?*" The woman leaned her elbows on her knees and shook her head. "I thought he'd be in jail by now."

"Katey! You *always* hated him but he's not *really* that . . . that. . . ."

Sobs jerked Brandi's shoulders and Dylan slid onto the sofa to take her in his arms. He smoothed her hair while she wept.

Kate got up to pace in front of the television. "They um . . . they were more *buddies* than boyfriend and girlfriend . . . but he got her in *so* much trouble in junior high. Cigarettes, skipping class . . . he took her joy riding in his dad's pickup before the kid even got his learner's permit, and the State Patrol pulled them over. I thought Mom was gonna stroke out when a couple of troopers brought her home."

Dylan nodded and lifted Brandi's chin. "He was still your friend last night, wasn't he?" She turned away but he held her closer. "Maybe his eyes were a little harder . . . maybe he was more sarcastic than he used to be . . . rougher around the edges . . . but still your buddy . . . still made you comfortable . . . and you felt like you could tell him *anything*."

"Yeah." Her whisper was almost lost in his chest.

"And he got a big kick out of it when you told him you had a professor who spanked you . . . but you wished he'd done a better job of it." More sobs wracked her bosom as she nodded. "What did he hit you with, Brandi?"

"Oh *God!*" She sniffled and sat up, wiped her eyes with a sleeve and stared at him. "His belt and . . . a curtain rod . . . and a rope . . . and his asshole *friend* held me duh-*down* while he . . . he. . . ."

"Shh . . . it's OK now. Come on."

He pressed her face to his shoulder while she wept, then he crooked a finger and Kate swiped her eyes as she walked over to sit next to her sister. Slowly and gently he turned the girl toward Kate's open arms. When the transfer was complete he puffed a breath, stood, and went to find the bathroom. He rummaged in the medicine cabinet for first-aid cream and then picked up a box of tissue, a handful of cotton swabs and a bottle of aloe lotion. His head jerked at the sound of shrill voices and he hurried back to the living room.

"I *knew* you'd pull that cop shit!" Brandi sat, arms folded, face

twisted in a thunderous scowl, at the opposite end of the sofa from Kate. "That's why I didn't wanna *tell* you!"

"All right, all right . . . settle down." He dropped the supplies on the end table and sat between the sisters. "Kate's not going to shoot *anybody* . . . and Brandi, *you're* going to quit screaming at Kate. Understand?" They huffed and looked away from him. "Kate, go change clothes . . . you need to get out of *authority* mode for a while."

She sneered. "Yeah, you'd know all about *that,* wouldn't you?"

"Don't get snide with *me!* You needed my help and you got it. Now go do what I told you."

"Jesus fucking *Christ!*"

He grabbed her arm, yanked her up as he stood, and then swatted her bottom. "One more F word and I will blister you *purple,* do you understand me? Go!"

She opened her mouth, then shut it, snorted and stomped down the hallway. Brandi sat, knees at her chin, and stared at him. He smiled and leaned over to pluck tissues from the box.

"Here . . . dry your eyes and blow your nose, and then I'll tend your wounds." He loosened his tie and slipped off his jacket while Brandi continued to stare. "What? I'm not going to blister anyone purple . . . that's professor code for 'I've had all I can take from you right now.'"

"I . . . I know, but. . . ." She blew three long blasts into the tissue and then shook her head. "She coulda broken your *arm* when you grabbed her."

"Probably . . . but I think she wanted an excuse to leave for a few minutes . . . collect her thoughts. Why don't you stretch out on your tummy?" He sat on the sofa edge and she wriggled into place. "Will you pull your pants down for me?"

"Um . . . it's OK. You can."

"All right."

His fingers stretched the elastic and he lifted the material clear of the bruises as he bared her to the knees. She watched his eyes and chewed a fingertip while he opened the ointment tube and dabbed antiseptic cream onto cotton swabs.

"Take your finger out of your mouth. Do you want a bullet to bite on while I do this?"

"No . . . unless you got one handy."

"I must have left them with the Taser." He winked. "But try not to clench your teeth."

She nodded, opened her mouth and panted while he spread ointment on the abrasions. The sting passed quickly and she sighed. He coated another batch of swabs and stroked on a second layer.

"I . . . I used to think he was so nice . . . was he *always* a jerk and I just didn't *notice?*"

"Travis? Possibly . . . but some people get worse with age, just as some improve. It sounds like he was a jerk-in-training even in junior high." He smiled and leaned down to kiss her forehead. "Let's not worry about him right now. I'll put the afghan on you and let the antiseptic soak in for a few minutes while I step outside."

"Huh? Where you going?"

"I have to deal with a couple of busybodies who followed me here."

"You're kidding!"

"I'm afraid not . . . just relax. I won't be long."

He snugged the knitted blanket over her back and went out the front door. The winter sun cast long, cold shadows and he thrust both hands into pants pockets. Michael's SUV sat on the other side of the narrow lane. He stepped over the snow bank at the end of the front walk and onto the pavement. Lisa and Teresa sat up when he rapped the driver's side door with his fist.

"*What* are you doing here, girls?"

Lisa turned the key and thumbed down the window. "Um . . . hi, Professor. Are you OK?"

"I'm fine . . . now answer the question."

"I *told* you he would be angry," Teresa muttered.

"But we just . . . we thought you might need *help*, that's all!"

"I appreciate your concern, but you disobeyed me and that does *not* make me happy. Teresa, do you have your key to my apartment?"

"I think so." She leaned into the back seat and opened a pocket in her satchel. "Yes . . . I have it."

"Good . . . go there and wait for me . . . *both* of you."

"But Professor, I. . . ."

"No *buts*, Lisa! I don't know *what* you two were playing at, and you may explain it to me later . . . *after* I punish you for pulling this ridiculous stunt."

"Uncle Dylan, *no!* How can you puh-punish us for merely being concerned with your welfare?"

"I believe you were *more* concerned with driving around on some silly adventure . . . and if it's *adventure* you want, just wait until I get home!"

"But I . . . I'm supposed to meet Greg for dinner and. . . ."

"Then you will have to postpone your date. Now go before I *do* get angry."

He slapped the truck's roof and backed away. Lisa scowled and switched on the engine. Tires scritched wet asphalt and Dylan turned toward the house. Lisa growled and glanced to her right.

"Sorry, Teresa."

The girl sighed and shut her eyes. "Yes . . . and now we shall *never* know what went on there."

"Sure we will . . . all we gotta do is look real pitiful after he spanks us and he'll tell us the whole story."

"He might have told us *without* this spanking, you know."

"Maybe . . . but this way we'll be sure."

"I think you are too curious for your own good."

"Yeah, I've heard that . . . but *you* wouldn't let me peek through the window."

"Of a *police officer's* house? I did not wish you to be *shot!*"

Lisa chuckled. "See? Nobody *dies* from getting spanked."

"No . . . one merely *wishes* they could. You *know* how embarrassing he can be."

"We could always drive to Mexico. He'd *never* find us there!"

Teresa gaped, then smiled and shook her head. "I have had *enough* adventure for one day, thank you. Perhaps there is some of the good sherry in his bar."

"*Now* you're talking!"

Lisa looked left at a stop sign, then turned right and sped along Main Street toward Dylan's apartment.

He scuffed damp grit from his shoes on the mat and opened the front door. Brandi looked up when he sat beside her and pulled down the afghan.

"Feeling better?"

"A little. Are you gonna put that aloe stuff on me?"

"Yes. Where's Kate?"

"In her bedroom, I guess. She didn't come in here."

Thick green gel dribbled into his palm as he squeezed the bottle, and he cupped his hands to warm it.

"Um . . . this isn't easy to ask, Brandi . . . but I have to."

"What? Mmm . . . that feels wonderful!"

She raised her hips while he smoothed relief over her bottom and thighs.

"Did he do anything *else* to you?"

"Hmm?" She opened her eyes and then opened them wider. "*No . . . he . . . you mean like . . . ?*"

"Like sex. He didn't . . . *use* you . . . in that way . . . did he?"

Her hair flew about her head as she shook it. "He . . . he *touched* me . . . there . . . kinda by accident . . . but I . . . I don't think he was interested in *that*."

"Not his *friend*, either?"

"No . . . it was like they just wanted to *hurt* me."

"This happened right at the party?"

"Um . . . there was a . . . a camping trailer in back of the house and . . . and he took me out there . . . said he wanted to spank me in private but then . . . then the other guy . . . Max . . . he came in and I got up off his lap . . . but he pushed me on the table and held me while . . . while Max looked around for stuff . . . to hit me with and . . . the more I screamed, the more they *laughed*."

Hot tears ran down her cheeks and Dylan wiped them with a tissue.

"Do you know where they are now? Where Travis is?"

"You . . . you're not going *after* him, are you? I already told *Katey* not to . . . to. . . ."

"No . . . I'm not the masked avenger . . . and no one is going to take control of this issue away from you. I just want to know if he's still around so I can warn my other girls."

"Um . . . OK. He's staying at his dad's house . . . he's on leave . . . from the Navy . . . and he's going back to his ship right after Christmas. That's what he *told* me, anyway." She sniffled and looked at him. "You said um . . . *other* girls. Does that mean . . . *I'm* one of your girls now?"

He smiled, drew the afghan over her and kissed her cheek. "Of *course* you are . . . and you enjoy the dubious distinction of having the sorest looking behind of any girl I've ever tended to."

"Yeah? Maybe you should take a picture so they can see what getting blistered purple *really* means."

"I think *not* . . . like all good hyperbole the phrase must never be defined, let *alone* depicted. Otherwise it will lose its magic aura."

She giggled. "Sure . . . if you say so."

"Why don't you rest while I check on Kate?"

"OK. Um . . . Professor?"

"Hmm?"

"Thanks for taking care of me and . . . can I have another kiss?"

"*May* I . . .?"

"May I have one?"

He leaned toward her cheek and she turned her head quickly and kissed his lips. She grinned at his mock frown and hid her face.

"*Rest*, young lady."

"Yes, sir," she said to the pillow.

The door to Kate's bedroom stood ajar and it swung open a few inches when he tapped with a knuckle. The shades were drawn but he could see her in the gloom, naked and curled like a fetus atop the counterpane.

"Sorry. Didn't know you were. . . ."

"Is she OK?"

"Sure. I'll just go back and. . . ."

"No . . . come in . . . please?"

He nodded, shut the door and sat on the bedside. She twined her arms around his thigh and rested her head on his knee. He sighed as he rubbed her back.

"Aren't you freezing? Why don't I pull down the covers?"

"Always taking care of people, huh, Professor?"

"When they let me . . . that's my job."

"Yeah . . . mine too . . . *serve and protect*. Ha!" She sobbed and he reached over to tug Kleenex from a box on the nightstand. "I . . . I can't even protect my own *sister* from assholes like Travis!"

"Kate . . . you of all people should know you can't protect her from *everything*. She's bound to make mistakes . . . and all you can do is help her learn from them."

"Like you did me?"

"I hope so. You *were* a handful at her age, but you turned out all right."

She sat up and blew her nose. "Yeah, well . . . I guess I don't have your *touch* with that stuff."

"Possibly . . . but I didn't *get* that touch overnight. When is Vick coming home?"

"Not until Friday . . . why? Scared he's gonna walk in and find you in bed with his naked girlfriend?"

He smiled and shook his head. "I'm *more* afraid you're going to beat yourself up over this until he gets around to spanking some *sense* into you."

"*God,* Dylan!" She threw her arms around his neck and wept. "He . . . he doesn't have your touch *either.*"

"Oh . . . um . . . I thought you told me he . . . took care of that for you."

"He *tries* but . . . with him it's more . . . *foreplay* . . . he hardly ever *really* punishes me!"

"I see. Did you *talk* to him about it?"

"*Dylan!* I can't just say . . . hey, Vick! Why don't you whack my ass until I scream 'cause I've been a bad girl? *Ow!*" She pouted and rubbed a hot handprint on her bare cheek. "What was *that* for?"

"You *know* better than to refer to your bottom as a head of livestock."

"You mean *ass? Ouch!* Quit it!"

"Then stop *saying* that in my presence."

"Don't you watch *television,* for Christ's sake? They say it all the *time!*"

"Which is one more reason for you *not* to. The language is degraded enough without people relying on the vast wasteland as a role model."

"Yeah, well I'd sound like a *girl* if I told Sarge I had to kick a perp's *bottom* 'cause he wouldn't submit."

"I didn't say you couldn't use it at work . . . but you aren't *at* work. Now . . . why *can't* you tell Vick you need a good hiding? Are you afraid of sounding like a girl to *him?*"

She took a deep breath and let it out. "He *used* to give me a hard lickin' every time I looked cross-eyed at him . . . but that was before we moved in together."

"Then perhaps you should *remind* him, in a non-judgmental way, of how much you appreciated his strictness in the past and would appreciate it even *more* in the future."

"Ya think?" He nodded and she frowned. "And I gotta do all that

before . . . um . . . before I get my uh . . . *tushy* whacked for not keeping better tabs on my sister?"

"Hmm . . . two days *is* a long time to carry such a burden of guilt, I suppose."

"You're damn *right* it . . . Dylan!"

He yanked her across his lap and swatted her cheeks hard. "I *told* you about the language, young lady!"

She yelped and reached back to cover her bottom when he slapped again, but he grabbed her wrist and twisted it up and onto her back. He rained quick, noisy smacks on her toned and trained behind while she kicked and wriggled, then pushed her head toward the floor to raise her bottom, and clapped as hard as he could at the base of her cheeks. She grunted and squirmed, and swiped hot, shameful tears from her face with her free hand. When his palm went numb he let go of her wrist and winced as he gave her a final sharp swat that spanned the cleft.

"Stand *up*, Kathryn. Now!"

"Owee! *Jesus*, Dylan, that really. . . ."

"*Hush*, girl! Go stand in the corner."

"No . . . I'm *not* one of your little. . . ."

"Don't tell me no!" He grabbed her arm and she stumbled as he dragged her to the wall next to the closet. "And don't you *dare* tell me you aren't one of my girls because you most certainly *are* . . . always were and always *will* be, as long as I have strength enough to lift a paddle! So just stand right there while I find something appropriate to use on a naughty *big* girl's heinie!"

"*Dylan!*"

The whine scratched her throat as the horrible, childish scolding burned her ears. She stamped her foot and rubbed her bottom with both hands. The hot flesh warmed her palms, just as his stern, sweet reminder warmed her heart. He stepped out of the closet and scowled.

"Kathryn! Put your hands on top of your head! You *know* better than to rub your behind when you're in the corner! What were you *thinking?*"

"Dylan . . . *Professor*, I . . . I'm *sorry!*"

"Turn around!"

Her feet shuffled and she sniffed back a tear as she faced him. He held something in his right hand and she blinked to focus. His

-- 237 --

lips curved in a tight smile as he held it up so she could see in the dimness. She gasped, crossed her arms over her breasts and backed into the corner.

"No *please?* That . . . that's *nasty!*"

"I imagine it will *sting* nastily. Go and kneel on the bed with your bottom well up."

"But I don't wanna . . . ow!"

He pinched her earlobe between thumb and forefinger, and she grabbed his wrist.

"Let *go,* Kathryn!"

"OK, OK . . . I *will* . . . just don't *do* that, please?"

She huffed and ran to jump on the bed when he released her ear. Hot blush burned her face and neck as she got up on all fours, her eyes focused on Vick's size-ten leather house shoe in Dylan's hand. It had a stiff but flexible rubber sole with tiny, raised traction dots, and her bottom clenched in anticipation of its awful burn.

"Head right *down,* young lady!"

"Oh *God!*"

Fat, hard nipples grazed the satin counterpane when she leaned forward and hid her eyes in her hands. Her cleft yawned and the hard, prickly rubber sole clapped tingly flesh. Bright white shock flowed along her spine and she panted long ragged breaths. The slipper smacked again and she curled her toes as she puffed away the pain.

Dylan rested a palm in the middle of her back and popped her quivery bottom, left cheek, right, then left again, over and over to drive out her guilty, remorseful demons. Twenty, thirty, forty sharp, measured pops echoed against the ceiling while he waited for the breakthrough sign, the signal she was ready to tear down her wall and let him in. Fifty, sixty, seventy, and he concentrated on the tender skin at the base of her bottom, all too aware of the long years of police work that had passed since he last chipped through the thick masonry of her innate stubbornness. Her pale skin darkened beneath the relentless slipper but she kept still while she uttered hoarse grunts.

Then, a kitten's wail, high and tremulous, burst from her throat and he smiled. The wail became a shriek, then a sobbing scream, and he stopped spanking but held the slipper tight across her cleft.

"You were a very silly girl to think Brandi's problems are *your* fault, Kate!" He lifted the shoe a few inches and swatted.

"*Ow* I know!"

"You will *not* blame yourself for this!" The sole stung again and she yelped.

"*OKaaay*, just *stop!*"

"When I think you have *learned! Your! Lesson!*"

"Ow! *Ow! Owee! Please!* No *more!*"

"Don't *tell* me how to punish your naughty *bottom,* young lady!"

"Hah! Haiee! I'm *sorry!*"

He leaned a knee on the bed, wrapped her waist with his left arm and peppered her red flesh with a dozen short, quick smacks.

"Are you sorry you were so *presumptuous* as to think your badge was a magic shield to protect her from *everything?*"

"Yuh . . . *yes!*" She squealed, kicked and finally reached a hand back to cover herself but he swatted it away.

"Don't you *dare, Kathryn!*" He pulled her closer and tighter, and turned his wrist to flick the sole lengthwise along her cleft.

"Dy! Lan! Not! Like! That! Aheee!"

"And you had *better* be sorry you tried to take away the little control she had left by offering to *shoot* that jerk!"

"Yah! Yee! *Yes!* I'm *sorreeee!*"

He slung the shoe across the room and gathered her in his arms. She sobbed and moaned as he turned and sat on the bedside to cradle her on his lap. Tight, hot buns heated his thighs while tears drenched his neck.

"Shh . . . it's OK now . . . it's all over and you're my good girl. Go ahead and cry."

"Guh-*God,* Dylan, you . . . you're just *mean!*"

"Of *course* I am." She looked up and he kissed her lips. "As mean as I *have* to be . . . and I'm surprised you forgot that already."

"I . . . I didn't *forget* . . . and what am I supposed to tell Vick when he sees the bruises on my a . . . *fanny?*" She wiped her nose and leaned on his shoulder.

Dylan hugged her and smiled. "With your iron butt? There won't be a mark on it by morning. But you might want to tell him anyway . . . could be a good lead-in to a conversation about discipline."

"Yeah maybe . . . I'll have to think about. . . ."

She gasped and turned toward the door when the latch clicked. It opened and Brandi held up a bottle.

"Anybody need the lotion?"

Kate squealed but Dylan shushed and held her tight. "Come in, Brandi . . . and close the door. That light is blinding."

"*Dylan!*"

"Hush! Your sister was very thoughtful and you should at least *act* appreciative."

"*God!*" Kate glared at Brandi. "Were you at the door the whole *time?*"

He crooked a finger and the girl sat beside them.

"No . . . I could hear pretty well from the living room . . . but when you started yelling I figured you could use this. Does he *always* spank you naked?"

"That's none of your *business!*"

"Kate!" He frowned and shook his head. "Not usually . . . actually, *never* that I can recall. But this *is* an unusual situation so I made an exception. Now why don't you both lie on the bed and I'll take care of you, hmm?"

"But I don't *want* lotion with *her* in the . . .!"

"Kathryn! Do you *want* me to use the slipper again?"

"No!"

"Then stop being so stubborn and lie down."

"*God,* Dylan!"

"Hush and do what I told you. You two can talk while I see to your injuries."

Brandi grinned, pushed her sweatpants off and climbed onto the bed. Kate huffed, glared at him for a second, then wriggled quickly off his lap when he squeezed a sore cheek. She lay beside her sister and tugged a pillow beneath her head. Brandi propped her chin in a palm and looked at her.

"Are you all right, Katey? How come he spanked you?"

"That's none of your. . . ."

"Kate! I said *talk* to her." He spread a bathrobe over her back and tucked it around her arms.

"*OK.*" She growled an expletive under her breath and then reached out to take Brandi's hand. "I um . . . I asked for it."

"But what did you *do?*"

"No . . . I mean literally . . . I asked him to . . . to punish me."

"But *why?* 'cause of *me?*"

"Sort of."

Dylan reached for the table lamp. "Close your eyes, Kate." She squinted when he switched it on and then took the Kleenex he plucked from the box and wiped her eyes. "Now pay no attention to the man behind the curtain. It's only the highly skilled but silent caregiver."

Kate nodded and blinked at Brandi. "Um . . . can I ask one thing?"

"Yeah . . . sure."

"How did you *get* here?" She shut her eyes and bit her lip when he spread lotion over her soreness.

"They uh . . . Travis called a cab . . . after they . . . got done with me."

"But . . . why didn't you go *home?*"

"I just . . . I didn't want to deal with Mom."

"You *called* her didn't you?"

"Sure . . . well . . . I asked Vick to . . . when he came in to tell me he was taking off. So anyway . . . I went to this party. . . ."

Kate bit her lip and listened while Dylan massaged and Brandi told her the details of the ordeal. He filled his palm with lotion again and again to coat the hot, red rash he had spanked into Kate's bottom, and to re-anoint the blue and green bruises on Brandi's. The two held hands and Kate sniffled but kept quiet while her sister talked. When the lotion bottle was empty he wiped his hands on a tissue and stood.

"I have to go . . . but you girls should keep talking."

They rolled off the bed and hugged him.

"Don't you want to stay for supper?"

"Not this time, Kate. I've got two little brats waiting at my apartment so I should run."

"Professor?"

"Hmm?"

"Can . . . can I do what Kate did?"

"What's that?"

"Just . . . *ask* for a spanking and get it?"

He laughed and kissed her forehead. "Maybe . . . *if* I think you need it. But I hope you're not in any great hurry."

"I'm not." She grinned. "But I bet I get over this pretty quick."

"*Quickly,* Brandi . . . and I'll bet you do, too. Don't forget to send me your class schedule for next semester, all right?"

"I won't." She hugged him and kissed his lips.

Kate shrugged into the robe and Brandi pulled on her pants. They walked him to the door, wished him merry Christmas and waved as he walked to the truck. He shivered while he started the Blazer and then headed for home. An image of Brandi's abused flesh glared in his mind and he shook his head, squinted, and smiled at the memory of her soft lips on his and the bright sparkle in her eyes when she kissed him.

CHAPTER 10
THE HEATING ELEMENT

TERESA GRUMBLED AND stared at the white tile floor in Dylan's guest bath. She knelt with her palms on the bathmat, her legs inside the tub and her tummy on its cold enamel rim. Lisa's hip rested next to hers only a few inches away. The girl looked at Teresa and sighed.

"Sorry . . . I didn't think he'd get *this* wigged out just 'cause we followed him."

"I *told* you he would embarrass us."

"I know I *know* . . . but I can't believe he made us get naked right in the *living* room."

A hot tear dripped from Teresa's eye and she swiped it away. "And with the curtains *open!*"

Lisa shrugged. "We're on the sixth floor . . . who's gonna see?"

"But I felt like everyone in the *world* was watching me take off my clothes!"

"Yeah, well . . . it's what he's gonna do *next* that worries *me.*"

"You *should* worry! It was very bad of you to take me on this wild bird chase after he told us to go home."

"Wild *goose* chase . . . and I *said* I was *sorry.*" She covered Teresa's hand with her own and squeezed. "So he never did this . . . this *bathtub* thing to you before?"

"Of *course* not!"

"I've heard of people getting *enemas* in the tub. You don't suppose he'll. . . ."

The latch clicked and the girls looked up as Dylan shut the door behind him. He wore sweatpants with court shoes and a faded, oversized Dodgers tee shirt. A white, hard plastic spatula swung from his fingers and the girls cringed.

"Do you need to use the toilet before I begin?"

They glanced at each other and grimaced, then Lisa turned to him.

"Yes, sir . . . if that's OK."

"Certainly . . . Teresa? Don't you need to go? Lisa didn't drink that entire bottle of Amontillado by herself."

Teresa squirmed as Lisa stood up, then she nodded her head. "Yes . . . sir. Are you . . . going to spank us with *that?*"

"Hmm?" He held the light utensil in the middle and it blurred like a propeller when he wriggled it between his thumb and two fingers. "I believe it will be effective . . . yes."

Lisa covered herself as best she could with her arms and hands, looked up at him and cleared her throat. "Excuse me . . . sir."

He put a hand on the doorknob when she reached for it. "Where are you going?"

"To . . . the other bathroom. You *said* I could. . . ."

"This toilet works perfectly, so go right ahead."

"But *Professor!*"

"Or get back into the tub . . . it's up to you."

"*God* . . . how can you be so . . .?"

"Don't push me any *farther,* young lady! Sit down and do your business, or kneel in the tub . . . before I become impatient!"

Teresa stood and her head spun with sherry as she leaned against the wall. Lisa grimaced, sat on the toilet and covered her eyes with her palms. Water hissed into water, and Dylan crossed his arms as he stared at the wall. She got up and put a hand on the toggle.

"Didn't you *forget* something, Lisa?"

"*Geeze!* Don't make me . . . do *that* . . . whuh-while you're standing right *there!*"

"*Wipe* yourself, young lady . . . or I'll do it for you!"

A blush warmed her face and neck as she unrolled tissue, turned her back to him and patted her vulva. She felt his eyes on her bare bottom, and frightened, excited butterflies danced in her tummy as

she dried pink, sensitive lips. The warm blush turned hot and she threw the paper into the bowl, flushed and shuffled over to stand next to Teresa.

"Go on, sweetie."

"I . . . I do not need to."

"Very well . . . but I want you on the side closer to the drain, so if you have an accident while I'm spanking you the urine won't. . . ."

"Uncle *Dylan!* Have you not embarrassed me *enough?* How can you say such . . .?"

"Teresa, stop that this *instant.* If you're embarrassed it's no more than you deserve for embarrassing *me* with your outlandish stunt . . . not to mention having a *party* while I was away! Now *go.*"

She blew exasperated breaths as she stomped to the commode. The seat was still warm from Lisa's bottom but Teresa shivered while her water splashed. She wanted to look up, to see if he were watching, but instead she hid her eyes and then took a deep breath as she tore paper and dried herself. The toilet roared when she pushed the handle.

"Back into the tub, girls . . . the way I had you."

"Whuh-what are you going to *do,* Uncle Dylan?"

"Spank you, of course. Now go on."

"But why in the *tub,* Professor?"

"So there's not a big mess when I put water on your bottoms."

"What? *Why?*"

He shook his head and held their arms while they stepped into the tub. "I haven't studied the actual physics, but I know that a girl's behind is *much* more sensitive when wet . . . so I don't have to spank as hard to achieve the desired effect."

Lisa knelt and gaped at him. "But . . . that's *horrible!* I mean . . . why do you gotta spank us at *all* when you already *embarrassed* us half to . . .?"

"Quiet! Down on all fours the way I had you . . . *now.*"

Teresa sobbed, knelt, and slapped her palms on the mat. Lisa puffed an angry breath and did the same. Their bottoms wriggled as they shifted their knees to find some semblance of comfort on the hard surface. Dylan took a washcloth from a pile on a shelf, then put it back and grabbed a hand towel. He ran water in the sink and drenched the towel, then sat on the tub's rim next to Teresa. She squealed when wetness bathed her cheeks.

"That's *cold*, Uncle Dylan!"

"I'll warm you up soon enough, so stop squirming."

Lisa yelped and dug her fingers into the bathmat when he sloshed water on her behind. "How come it's gotta be cold, huh?"

"I believe it's because the nerve endings respond more quickly when they're chilled . . . but I'll be happy to experiment with a range of temperatures . . . if you're that curious." She scowled at him and shook her head. "No? Then perhaps you're ready to *curb* the curiosity that got you into this predicament to begin with?"

"We just wanted to *help*, Professor!"

"That's your story and you're sticking to it?"

"Um . . . *yeah*. And . . . and we don't *deserve* to get spanked for being *helpful!*"

"That's nonsense and you know it. Now keep still while I remind you *not* to put your impertinent little noses where they don't *belong*."

He raised his arm and Teresa grimaced. His hand fell on tender, wet flesh and she gasped at the sting. He gave her ten swats and then leaned forward to treat Lisa's wriggly behind to the same. She grunted and her bottom twitched as the sting began to burn.

"Owee! *Geeze*, Professor!"

"You're starting to appreciate the effectiveness of the method?" She nodded. "For sure . . . it's um . . . it hurts *real* bad!"

"Very *badly*, Lisa . . . just because you're in distress is no reason to abandon good grammar."

"How can you be such a . . .?"

"*Hush*, girl!" Tiny water drops flew through the air as he smacked Teresa's behind, then he frowned at Lisa and she turned away and gritted her teeth while his hand clapped her wet bottom. "I can only imagine what got into you two, but I plan to see that it doesn't happen *again*."

"Buh-but it *won't*, Uncle Dylan . . . honestly!" Teresa sniffled and yearned to rub the sharp ache from her behind.

"I should hope *not* . . . now be still so I can dampen your bottoms." He squeezed the towel and once more bathed their cheeks. "The problem with wet spanking is that the water bounces off and must be reapplied frequently."

"Yeah . . . my heart *bleeds* for you," Lisa muttered.

He shot her a quick glance and then picked up the spatula. "Although I have *heard* of a method to prevent that happening."

Teresa stared at the horrid, flexible implement. "Whuh-what is that, Uncle Dylan?"

An ironic smile curved his lips. "I know you're *fascinated* by the subject . . . and of course while I'm *telling* you I won't be *spanking,* true?" She grunted and shrugged. "All right . . . it was in a letter to a magazine . . . the writer said she used a mixture of water and glycerin to coat her daughter's bottom, and that it kept the skin wet for as long as she cared to spank."

"Have *you* ever tried that, Professor?"

He shook his head. "Somehow I never think to put glycerin on my shopping list . . . but I'll do that right now, if you'd like to be my test subject."

"*No* . . . never mind . . . that's OK."

"I thought it might be . . . now are you through stalling?"

"Well, *geeze,* Professor! You brought it *up!*"

"That's a very impudent tone for a girl whose sarcastic remark I chose to ignore only a moment ago."

Lisa grunted and glared at the floor. "I didn't *mean* anything."

"Yes, I'm *quite* sure."

He patted their behinds, rubbed his fingers together, and then leaned over to twist open the tap. A trickle ran from the spigot and he doused the towel. The girls shivered when he rewetted their behinds, and their hearts pounded in dreadful anticipation. He raised the spatula and Teresa squeaked when hard, flat plastic popped a sore, moist cheek. It popped again on the other cheek, and she gasped as the water magnified the sting and flashed it straight to her brain. She raised her upper body but he put a hand on her back to hold her while he fanned her bottom with quick, light swats that covered her in wet fire. Lisa yelped, then bit her lip when he reached over and dealt ten flaming smacks to her round tenderness.

Water sprayed from tight skin with each clap, and the girls panted, moaned, and then squealed as he alternated from one bottom to the other. He stopped to dribble more water on sore flesh, but that gave them no relief since they knew it was only a brief respite before the infernal implement returned to heap coals on the fire. When their skin glowed warm pink he dropped the spatula to the floor and rubbed their backs.

"All right, girls . . . it's over. Step out of the tub and give me a hug."

Faces redder and wetter than their bottoms, they grabbed the tub rim and pushed themselves up. Quivery arms surrounded him as they stood on the mat. His shirt and pants were wet through and they shivered while he hugged them.

"Wuh . . . we're sorry, Uncle Dylan!"

"Yeah and . . . we won't ever do it *again*."

"I know you won't." He kissed their tear-damp cheeks and patted their bottoms. "Let me wrap you up, hmm?"

They stepped back and he grabbed bath sheets and draped them over quaky shoulders. Lisa clasped terrycloth to her throat and tiptoed to the vanity mirror. She turned and reached down to lift the towel, then grimaced at the reflection.

"It *feels* like it oughta be a lot redder." She glared when Dylan chuckled. "You're not gonna tell Michael about this wet spanking thing, are you?"

"I *could* if you like."

"Don't be so mean! Do we get cold cream now or *what?*"

"Are you going to ask nicely or *what?*"

Teresa stamped a foot. "You *are* being mean, Uncle Dylan! You are supposed to *forgive* us now and not *tease* us anymore."

"Yes, yes . . . very well. You're forgiven . . . now dry your legs *and* your faces, then come into the bedroom."

The door shut and Teresa moaned while she rubbed soreness from her bottom with terrycloth. Lisa looked at her and raised an eyebrow.

"Don't forget, now."

"What?"

"To *ask* him! He *owes* us a story for what he did . . . yeesh!" Lisa flicked off the towel and hugged it to her breasts. Her rear cheeks jiggled as she danced to release the pain.

Teresa smiled in spite of the discomfort in her own behind. "Let us hope he will read no *more* of these letters in magazines."

"No *kidding!* That spatula really *does* sting on a wet butt." She wrapped up in the towel and bit her lip. "But you gotta wonder what kind of magazine would *print* a letter like that."

"Um . . . *Sports Illustrated?*" Teresa grinned when Lisa laughed.

"More like *Spankers Illustrated* . . . we should look in his underwear drawer."

"Lisa! Are you still *drunk?*" She fluffed her hair in the mirror

and scowled at the girl. "Your curiosity has already brought me *one* spanking and I do not wish to try for *another*."

"OK, OK . . . let's go see if he's ready to be *nice* to us now."

Dylan walked in from the hallway as the girls came out of the bathroom. He wore a crisp cotton shirt and denim slacks, and carried a jar in his hand. Two long-sleeved jerseys were draped over his forearm.

"Here . . . slip these on and lie down." They dropped their towels and pulled the cotton shirts over their heads, then lay side by side on the bed. "A little closer, Lisa . . . so I don't have to stretch so far."

She wriggled over until her hip touched Teresa's. "Your arm bothering you, Professor?"

"Not particularly . . . but thanks for asking." He opened the jar and slicked white cream over sore pinkness.

"I just wondered, you know . . . thought maybe you wore yourself out this afternoon."

"Hmm?" He dipped more cream and swirled his fingers around their tight bottoms.

"I mean. . . ." Lisa licked her lips and Teresa covered her eyes with a hand. "You couldn't of got that tired whacking *our* fannies . . . so I thought maybe you had to do something *else* that. . . ."

"Lisa! Your subtleness will only *aggravate* him." Teresa turned her head. "She wants to know why you had to go to Kate's house, so please *tell* her . . . or tell her to shut up . . . before she gets us in any *more* trouble!"

He stared at her for a moment and the girls held their breaths. Then he chuckled, rubbed his hands together and continued to massage.

"You sound just like your Papa."

Teresa exhaled and swallowed. "Truly?"

"I don't think the word *subtle* was in his vocabulary in *any* language. That was one reason I liked him so much."

Lisa waited as long as she could while he caressed them and stared into space. "*Dylan?*" She bit her lip and grimaced at the petulant whine in her voice.

"Hmm? Oh . . . yes . . . it turned out Brandi was beaten, almost bloody, by someone she thought she could trust . . . and Kate couldn't get a straight story out of her."

– 249 –

"But *you* did?"

"I believe so."

"Why wouldn't she tell *Kate?*"

"Well . . . Kate has always been overprotective, and her badge and gun only complicate matters. The worst thing one can do when a girl has been abused is to take it upon oneself to seek revenge on her behalf."

"How come?" Lisa leaned up on an elbow. "I mean . . . if *my* sister had a badge and a gun and some guy beat the hell out of *me*, I'd say sure . . . go ahead! Blow him away!"

"You think so *now* . . . but that sort of thing actually disempowers the victim and makes her feel even *less* in control of her own life."

"So . . . nothing's gonna *happen* to this guy?"

Dylan shrugged. "I don't know for sure. *Kate* won't do anything . . . I think I convinced her not to, anyway."

Teresa smiled. "You can be *very* persuasive, Uncle Dylan. Did you give *her* a wet spanking also? *Au!*"

He rubbed sting from the soft swat and clicked his tongue. "You're being *nosy* again." She pouted until he leaned down and kissed her. "The problem is . . . Kate can't do anything *official* without making the whole thing public, which Brandi doesn't want . . . and if she acts *unofficially* she could get into a *real* mess."

"Rogue cop shoots civilian for no apparent reason, huh?" Lisa smirked and he nodded. "So why don't *we* do something? Who *is* this guy, anyway?"

"Don't even *think* about it, Lisa! And you had *better* not mention it to Brandi, either. But I *will* tell you his name . . . in case you run into him. It's Travis Hunter."

"You're *kidding!*"

"You know him?"

"Well yeah . . . kinda. Mandy used to hang out with him . . . like *years* ago. He joined the army or something, didn't he?"

"Navy . . . did your sister have any problems with him?"

"She never said anything if she did . . . but it didn't last long. I just remember him 'cause he was a lot dweebier than the other guys she hung with."

Dylan laughed. "Is *dweebier* actually a word?"

"Now don't get all professory!" She grinned when he moaned.

"So how come . . .? Oh! *Travis* . . . Travis! Kate thought Brandi was talking about *you* and *that's* why she busted in like *Lethal Weapon* . . . OK, mystery solved. So *see?* You coulda saved yourself all that trouble and just *told* us to begin with!"

"Except that I didn't *know* until I pried the story out of Brandi . . . and really, it's no trouble at *all* to spank your impudent fannies."

"No trouble for *you,* Uncle Dylan." Teresa sighed and her legs parted when his palm stroked the deep divide between her sore cheeks. "But it is a good thing we care so much for you . . . or we would be angry that you were this strict to us."

Lisa moaned and closed her eyes as his thumb slicked cream along the edge of her cleft. "Whadaya mean *we?* I'm mad as hell . . . *heck* and I'm not gonna take it anymore."

He chuckled when she grinned. "You watch too many movies, Lisa."

"I told her this also." Teresa grunted when Lisa's foot flicked her calf.

"Greg's always quoting stuff at me . . . I musta picked it up from him." She blinked and looked at Teresa, but the girl's mouth hung open, her eyes were shut, and she was lost in his smooth caress.

Hot pink skin paled as he kneaded and he shook his head to clear the image of Brandi's battered flesh from his mind, and then watched their closed eyelids flutter. Lisa's toes clenched, relaxed, and she whimpered as she spread her thighs. He inhaled the aroma of her excitement and then gritted his teeth when Teresa bent her left knee, pushed it sideways, and exposed damp, swollen labia. His arms quivered and he kept his fingers flat and rigid while he circled the creamy summits. Teresa whimpered, arched her back, and the tiny rose of her anus peeked at him. He looked at their faces, turned toward one another on the pillows, so serene, yet flushed so warmly red. Lisa's tongue darted at the corner of her mouth, then she swallowed and moaned as he took a deep breath and slid his thumbs inside their open grooves.

Teresa gasped and then squeezed her eyelids tighter when he touched her moist cleft. She felt Lisa's warm breath on her face, wondered if he was touching *her* the same way, but the thought drifted away on a flood of exquisite sensation. His thumb pad slicked along the tender crease toward her spine, and blissful tremors bathed her from head to foot as she bit her lip to suppress an animal grunt.

Lisa's heart pumped hot, needful blood through her breasts and straight into her vagina. Wanton images danced behind closed eyelids and lightening flashed through spank-stung cheeks to spark lascivious tingles in her puffy lower lips. A vague sense of unease made her open her eyes a slit, but Teresa's rapt expression reassured her and she abandoned herself once more to his sensual fingers.

Dylan squeezed the firm, round bottoms, reveled in their smoothness and the electric quivers that shuddered through them when he caressed the deep valleys, his thumbs scant millimeters from their tight, puckered holes. His eyes shifted from the sweet, open fissures to Teresa's face, and outraged conscience snapped at the back of his mind. He sought to quell its sharp teeth with thoughts of what could happen to *her* if he refused the attention she so obviously needed, as he had with Brandi, but then he grimaced at his own hypocrisy, evident in the stiffness inside his trousers, and drew back from the slippery inner slopes to massage the innocent flesh of their cheeks.

The telephone jangled, shrill as the Trumpet of Doom, and he cursed under his breath as he grabbed the towels from the floor and draped their nakedness. They hugged themselves and curled on their sides when he picked up the receiver.

"Yes?"

"Dylan?"

"Oh . . . hi, Gwen. Can you give me a minute? I was right in the middle of something."

"That's OK, I . . . I'll call back later."

"Um . . . why don't I call *you* back?"

"Sure . . . yeah. When . . . do you think?"

"Ten or fifteen minutes . . . are you all right?"

"Yeah sure . . . I just . . . need to talk, OK?"

"You're *not* all right . . . I can hear it in your voice. Did something happen?"

"Just . . . just *call* me, OK?"

He puffed his cheeks and nodded. "I will . . . very soon . . . don't go away."

"I'll be here."

The phone clicked and he set it in the cradle. Teresa rose to her knees, wrapped the towel and secured it at her waist, then crawled over and sat next to him. Lisa knotted her bath sheet and went

– 252 –

around to the other side. They grabbed an arm apiece and he patted their thighs while he bit his lip and blinked at nothing.

"She is not OK?"

"Doesn't sound like it, sweetie." He took a deep breath and then kissed their foreheads. "Are you OK, Lisa? I mean . . . um. . . ."

She nodded and grinned. "Yeah . . . you took care of us pretty good."

"Pretty *well*." He looked at Teresa and a blush colored his cheeks. "Are *you* all right?"

A deeper blush painted her face as she nodded. "Certainly . . . um . . . thank you for the cold cream."

"Yes, well . . . why don't you put your clothes on?"

"OK." Lisa kissed his cheek.

Teresa hesitated then did the same, and the girls ran to the living room. They collected their neatly folded uniforms from the coffee table and scurried back to the bedroom. Dylan flattened against the wall when they dashed past, then went to the bar and poured a large whisky. He let smooth malt caress his tongue before he swallowed, then gazed at the empty sherry bottle. The phone beeped when he picked up the handset, but he set it down and sipped more whisky.

Teresa watched Lisa from the corner of her eye, and frowned as she removed her towel and looked over her shoulder at the mirror. "I . . . I cannot believe the spatula left no marks."

Lisa stood next to her and twisted her bare bottom from side to side. "Guess he *didn't* smack very hard . . . stung like blazes, though."

"Perhaps it will bruise later?"

"Maybe . . . sure *feels* better."

Teresa bit her lip and pulled off the cotton shirt. "Yes . . . perhaps *too* much better."

"Um . . . yeah." Lisa threw her jersey at the bed and grabbed her panties. "He . . . uh . . . got a lot more . . . intimate . . . than usual . . . or was that just me?"

"No . . . I think with me also." Teresa pouted and zipped her skirt. "Do you think he *meant* to . . . to . . .?"

Lisa smirked as she snapped on her bra. "I don't know . . . he could of just got carried away 'cause . . . um . . . we were in bed?"

"Perhaps . . . but he has given me lotion on the bed before and he never. . . ."

"Yeah . . . but he had two sexy heinies to play with this time . . . maybe we overwhelmed him." She grinned and stuffed her blouse tail into her waistband.

Her fingers trembled as Teresa fumbled with blouse buttons. "So . . . if the phone had not rung. . . ."

"I don't think so . . . it felt like he kinda backed off before the phone rang." Lisa straightened Teresa's collar and kissed her cheek. "He is a man . . . and sometimes they forget what they're doing . . . especially when they've got a, um . . . but nothing *happened*. Which is good, 'cause you'd have been really mad at me if I was right there with you the first time." Teresa's eyes bulged and she looked away. Lisa grinned and grabbed the girl's shoulders. "What's *that* all about? Huh? Come on . . . tell Aunty Lisa."

"But I . . . he. . . ." She licked her lips and scowled.

"That's great! When? While he was spanking you?"

Teresa nodded and released a long breath. "That day . . . after . . . I ran away, he . . . he spanked me, and. . . ."

"And you got *off?*" Lisa giggled and hugged her. "Welcome to the club!"

"Lisa! It . . . it was very disturbing to me! He *is* my uncle, after all."

"Yeah, well . . . we won't go into *that* again. But at least you're learning what to look for in *other* men, huh?" A hot blush bathed Teresa's face and Lisa gasped. "Omigod! *Who? Where?* Oh, shit . . . we gotta get out of here." She held Teresa's arm as she stepped into her loafers. "Come on . . . have dinner with me and Greg, then we'll go to Suds and have a *long* talk while he plays pool, OK?"

"Well . . . I. . . ."

"Look, you don't wanna hang around while he's on the phone with *her*, do you?"

"No . . . but. . . ." She glanced at her watch. Her new friend always arrived in the chat room late at night, so she nodded. "I must call Fel and tell her where I am going."

"Call from the car . . . now put your shoes on and let's *go*." Lisa bit her lip when they entered the living room and she saw Dylan staring at the sherry bottle. "I'm OK to drive, honest!"

"Hm? Oh . . . yes . . . I suppose the alcohol has had time to metabolize."

"Yeah, and you um. . . ." She took the hand he offered and squeezed it. "You *spanked* it out of me!"

"Indeed? Well, see that you remain sober the rest of the evening."

"OK, Professor . . . anything you say." Lisa grinned and backed toward the coat rack by the door.

He held out his arms and Teresa hugged his neck. "Are you going home, sweetie?"

"Well . . . Lisa has invited me to dinner . . . and you must call *her* . . . um . . . Gwen . . . so I will leave you in peace."

"I *would* ask you to stay, but I have a pile of finals to grade by Friday so I won't be very good company anyway."

He kissed her lips and patted her bottom as she turned to take her jacket from Lisa.

"'Bye, Professor . . . and thanks for . . . um . . . for the sherry. It was really good."

"I'm so glad you liked it, Lisa. I'll buy more for when you come to help me with the glycerin experiment." He smiled and winked.

Her nose wrinkled and she stuck out her tongue, then opened the door and pushed Teresa into the hallway. Dylan finished his drink and poured another, but even the smooth malt, redolent of sea salt and peat fires, could not drive the scent of cold cream and girlish arousal from his nose. He sipped, picked up the phone and thumbed a speed key. Gwen answered at the first ring.

"Hi, Dylan . . . um . . . I didn't mean to worry you."

"Oh, *really* . . . just practicing for when you do mean to worry me?"

"Don't yell . . . I had a bad day."

"I didn't yell, but . . . all right. Do you want to tell me about it?"

"Sure . . . um . . . what were you doing when I called?"

"You first."

"OK . . . well . . . you know how you've been after me to move out of Boston?"

He frowned and set his glass on the bar. "I haven't been *after* you, Princess."

"Yeah well . . . you *suggested* it a few times."

"And you always told me how much you'd miss it . . . family and church and all. Why? Are you considering it?"

"Um . . . now might be a good time."

"I see." He took a deep breath. "What happened to change your mind?"

"I um . . . kinda got fired."

His eyes widened and he grabbed the glass. "Well that's . . . surprising. By the insurance company or Treasury?"

"The company . . . Calvin told me today my position is being eliminated, so . . . um. . . ." She coughed and then sighed.

"That's not *really* what's going on, is it?"

"No. You remember those kickbacks I told you about?"

"The cement factory? Yes . . . and?"

"Well . . . I sent my report to Randy and it opened a *big* can of worms."

"How so?"

"The cement company is just the tip of the iceberg . . . there are twenty other businesses involved, most of them a lot bigger, and they've got interlocking ownership . . . so when the guys in DC started poking around they *really* stirred up a hornet's nest."

"*All* these companies are taking kickbacks?"

"Not kickbacks . . . money laundering . . . from illegal immigrant prostitution."

"Oh for pity's sake . . . slave traders?"

"Basically, yeah. So the INS, FBI, Treasury . . . probably the Interstate Commerce Commission . . . everybody in Washington is going nuts issuing writs and subpoenas, and they've got agents climbing all *over* these guys. It'll be bigger than Enron when it hits the papers."

"But that . . . that's *great!* I mean . . . congratulations, Princess! You're the Lone Ranger!"

She huffed. "You got *that* right . . . *all* alone."

He sighed and shook his head. "OK . . . tell me the rest."

"Every one of those businesses has multiple policies with us . . . um . . . with the company I *used* to work for, so now. . . ."

Her voice trailed off and he grimaced.

"Well *drat* . . . so they're saying *you* killed the golden goose?"

She snorted. "Of *course* not . . . that would make me look like a whistle-blower, and whistle-blowers are protected. But once those companies go belly up from fines and penalties and indictments, they won't be shelling out three and half million in premiums every year."

"I suppose not . . . so the insurance company can make a case that you really *are* being downsized . . . because of lost revenue and not as retaliation."

"Yep . . . that's about it. Calvin was real careful what he said to

me . . . and he even brought in a stenographer to record our meeting."

"Oh boy . . . I'm *really* sorry, Princess."

"Thanks. So merry fucking Christmas, huh?"

"Gwen! There's no reason to. . . ." He drained the whisky and coughed. "OK, maybe there is. Have you told your family?"

"Yeah . . . sort of. I called Aunt Phoebe and told her I'd been laid off . . . so the immediate *world* will know by tomorrow."

"Will you have Christmas at her house?"

"I suppose. Life goes on, right? You're still coming for New Years, aren't you?"

"Absolutely! I'd come right *now* but. . . ."

"I know, I know. I'm OK, really . . . but I could sure use a hug."

"So could I. Then um . . . you're seriously thinking about moving?"

"Yeah . . . I'm so fucking pissed off at this town right now I could. . . ."

"Gwendolyn! I let you slide on one bad word, but you're really pushing it."

"But *Dylan.*"

She sobbed and his heart nearly broke, but he took a deep breath and let it out.

"Young lady, this is *not* the end of the world and I *forbid* you to make any rash decisions before we sit down and talk about your options. Do you understand me? Gwen?"

"Yuh . . . yes, sir." She sniffled and cleared her throat. "I'm OK . . . and . . . and I'm sorry I said those words."

"Are you? We'll discuss *that* as well, when I see you next week."

"*Nooo.*"

The whine brought a smile to his lips. "Indeed we *will* . . . you know better."

"You . . . you're not gonna s-*spank* me, are you?"

"I most certainly *am* . . . because you *need* to be spanked, and *hard.*"

"Nuh *uh* . . . I *don't!*"

"No arguing. If I *didn't* spank you for saying bad words, you might think I don't love you . . . and I do . . . very, very much."

She huffed. "I know, but . . . you could just only *hug* me and *kiss* me . . . you don't gotta *spank* me to show me you love me."

– 257 –

"Oh but I *do* . . . right on your little bare fanny."

"You're so *mean* to me!"

"No . . . merely strict . . . when you're naughty."

"Yeah, but you think I'm *always* naughty."

"Not always . . . often enough, though."

"Only *some*times. But . . . so . . . if I decide to move out west are you gonna be *nice* to me?"

He frowned. "*Now* you're moving to LA? After all the years I tried to talk you into . . . ?"

"*No*, silly . . . to Iowa! Why would I wanna move to *LA?*"

"Oh!" He laughed. "I still think of this as *back east*, I guess . . . but I would be *thrilled* if you did."

She giggled. "That *doesn't* answer my question, you know."

"Hmm? Will I be nice to you . . . if you move here? Define *nice.*"

"Yeah . . . that's what I *thought*. You'll spank me so much my bottom's *always* gonna look like I sat on a wasp nest."

"There you go with the hyperbole again . . . but don't forget all the hugging and kissing and cuddling that accompany a sore fanny."

"Mmm . . . you better quit that . . . or I'll forget how depressed I am."

"Good. Should I start saving the real estate listings for you?"

"Sure but . . . Randy said the Department would help me relocate."

"That's wonderful! So we *do* have something to celebrate this New Years."

"Yeah . . . so um. . . ." She grinned. "So you don't gotta spank me for saying those words, right?"

"Ohhh . . . that's so *cute*, Princess! Totally off the mark and incredibly naïve . . . but cute, nonetheless."

"Dylan! You're not being *reasonable!* How can you *possibly* . . . ?"

He smiled and leaned back, poured more whisky, and they chatted and bickered until red dawn washed the stars from an inky velvet night.

CHAPTER 11
GREEN EYES IN THE EAST

CHRISTMAS DAY CAME and went, joyfully, peacefully, with no problems other than Felicia's plum pudding, which crumbled in the boiler. Mac consoled her while they watched movies after the turkey dinner, and then they went to his apartment. Dylan and Teresa sat at the kitchen bar and played cribbage on an ebony board, her gift to him. She thumbed the diamond tennis bracelet he gave to her and smiled.

"Is now a good time to talk about where I will live?"

"Well . . . yes . . . but I should tell you something first."

She put her cards down and counted eight. "What is that?"

"Gwen may be moving to Iowa."

"*What?* When?"

"It isn't decided yet. She's looking for a job now, but it will be in the next few months . . . if it happens at all . . . take your nobs for the jack, sweetie."

"Oh! Yes . . . thank you." Her heart pounded as she moved the peg one more space. "She will find a job *here?*"

"Possibly . . . but more likely in Des Moines or Omaha . . . double run for ten."

"But if . . . if she finds work *here* . . . will she *live* with you?" She coughed to cover the whine in her voice.

"We've discussed it . . . but a lot is still up in the air." He

sipped whisky and watched her shuffle. "She'll probably buy a house of her own, wherever she winds up . . . assuming she can sell the one in Wellesley. I take it you'd rather she didn't . . . move in with me."

She set the deck down and picked up her wine glass. "I . . . I think your apartment is very small."

"Which is why I've been looking at townhouses."

"You have?"

He nodded. "Since you'd rather not stay on your own, I'll be glad to have you with me . . . but I've been on *my* own for so long, we'll need lots of space so we don't step on each other's toes."

Teresa bit her lip and set her glass down. "If you think this is best, Uncle Dylan."

"Don't *you?*" He held out his arms and she got up to sit on his lap. "I'm sorry the situation has been so uncertain lately, and I know you've felt insecure. Do you need some time to think about it?"

"No . . . I *want* to live with you, only. . . ." She cleared her throat. "Will there be room . . . in this townhouse . . . for anyone else?"

"You mean Gwen." He took a deep breath. "I don't plan on her living with us . . . not in the townhouse, anyway."

"Oh! Then . . . um. . . ." She coughed and wriggled on his lap. "You merely surprised me . . . that you already have made up your mind."

"I was so sure you *did* want this I went ahead and planned for it . . . but nothing is written in stone. The student apartment is still an option."

She shook her head and kissed him. "I *do* want to live with you . . . so . . . so that I can take care of you."

He chuckled. "You think I *need* to be taken care of?"

"Yes . . . because you are so busy taking care of others you have no time for yourself . . . or to have any fun."

"You may have a point . . . but you won't break me of my care-taking habits overnight, you know."

"I would not try . . . but at least I will make you a good breakfast before school." She giggled when he squeezed her.

"*That* couldn't hurt . . . just keep in mind that I'm *still* your professor, and the fact that you feed me doesn't get you any special treatment in class . . . plus, I'll *know* whether the dog ate your homework."

Her mouth dropped open. "We will have a *dog?*"

He laughed. "That means you'll have no excuses for not doing your work . . . because I'll have my eye on you *all* the time."

"I know . . . and this makes me feel *very* secure."

"Good . . . but I have to ask one thing."

"What?"

"Do you think you can be civil to Gwen when you meet her?"

"Of *course!* I am civil to *all* of your friends."

"Yes, well . . . you've never met a friend who is quite so . . . *close* to me, have you?"

"No . . . I have never met any of your *lovers,* if that's what you mean."

He leaned back and put a palm under her chin. "What do *you* mean . . . *any* of my lovers?"

She grinned. "Fel told me that you have had many girlfriends . . . and I cannot *believe* they were merely platonic relationships."

"Oh you *can't?*"

"No . . . you are much too handsome and sexy for girls to keep their hands from you."

"I see!" He faked a scowl. "Do you know what *I* believe?"

Her eyes widened and her heart throbbed. "What?"

"That your bottom is too sassy and impertinent for me to keep *my* hand from *it!*"

"No, Uncle Dylan!"

He laughed and she squealed when he lifted and draped her across his thighs. Tight cheeks inside snug wool trousers jiggled as he clapped them softly a dozen times, and then he pulled her up onto his lap once more. She glared and battled to keep the pout on her lips, but it dissolved when he kissed her.

"Now . . . do you *believe* that I have room in my heart for both you *and* Gwen?"

"Um . . . yes, Uncle Dylan."

"You don't sound convinced . . . but it's getting late so we'll talk about that another time."

"All right. Will you go home now?"

"No . . . I've had a bit too much Christmas cheer to drive. I'll sleep in Fel's bed."

She snuggled into his chest and sighed. "So . . . what will you do for New Years?"

"The usual . . . dinner and dancing . . . champagne at midnight. Do you have plans?"

"Well . . . there is a party. May I go?"

He chuckled. "You waited until I'd had sufficient whisky to ask me that?"

"Of *course* not."

"Where *is* this party?"

"At the home of Greg's friends . . . I have been there before."

"Ah, yes . . . where you met my illegitimate son. Siberian, wasn't he?"

She grinned and slapped his shoulder. "Slovenian! And he could *not* be your son because he was not nearly as silly as you."

"Is that so?" He hugged her until she whimpered, and then he smiled and kissed her cheek. "Will you be the designated driver again?"

"No . . . Lisa says we should take a taxi, so no one has to drive."

"Uh *huh* . . . does that mean you intend to *drink,* young lady?"

"*No* . . . only it is very dangerous on the roads late at night on New Years."

"True . . . maybe instead of a taxi, I'll ask Kate to take you home in her squad car."

Teresa glowered and squirmed off his lap. "And maybe *you* should go to bed because you are becoming delirious!"

"All right, all right." He let her pull him to his feet. "Just be sure you're home by one o'clock."

"Uncle *Dylan* . . . on New Years *Eve?* We will *leave* the party at one o'clock, OK?"

He sighed. "Very well . . . but *at* one o'clock . . . not one-oh-five or one-fifteen. And order the taxi in advance so it's waiting."

"*Yes,* Uncle Dylan . . . I *will,* Uncle Dylan . . . go to *bed,* Uncle Dylan." She squeaked when he swatted her seat.

"And *don't* let me hear that you got home late."

"Do not *worry* so. You will get an ulcer."

"It's my *job* to worry about you. Now go put your pajamas on."

She smiled when he tucked her in, kissed her, and turned out the light, then she waited to hear his snores before she got out of bed and logged onto the internet. Her eyes glowed when she saw *daddy4grlz* in the chat room and she bit her lip as she typed a long, sassy hello to him.

Dylan arrived at Gwen's house early on the evening of the thir-
tieth. A For Sale sign hung from a bracket at the curb and he
frowned as he got out of the car. Mel opened the trunk and took
out his suitcase.

"She's moving, Professor?"

"Looks like it." He signed the voucher Mel handed him. "I
should have known she wouldn't waste any time."

The man grinned and gave Dylan the receipt. "Women, huh?
They're never in a hurry . . . unless you don't *expect* them to be."

"So always expect the unexpected."

"Exactly! That's how I stayed married for twenty years."

"Then you're better at it than most." Dylan smiled and held out
a hand. "Happy New Year, Mel . . . see you on the second."

"Same to you, Professor. Take care!"

Gwen met him at the door and pulled him inside. She wore a
long, diaphanous blue nightgown that revealed more than it concealed, and his hands roamed over her silken contours while they
kissed. Her eyes sparkled with mischief as she looked up at him.

"You like my outfit?"

"Very much . . . what there is *of* it. Christmas present?"

"Uh huh . . . from Aunt Phoebe, if you can believe *that*."

He chuckled and patted her bottom. "She probably thought
you'd wear a full slip under it . . . or at least panties."

"Actually I think it's a hint I oughta get married and make her a
great-aunt."

"Man bait? Well, it's working."

She licked her lips. "Yeah? So you wanna go to bed?"

"*Very* soon . . . but don't you want your Christmas present
from *me*?"

"Uh huh . . . long as it's not a stocking full of switches!"

"Of *course* not." He led her into the living room and she curled
beneath his arm as they sat on the sofa. "I'd never give you the
same present two years in a row."

Lights on the tree twinkled and he stared at them, a wistful
smile on his lips. The cat amulet at her throat sparkled while she
toyed with it.

"Well?"

"Hmm?" He blinked and kissed her lips. "What did you do with them, anyway?"

"Do with *what?*"

"The switches I gave you."

"Dylan! I used them to start a fire, what do you *think?*"

"Oh dear! Makes me wonder if I should give you *this* year's gift, since it's made of paper."

"*Paper?*" She huffed, then grinned and slipped her hands inside his jacket. "Will you quit teasing and give me my *present?*"

"Don't tickle! Gwendolyn!" Hard, sharp nails dug into his ribs and he howled.

"Nuh *uh! I'm* not naughty 'cause *you* started it!"

"All right . . . all right. Here." He panted and slipped an envelope from his inside pocket.

She grabbed it and her brow furrowed as she unfolded a printed page and turned it toward the light, then she threw her arms around his neck. "Omigod omigod *omigod! Dylan!*"

He laughed and hugged her while she covered his face with kisses. "I take it you're pleased."

"Oh *God* am I ever!" She glanced at the paper and gasped. "But I gotta go on a diet *now.*"

"*What?* You're not in the *least* overweight."

"Deb went on one of these cruises and she gained a pound a *day!* All they *do* is feed you!"

"Yes, well . . . perhaps I can think of enough strenuous activity to keep your mind off the midnight buffet, hm?"

"Yeah . . . I bet you *can.*" She sighed and their lips met in a long kiss. "Thank you *so* much . . . I really need to get the hell *out* of this town, ya know?"

He nodded and squeezed her silky behind. "I guessed you might . . . and I notice you already put the house on the market."

"Um . . . yeah. I was gonna tell you about that but . . . oh!"

She wriggled off his lap and ran to the tree, her nakedness enhanced by a cloud of blue silk. Her round bottom beckoned him as she bent to take a flat package from the tree skirt, and then she grinned as she came back and knelt by his side on the sofa.

"Oh, Princess . . . you got me a tie. How thoughtful."

"Uh huh." She covered her mouth and giggled while he tore off ribbon and wrapping. "You like it?"

He held up the strip of dark red silk and peered at it. "What in the *world?*"

"It's the Grinch! See? There's his face . . . and a little Who right there."

"Ah! Yes . . . *very* cute." He smiled and kissed her lips. "Thank you."

"Don't throw away the box!" She sat back and chewed a fingertip. "There's um . . . something else in it."

His eyes widened when he pulled out a cardboard panel, and then turned the package over. A foot-long leather strap dropped into his hand and he grinned as he thumbed its supple smoothness.

"You are a *very* brave girl . . . *extremely* naughty, but brave."

"Now just remember this is a *Christmas* present . . . so it's a *toy* . . . and you can't use it to be *mean* to me, OK?"

"I'm *never* mean to you!" He wrapped his arms around her and held tight while they kissed. "So . . . did you get this for our discussion about your bad language on the phone the other night?"

"No! I found it on the web a couple months ago. Can you see these? Hold it up."

He shifted her onto his lap and examined the strap. "What does it say? *Ouch?*"

She giggled. "But look at the letters. They're *backward* . . . like, mirror image . . . and embossed into the leather so they'll um. . . ."

"Well of *course!* Print little red *ouches* on your little red fanny! This is *too* precious and I have *got* to try it out."

"OK . . . maybe later after we . . . *Dylan!*"

Silk billowed as he tossed her across his knees. She squealed while he laughed and swept blue gossamer away to bare her bottom.

"Thank you, thank you, *thank* you for the lovely gift," he said, and clapped her cheeks with each thank you.

"Ow . . . ow . . . owee!"

"No . . . it's ouch . . . ouch . . . *ouch!* Didn't you read the instructions?"

"OK! Geeze!" She grinned at him while leather popped softly. "So . . . *ow!* Can you see the *ouches* yet?"

He ran his fingertips across her smoothness and bent to inspect

the pink skin. "No . . . I think I'd have to be more serious for *that* to happen."

"Um . . . never mind. You don't wanna use up *all* the fun on the first day, right?"

"I really *should*, you know. Test it to make sure it's not faulty."

"No that's ☉K! It works real good, honest!"

"Really *well* . . . and it's *my* toy . . . so I get to play with it *my* way!"

"Nowee! Yow! *Ouchee!*"

"*Aha!* There we go!" He caressed her bottom with his thumb and then planted a kiss on the crown of a cheek. "The words are a *little* bit darker pink than the rest of the stripe, and quite readable . . . so I would call that a successful test, wouldn't you?"

She sniffled. "Yeah . . . terrific. *Now* can I get up?"

"No more testing?"

"No! That's enough!"

Her arms trembled as he sat her on his lap and hugged her.

"*This* is odd, Princess."

"Huh? What is?"

"Usually when you're on my lap with a sore bottom I forgive you for something . . . but it seems I have nothing to *forgive*."

"Um . . . you *could* forgive me for those words the other night."

"Hmm? But I didn't *scold* you . . . how can I forgive you without a good scolding?"

"Call it a Christmas present?" She grinned and kissed his lips.

"A Caribbean cruise isn't *enough?*"

"I gave *you* two presents!"

He smiled and squeezed her. "That's true. All right . . . you're forgiven for your atrocious language."

"OK . . . um . . . thanks. Can I take off your clothes now?"

"*May* I . . . oh never mind. Shall we go to the bedroom?"

"Sure . . . or you could nooky me right here on the sofa."

"Gwen! *Nooky* is *not* a verb! I'm not even sure it's a *word*."

She rolled off his lap and giggled as she grabbed his lapels. "Let's *go*, Professor!"

"Yes, ma'am!" He leaned against her tummy and draped her over his shoulder as he stood. "We'll go right *away*, ma'am!"

Her palms slapped his back and her legs scissored. "Dylan! Put me *down!*"

"OK . . . you're short . . . you're not married . . . and you're a terrible disappointment to Aunt Phoebe."

"That's *not* what I meant!" She laughed and then screeched when he picked up the strap and swished it across her bottom. "Owee!"

"No . . . it's *ouch!*"

"You're not playing *fair!*"

The strap flicked her wriggly behind and she shouted unlikely threats as he carried her down the hall and dropped her onto the bed. She watched him undress and rubbed warm sting while warmth of another sort tingled her vagina. He dropped his clothes onto the bureau and she licked her lips when he stretched out, naked, beside her. She rolled into his arms and his growing stiffness pressed her thigh. They kissed, long and wet, as he tugged wispy silk up her body and gathered it at her neck. She broke the kiss and raised her arms so he could pull the gown over her head, then thrust her tongue into his mouth once more.

His organ throbbed against her belly and his hands covered and squeezed her tender rear cheeks. Fingers delved into her moist furrow, spread it wide, and caressed the tight, tiny opening within. She wriggled upward and bent a leg over his hip, and the steamy moisture between her thighs inflamed his manhood. He moaned, pushed, and lay on top. Her heart pounded and her knees quivered as she lifted them. Wet petals opened and he raised his hips. The fiery arrow pierced her soul and she growled, wrapped her arms and legs around him as his shaft withdrew, thrust slowly, and retreated again. Quicker and quicker he stroked and her bottom bounced while their bellies clapped. His fire blazed within and fed her furnace of desire, pumped her like a bellows until the heat burst, showered her with throbbing, quivering sparks, consumed her in its inferno, and left her spent beneath him.

He panted and licked his lips, then grunted when she used her special muscles to squeeze out one final drop of lust. His shoulders trembled as he lifted himself onto his elbows and kissed her.

"*You* are a little devil, you know that?"

She grinned and squeezed again. "Good nooky, huh?"

"Gwen!" He laughed and then coughed as he rolled and flopped onto his back.

"Hey!" She folded her arms on his chest and gazed into his half-shut eyes. "I wasn't *done* with you. Ow!"

"Your little fanny's going to be *well* done if you don't settle down."

"*OK* . . . but don't go to sleep yet."

He sighed and wrapped her in his arms. "Somehow that never seems to be an option."

"Nope . . . and anyway I gotta tell you about the house."

"Oh . . . all right. What about it?"

"Well, my cousin Eddie just got his real estate license, so he doesn't have a lot of listings . . . and he'll cut his commission in half just to get the sale under his belt."

"Not a bad deal. Is that why you jumped so quickly?"

"Yeah . . . and I got a bunch of interviews lined up."

"Already? Where?"

"A couple in Des Moines, one in Omaha . . . one someplace on Main Street. If they use logical street numbers, it's about five blocks from your apartment."

"What? *My* Main Street?"

"Uh huh."

"*That's* good news . . . and fast work for a bureaucracy."

"Yeah . . . Randy got real ticked off when I got fired, so he's kinda pushing this."

"Well bravo for Randy! He's going to fool around and change my entire opinion of bureaucrats if he's not careful." He smiled and kissed her. "But what about the cruise? I thought you'd be unemployed for a while so. . . ."

"Oh I'll *go* . . . even if I have to shuffle the interviews around." She grinned. "I think I'll buy a thong bikini to lie around the pool in."

"You think *what,* young lady?"

"Nooo!" She laughed, wriggled and screeched while he slapped her bottom. "Dylan! OK! No thong!"

"I should say *not.* The very idea!"

She rubbed hot handprints and pouted at him. "You know . . . most guys *like* thongs . . . think they're sexy."

"When have I ever been *most guys?*"

"Yeah . . . you're one of a kind, *that's* for sure. I'm still trying to figure out *what* kind."

He grinned. "You'll let me know, won't you? When you find a label for me?"

"Huh! I got a *bunch* of labels for you."

"And I think you'd better keep them to yourself, if that naughty smirk is any indication." He kissed her and she giggled. "Oh! I should tell *you* something . . . since we're so full of surprises tonight."

"What?"

"I won't be *at* the Main Street address much longer."

"You're giving up your beautiful penthouse? How come?"

He laughed and patted her bottom. "It's hardly *that* . . . but I've decided to have Teresa stay with me . . . until she feels more sure of herself."

"Oh . . . um . . . but not at the apartment?"

"No . . . it's really too small . . . but I found a townhouse that I think will work for us."

"Yeah?"

She bit her lip and sat up, then tugged the covers down and wrapped the duvet around her shoulders. He frowned and shook his head.

"What's the matter, Princess?"

"Nothing. I just got chilly."

His lips fluttered as he blew a breath. "Is there a *problem* with her living with me?"

"'Course not . . . why would you think that?"

"Because I just got very chilly, too. Why do you suppose *that* is?"

"Um . . . 'cause you're naked and sweaty?"

"Gwen, you can't *possibly* be jealous of Teresa! She's a child!"

"Yeah, but . . . she's a *well-developed* child . . . from those pictures you showed me. What is she twenty . . . twenty-one?"

"Nineteen!" He huffed, jumped off the bed and grabbed his robe from the closet. "And it wouldn't matter if she's thirty-eight, she's my *niece!*"

"OK, OK . . . I *said* there's no problem. It's just um . . . you never lived with *anybody* before . . . I mean, after you left home."

"And your point is . . . ?"

"Well . . . she's gonna be right *there* . . . and . . . and running around the house in her underwear, and. . . ."

"Oh for pity's sake . . . she *won't* and what if she *did?*"

"Well, *Christ,* Dylan! You already spank *her* bare butt more than you do *mine,* and I *know* what that does to you!"

His teeth clenched and he took a long breath through his nose. "Gwen, that is *enough*. I *love* you . . . I *adore* you . . . and I *won't* have you thinking I love *her* more than I do you!"

She sniffled and wiped her eyes. "But . . . but you never asked *me* to live with you!"

"What are you *talking* about? No more than forty or fifty *times!*"

"Nuh *uh!* You . . . you only said to . . . to come *stay* with you . . . for a while."

"Well yes, but. . . ." He sat and she wriggled as he pulled her onto his lap. "Shh . . . stop fighting me. You *hate* LA . . . so I was trying to *ease* you into the idea of living with me."

"Hah! You're *never* that subtle when . . . when you want me to do something."

"Yes, all right . . . that was a mistake. I'm sure it wasn't my first." He hugged her and she turned her head when he tried to kiss her. "So . . . um . . . would you like to live with me *now?*"

"Yeah *right* . . . me and Teresa in *your* townhouse. *That'll* work."

"Princess, I don't know what you want me to *do*. Should I *make* her live with Fel and Mac? Send her back to *Germany?*"

Tears streamed from her eyes and she threw her arms around his neck. "*No* just . . . just hold me!"

He hugged her and rubbed her back while she wept. "It's all right . . . we won't worry about it now . . . and we'll figure out something that *will* work."

"I . . . I'm *sorry*, Dylan!"

"Shh . . . I know . . . lots of stress lately . . . way too much. Should we have a glass of wine before we go to bed?"

She nodded and swiped tears as she looked at him. "You really *do* love me?"

"More than life itself. You're my one and only princess . . . now and forever."

"I love you too."

"Then everything's all right. Let's put something warm and cozy on you, hm?"

He kissed her lips, went to the closet and pulled out the peach sweat suit. Her wet green eyes gleamed and she rubbed her tingly red bottom while she waited to once more feel his tender, loving touch.

Confessions D'Amour
Anne-Marie Villefranche

Confessions D'Amour is the culmination of Villefranche's comically indecent stories about her friends in 1920s' Paris.

Anne-Marie Villefranche invites you to enter an intoxicating world where men and women arrange their love affairs with skill and style. This is a world where illicit encounters are as smooth as a silk stocking, and where sexual secrets are kept in confidence only until a betrayal can be turned to advantage. Here we follow the adventures of Gabrielle de Michoux, the beautiful young widow who contrives to be maintained in luxury by a succession of well-to-do men, Marcel Chalon, ready for any adventure so long as he can go home to Mama afterwards, Armand Budin, who plunges into a passionate love affair with his cousin's estranged wife, Madelein Beauvais, and Yvonne Hiver who is married with two children while still embracing other, younger lovers.

"An erotic tribute to the Paris of yesteryear that will delight modern readers."—*The Observer*

A Maid For All Seasons I, II – Devlin O'Neill

Two Delighful Tales of Romance and Discipline

Lisa is used to her father's old-fashioned discipline, but is it fair that her new employer acts the same way? Mr. Swayne is very handsome, very British and very particular about his new maid's work habits. But isn't nineteen a bit old to be corrected that way? Still, it's quite a different sensation for Lisa when Mr. Swayne shows his displeasure with her behavior. But Mr. Swayne isn't the only man who likes to turn Lisa over his knee. When she goes to college she finds a new mentor, whose expectations of her are even higher than Mr. Swayne's, and who employs very old-fashioned methods to correct Lisa's bad behavior. Whether in a woodshed in Georgia, or a private club in Chicago, there is always someone there willing and eager to take Lisa in hand and show her the error of her ways.

My Secret Life
Anonymous

Over two million copies sold!

Perhaps the most infamous of all underground Victorian erotica, *My Secret Life* is the sexual memoir of a well-to-do gentleman, who began at an early age to keep a diary of his erotic behavior. He continues this record for over forty years, creating in the process a unique social and psychological document. Its complete and detailed description of the hidden side of British and European life in the nineteenth century furnishes materials for the understanding of the Victorian Age that cannot be duplicated in any other source.

The Altar of Venus
Anonymous

Our author, a gentleman of wealth and privilege, is introduced to desire's delights at a tender age, and then and there commits himself to a life-long sensual expedition. As he enters manhood, he progresses from schoolgirls' charms to older women's enticements, especially those of acquaintances' mothers and wives. Later, he moves beyond common London brothels to sophisticated entertainments available only in Paris. Truly, he has become a lord among libertines.

Caning Able
Stan Kent

Caning Able is a modern-day version of the melodramatic tales of Victorian erotica. Full of dastardly villains, regimented discipline, corporal punishment and forbidden sexual liaisons, the novel features the brilliant and beautiful Jasmine, a seemingly helpless heroine who reigns triumphant despite dire peril. By mixing libidinous prose with a changing business world, *Caning Able* gives treasured plots a welcome twist: women who are definitely not the weaker sex.

The Blue Moon Erotic Reader IV

A testimonial to the publication of quality erotica, *The Blue Moon Erotic Reader IV* presents more than twenty romantic and exciting excerpts from selections spanning a variety of periods and themes. This is a historical compilation that combines generous extracts from the finest forbidden books with the most extravagant samplings that the modern erotica imagination has created. The result is a collection that is provocative, entertaining, and perhaps even enlightening. It encompasses memorable scenes of youthful initiations into the mysteries of sex, notorious confessions, and scandalous adventures of the powerful, wealthy, and notable. From the classic erotica of *Wanton Women*, and *The Intimate Memoirs of an Edwardian Dandy* to modern tales like Michael Hemmingson's *The Rooms*, good taste, passion, and an exalted desire are abound, making for a union of sex and sensibility that is available only once in a Blue Moon.

With selections by Don Winslow, Ray Gordon, M. S. Valentine, P. N. Dedeaux, Rupert Mountjoy, Eve Howard, Lisabet Sarai, Michael Hemmingson, and many others.

The Best of the Erotic Reader

"The Erotic Reader series offers an unequaled selection of the hottest scenes drawn from the finest erotic writing." — *Elle*

This historical compilation contains generous extracts from the world's finest forbidden books including excerpts from *Memories of a Young Don Juan, My Secret Life, Autobiography of a Flea, The Romance of Lust, The Three Chums,* and many others. They are gathered together here to entertain, and perhaps even enlighten. From secret texts to the scandalous adventures of famous people, from youthful initiations into the mysteries of sex to the most notorious of all confessions, *Best of the Erotic Reader* is a stirring complement to the senses. Containing the most evocative pieces covering several eras of erotic fiction, *Best of the Erotic Reader* collects the most scintillating tales from the seven volumes of *The Erotic Reader*. This comprehensive volume is sure to include delights for any taste and guaranteed to titillate, amuse, and arouse the interests of even the most veteran erotica reader.

Color of Pain, Shade of Pleasure
Edited by Cecilia Tan

In these twenty-one tales from two out-of-print classics, *Fetish Fantastic* and *S/M Futures*, some of today's most unflinching erotic fantasists turn their futuristic visions to the extreme underground, transforming the modern fetishes of S/M, bondage, and eroticized power exchange into the templates for new sexual worlds. From the near future of S/M in cyberspace, to a future police state where the real power lies in manipulating authority, these tales are from the edge of both sexual and science fiction.

The Governess
M. S. Valentine

Lovely Miss Hunnicut eagerly embarks upon a career as a governess, hoping to escape the memories of her broken engagement. Little does she know that Crawleigh Manor is far from the respectable household it appears to be. Mr. Crawleigh, in particular, devotes himself to Miss Hunnicut's thorough defiling. Soon the young governess proves herself worthy of the perverse master of the house—though there may be even more depraved powers at work in gloomy Crawleigh Manor . . .

Claire's Uptown Girls
Don Winslow

In this revised and expanded edition, Don Winslow introduces us to Claire's girls, the most exclusive and glamorous escorts in the world. Solicited by upper-class Park Avenue businessmen, Claire's girls have the style, glamour and beauty to charm any man. Graced with super-model beauty, a meticulously crafted look, and a willingness to fulfill any man's most intimate dream, these girls are sure to fulfill any man's most lavish and extravagant fantasy.

The Intimate Memoirs of an Edwardian Dandy I, II, III
Anonymous

This is the sexual coming-of-age of a young Englishman from his youthful days on the countryside to his educational days at Oxford and finally as a sexually adventurous young man in the wild streets of London. Having the free time and money that comes with a privileged upbringing, coupled with a free spirit, our hero indulges every one of his, and our, sexual fantasies. From exotic orgies with country maidens to fanciful escapades with the London elite, the young rake experiences it all. A lusty tale of sexual adventure, *The Intimate Memoirs of an Edwardian Dandy* is a celebration of free spirit and experimentation.

"A treat for the connoisseur of erotic literature."
—*The Guardian*

Jennifer and Nikki
D. M. Perkins

From Manhattan's Fifth Avenue, to the lush island of Tobago, to a mysterious ashram in upstate New York, Jennifer travels with reclusive fashion model Nikki and her seductive half-brother Alain in search of the sexual secrets held by the famous Russian mystic Pere Mitya. To achieve intimacy with this extraordinary family, and get the story she has promised to Jack August, dynamic publisher of *New Man Magazine*, Jennifer must ignore universal taboos and strip away inhibitions she never knew she had.

Confessions of a Left Bank Dominatrix
Gala Fur

Gala Fur introduces the world of French S&M with two collections of stories in one delectable volume. In *Souvenirs of a Left Bank Dominatrix*, stories address topics as varied as: how to recruit a male maidservant, how to turn your partner into a marionette, and how to use a cell phone to humiliate a submissive in a crowded train station. In *Sessions,* Gala offers more description of the life of a dominatrix, detailing the marathon of "Lesbians, bisexuals, submissivies, masochists, paying customers [and] passing playmates" that seek her out for her unique sexual services.

"An intoxicating sexual romp." —*Evergreen Review*

Don Winslow's Victorian Erotica
Don Winslow

The English manor house has long been a place apart; a place of elegant living where, in splendid isolation the gentry could freely indulge their passions for the outdoor sports of riding and hunting. Of course, there were those whose passions ran towards "indoor sports"—lascivious activities enthusiastically, if discreetly, pursued by lusty men and sensual women behind large and imposing stone walls of baronial splendor, where they were safely hidden from prying eyes. These are tales of such licentious decadence from behind the walls of those stately houses of a bygone era.

The Garden of Love
Michael Hemmingson

Three Erotic Thrillers from the Master of the Genre

In The *Comfort of Women*, the oddly passive Nicky Bayless undergoes a sexual re-education at the hands (and not only the hands) of a parade of desperate women who both lead and follow him through an underworld of erotic extremity. The narrator of *The Dress* is troubled by a simple object that may have supernatural properties. "My wife changed when she wore The Dress; she was the Ashley who came to being a few months ago. She was the wife I preferred, and I worried about that. I understood that The Dress was, indeed, an entity all its own, with its own agenda, and it was possessing my wife." In *Drama*, playwright Jonathan falls into an affair with actress Karen after the collapse of his relationship with director Kristine. But Karen's free-fall into debauchery threatens to destroy them both.

The ABZ of Pain and Pleasure
Edited by A. M. LeDeluge

A true alphabet of the unusual, *The ABZ of Pain and Pleasure* offers the reader an understanding of the language of the lash. Beginning with Aida and culminating with Zanetti, this book offers the amateur and adept a broad acquaintance with the heroes and heroines of this unique form of sexual entertainment. The Marquis de Sade is represented here, as are Jean de Berg (author of *The Image*), Pauline Réage (author of *The Story of* O and *Return to the Château*), P. N. Dedeaux (author of *The Tutor* and *The Prefect*), and twenty-two others.

"Frank" and I
Anonymous

The narrator of the story, a wealthy young man, meets a youth one day—the "Frank" of the title—and, taken by his beauty and good manners, invites him to come home with him. One can only imagine his surprise when the young man turns out to be a young woman with beguiling charms.

Hot Sheets
Ray Gordon

Running his own hotel, Mike Hunt struggles to make ends meet. In an attempt to attract more patrons, he turns Room 69 into a state-of-the-art sex chamber. Now all he has to do is wait and watch the money roll in. But nympho waitresses, a sex-crazed chef, and a bartender obsessed with adult videos don't exactly make the ideal hotel staff. And big trouble awaits Mike when his enterprise is infiltrated by an attractive undercover policewoman.

Tea and Spices
Nina Roy

Revolt is seething in the loins of the British colonial settlement of Uttar Pradesh, and in the heart of memsahib Devora Hawthorne who lusts after the dark, sultry Rohan, her husband's trusted servant. While Rohan educates Devora in the intricate social codes that govern the mean-spirited colonial community, he also introduces his eager mistress to a way of loving that exceeds the English imagination. Together, the two explore sexual territories that neither class nor color can control.

Naughty Message
Stanley Carten

Wesley Arthur is a withdrawn computer engineer who finds little excitement in his day-to-day life. That is until the day he comes home from work to discover a lascivious message on his answering machine. Aroused beyond his wildest dreams by the unmentionable acts described, Wesley becomes obsessed with tracking down the woman behind the seductive and mysterious voice. His search takes him through phone sex services, strip clubs and no-tell motels—and finally to his randy reward . . .

The Sleeping Palace
M. Orlando

Another thrilling volume of erotic reveries from the author of *The Architecture of Desire*. Maison Bizarre is the scene of unspeakable erotic cruelty; the Lust Akademie holds captive only the most debauched students of the sensual arts; Baden-Eros is the luxurious retreat of one's most prurient dreams. Once again, M. Orlando uses his flair for exotic·detail to explore the nether regions of desire.

"Orlando's writing is an orgasmic and linguistic treat." —*Skin Two*

Venus in Paris
Florentine Vaudrez

When a woman discovers the depths of her own erotic nature, her enthusiasm for the games of love become a threat to her husband. Her older sister defies the conventions of Parisian society by living openly with her lover, a man destined to deceive her. Together, these beautiful sisters tread the path of erotic delight—first in the arms of men, and then in the embraces of their own, more subtle and more constant sex.

The Lawyer
Michael Hemmingson

Drama tells the titillating story of bad karma and kinky sex among the thespians of The Alfred Jarry Theater.

In this erotic legal thriller, Michael Hemmingson explores sexual perversity within the judicial system. Kelly O'Rourke is an editorial assistant at a large publishing house—she has filed a lawsuit against the conglomerate's best-selling author after a questionable night on a yacht. Kelly isn't quite as innocent as she seems, rather, as her lawyer soon finds out, she has a sordid history of sexual deviance and BDSM, which may not be completely in her past.

Tropic of Lust
Michele de Saint-Exupery

She was the beautiful young wife of a respectable diplomat posted to Bangkok. There the permissive climate encouraged even the most outré sexual fantasy to become reality. Anything was possible for a woman ready to open herself to sexual discovery.

"A tale of sophisticated sensuality [it is] the story of a woman who dares to explore the depths of her own erotic nature."—*Avant Garde*

Folies D'Amour
Anne-Marie Villefranche

From the international best-selling pen of Anne-Marie Villefranche comes another 'improper' novel about the affairs of an intimate circle of friends and lovers. In the stylish Paris of the 1920s, games of love are played with reckless abandon. From the back streets of Montmartre to the opulent hotels on the Rue de Rivoli, the City of Light casts an erotic spell.

The Best of Ironwood
Don Winslow

Ostensibly a finishing school for young ladies, Ironwood is actually that singular institution where submissive young beauties are rigorously trained in the many arts of love. For James, our young narrator, Ironwood is a world where discipline knows few boundaries. This collection gathers the very best selections from the Ironwood series and reveals the essence of the Ironwood woman—a consummate blend of sexuality and innocence.

The Uninhibited
Ray Gordon

Donna Ryan works in a research laboratory where her boss has developed a new hormone treatment with some astounding and unsuspected side effects. Any woman who comes into contact with the treatment finds her sexual urges so dramatically increased that she loses all her inhibitions. Donna accidentally picks up one of the patches and finds her previously suppressed cravings erupting in an ecstatic orgy of liberated impulses. What ensues is a breakthrough to thrilling dimensions of wild, unrestrained sexuality.

Blue Angel Nights
Margarete von Falkensee

This is the delightfully wicked story of an era of infinite possibilities—especially when it comes to eroticism in all its bewitching forms. Among actors and aristocrats, with students and showgirls, in the cafes and salons, and at backstage parties in pleasure boudoirs, *Blue Angel Nights* describes the time when even the most outlandish proposal is likely to find an eager accomplice.

Disciplining Jane
by Jane Eyre

Retaining the threatening and sadistic intent of Charlotte Bronte's *Jane Eyre*, *Disciplining Jane* retells the story with an erotic twist. After enduring constant scrutiny from her cruel adoptive family, young Jane is sent to Lowood, a boarding school where Jane is taught the ways of the rod that render her first in her class.

---

66 Chapters About 33 Women
Michael Hemmingson

An erotic tour de force, *66 Chapters About 33 Women* weaves a complicated web of erotic connections between 33 women and their lovers. Granting each woman 2 vignettes, Hemmingson examines their sexual peccadilloes, and creates a veritable survey course on the possibilities of erotic fiction.

The Man of Her Dream
Briony Shilton

Spun from her subconscious's submissive nature, a woman dreams of a man like no other, one who will subject her to pain and pressure, passion and lust. She searches the waking world, combing her personal history and exploring fantasy and fact, until she finds this master. It is he, through an initiation like no other, who takes her to the limits of her submissive nature and on to the extremes of pure sexual joy.

S-M: The Last Taboo
Gerald and Caroline Greene

A unique effort to abolish the negative stereotypes that have permeated our perception of sadomasochism. *S-M* illuminates the controversy over the practice as a whole and its place in our culture. The book addresses such topics as: the role of women in sadomasochism; American society and Masochism; the true nature of the Marquis de Sade; spanking in various countries; undinism, more popularly known as "water sports"; and general s-m scenarios. Accompanying the text is a complete appendix of s-m documents, ranging from the steamy works of Baudelaire to Pauline Reage's *Story of O*.

Order These Selected Blue Moon Titles

My Secret Life	$15.95	The Uninhibited	$7.95
The Altar of Venus	$7.95	Disciplining Jane	$7.95
Caning Able	$7.95	66 Chapters About 33 Women	$7.95
The Blue Moon Erotic Reader IV	$15.95	The Man of Her Dream	$7.95
The Best of the Erotic Reader	$15.95	S-M: The Last Taboo	$14.95
Confessions D'Amour	$14.95	Cybersex	$14.95
A Maid for All Seasons I, II	$15.95	Depravicus	$7.95
Color of Pain, Shade of Pleasure	$14.95	Sacred Exchange	$14.95
The Governess	$7.95	The Rooms	$7.95
Claire's Uptown Girls	$7.95	The Memoirs of Josephine	$7.95
The Intimate Memoirs of an		The Pearl	$14.95
Edwardian Dandy I, II, III	$15.95	Mistress of Instruction	$7.95
Jennifer and Nikki	$7.95	Neptune and Surf	$7.95
Burn	$7.95	House of Dreams: Aurochs & Angels	$7.95
Don Winslow's Victorian Erotica	$14.95	Dark Star	$7.95
The Garden of Love	$14.95	The Intimate Memoir of Dame Jenny Everleigh:	
The ABZ of Pain and Pleasure	$7.95	Erotic Adventures	$7.95
"Frank" and I	$7.95	Shadow Lane VI	$7.95
Hot Sheets	$7.95	Shadow Lane VII	$7.95
Tea and Spices	$7.95	Shadow Lane VIII	$7.95
Naughty Message	$7.95	Best of Shadow Lane	$14.95
The Sleeping Palace	$7.95	The Captive I, II	$14.95
Venus in Paris	$7.95	The Captive III, IV, V	$15.95
The Lawyer	$7.95	The Captive's Journey	$7.95
Tropic of Lust	$7.95	Road Babe	$7.95
Folies D'Amour	$7.95	The Story of O	$7.95
The Best of Ironwood	$14.95	The New Story of O	$7.95

Title	Quantity	Price
_____	____	_____
_____	____	_____
_____	____	_____
_____	____	_____

Shipping and Handling (see charges below) _____

Sales tax (in CA and NY) _____

Total _____

Name _____

Address _____

City _____ State _____ Zip _____

Daytime telephone number _____

❏ Check   ❏ Money Order   (US dollars only. No COD orders accepted.)

Credit Card # _____ Exp. Date _____

❏ MC   ❏ VISA   ❏ AMEX

Signature _____

(if paying with a credit card you must sign this form.)

Shipping and Handling charges:*

Domestic: $4 for 1st book, $.75 each additional book. International: $5 for 1st book, $1 each additional book
*rates in effect at time of publication. Subject to Change.

Mail order to Publishers Group West, Attention: Order Dept., 1700 Fourth St., Berkeley, CA 94710, or fax to (510) 528-3444.

PLEASE ALLOW 4-6 WEEKS FOR DELIVERY. ALL ORDERS SHIP VIA 4TH CLASS MAIL.